Invitation to Love

"Would they worry, Deborah, if they knew you were staying with me for a day or so? We could arrange to give them a message."

Before she answered she surveyed the beauty and the tranquility of the river and valley. Somewhere on shore chimney smoke was rising to drift lazily across the water and bring to her its fresh and acrid scent. The chugging of the launch's engine seemed very loud and insistent. So . . . suddenly did the beating of Deborah's own heart. Her hand reached up to smooth his hair; her eyes were clear and peaceful as she whispered, "Yes, Robert, take me ashore with you."

Other Avon Books by
Clyde M. Brundy

GRASSLANDS
HIGH EMPIRE

CALL UP THE MORNING

Clyde M. Brundy

AVON
PUBLISHERS OF BARD, CAMELOT, DISCUS AND FLARE BOOKS

CALL UP THE MORNING is an original publication of
Avon Books. This work has never before appeared in book
form.

AVON BOOKS
A division of
The Hearst Corporation
959 Eighth Avenue
New York, New York 10019

First Avon Printing, June, 1983

AVON TRADEMARK REG. U. S. PAT. OFF. AND IN
OTHER COUNTRIES, MARCA REGISTRADA, HECHO EN
U. S. A.

Printed in the U. S. A.

WFH   10 9 8 7 6 5 4 3 2 1

To
SYLVIA, STEVE *and* MAX
Who all somehow got into these pages

PART ONE

Chapter 1

FROM THE crest of a gradually ascending hill, Deborah Dexter stared silently back across the prairie toward broken dreams. The upward pull along this rutted western Nebraska road had caused her team, a mismatched white horse and a tan mule, to breathe heavily. She drew them to a stop. The day was beginning with warm sunshine; the song of a meadowlark proclaimed the nearness of summer in this year of 1889.

The homestead was two miles behind them, and already its small buildings were blending into the solitude and the vastness of pioneer Banner County. Her gaze could no longer distinguish the small, fenced area where only a month before they had buried her father, Tom Dexter, a victim of lightning that had accompanied an evening shower.

As her mind swept both the homestead and the past, Deborah used a wind-tanned fist to wipe away tears. She was sixteen years old and without brothers or sisters. She sensed today that something of her childhood would remain on the half section of land from which each step of the farm team would carry her and her mother farther away. She turned to face southward along this road to Box Butte, in neighboring Kimball County; with a slap of the reins she urged the team into motion. The sunlight silhouetted her on the greening grass, a slender girl who stood five feet four and might weigh a hundred fifteen pounds. Just now, a straw hat with wide brim hid some of her brown hair and shaded eyes that were dark . . . steady . . . anguished.

Presently Deborah realized that her mother, seated beside her on the swaying seat of the farm wagon, was speaking. It was the first time Rose Dexter had uttered a word since they had turned from the homestead lane onto the county road. She was a plump woman in her late thirties, now clad in a starched sunbonnet and a checked gingham dress. For a long time she had kept her eyes fast, in a stoniness, to the road ahead.

"He was a dreamer, Debbie. That's what caused your father to fetch us out here on the prairies when you were only ten years old."

"And now we are running away. Leaving our home and—" The girl's words trailed off as she ran an appraising gaze over their load of household belongings, the crate of red hens tied to the wagon's tailgate, and the haltered milk cow that plodded a reluctant way behind them. Deborah caught a wistful breath and then went on. "Perhaps, Mom, we should have stayed on the claim. We could have managed somehow. Weather conditions look better this spring. By next year—"

"By next year you will be finishing a term of schooling in town," Rose Dexter interrupted. "There is bound to be some kind of work I can find in Box Butte to keep a roof over our heads."

"But Daddy was sure that things would turn out real well at harvesttime."

"I know, Deborah. How well I know. For your father, *tomorrow* was always certain to be the best

4

of days—or years. He could hardly wait for some great, shining time that somehow seemed to elude us but must lie beyond the horizon of tomorrow."

"What is wrong with that sort of faith?"

Rose Dexter was quiet a little while before answering. Then her words came in a studied and perplexed way. "Lately, honey, I keep asking myself just that. What is wrong in putting so much faith in the future? It kept us going through hailstorms, drought, grasshopper plagues, and blizzards. But it was also breaking our bodies and our hearts . . . making your father and me old beyond our years." As her words ended, Rose Dexter lifted the reins from her daughter's hands. "Lay your head on my lap, Debbie, and sleep a bit; you've been up since long before daylight."

It took them two full days to drive to the town of Box Butte, which had sprung up on the main line of the Union Pacific Railroad. Evening was coming on when they drove slowly into town and stopped on a large vacant lot that offered both grass and dry branches from an old cottonwood tree. Water could be carried from a pump they had noticed beneath a nearby windmill. They yearned for a hotel room, a bath, and restaurant cooking; prudently they forced themselves to gather wood and start a fire over which to prepare their supper. They could spread bedding on the grass and sleep beneath their wagon while the picketed horse, mule, and cow grazed nearby.

Twilight was deepening into night when two men, astride tired horses, rode by them and stopped a hundred feet away. Behind the saddle of

5

each was a tightly roped bedroll. The men seemed to have no rifles or handguns. Deborah watched them curiously as they alighted and stood in quiet conversation. She had never seen men such as these, dressed in black suits and with white shirts. Their hats were also black, with broad brims and rounded tops.

Presently one of the strangers strode toward the Dexters' wagon and removed his hat. Despite his heavy beard, Deborah sensed that the man was young, perhaps in his early twenties.

"Miss," he said after a bow, "I am Elder Nephi Oakes, a missionary of the Church of Jesus Christ of Latter-day Saints—the Mormon faith."

His words caused Rose Dexter to leave the campfire and move closer. He repeated his name and that of his church. Then he added, "We usually make camp here because of the grass. However, ladies, if you would rather we went elsewhere tonight, I am sure we can find a spot."

The respect with which he spoke caused Deborah to peer searchingly into his face. Then she asked, "Is the man with you also a preacher?"

A smile tugged at the stranger's mouth. "Not exactly. He is a missionary . . . the same as I. Our church has no ministers or preachers." He motioned for his companion to join them. When he did, Deborah instantly surmised that the second stranger was even younger than Elder Nephi Oakes.

"This is Elder Lemuel Froman, also of the faith. We have come—" The words of the older stranger broke off as a delighted laugh escaped the girl. Presently Deborah muffled her mirth, but her dark brown eyes remained alive with interest. "It seems odd," she remarked, "and downright funny that you two call yourselves *elders*. Why, neither one of you is much older than I am."

Rose Dexter, who had listened in silence, now cast a disapproving glance at her daughter. "That was a downright disrespectful thing to say, Deborah." She turned to face the men squarely. "I am Rose Dexter and this is my daughter, Deborah. As for your camping close by tonight, I . . . I hardly know what to say."

"Oh, Mom, let them stay. We'll be all right." In the girl's voice was yearning for companionship and a trace of the loneliness of their now-deserted Banner County homestead.

Rose Dexter considered the situation, then with some reluctance said, "It might be best if others were within calling distance. Stay the night, the two of you. Then we'll see what tomorrow brings."

With a word of thanks, the missionaries returned to their horses and unsaddled and picketed them. Soon they too had a small fire lighted and went about preparing a meal.

Time wore on and the Dexter women spread their blankets and prepared to seek a night's sleep. It was then that their attention was again drawn to the two strangers, whose voices had joined together in song.

Come, come, ye Saints, no toil nor labor fear;
   But with joy wend your way.
Though hard to you this journey may appear,
   Grace shall be as your day.
'Tis better far for us to strive

7

Our useless cares for us to drive;
Do this, and joy your hearts will swell—
All is well! All is well!

The words sounded clearly and pleasantly across the quiet coolness of the spring night. They were followed by the older missionary reading briefly from the New Testament of the Bible, and then by a short prayer uttered by the more boyish voice of Lemuel Froman. Then silence was across the campsites. For a time Deborah, in spite of her drowsiness, heard the words of the hymn running through her mind. "Mom," she said presently, "it was almost as though they understood our troubles and were singing just for us. You know . . . those words about 'hard to you this journey may appear.' Have you ever heard of such a religion? *Saints,* they call themselves. Latter-day Saints."

"I have read of them, Deborah. They are a persecuted people, the Mormons. They were driven out of both Kirtland, Ohio, and a place called Nauvoo, Illinois. That happened about fifteen years before the Civil War, and many of their leaders were killed. Later they crossed the Missouri River and then trekked westward to the Great Salt Lake Valley, out in what is now Utah."

"What do you suppose these two are doing here? In a railroad settlement in western Nebraska?" Deborah asked.

"Likely they have been sent out to recruit new members for the Church. The Mormons always want more settlers for that big frontier country out there. Also, I have heard it is part of their creed that the entire world should be told of their beliefs."

Deborah snuggled deeper into the blankets. "Anyhow, Mom, I feel safer with the two of them being off there a little way." Then she giggled. "I wonder if they ever get fleas in those big beards."

"Debbie, for heaven's sake, go to sleep," her mother replied.

The sun's rays, breaking over an eastern ridge, brought Deborah fully awake. She cuddled in the blankets spread beneath their wagon and looked about. Her mother was already up and just now was seated on a small stool and milking their cow. A curl of blue woodsmoke lifted lazily from their fire into the stillness of an early hour. Deborah shifted her gaze toward the missionaries' camp; already the two had broken camp and left. "They didn't have to up and run away like that," she muttered.

When Rose Dexter finished milking and carried the pail close to their wagon, Deborah had already left the quilts and dashed cold water onto her face from the pump. They repicketed their horse and mule to grassier spots, threw grain to the crated chickens, and then prepared breakfast. Rose stood looking over the part of Box Butte that lay within view. "It isn't as large a town as I'd hoped it might be, Debbie. Just the same, someone is going to need help. Perhaps in a store or a boarding-house."

"Can we leave our outfit here while we go down on the main street?" Deborah queried.

"It would be a foolish thing to do."

The girl turned to hide her disappointment from her mother, then said, "I'll stay and look after things. It is so short a way you can walk into town. But . . . but Mom, be right careful."

"We'll do nothing of the kind, honey. We will stay together. Help me hitch up, then tie the cow's lead rope to the wagon. We'll drive into town."

They came onto the single main street of Box Butte and presently drew up in front of a sizable general store. Their arrival drew few curious glances, for theirs was not the first heaped wagon to come and go along the dusty, pioneer street.

Within an hour Rose Dexter's face grew worried. Inquiry at several places had drawn but a shaking of heads and realization that work for a farm woman was probably not to be had without a long wait and after having become acquainted with the townspeople.

"I'll find something, Debbie," the woman said determinedly. "If needs be, we will find a shack somewhere abouts and I can take in washings and ironings."

"You would do that just to get me into a town school?" Deborah's words carried a bit of awe. Then she spoke words of firm conviction. "We'll make out, Mom. There will be something better than scrubbing floors or filthy work shirts."

Rose studied her daughter's face. "I wish I had some of your endless hope . . . that trust that time will solve everything in a wonderful way. It's something of your father in you. Likely it will be with you all of your life—for either good or for disaster."

"But you will find work, Mom. I just know you will."

"Then I wish it would show up real quick," Rose answered.

At noon they drew the wagon and livestock into the shade of a north-fronting structure that was Box Butte's elite hotel, restaurant, and barber shop. Off to one side stood a less pretentious two-story frame building with a sign designating it as a saloon.

"Pretty soon," Deborah said, "we'll have to go back to the place where we camped so the team can have water. Maybe tomorrow—" Her words were drowned by a new sound, the blast of a locomotive whistle. Her team moved nervously about but she kept a firm hold of the reins and quieted them. Soon a train rattled into town and stopped with its cars blocking one end of the street. Debbie watched, fascinated. "Wouldn't it be fun to travel on that—just take off for somewhere beyond a lot of hills—maybe even all the way to Idaho Territory!"

Her mother's eyes widened. *"Idaho.* Debbie, what on earth gave you such an idea? What do you know about Idaho Territory? It's out in the wilderness somewhere."

"I don't care how far away it is," Deborah replied quickly. "I read about it in a magazine and our school encyclopedia. There are forests out in Idaho country . . . and big rivers . . . and even fruit orchards."

Rose sighed, then said, "Another one of those wonderful places beyond a rainbow. Just like this end of Nebraska was talked up as a sort of paradise when the railroad and the land agents wanted settlers out here. Your father was so enthusiastic—"

11

Their conversation was cut short as they watched a man come onto the plank sidewalk and approach their wagon. He was dressed in a tailored blue suit and a homburg hat and appeared to be in his early forties. He came closer and cast a sharply appraising eye over the mismatched team, the clutter of household goods, and the two women. Then he spoke to Rose Dexter.

"I hear that you are looking for work," he said bluntly.

"That is right," Rose replied. "I am Mrs. Dexter, and this is my daughter, Deborah. If you are needing help, I can do housework or cleaning, or even help in a store."

The man's eyes swept over her and then fastened on Deborah. "I'm well supplied with such help. But I might have something to offer the young lady."

"Like what?" Rose asked guardedly.

He nodded toward the saloon. "I could use another dancer; we put on a show of sorts every night." He waited a bit, then added, "Think it over. My name is Carswell. Henry Carswell."

A flush of anger crossed Rose Dexter's face. "I've already thought it over, Mr. Carswell. The answer is *no!* This girl is only sixteen years old."

"So what?" Carswell grinned in an unperturbed way. "A job's a job these days. Hard to find. Think it over." He turned to stride away.

Moments later Deborah looked squarely into her mother's face. "You didn't give me a chance to say one word," she said heatedly. "Mom, maybe I could learn to be a dancer. We need money and a place to live." The stark reality of their future lay in her thoughtful eyes.

"Do you realize what being that sort of dancer really means, Debbie? In a place like that man is talking about? Well . . . I'll tell you. He wants saloon girls. Girls to dance with his customers—and perhaps to go upstairs with them. Railroaders. Cowboys. Homesteaders in town for a fling."

"Perhaps we would be better off in Idaho," Deborah breathed.

"Just what makes you think there aren't such places—and such men in Idaho?" her mother demanded.

"But what if we can't find work, Mom? What if that dancing job is all—?"

"Then we will move on, honey. It's only a couple of days' drive to Cheyenne. It is a lot bigger town and bound to have more jobs." Rose looked into the troubled face of her daughter and thought: She is too young for such uncertainty and so little security.

Then instant resolve swept Rose Dexter, and she said, "After a bit, Debbie, we'll drive back to the vacant lot. But you know what? Right now we are going to walk over to that restaurant across the street and have a real dinner—anything they have that we want."

When they returned to their campsite there were again horses and men on the vacant lot.

"It's the elders," Deborah said excitedly. "They have set up camp again. I hope they sing again this evening."

They were climbing from the wagon when the older missionary approached again and doffed his hat. As he spoke, he began to help unhitch the white horse and the tan mule. "If you ladies are to remain here a night or so, we have a tent we would like you to use." He pointed toward a rolled and wrapped canvas and added, "Lemuel and I can set it up for you. Those dark clouds gathering off westward likely mean rain, and the tent would—"

Debbie gave her mother no chance to refuse the offer. "A tent! A real tent. I've never slept in a real tent. Could you set it under a shady tree?"

"We could," Nephi Oakes nodded, "but it would be best to have it in the open . . . away from any tree. Just in case of lightning."

At his words, the girl threw her hands to her face. A shudder ran its way over her. Her mother threw a protective arm about Deborah, then explained. "She lost her father to lightning."

Nephi Oakes shook his head. "What a blunder on my part to have spoken so."

"You had no way of knowing," Rose Dexter said. "And we would appreciate use of the tent."

It was erected none too soon, for the rain began before dusk. It was not a blustery storm with wind and lightning and thunder, but rather a gently persistent drizzle that might continue throughout the night. Deborah watched its coming and then spoke accusingly to the two missionaries. "You've provided us with shelter and now have none for yourselves."

As the men threw black rain slickers about themselves, young Lemuel Froman answered. "Don't worry about us. We have arranged for an empty building just off main street. We're using it a night or so for church services. We can bed down there afterward."

"Services," Deborah repeated curiously. "I thought you Mormons did not have preachers."

"Does one have to be a preacher to speak of what is closest to his mind and heart?" Froman challenged.

"Of course not." In Deborah's reply was something of her reluctance to have them leave, to face the lonesomeness of the camp and the oncoming night.

Nephi Oakes studied her face, then said, "If you ladies would care to attend our church services, we shall escort you to and from our building."

An exciting possibility struck the girl, and she asked, "Aren't you from Utah? Close to Idaho?"

Oakes nodded. "Indeed we are. In fact, miss, we left Ogden only three weeks ago."

"Have you ever been to Idaho?" she asked quickly.

"I was born and grew up in Idaho," Lemuel Froman replied.

"If we come to your meeting, will you tell us something about Idaho?" Deborah asked excitedly.

"Of course," Nephi Oakes replied, grinning. Then he grew serious. "But we will speak also of other times and of other places. Of the land and the time of those the Master termed his 'other sheep.'"

A light rain continued as darkness fell. The dirt roads of the town became muddy and puddled, except for a single block of the business street; along this stretch, gravel had been spread and reached almost to the plank sidewalks. Accompanied by

Nephi Oakes and Lemuel Froman, the two women left the shelter of their tent and walked into town. There was the pleasant scent of woodsmoke in the air; from a roadside ditch came the springtime challenge of half a dozen frogs.

The building to which the missionaries led the way was a small clapboard structure that for a time had housed a harness shop. Now it had been swept, dusted, and rearranged to accommodate a few chairs. There was a small varnished table on which the missionaries had laid two books. Deborah knew one of them to be a well-worn Bible. She noticed the embossed title of the other—the Book of Mormon.

Seven o'clock, set for the service, came and passed. Although Deborah and her companions glanced often toward the door, no other person entered. A full half hour passed, and there was only the murmur of the rain on the roof and an occasional word among the four. Then Elder Nephi Oakes rose and said, "Perhaps we should begin our devotions."

"But there's nobody here," Deborah spoke up in surprise. "That . . . that is, except my mother and me."

"It was said by the Lord," Oakes replied, "that wherever two or more gathered in His name, there would He be also."

The services were not long, but from them, both Deborah and Rose Dexter learned much of the belief of these two men. After a concluding prayer, Lemuel Froman handed the women small pamphlets. "These tell of a race of people we believe lived in the North and South American continents long before the discoveries of Columbus. You will read of things that may amaze you. You may also have your doubts. Perhaps we can discuss these things at a later meeting." He paused, then added, "Miss Deborah, you asked to be told something of Idaho. Do you have questions I might answer?"

"Is it really so beautiful a place . . . streams . . . meadows . . . woods?"

Froman smiled and would have replied. Instead, the attention of the four suddenly centered on raucous and jeering voices from outside the building. There was a yell, then a fist-sized rock shattered a pane of the store's side window. A high-pitched voice called out, "Come on out and preach in the street, you infidel Mormon Saints."

Deborah noted the glances between the two young missionaries. She sensed that they had experienced this before. Both men strode to take strategic places beside the door opening onto the street. Anyone entering would be in for a rude and rough surprise, for into the capable-looking hands of both Oakes and Froman had come tools of self-defense—effective-looking clubs capable of quelling a small riot.

Another voice sounded from outside. "I say we go in and drag the proselyting bastards out."

A calmer voice cut in. "There are women in there. We're not going to harm women."

"How do we know they're not being harmed now? Besides, that young one is a good-looking filly. About right for me to—"

The words that would have followed were lost in the sudden yanking of the door open by Nephi Oakes. He had shed his coat and now stood on the building's outer step with anger-touched face and voice.

"This building is a place of worship. If any one of you wants to defile it, get ready for battle."

Through the open doorway and the mistlike rain, Deborah noted that the outer crowd was larger than she had at first thought. She was aware too that Lemuel Froman had stationed himself in a way that would offer protection for her and her mother. These missionaries might take a beating, but it would be after a mighty fight.

One figure detached itself from the crowd and shuffled toward the waiting Nephi Oakes. "I can give both of these preachers a going-over," he boasted. He stepped closer and took a hefty, looping swing at Oakes. Had it landed full force, Oakes might have been knocked into the muddy street. Oakes saw it coming and sidestepped the smash. In a reasonable tone, he said, "You're pretty drunk, fellow." Then the missionary appealed to the crowd. "Why don't you take him home for a sobering sleep?"

Again there was a forward movement of several men; Deborah knew now the nasty mood of the intruders and the danger lurking for the missionaries. She looked about for something she could grasp and use in their defense. There was a chair or so, but these were heavy and could be swung aloft and used to bash a head or two. She was moving to grab a chair when her eyes fixed in astonishment on her mother. Abruptly, Rose Dexter was standing in the open door and from somewhere within her clothing had brought forth a stubby but deadly-appearing pistol. She lifted it so it was seen by the mob outside. "Now just hold everything," she snapped. "I mean every one of you silly idiots."

"Are you a Mormon believer too?" someone asked.

"I'm a Methodist. A fighting Methodist. And right now I mean business."

"All we want to do, lady, is run these Mormons out of town. Nebraska doesn't need the likes of them."

Rose stared at the speaker, then seemed to dismiss him with contempt. Her gaze had riveted on another man who was standing at the edge of the crowd. She recognized him as the saloonowner who had offered Deborah a job. Keeping the crowd aware of the weapon in her hand, she challenged the saloonkeeper. "Is this the sort of riffraff you wanted my daughter to dance with . . . entertain?"

Henry Carswell studied her in an unperturbed way, then said, "You know, sister, maybe I do have a job for you." He turned to the restless crowd. "Drinks are on the house for fifteen minutes. Let's get in out of this infernal rain."

For a moment there was hesitation, with the attention of the crowd shifting among the crouching and ready Nephi Oakes, the pistol-holding woman, and Carswell's unexpected offer.

"Let's get downtown for a snifter," an older man urged. "Hell, we can chase Mormons out of town any day. Old Carswell don't spring for free drinks once a year."

Within a couple of minutes the mob had dispersed and a quietness was upon the small meeting place. Deborah managed a relieved smile, put down an oak chair, and smiled at Lemuel Froman. "You never did get to tell me about Idaho."

Froman started to reply and then remained silent as a serious-faced Nephi Oakes laid down his club and spoke. "We can do better than tell you of Idaho, Deborah. People like your mother and you are needed there. We can arrange for you to have safe conduct to Idaho . . . and attend school while your mother has decent employment."

Deborah's mouth fell open, then seconds later she asked, suspiciously, "Would we have to join your Latter-day Saints? Become Mormons?"

"Only if the time comes that your heart dictates such a decision."

Rose Dexter had listened, and now she spoke. "Idaho is far away, Debbie. It would cost about everything we have to get there. Besides, I'm wondering what sort of job that conniving Mr. Carswell is going to offer me."

Deborah looked at the missionaries in a troubled way. Presently she asked, "Are you going to stay around here, in Box Butte, with so much trouble stirred up? With those men threatening you?"

"We must remain until our mission is completed," Lemuel Froman answered.

The girl was pensive and subdued as she shrugged into her coat. Why must Idaho always seem but a dream, a distant and enchanted land of beauty but unreality?

The Dexters did not have to wait long to learn what Henry Carswell had in mind for them. They were scarcely out of bed the next morning when he drove up to their camp in a polished buggy drawn by a pair of spirited black horses. He greeted them in a friendly but brusque way, centering his attention on Rose after a sweeping glance about their camp. "Roughing it like this can get people old in a hurry," he commented. "It's no way for womenfolk to exist."

Deborah stared briefly at him, then responded tartly, "It's better for us than what you tried to hire me for—saloon bait for drunks."

Carswell grinned broadly. "A spitfire, aren't you? Well keep it up, sis. There are too many meek and wishy-washy people these days." He turned to Rose Dexter. "Lady, I need someone to take over a restaurant I own downtown. I've an idea you can cook . . . and for sure you know how to handle trouble."

As Rose absorbed the offer, Carswell sized up the part of the lot where the two missionaries were dampening their campfire and preparing to ride away. "I hope," Carswell said aloud, "that those Mormons clear out right soon. Leave this corner of Nebraska."

His tone caused Deborah to bristle. "I hope they stay right here in Box Butte," she said. "At least we can trust them. Both Mr. Oakes and Mr. Froman are friendly. And helpful."

Carswell chose not to answer but spoke again to the girl's mother. "Mrs. Dexter, if you take on the restaurant for me, it will be strictly a business deal. The pay will get you by and we can provide a small house."

"Are you sure this has nothing to do with your other business, your saloon and dance hall?" Rose questioned doubtingly.

"Listen, lady, money is what interests me. You make my eating place show a profit and nobody's going to bother either you or your feisty girl. Besides, if you don't like the arrangement—say, after two or three weeks—the road will still be open for you to leave this town."

Rose glanced toward the missionaries, who were now standing in conversation. She sensed that they were waiting for Carswell to finish his visit and leave. Now she said, "Mr. Carswell, I would like until tomorrow to think this over, but I do appreciate your offer."

He tipped his hat and turned to leave. "I'll wait for your decision, ma'am."

When he was out of sight, Rose motioned Deborah to her side and walked over to the missionaries. "Thank you for standing by," she said. "Mr. Carswell has offered me work handling a restaurant he owns."

"Can that man be trusted?" Deborah asked bluntly.

Nephi Oakes answered. "Carswell owns a big slice of this town, and money is his chief concern. If you can build a business for him, you'll make a good amount of money."

"He said he hoped you two get out of this part of Nebraska right soon," Deborah said.

Lemuel Froman nodded. "He realizes that our ministry can cut into the profits of his less-desirable enterprises. But, Deborah, I sense something beyond that: Henry Carswell is concerned for our safety."

"But he isn't a Mormon, is he?"

"Of course not. But behind that facade of not caring is a man of spiritual worth."

Rose Dexter had listened, and now her decision was reached. "Deborah, I am going to take the restaurant job with Mr. Carswell. We can't live underneath a farm wagon much longer."

Two weeks went by. The Dexters found the house provided by Carswell to be warm, solid, and clean. With the furniture they had brought from the homestead, they made it comfortable. On the edge of town was a fenced pasture in which they could graze their horse and mule and the cow for a small rental.

Rose turned to the affairs of the restaurant on the town's main street. For a week she and Deborah went about in old clothing and with rolled sleeves as they cleaned and scrubbed and polished. Then it became a matter of ordering and organizing their food and supplies. Menus were planned and a small advertisement placed in the *Box Butte Bugle*. The time passed so busily that they scarcely realized that several days went by without their seeing either Nephi Oakes or Lemuel Froman. Business at the restaurant picked up. Rose began making inquiries about the local school and courses that Deborah could take.

On another night of pouring rain, the missionaries returned. It was nearing midnight when Deborah, with her mother close behind, jumped from bed, threw a robe about her, and answered an insistent pounding on their door. In the dim light they could make out the forms and faces of Oakes and Froman—and between these two was the limp form of a third man. A single glance at the stranger caused Deborah to cry out in alarm, "My God, who is he? What has happened to him?"

23

Oakes answered in a weary and concerned voice, "We don't know his name. He is a sheepherder. A Basque. His flock was slaughtered . . . a few miles north of here." Oakes drew a long breath and continued. "This man was beaten and left in a ditch—half dead."

Rose Dexter turned to touch a match to the kitchen's kerosene lamp. "Bring him in here. Then go find a doctor."

Oakes shook his head. "It would be better if we try to dress his wounds and then take him to our meeting hall."

"Why?" Deborah cried out. "Look at his face. And that broken arm. He needs a doctor. We can fix a bed for him here."

Lemuel Froman laid his hand firmly on her shoulder, and his eyes were solemn. After a moment he asked, "Do you realize what you are saying, Deborah? This man is a sheepherder in cattle country. Anyone who helps him may be in great trouble."

Rose had already moved into the kitchen and was dampening a washcloth. At Froman's words, she looked up but remained silent. It was as though she had already made up her mind and was waiting only for Deborah to concur.

After a thoughtful moment, the girl asked, "If it is so dangerous to help a beaten man, what causes you and Elder Oakes to take such risks?"

The missionaries remained silent as they lowered the stranger onto the narrow cot toward which Deborah pointed. They would have drawn a stained saddle blanket about him, but instead used a patchwork quilt that Rose handed them. Deborah looked from the face of Oakes to that of Froman, and her chin took on a determined thrust. "How can we be less caring . . . less compassionate than you?" Her eyes held a resolute steadiness as they searched the sheepherder's bruised and discolored face, noting its youthfulness. "Jesus," she murmured, "he isn't really a man—just a boy . . . maybe eighteen. Or nineteen."

"Leave him with us," Rose nodded. "But first look in our woodshed for something we can use as splints on his arm."

"I've been taught how to set such a break," Oakes said. "It would be best if we can do it before he regains consciousness. Sometimes the pain proves almost unbearable."

Their task was almost finished when the young herder's eyes opened and his breath quickened in pain. To their surprise, no cry escaped him. He lay silent, then after a time let the gaze of his dark eyes roam their faces and the room. When Rose slipped a pillow under his head and helped him to sip water from a glass, he smiled tiredly. Three low spoken words followed, but none of those present knew their meaning.

"Probably he speaks the Basque tongue," Lemuel Froman explained. "It is a difficult language. Some say it was spoken in the Garden of Eden."

Nephi Oakes studied a window, noting that now it was touched by the first faint light of dawn. He shrugged into his coat, then said firmly, "Lemuel, if we're to leave here unseen, we have little time to get started."

"But you . . . both of you . . . will need something to eat," Deborah protested.

"Thank you, but another time, Deborah," Lemuel Froman spoke up. "There is no sense in causing you more danger than we already have."

Moments later both missionaries went quietly into the outer gloom, mounted their horses, and were lost to sight.

Chapter 2

THE DAY dawning outside was Sunday. Rose heaved a sigh of relief as she realized her restaurant would remain closed and she could stay home. She made the stranger as comfortable as possible, then seeing that Deborah had fallen asleep in a chair, she roused the girl and helped her to bed in their small room that opened off the kitchen. After a while the injured man stirred restlessly. Rose sensed his need, sought out an empty tin pan to place near him, then left the room. Later she emptied the pan and again bathed his swollen face.

The day wore on without incident. When the shadows of evening were lengthening, a refreshed Deborah awakened and began preparing supper. Rose went again to the bedside of her patient. He had awakened, and there was less pain and bewilderment about him. When she made signs as to whether he was hungry, he nodded and smiled tentatively. At that moment he seemed little more than a child, and Rose placed her hand reassuringly over his. His eyes softened, and for the first time she knew him to be fully conscious. His lips moved; in tones scarcely audible across the room he said, "Me Antonio—Antonio Onederra."

Deborah had entered the room with a poached egg, a bowl of soup, and a cup of tea. She drew a chair close to the cot and placed the food upon it.

Then she pointed to her mother. "Rose," she said and then slowly repeated the name. He uttered it aloud clearly, but when she pointed to herself and said, "Deborah," it took him a little time to master the sounds. Later, after he had eaten, he spoke one word in a fretful and concerned way. "Sheep," he said worriedly, and they knew he was inquiring about the flock that had been in his care. All they could do was shake their heads, then move their hands in an unknowing, helpless way.

At her cafe the following day, Rose Dexter noticed a changed atmosphere among her customers. Usually there was joking and talk of events about the town and grasslands, but now the men and women there had become quiet and noncommittal. There was a little talk of a slaughtered band of sheep and the disappearance of their herder, but it was mentioned guardedly and with no opinions offered.

It was nearing two o'clock and she was preparing for the evening meal when a slight noise from the street caused her to peer out of a large window beneath which she had set half a dozen potted geraniums. A stranger was knotting bridle reins about her hitchrail, and when finished he turned to stroke the flank of his horse. Rose watched in fascination. She had seldom seen a horse such as this, yet she realized that it must be a purebred Arabian stallion. It stood sleek and proud, frequently tossing its shapely sorrel-hued head. Its trim but well-muscled legs seemed to speak of both speed and stamina.

Her interest and curiosity quickened as she assessed the man who had spoken aloud to the horse and then begun walking toward the cafe's door.

28

He was tall enough that he had to lower his head to enter. His hat was in his hand, and with the hat he beat dust from well-cut trousers and coat. He was middle-aged, with dark hair and moustache. About his face, tanned and furrowed, there seemed neither friendliness nor dislike. The reserve seemed to center in his gray eyes, which were quiet and watchful and aloof.

He chose a seat facing the door through which he had entered. When Rose took his order, she was aware of his close scrutiny of her and was keenly conscious of the weapons strapped to him: two mahogany-handled pistols whose holsters hung from a belt inlaid with silver. He chose a breakfast order and ate it leisurely. When the only other customer in the cafe had left, the gunbearing stranger motioned Rose toward him. Then he spoke, and his voice surprised her. It was well modulated but firm; it seemed also to hint of southern days and schooling.

"Ma'am," he said, "I presume we are alone. That there is no one else about."

Her first impulse was to parry the question, not give him certainty of her being by herself. But for some reason unknown to her she nodded, then explained, "I have only a part-time waitress and dishwasher. She left half an hour ago."

A small, pleased smile touched his face. "That is good, Mrs. Dexter. What I have to say is for your hearing only."

Rose must have let her surprise show. How had this stranger known her name . . . her identity?

He seemed to read her thoughts. "Two men of the Mormon Church spoke of you. They asked me to let you know they are both well."

"The missionaries," Rose said, relieved. "Elders Oakes and Froman."

He nodded, then looked about to confirm again their aloneness. "The young herder—the one who was beaten—how is he doing?"

She dropped into a chair across the table from him, studied his face, then asked, "Just who are you?"

"Does it really matter, Mrs. Dexter? I know that you have risked much by taking in one of us—a young Basque, Antonio Onederra. You are caring for him at your home. And his whereabouts are still unknown, although vicious and merciless men are seeking him."

"He is better," Rose said on impulse. "He has a beaten face and a broken arm. Thank God that is all."

The stranger rose to his feet, inquired the price of his meal, and drew a small leather pouch from his shirt pocket. Presently he laid two gold pieces in her hand. "The meal was very good and very welcome," he said almost gratefully. "And I am sure the care of Antonio is also excellent." She started to make change, but he waved her hand away. "You may need supplies. Medicine. Keep the change. You have done something brave. It is appreciated." He turned to leave, then hesitated momentarily. "I do regret not having met your courageous daughter. She must be quite like you." Without another word, he passed through the doorway. Rose watched, perplexed, as he swung easily into the saddle and reined his sorrel mount in a direction that would take him quickly out of Box Butte.

He had scarcely been gone half an hour when

another man arrived at the cafe. It was Henry Carswell, owner of the property, and although he came afoot from his saloon, Rose sensed anxiety and urgency about him. For a few moments he stood in thoughtful silence, with one foot on a chair while his finger traced idle lines on a red-checked tablecloth. Then he asked abruptly, "Do you know who that rider was . . . and why he was here?"

Rose moved to where she could look steadily into Carswell's face. "I know only what he saw fit to tell me, Mr. Carswell. He gave no name and no indication of his business. He merely mentioned someone he knows and whom he feels I may have met."

Carswell's hand formed into a fist and beat nervously on the table. "Someone you have met, Mrs. Dexter—like the Basque sheepherder you are harboring within your house?"

Rose's face displayed no surprise or disturbance at his blunt question. She had dealt with Henry Carswell before. "Yes, Henry," she answered, stressing his first name. "Deborah and I are taking care of a badly beaten young man, one who understands but a few words of our language. We only know that his name is Antonio Onederra . . . that he has a badly beaten face and a broken arm . . . and that he was brought to us in the middle of the night after his flock was destroyed."

Carswell had listened without interrupting. Now he smiled for the first time. "Suppose we sit down like a couple of sensible people and discuss this over coffee and a slice of your lemon pie." When she had served him and sat with a cup in her elbow-propped hand, he added, "Rose, you're about the most honest and outspoken woman I've ever met. You've made a real winner out of this dinky cafe. But now I am worried. There are things you should know."

"Like what?" she encouraged.

"Like the news that was brought into my saloon an hour ago. Last night several head of range cattle were killed or badly injured close to where the sheep were destroyed. The cows and a couple of bulls were hazed off a fifty-foot ravine embankment."

Rose shuddered, then asked, "Henry, what is all of this senseless brutality leading to?"

"I wish to God I knew for sure. It's the old story of not enough room or graze for both cattle and sheep on our corner of the grasslands. It is likely to get nasty, Rose, with men injured or killed as well as livestock." Carswell was silent a bit, then went on. "The stranger who came here to the cafe? Was he aware you are caring for the herder?" Without awaiting her answer, he continued, "He must have been.

"Rose, that man, the rider on that Arabian stallion, is Jeff Harding. He used to be a gunfighting lawman in Wyoming. Now he is working for the big sheepmen of the West. Wherever these range wars loom up you'll find Jeff Harding—and his guns.

"What concerns me now is safety—for you, for that spitfire girl of yours. You know, Rose, I got to admire your sheer guts if not your wisdom. Before long the cattlemen, particularly the crazy ones who slaughtered those sheep, are going to find out you are hiding the herder. In a small town like this there's no way it can be kept a secret."

"What should I do then? I can't force a sick and bewildered boy out into the night. Not until he has healed some."

He dug in his pocket and handed her a serviceable-looking pistol. "I know you already have one of these. I would suggest that both you and Deborah keep one close at hand. Just in case." Carswell managed a somewhat reassuring smile, then rose to leave. Then he said, "It's close to closing time. Why don't you go home now. And, by the way, don't be surprised if you happen to see a man or so watching your house. Likely the cattlemen don't suspect you yet—but if I know Jeff Harding, the sheep association has already set a guard over your house."

A strangely persistent thought was upon Rose Dexter as she locked the cafe and hurried homeward: Is Debbie so impractical . . . so crazy . . . after all, to think there may be a better life for us out in Idaho?

Within their cottage, Deborah was standing at a window watching a few cars being shunted about by an engine on the Union Pacific's tracks nearby. There was a pensive look upon her face, but it vanished when she looked up and greeted her mother, who asked about the condition of their patient.

"I guess he's better," Deborah said, laughing. "He insists on hiking to the outhouse. Won't have a thing to do with our chamber pot. And he insists on sitting up and laying out some sort of game for himself with a deck of cards."

"It sounds like he's on the mend," Rose said. "And it is better so. Debbie, there is more trouble. A bunch of cattle were killed last night, probably in retaliation for the sheep." Rose settled into a rocking chair, flexed her toes, then told of the rider who had inquired of their patient. "Somehow, Deborah, it was almost as if he were two persons. Warm and concerned about our Basque boy, courteous to me. Yet I sensed that he has faced death and danger and has brought them to others—to his enemies. That man can be an avenger—a deadly one."

As she became silent, Rose noted that her daughter was again at the window, staring into the twilight. Then Rose asked, "Debbie, in heaven's name what do you see out there? You've scarcely—"

Deborah motioned for her mother to stand beside her. "Mom, do you see that boxcar? The red one over there on the siding? There are men in it. Two men. And I am sure they are watching our house, spying on us."

"Likely so, honey. Mr. Carswell seemed sure that the mysterious rider, that Jeff Harding, would leave someone to watch over us."

Deborah pointed to another car. "I like that one better, Mom, the one with doors shut tight. Know what it is? It is an *emigrant* car. The kind the Union Pacific uses to move families and their belongings to a lot of places far up their lines."

"Like maybe to Idaho country?"

"If the railroad goes there. I'm not sure it does yet." The girl peered into the fast-gathering darkness, then added, "Lemuel Froman told me a lot of Mormons go to Utah nowadays in emigrant cars. It's faster and safer and a sight more comfortable than a covered wagon."

Before she could say more, they were interrupted by the young Basque passing through the room. He was obviously embarrassed and clutched about him a faded robe that Rose had given him. He moved into the backyard and headed for the privy.

"How often has he done that before, in daylight?" Rose asked sharply.

"Only twice."

"Twice too often," Rose said, worried. "If he hasn't already been spotted, he surely will, come tomorrow."

While Antonio Onederra was still outside, a rapping sounded at their front door. Before opening it, Rose made sure her hand was on the pistol Carswell had given her. But there was no cause for alarm; their visitors were Nephi Oakes and Lemuel Froman. Their clothing was dusty, and the faces of both were heavy with fatigue.

As Rose motioned them inside, Oakes asked, "How is he, ma'am?"

"He is already up and about," Rose assured them. She waved the missionaries to chairs, then asked, "But how about you two? You look exhausted. Where have you been?"

"On what I fear has been an impossible errand," Nephi Oakes answered despondently. "Lemuel and I hoped to visit some of the more reasonable stockmen, those who run cattle, and the few sheepmen, to persuade them to avert a catastrophe."

"Feelings are running pretty high and ugly here in town," Rose commented. She then told them of the visit of the stranger, Jeff Harding, to the cafe, and also of Carswell's certainty that the sheepmen had posted guards to protect her and Deborah and also the young Basque.

"There is apt to be bloodshed before this mess straightens out," Lemuel Froman cut in decisively. "I wish there was some way we could get that beaten herder out of Box Butte. I feel responsible for what might happen—"

His words dropped off as the rear door opened and Antonio Onederra came into the room. He stopped short, both frightened and wary of the missionaries. It wasn't until Oakes offered him a hand and a smile that the herder lost some of his fear.

"He doesn't recognize you," Rose surmised. "You know, he was unconscious when you brought him in." She was watching Onederra speculatively as he stood looking uncertainly from one face to another. "I fear what will happen if he is here tomorrow and persists in going outside," she said.

"But he needn't be here tomorrow. None of us need be," Deborah spoke up, her voice full and firm across the room. "It's so simple we should have realized all the time." She had the full attention of the others.

"Realized what?" Rose asked.

"If we act right away we can be—" She became silent. There was a low but insistent rapping at the front door. It brought concern to the face of everyone in the room. Again Rose Dexter's hand knew the comfort of the pistol in her pocket as she stepped close to the door and asked, "Who is it?"

"It's me, Rose. Henry Carswell. Let me in, please. Hurry."

The urgency of his tone caused Rose to throw

open the door. He came in and closed the door quickly behind him. "There is apt to be hell in town before morning. Some of the riffraff are playing the sheepmen and cattlemen against each other." He turned to the missionaries. "You know the stupid jackasses I mean. The same ones who wanted to run Mormons out of town—or worse." Carswell dropped worriedly into a chair, stared at the glowing chimney of a kerosene lamp, and added, "Maybe I can come up with a plan. It won't be easy this time. Every bastard in town seems to be packing a gun and panting for trouble."

Suddenly sixteen-year-old Deborah Dexter moved to stand facing them all. There was excitement and concern on her face. "Listen to me. We can all be out of this town before morning. We can take Antonio and go wherever we want . . . as long as it is farther west."

Carswell would have interrupted with a doubting question, but she gestured him to silence. "Right out there on the railroad siding is an empty emigrant car. It isn't fifty yards from this house. We could be in it, and have the things we need, within an hour. A westbound freight train comes through here between two and three o'clock in the morning. If we could arrange"—her voice lost some of its confidence as she thought aloud —"if we could arrange to have that car switched onto the train. But . . . but likely we couldn't. The train people would never do it without our paying a lot of money."

"It just might work," Nephi Oakes pondered aloud. "Many of our Saints traveled to Utah in such cars."

Henry Carswell ran thoughtful fingers through

his graying hair as they sat for a time in subdued silence. Finally he strode to the window, pulled aside a heavy curtain, and peered into the night. Then with a wry smile he faced the others. "I never thought I'd be fool enough to say what I am going to tell you. I can get that emigrant car on its way without any trouble. All I'll have to do is fork over the right freight charges to the Union Pacific night telegraph operator, then tell him it'll be loaded in time to be moved out on the morning train." He broke off, and his voice had changed to an amused irony as he went on. "Imagine me— Carswell, the tightfisted saloonkeeper—agreeing to ship off the best damn cafe manager I ever had. Along with her spitfire kid, a couple of preachers who think they are Saints, and a broken-winged kid who can't speak one word of American lingo. Jesus!"

A delighted laugh escaped Deborah. She walked quickly to Carswell's side, threw an arm about him, and looked at him excitedly. "You're willing to do that, Mr. Carswell? You really are? Maybe I should have taken the job dancing at your honky-tonk."

For a minute he squeezed her hand; then he pushed her aside. "Doggoned if it won't be great to have you and your ideas out of town. Now get busy. All of you. Get everything into that car you possibly can. Food, bedding. Your clothes. Any medicines you have." He turned to Nephi Oakes. "Elder, you ought to take charge. These folks will be heading toward your home stamping grounds."

Rose had listened with mingled eagerness and consternation. Now she said, "Mr. Carswell . . . Henry . . . I can't just up and leave the cafe after what all you've done for us. And . . . and besides, what would Deborah and I do with our cow . . . our horse and mule . . . our wagon?"

"The last part is the easiest," Carswell said with obvious emotion. "I will arrange to sell your belongings and send the money to you, Rose. You will need to let me know where to send it. About the cafe: You've done a fine job, and I wish I could keep you here. But if there is trouble in which any of you could get hurt or . . . or . . . Damn it all, Rose, get out of this powder keg before it blows a lot of innocent people to smithereens along with the idiots who stir up the trouble." He paused, baffled, then asked, "Where do you suppose you'll find a home spot out West?"

"We're going to Idaho Territory," Deborah answered quickly. "Out where there're mountains and rivers and lots of green things. Like big trees."

"Idaho, eh?" Carswell commented. "I was out there once myself, to a place called Bonanza, up on the Yankee Fork of the Salmon River. Way in the wilderness but rich with silver and gold. I'll give you the names of a couple of people there. Be sure to look them up if you get that far into Idaho." He grabbed his hat. "Now I'd better get down to the UP depot."

When he had left, a flurry of excitement broke across the others. Each realized that what they were about to attempt was daring and perhaps dangerous. It was quiet, thoughtful Lemuel Froman who put them at ease as he said, "Nephi, I know we are scheduled to return to Salt Lake City soon, but what will the Church officers say to our journeying west in an emigrant car?"

"Considering the circumstances, Lemuel, and the distinct possibility of a mob taking their frustrated fury out on us, I am sure the Church will agree that our mission here be postponed, or closed."

"What about your saddle horses?" Deborah asked.

"They are rented animals, belonging to a livery stable here in Box Butte. If we unsaddle them and turn them loose, I am sure they will be close to the livery stable when morning comes. The rest of our gear is pretty scant; we can stow it in a corner of the boxcar."

Rose said, concerned, "I surely hate to leave our cow. She is due to have a calf any day. Out West we likely will need a good milk cow. Can't we load her?"

"We could if there was time and we had a loading chute." Oakes pointed out. "There may be precious little we can get lifted into the car."

The answer came nearly an hour later, when they had packed what they knew they must take and began to carry it toward the emigrant car. Rose stood near the car and peered eastward along the siding, then whispered urgently, "If we could somehow push this car sixty feet or so that way, there is an embankment along the track."

"You're right, Mom," Deborah responded. "There are some heavy planks there, too. Or there were last week. Remember? Some plows and cultivators were unloaded."

All five pushed on the heavy mass of the car, but its iron wheels failed to move.

"We're crazy," Rose said, panting. "The brakes

are set. Those railroaders always climb up on top and turn that wheel when they leave a car."

Without a word Lemuel Froman sought out the iron steps of a ladder and climbed aloft. Then he hurried down. "It's released."

Despite the free brake and all of their strength, the car moved at an agonizingly slow pace. They had gone less than ten feet when sudden movement behind them caused them to whirl about. Two men had appeared out of the gloom. They wore bandana handkerchiefs across the lower part of their faces. They carried rifles and had holstered pistols at their sides.

"What goes on here?" one demanded in a low, accented voice.

Before either the Dexter women or the missionaries could reply, there was a muffled exclamation from Antonio Onederra as he pushed close to the speaker. Suddenly words burst from him in what seemed an unintelligible torrent. As he finished, his free arm was outthrust and his hand lay on the shoulder of the stranger who had challenged them.

This stranger spoke again. "This boy. He is Basque. He says you took good care of him. Set his arm. Doctored his face. Why did you do that for a sheepherder?"

"He wasn't a sheepherder to us," Rose said tersely. "He was a boy. And hurt. We would have done the same for a railroader, or . . . or a cowboy."

The second stranger had not spoken. Now he faced Rose and spoke in a cautious voice. "Don't be afraid of us, lady. We were sent here by Jeff

Harding in case you were threatened or needed help."

Rose again peered toward the gloom of the embankment ahead. "We need to get this car down there and load it. Box Butte may be a sizzling hell for all of us come daylight."

With the strength and weight of seven people, the car ground easily on the rails. Within five minutes it was at the embankment, the crucial planks had been placed, and a hurried loading began.

"At least we can get our cow aboard," Rose exulted. "But it's like me to leave some of my things at the cafe just at a time like this."

"Like what?" Deborah inquired in irritation.

"Don't be so cross, Debbie," her mother said tiredly. "You know I liked having some personal things at the cafe. A few of my own utensils. A couple of books. My Bible. Some pictures of you and your father."

A surge of compassion touched Deborah. "I understand, Mom. Of course you've needed a few of the things that make our leaving the homestead bearable." She waited a moment, then said decisively. "We're not going to leave those things behind, Mom. I'll go get them for you—right away."

Rose gasped aloud, then near-panic edged her answer. "Don't you dast, Debbie. We can't take the chance. Anything might happen to you if you went uptown alone."

"I am going, Mom. We have lost enough already. Just about everything we had."

Rose started to protest again, but the grimness of her daughter's face, revealed in the scant light, caused her to refrain. Instead, Rose drew the pistol from her pocket and put it in Deborah's hand. "Take this, child. I have another one. Mr. Carswell made me take it. And I am going with you to the cafe."

"You can't. One of us has to be here to make sure our things are loaded."

"She won't be alone." The words caused both women to whirl and face the men already busy getting the reluctant cow into the car. The taller of the two strangers had detached himself from the crew and was facing them. "Ma'am, where she goes, I go."

Rose stared in wonder as new confidence marked Deborah's face and she moved quickly toward the cafe. Within a few steps the darkness had obscured both her and the armed man who kept pace with her.

"Oh, my God," Rose reproached herself. "Why did I let her take such a chance? If only I knew I can trust that man."

"Mrs. Dexter, that man was placed here by Jeff Harding," Nephi Oakes said. "You can well believe he has no desire other than to guard Deborah—with his life, if need be."

Even in darkness it was only a five-minute walk through the darkened streets to the cafe. Deborah knew where a key to the back door was kept under the eaves of a lean-to. She found the key, unlocked the door, and went in. She noticed how the man who had accompanied her moved quickly into a position that would offer sight of both approaches to the building, then seemed to blend into the shadows. Inside, she groped about trying to locate the items her mother had mentioned. Soon she was panting in frustration. It would require light—and light was the last thing she wanted to risk. Her teeth were clamped desperately on her lower lip as she touched a match to the wick of a coal-oil lamp.

Aided by the light's pale and flickering glow, she quickly rounded up Rose's personal possessions in a large cloth bag. Deborah was smiling with satisfaction as she bent over to blow out the flame. Then she froze into rigid and fear-touched expectancy. Voices had sounded at the outer side of the door from which she had entered. There was a sound of scuffling and then the outraged voice of Henry Carswell. She moved to the door and jerked it open. The lamplight still cast its uncertain glow, for she had been too startled to finish blowing out the flame. Now the light revealed two men. Carswell stood staring angrily through the doorway. He could move no farther, for his way was blocked by the stranger who had accompanied Deborah here. His back was toward her now and with powerful shoulders and uplifted arms he was holding his rifle against Carswell's chest.

"Let him in," Deborah half shouted. "You hear me? It's all right. It's Mr. Carswell, who owns this place." As her guard slowly lowered his weapon, she smiled in relief at her mother's employer. Then she said, "My goodness, Mr. Carswell! What brings you here?"

"I might ask you the same thing, young lady. I was across the street coming back from the depot and saw a light in here." He was inside and had closed the door when he demanded, "Deborah, who is that big fellow outside?"

"I don't know his name. But he is one of those men the sheep people set to watch over the Basque

44

herder—and my mom and me." His face still showed his confusion. "My mother left some important keepsakes here. I couldn't let her leave town without them, so I—"

Carswell shook his head and for the first time managed to grin. "So you took one hell of a chance and came up here to break in. Girl, don't you realize what is happening? The mood of this town? Just one shot, or perhaps one shout, can set off a blind and irresponsible mob."

"We caused it. Me. My mom. The Mormons. When we took in that sheepherder. But Mr. Carswell, what would you have done if he'd been brought to your door?" When he failed to answer, she went on. "Did you see the agent for the railroad? How much is the car going to cost us?"

"Never mind about the money," Carswell growled. "It's arranged for switch pickup. It's already billed all the way to Utah."

"Utah?" she repeated weakly.

"Well, where else in kingdom come could I send you? You're going to Ogden. Ogden, Utah. Right out where those missionaries hail from." Carswell looked hastily about, then blew out the lamp. "Now let's get out of here. I suppose the others have the car about loaded. I hope so. Right now even some of the most responsible stockmen of western Nebraska are over at my saloon, half inclined to search every house in Box Butte for that Basque kid. Some of the wiser heads want this fracas cooled down. Others want to stir up a bloodletting range war."

Presently they were standing on the dark street close to the cafe. Deborah had listened to Carswell's anxious summary of circumstances in stony silence. Suddenly she straightened so that an errant ray from lights in the nearby saloon touched her face. Her eyes had narrowed and her fingers were tightly clenched. "Mr. Carswell, I am going to talk to them . . . those stockmen at your saloon."

"My God! No, Deborah!" he half shouted. "They wouldn't listen to you. Likely they wouldn't even allow you through the door."

"Because I am young? Because I am a girl? Mr. Carswell, I am old enough to have seen my father's love of these prairies and his faith in acres that were fenced and plowed. Sure I'm a girl. Who more than women know the stupidity and waste of slaughtering the cattle—or the sheep—that some family depends on to keep their children in clothes and schoolbooks and even with something to eat?" As her words ended, she was already striding across the street toward the door of the saloon. In wordless wonder, Henry Carswell plodded along after her. Neither of them noticed that another man followed almost as a silent shadow—the stranger who had been always on watch since they had left the emigrant car.

Carswell quickened his gait and was first to reach the door. "At least let me lead the way, girl. Sort of quiet things down and introduce you."

"They don't need to know who I am," Deborah said with anger. "I'm just going to tell them what I think. And it's probably the same as most of their wives would say if these foolish stockmen had sense enough to hear them out."

"If you're set on doing it, Deborah, for Lord's sake tell *them*. Not me."

Inside, as he kept close to her side and led the

way toward the far end of the well-lighted but smoke-hazed room, she looked about. She judged that there were thirty men in the saloon. Some of them were lined up at a polished bar, while others sat in small groups at tables upon which there were glasses, decks of playing cards, and receptacles for cigars and stubs of cigarettes. Her eyes widened at the long array of bottles on a mahogany back bar and the size of its reflective mirror. Above the bar, at midcenter, was a huge gilded frame enclosing the reclined form of a painted nude. She was aware also of the revealing silk and lace costumes of four girls who moved about the tables with smiles and banter.

An obviously flustered Henry Carswell lost no time coming to the point. "Listen . . . everybody. . . listen to me." He had grabbed a sturdy wooden box and was aiding Deborah to step onto it. "This pretty gal ain't going to tell any of you her name, but maybe a few of you already know her. She says she hails from up in Banner County. And she's got something she wants to tell you. If you're wise, you'll listen. This young lady has sense as well as pretty hair and eyes. I found that out when I tried to hire her and was flat turned down." He looked in a challenging manner about the room, then grinned nervously at Deborah. "Go ahead, gal. Get it said. Don't take too long; this speech time is costing me money when these dudes quit bellying up to the bar."

Deborah Dexter swept a seemingly contemptuous gaze over those staring at her. They seemed little different from the men she was accustomed to seeing each day on the streets, or those who had been neighbors when her father had been alive and they had lived in Banner County. She smiled at them tentatively, then after a deep breath said aloud, "Most of you are probably not going to like what I have to say. That's too bad. Why? Because I am going to tell you just how much a bunch of blasted fools you are. In ten years—and maybe a lot less time—neither cattlemen nor sheep growers are going to own and control the grasslands."

There was a murmur of doubt among them, but the crowd moved forward and seemed under the spell of her derision and her intensity.

"I grew up on a little homestead. Up in Banner County. We would still be there, my mother and me, if my dad hadn't been killed by lightning a couple of months ago." Deborah paused, then looked with level and challenging eyes into the grizzled face of an older and wiser-looking rancher. "My folks didn't have many acres . . . no big and powerful spread . . . but they had something a lot more precious: my father's way of looking ahead. He knew that the time of the Indians and the buffalo was about gone. And . . . and was just as sure that a few years will see the end of the too big and too wasteful cattle and sheep operations. The homestead laws will see to that. So will miles of barbed-wire fence. And plows. And harrows. And threshing machines. There's a saying my dad had that the future belongs to those who prepare for it. Right now, you fellows aren't preparing for anything except to kill off each other's herds and probably quite a few of yourselves."

Deborah fell momentarily silent, knowing that she was perilously near to tears. There seemed little agreement or sympathy on the faces of the men. Now one of the younger ones shouted, "Shit

. . . if we can run the herders and their stinking sheep off our range, we sure can handle a few hayseed homesteaders."

"Sure you can," Deborah blazed. "And for every one you chase off—or kill—you'll soon see a dozen more in his place. And remember this: Every one of them will soon have legal deed to the land he claims. There're likely to be courts, and even federal troops, to back them up." She threw her arms into the air, then shouted, "Damn it, why do I waste my time and breath? None of you will listen!"

She failed to hear the low comment of a thin, middle-aged man in rancher's garb who carried worry in his eyes. "You're wrong, young lady. Some of us have listened. Listened good."

Deborah turned to leave, then, over her shoulder, said in a tone that echoed throughout the room, "You stockmen will be swept away like the wind unless you use your God-given wits. Forget fighting. Build fences and let them instead of guns determine where sheep or cattle will graze. Otherwise the homesteaders will see the end to every last stupid one of you."

With Henry Carswell at her side, she moved toward the door. She had expected a roar of angry disapproval; instead, most of those present seemed stunned and uncertain.

They had slipped through the doorway into the outer darkness when an astonished Henry Carswell chuckled and said, "Hell, you've given 'em something to chew on and think about—at least those with brains, and they are the ones who count. Now . . . let's skedaddle and get you and your mother and that herder inside the emigrant car." Carswell gazed about, taking comfort from his sudden realization that the guard who had accompanied them to the saloon was following a few paces behind them.

They moved in silence toward the loading embankment and the car and soon were among those standing beside it waiting for them. Then abruptly there was a new sound. From the direction of the town's main street came the thud of running feet and the angry shouts and curses of several men. Henry Carswell tensed, knowing that already a mob had formed. "Are you through loading?" he demanded of Nephi Oakes.

"All that we believe it wise to attempt loading," the Mormon replied quietly.

"Then get inside. All of you. Quick." With surprising strength, Carswell lifted Deborah Dexter from her feet, held her close for a moment, and then placed her inside the car's half-open doorway. He motioned the men inside and said, "I'm going to slam the door shut and slap on a Union Pacific seal. Even damn fools hesitate to tamper with a UP seal. It can mean having a dozen railroad detectives and federal lawmen on their tail in a hurry."

As Lemuel Froman was entering the car, Carswell gripped his hand. "So long, Elder. Knowing the persistence of you Mormons, I suspect you and your partner will be back in Box Butte within a year. And by the way, if you need to break out of this car in a hurry, any sort of iron bar will pry off the hasp; it's made that way." He turned to grasp the hand of Rose Dexter, who had tarried outside and was the last to enter. "You're a strong and steady woman, Rose. Damn . . . I wish I could

50

keep you here. If you get to Idaho be sure to look up those people in Bonanza." He would have said more, but there was the loudening hue and cry of the searching mob. He pushed Rose into the car, then to her utter surprise kissed the hand he was still clutching. The car door was slammed shut, and there was the faint sound of the latch being closed and sealed. After that there was nothing but the darkness, the tenseness among them, and the urgent hope to be moving soon onto the main track . . . out of Box Butte . . . onto the long westward-pointed rails toward an unknown future. They did not know that already Henry Carswell was moving swiftly toward a waiting switch engine, or that near the boxcar's door a single grim-faced guard, with alert eyes and ears and a ready rifle, was still fulfilling the task that had been set for him by the sheepmen's enforcer, the man called Jeff Harding.

Although it seemed a long wait, it was only about fifteen minutes until there was a rumbling sound outside and then the slamming jerk as the switch engine coupled with their car. It began slow movement and then picked up speed. Silent but alertly listening, Deborah was sure she knew the moment when they were off the siding and moving toward the through train. This was confirmed by a second jolting coupling, the muffled voice of a trainman, and then the sound of a train's whistle signaling departure. Within minutes, the increased tempo of wheels moving over rail joints, and the slight swaying of their car, told them that they were indeed well out of Box Butte and rolling along through the night. None of them were aware that they had been given precious moments by a ruse of their mysterious guard. He waited near the car for the approach of prowling troublemakers, then deliberately let himself be seen entering the Dexter house. When the mob gathered about this house, ignoring the switching of a Union Pacific boxcar, the guard judged his timing and then quietly left through a window of the house. When the mob at last worked up courage to break into the house, they found it deserted.

Chapter 3

THOSE IN the westward-moving emigrant car sat for a time in darkness. There was silence about them, as though each was pondering the danger that lay behind, the narrowness of their escape, and the reality of the unknown before them. Presently Deborah heard someone groping toward her, then knew it to be her mother's comforting arms encircling her. She pressed her head upon Rose's shoulder. With the cheerful confidence she had inherited from her father, Deborah spoke aloud. "Things are going to be all right now, Mom. Up ahead there is Cheyenne. Then the country Mr. Oakes and Mr. Froman came from . . . the Mormon country. Best of all, Mom, we'll be closer to Idaho . . . to its big, clean greenness . . . to a real chance for you and me."

Her words seemed to break the tension within the car. Soon Nephi Oakes located a lantern and touched a match to its wick. A pale yellow glow drove back the darkness of the car and enabled them to seek more comfortable positions. After a short time of conversation and of assuring each other of the likelihood of their safety, they tired. Soon the light was extinguished and there were only the sounds of breathing, the rumble of wheels on rails and, infrequently, a whistle far ahead.

* * *

They were awakened hours later by the train's grinding to a stop. Outer light, coming through small cracks around the sealed door, told them daylight had come. Presently there was the sound of footsteps outside, coming to a halt at the door. There was enough light for Deborah to see both missionaries quickly stand before the door in readiness. She was aware too that her mother now stood with her revolver in hand.

There was a snapping sound, the rattle of a hasp being slid free, and then abruptly the car's door was slid aside about four feet. Daylight poured in, causing them to blink and then to stare. Peering into the car was an overall-clad trainman with red signal flag and a small cutting tool in his hands. Beyond him and across a couple of empty tracks were the streets and buildings of a town. And far beyond, in brilliant morning sunshine, was a vast sweep of prairie that rose to the darkness of forested mountains and a ridge of snowy peaks.

The trainman stood with a smile breaking across his weather-seamed face. "Hi, folks," he greeted them in an Irish brogue. "Now, don't ye be gettin' riled up or afraid. It's just that back in Box Butte Mr. Henry Carswell asked me to look in on ye." He paused to wave an arm toward the settlement outside. "Ye're in Cheyenne now. Cheyenne, Wyoming Territory." His eyes swept appraisingly across them, then he added, "Seems ye're all in good shape. If ye want to get out and mosey around a bit, it'll be most of two hours before this train moves out toward Laramie."

Deborah walked to the door and gazed tentatively about. "How far are we from Box Butte?" Her voice carried lingering concern.

The trainman studied her form as she stood in the doorway, then let his gaze lift to her firm chin, her steady, brown eyes, and her dark hair. There was appreciation of what he saw in both his stare and his voice as he answered her question. "Ye're better than fifty miles out of Box Butte now. Ease down, lass; ye don't have to keep lookin' fer troublemakers now." Suddenly he swept a soot-darkened cap from red and unruly hair and then thrust out a hand. "I'm Tim O'Fallon . . . a brakeman on this drag. I'll be with ye until we are over the hump to Laramie."

Rose had listened. Now she repeated in a puzzled voice, "Over the hump. What do you mean, Mr. O'Fallon?"

He pointed his red flag toward the sun-touched hills to the west. "We gotta climb that hump . . . them mountains. It's a steep crawl up to 8,000 feet atop Sherman Hill, then back down a couple a' thousand into Laramie City." He paused as his gaze encountered the two missionaries and the injured Basque. "Five of ye I see already. How many more have ye stowed away in there?" As though to satisfy himself, he climbed through the doorway and stood upright in the car.

Moments later Deborah laughed aloud at his astonishment. "Now that you've seen all five of us, maybe you can figure out how we can get something to eat. I'm hungry."

"Lass, there's a railroad eatin' place, a beanery, a few car lengths up the track near the depot. Or you can buy grub at a grocery an' meat market up the block." He pointed to a far corner of the car. "These emigrant cars are fixed up with a stove of sorts an' some kindlin' and coal." He shook hands with Rose and Deborah, waved good-bye to the missionaries, and then eyed the Basque sheepherder speculatively. "Likely," O'Fallon declared, "it is a good thing you got this young fellow out of Box Butte. I hope he doesn't get any ideas of stickin' around Cheyenne. This is cattle country."

He jumped from the car and leisurely sauntered away. Later Deborah had her mother write a list of their most urgent grocery supplies. Then with Nephi Oakes and Lemuel Froman she left the car, crossed the tracks, and ventured up the town's main street. There were more stores, more hotels, and more people on the street than she had ever seen in one place. And there was the constant movement of wagons, surreys, and men on horseback. She was aware of some of the strangers staring at her and the black-coated missionaries, but no one stopped or questioned them. Within an hour they had purchased the supplies and returned to the railroad car.

At its open door, brakeman Tim O'Fallon was again standing, now in animated conversation with Rose Dexter. He smiled toward Deborah and then drew a bulky silver watch from his vest pocket and studied it. "We'll be pullin' out for Laramie City in ten minutes or so. I'm gonna close this car door, but it won't be latched or locked. After a bit, when we're a few miles out of Cheyenne, you can push the door open if you wish. You'll see some country that's fresh from the hand of God when we get atop Sherman Hill. Be sure an' look southwest, over into the mountains of Colorado. We'll stop now an' then, but I wouldn't climb out and wander far from the train. We start up sorta suddenlike."

Of the long trip across Wyoming Territory, Deborah would remember many things. The vast, far-horizoned distances, the strong wind that seemed to blow constantly, and the smallness of the towns strung out along these railroad tracks and the line of telegraph poles that seemed always to seek some even more distant range of mountains or treeless and sage-strewn plain.

The nights through which they rumbled were cold enough to make them seek quilts and blankets, yet the sunlight-drenched days enabled them to spend much time with the door open as they watched the ever-changing panorama of scenery.

Sometimes they spotted herds of cattle, belonging probably to the widely separated ranches. Twice they passed bands of sheep, and sight of them created deep interest and a tinge of excitement within Antonio Onederra. The young Basque was healing rapidly now, and only a flour-sack sling in which he carried his broken arm remained as a token of the beating he had endured and of the days of suffering and anxiety that had followed as Deborah and Rose Dexter had risked their own safety to care for him.

The missionaries had managed to rig a few sticks of lumber and a roll of tar paper to give the Dexters a sort of private room at one end of the car. Both Oakes and Froman spent much time reading; Deborah wondered if these men ever for a single hour were without their Bibles, the Book of Mormon, and other tomes dealing with their faith.

It seemed that their train spent as much time at small stations and sidings as it did moving forward, and Deborah surmised that this main line of the Union Pacific, which had been built only ten years before, was the delicate and vulnerable supply line not only to the cities of the Pacific Coast, but also to an immense inland area. Nephi Oakes confirmed this, telling her that at some points wagons came as much as two hundred or three hundred miles to receive freight left by the trains.

Deborah's excitement grew with each passing mile. Now the green wonderland of Idaho was always nearer. Occasionally, as she stood or sat in the car doorway and studied the harsh and barren vistas of the Laramie Plains, the North Platte River country, and the Red Desert, she wondered if there could be a great and urgent change. Perhaps she had been fooled. Perhaps Idaho too would be desolate and windswept and made up of boldly looming but treeless buttes, of great brush-covered valleys, and of mountains that remained far away and elusive.

She voiced the fear to Lemuel Froman. He took her hand, held it reassuringly, and drew her to the open doorway. "Things will change, Deborah. They're already beginning to. See that valley off south? And the stream? It's the Black's Fork River. And that high wall of snowy peaks is the Uintah Range. Beyond those mountains is the great Wasatch Range—and then the Salt Lake Valley. Yes, Deborah, there will still be deserts to cross, but the beautiful land is out there too."

"It is just as though I am traveling into some shining tomorrow," Deborah said with a sigh.

"My father was like that. I remember how I sometimes wakened real early, back there on our homestead in Banner County. Daddy would already be up and looking out across the fields and the prairie. There was an eagerness on his face, just as if he was sure something great was about to happen." She hesitated and then added brokenly, "But . . . but it never seemed to come true."

"Don't be so sure it didn't," Lemuel Froman said, and his words carried conviction. "Didn't your father have land of his own . . . and you . . . and your mother . . . and the knowledge that each of you loved him?"

"I miss him," Deborah whispered. "And now he seems so far away."

"You carry a lot of him with you, Deborah. Most people, and especially women, would be doubt-ridden and fearful coming into a new and strange country. But you carry an eagerness to see the wonder of tomorrow and of the vistas beyond the next purple ridge or the next range of mountains. You're . . . you're a brave and understanding person, Deborah. A very special person."

She looked into his face, started to speak and then became silent. His words had revealed something she had vaguely sensed. Lemuel Froman, a missionary of the Church of Jesus Christ of Latter-day Saints, a young Mormon from Idaho Territory, carried deep feelings. Feelings that someday might lead him toward her tomorrows and her world.

Before they could say more, Rose Dexter motioned excitedly for all of them to come to the open doorway of the car. "Look!" she said excitedly and pointed outside. "The country has changed and we are in a valley, one that seems to be turning into a mountain canyon. There is a river. And green trees. Maybe at last we're beyond the desert."

Nephi Oakes shook his head. "No, Mrs. Dexter, there are vast deserts ahead. But just now we're about to enter Echo Canyon, a natural pass through the Wasatch Range of mountains. Within a few hours now we'll reach Ogden . . . Ogden, Utah Territory. We will be at journey's end as far as this emigrant car is concerned. Ogden is only about thirty-five miles from my home—Salt Lake City."

Rose scanned the sky and noted that the sun was dropping toward a serrated skyline. "Will we reach Ogden before dark?" she queried.

"Likely," Oakes nodded.

"What does it matter?" Deborah said and shrugged. "There will be no one there expecting us."

Neither of the missionaries answered, but Deborah was puzzled by the manner in which Lemuel Froman smiled at Oakes, and the older missionary's acknowledging nod.

They did not reach Ogden before dark. At a small siding named Devil's Slide their train drew to a halt and for almost two hours cars were banged about as loads of rock and lumber were coupled on. Then the train crew set lanterns as warning signals and took off for an eating place near the base of an awesome cliff. The impatient five people in the emigrant car from Box Butte, Nebraska, settled down for another night aboard. Later the freight train got under way again, but Deborah was too drowsy to pay much attention.

She was awakened by considerable noise outside the car. There was no train movement; daylight and a shaft of sunlight pouring in told her that the car door had already been pushed open. She noted that her mother was already up and about, having left their small tar-papered cubicle. With a tin basin and a scant supply of water, Deborah managed to freshen up and then to comb her tumbling curls into place. She had donned a light sweater and a slightly wrinkled calico dress when she walked expectantly to the car doorway and gazed out. So this was Ogden. Her first impression was of a larger and busier town than she had expected. There were mountains behind the town, and their height caused her to catch her breath. The sun was just now cresting them and throwing its warmth across streets that were bordered by stores and warehouses and various business buildings. There were several railroad tracks, and their car had been spotted alongside a plank platform that would facilitate unloading.

She looked about their car and saw that only her mother and Antonio were there. Deborah started to inquire about the missionaries but her mother, busy stacking some of their possessions near the open doorway, was already explaining. "Good morning, sleepyhead. I thought you would be up at break of day to see this Mormon town . . . this new Jerusalem in the wilderness." She paused and motioned Deborah toward her. "Here. Grab hold of this trunk and help me shove it along. Mr. Oakes said before he left—"

"Where did they go? Mr. Oakes and Lemuel?" Deborah asked and tugged hard at the trunk.

Rose Dexter's response was a bit slow in coming. Her mind was absorbing a fact: She called him Lemuel, instead of Mr. Froman. It's the first time Debbie has done that. I . . . I wonder if . . . She stowed away her sudden curiosity and said in a matter-of-fact way, "Both of the missionaries left real early this morning. But they will be back. They asked that we get everything in order for unloading and then wait."

"We won't have much longer to wait," Deborah replied. She was staring along the siding and watching two horse-drawn wagons approach the platform. In one rig was a tall and husky-looking driver clad in homespun work clothing. With him was another man of similar age and build and Elder Nephi Oakes. The second wagon, trailing close behind, held four more people. Handling the reins was Lemuel Froman, now busily engaged talking to a middle-aged, heavyset man who was clad in the dark garb and wide-brimmed hat of the Mormons. There was also a woman of similar age and a blond and bareheaded boy of perhaps twelve years. He was wearing faded blue trousers from the hip pocket of which protruded a slingshot made of a willow branch and a length of rubber that had apparently been cut from a worn-out overboot.

In silent amazement, Rose and Deborah watched all of these people climb from the wagons. Presently the teams were secured by hitching their bridles to a pole railing that encircled the unloading platform. Then, with Nephi Oakes and Lemuel Froman and the middle-aged stranger leading the way, all seven people trudged across the platform and drew into a group beside the open doorway of the emigrant car.

Nephi Oakes was the first to speak. His words, spoken briskly and with a confident smile, took into consideration the questioning dismay on the faces of Rose and her daughter. "Don't be alarmed. You're among friends." Oakes gestured toward the older man, then added, "Mrs. Dexter . . . Miss Dexter, this is Bishop Joshua Stannard of our Church. He has already arranged temporary living quarters and pasture for your livestock."

Rose held out her hand toward that offered by the stranger. "But how?" she gasped. "We just got here. You had no way of knowing."

Bishop Stannard had removed his hat, revealing a thickness of iron-gray hair. His face was smiling, but it also carried something of intensity and authority. He was appraising both of the Dexters with steady gray eyes as he explained. "We have known for several days that you were on your way from Nebraska—along with our two elders and an injured Basque lad. Elder Oakes used the telegraph. At Cheyenne."

Lemuel Froman's eyes were on Deborah as he spoke for the first time. "You probably wonder who the rest of us are. And what we're doing here." He motioned the woman to his side. "Aunt Martha, I want you to meet Mrs. Rose Dexter and Deborah, her daughter. I'll let you tell them that your name is Martha Rockwell . . . and that this towheaded young fellow is your son, Ted." He paused to indicate the two other men. "You should also know the names of these hard workers. They are the Milles brothers. They are Swedish, and as yet do not speak much English. But they really know the hauling business."

At sound of their name, the brothers bowed and touched their hats. Then as if prearranged, they broke from the group, returned to the empty wagons, and skillfully maneuvered their teams to bring the first wagon to the emigrant car for loading. Within half an hour the railroad car had been emptied, and the two wagons, now carrying Rose and Deborah, Antonio, and Martha Rockwell as well as the drivers, moved up a wide but dusty street of Ogden. A bishop and two elders of the Church of Jesus Christ of Latter-day Saints followed, walking behind the wagons—and occasionally chiding a bareheaded boy who eagerly aimed his slingshot at any object that seemed to be a likely target.

Within a week Rose and Deborah Dexter had settled into the pace of life in the busy and rapidly growing town of Ogden. It seemed that no one long remained a stranger here, for although they were Gentiles in a Mormon community, the activities of the Church continually touched their lives. They found that the residents of Ogden were of widely varied backgrounds; largely, these pioneers had been recruited by the Church from the eastern states and from England and the Scandinavian areas of Europe. Already an invitation had been extended for the Dexters to join the Church, and Deborah sensed that growing pressure would be put upon them to become Mormons. Rose was aware of this too, and as the first days passed she sensed that these settlers were building a flourishing and satisfying life-style based on the spiritual values and creed of the Mormons.

Upon their arrival in Utah, Deborah had been

concerned about the future of the young Basque. She need not have worried. They had been in Ogden less than two days when work was secured for Antonio on a farm on the edge of Ogden. His work was satisfactory. Likely he would have remained a farm worker had not a letter arrived one week later postmarked at Scottsbluff, Nebraska, and addressed to Rose in care of Elder Nephi Oakes.

But it was not Oakes who brought the letter to the Dexters. Instead it was delivered early one evening by Bishop Stannard. He drove up in a polished black buggy, tied his team of black mares to a hitching post, and mounted the steps of the small cottage. Rose had just returned from downtown Ogden, where she had talked to a restaurant owner about the possibility of her securing work. At the time, Deborah was away from home, having been invited to a youths' twilight service at a nearby ward of the Mormon Church.

As she opened the door in response to Stannard's knock, Rose was aware of his charm and vitality. His self-confidence and innate courtesy were those of a well-educated man and a born leader. Something stirred within Rose Dexter . . . something a bit unsettling and yet exciting. For the first time since her husband's death she thrilled to the presence of a man near her.

He came quickly to the point, grasping her extended hand and peering intently into her face. "Mrs. Dexter, I decided to bring this letter in person. Elder Oakes is in Salt Lake City attending a conference." There was a deepness and modulation about his voice that marked this churchman as a trained and experienced speaker.

"Please sit down, Bishop Stannard," Rose said, and she indicated a nearby chair. "I appreciate your thoughtfulness in bringing this letter. Would I be rude to open it now? I am very curious."

As her gaze scanned the few lines of the letter, a gasp of surprise swept her.

Dear Mrs. Dexter:

The officers of our association have asked me to write to you and forward this bank draft for $150.00, together with our sincere thanks for the care you and your daughter gave the young herder, Antonio Onederra. Yours was a courageous act.

We would be grateful if you would now buy a railroad ticket for Antonio to Boise, Idaho. Also, will you send a telegram to Ramon Echiverri at Boise (you will not need further address) telling him when Antonio will arrive. Kindly give our herder enough money for his meals en route to Boise. We desire that you keep the remainder of the $150 for yourself, as a token of our appreciation.

Your obedient servant,

Jeff Harding, for
the sheepmen of western Nebraska

She was quiet and thoughtful as she replaced the letter and the bank draft in the envelope. "I wonder," she murmured aloud, "if there are other Basque people in Idaho."

"Indeed there are," Stannard answered. "Boise is becoming a sort of population center for them, largely because of the Idaho, Oregon, and Nevada sheep industry. But why do you ask, Mrs. Dexter?"

She told him of the contents of the letter, then listened as he said, "Likely it is better for the young man to journey on to Boise. The work we can offer him here is temporary." He waited a moment then added, "Besides, he is of the Roman Catholic faith."

"Is that so important, Bishop Stannard? I, myself . . . and my daughter . . . are not Mormons. We are Methodists."

"I am aware of that," he said with a disarming smile. "Perhaps at a later time you will see fit to join our Church. You would be most welcome."

"Are you attempting to convert me?" Rose asked, meaning to dispel the seriousness of the moment.

"Right now," Stannard answered, "I am merely planting in your mind a possibility to think about. Later our elders will call upon you and your daughter to explain the rudiments and the joy of our faith." He rose from the chair, seemed suddenly to take on a somewhat boyish air, and asked, "Rose, I have to drive out in the country to one of our farms. I would like the pleasure of your company if you would care to go along. The farming area is green and quite pretty where we have brought it under irrigation. Besides, I am sure you haven't been more than half a mile from this cottage since you arrived."

Rose studied the eagerness on his face. Suddenly she wanted greatly to accept his invitation, to ride beside this handsome and well-mannered man in the black buggy, and to enjoy the trotting

67

of spirited horses and the wind in her face. One question was foremost in her mind, but for some reason unknown to her she failed to ask it. Instead she peered into his face and said, a bit breathlessly, "Bishop, are you sure it is proper for a churchman of your standing to ask a lady to go buggy-riding with him?"

His face was calm and unperturbed when he answered. "The doctrine of my faith does not deny any man such companionship."

"I'll be ready in five minutes," Rose said. Her face became livelier . . . younger . . . more eager. She had for now sidestepped the question: Was this Mormon Bishop, who had sought her out for companionship, already a married man?

Three days later they put Antonio Onederra on a train bound for Boise. At first he had seemed reluctant to leave the small farm, but mention of Jeff Harding changed the herder's attitude at once. He accepted the trip as though it was something ordained for him to do.

Deborah's almost wistful words broke the silence as they trudged homeward from the depot. "Mom, I wish we'd been going with Tony on that train. Somehow Idaho seems so close now. People tell me it is only about fifty miles to the border." Her breath quickened. "Just think of it. The great mountains. The forests. The shining rivers."

"Just wait a minute, Debbie." Rose's words were a bit caustic. "Tell me what is wrong with Ogden. There are mountains here. Big and high enough for me, at least. What would be wrong with settling down here? I could get a job. You could get set for school."

Deborah stopped in her tracks and stared into her mother's face. "Mom, we're in Utah—Mormon country."

"The Mormons have been kind to us—and helpful."

"Of course they have. But you and I will never really be a part of this town . . . this state . . . unless we join their Church. Unless we become Mormons."

Rose's face took on stubbornness as she clutched her daughter's arm, then said, "Honey, would that be so terrible? Becoming Mormons? Many people are finding it a rewarding choice. Why, Bishop Stannard told me—"

"Mom," Deborah cut in with softly, "are you in love with Bishop Stannard?"

"Why . . . why!" Rose Dexter gasped.

Deborah studied her mother's flushed face and revealing eyes. "Yes, Mom, you are. And I am glad. You can't hang onto Daddy's memory. We loved him. But he is dead now." Deborah fell silent, then seemed to drag resolute but painful words from herself. "But Mom, surely you know— Bishop Stannard is already married. In fact, he has two wives."

"I didn't . . . he never . . ." Rose words were despairing. "Are you sure, Debbie?"

"Very sure, Mom. In fact, when I attended that young people's meeting I was introduced to one of his daughters." She threw her arm about her troubled mother. "Don't hate the bishop for this. I'm sure he would have told you—later. But this is Utah. He is a Mormon, and I believe a wealthy one. And his faith and creed teaches the sanctity of a man's having more than one wife."

69

One word escaped Rose, but it carried neither approval nor condemnation. "Polygamy."

The week that followed was a restless one for Deborah. Rose was called upon to take over a small cafe temporarily when its owner was called to San Francisco. It demanded much of her time; when she returned home evenings, she was tired and quiet. On Friday evening the bishop's well-kept horses and rig again appeared in front of their house, and Stannard, with smiling graciousness, requested that both Rose and Deborah take a drive and then have dinner with him. Deborah exempted herself with a polite bit of evasion. She sensed that both her mother and Stannard should have this time to themselves and surmised also that her mother had arrived at a decision about the bishop.

For a time after they had driven away, Deborah puttered about the house. Lately a restlessness had been growing within her. She sensed that an active future lay ahead, but she could not see herself settling down to a school-and-church routine. Near sunset she left the cottage, and walked eastward on a street of scattered homes. Soon she was surprised how rapidly the street became but a rutted roadway and climbed in a zigzagging way onto a mountain that was taking on the rose and purple hues of oncoming evening.

When she finally stopped to catch her breath and gazed back into the sunset, a quick breath told of her surprise and wonder. Ogden had dwindled to shadowy streets and distant, muted sounds. Beyond, an immensity stretched out, land that lay dappled by the sunset's light and shadows as it led to far-distant mountains. Then she was staring at an expanse of water westward that seemed to her to be an inland ocean. She had caught her first good view of the Great Salt Lake and its surrounding valley—the country of which Mormon leader Brigham Young had said: "This is the place."

The swiftly nearing sunset warned her to return to the town below. But she was reluctant to do so. It seemed that for the first time she realized the tremendous distances of the West. She had sensed them on the long train trip from Nebraska, but that was a moving panorama. Now her gaze could capture and hold distance. Out there somewhere must be Nevada and California. She moved to let her searching eyes roam along the vast escarpment of the Wasatch Mountains leading northward. Far off, and seemingly detached from the chain of mountains, stood a great butte, its crest burnished gold by the last rays of day.

Suddenly she knew. That far-off landmark must be nearly half a hundred miles distant—and that would place it in Idaho. For the first time she had seen at least one small part of the land that had so long excited her imagination and been a beckoning goal. Her impulse was to begin walking toward the butte, to be even a few feet closer to the territory called Idaho. At that moment her decision was made. Nothing would hold her here in Ogden. Even though her mother chose to remain, she must somehow go on—and not be content until the promise of Idaho had been realized. Her steps were sure and her heart was pounding its excitement as she raced the oncoming night toward the valley, the town, and their cottage.

Her mother had arrived home, lighted a kerosene lamp, and sat beside a street-fronting window for her return.

"Mom, I hope you haven't been worrying; I've just been out for a walk. How was your drive and supper with the bishop?"

Rose got up from her chair and fingered the lamp so it gave a brighter glow. Then she reached for her daughter's hand and said simply, "Deborah, Bishop Stannard has asked me to marry him." As if to stave off the girl's question, she added quickly, "Yes, honey, he told me truthfully of his other wives."

Deborah's arms encircled her mother and for a moment held her tight. Then she said in a steady voice, "Mom, you know I love you, want happiness for you. I am sure that with the Bishop you will find it." She paused, searching the composure of Rose Dexter's face. Then she added hesitatingly, "But there is something else, Mom. I can't stay with you here in Utah. I must go on to Idaho—it has been my dream for half of my life."

Rose had listened in silence. Now, as she answered, her voice carried a sureness Deborah had not heard for a long time. "Debbie, you are too prone to jump to conclusions. Of course you're going to Idaho. You will go as soon as we can make arrangements—and I am going with you."

"You mean?" Deborah managed to gulp.

Rose nodded. "Yes, honey, I may marry Bishop Stannard. But I have to have time to think it over. After all, your father has been gone but a few months; he still seems part of me. Deborah, we are going to sell our belongings and strike out. I told Mr. Stannard that I would know my answer . . . deep in my heart . . . by Christmas."

"So we'll get tickets to Boise, like the one Tony had?"

"No," Rose said, smiling. "We don't know a soul in Boise—or even in Idaho. But remember what Henry Carswell told us about a place in Idaho called Bonanza?"

"Of course I remember," Deborah giggled excitedly. "He said Bonanza is on the Yankee Fork of the Salmon River—way in the wilderness, but rich with silver and gold."

"That's right. And he gave me the names of people we should look up when we get there."

Deborah moved to the window and before closing the curtains stared out across the night lights of Ogden. From somewhere along the railroad came the lonely sound of a fading train whistle and the rattle of cars.

Chapter 4

IT WAS a small mixed passenger and freight train on the Utah and Northern Railroad that finally carried Deborah Dexter and her mother into Idaho Territory. The train ran northward through a series of small farming towns and alongside rivers bordered by meadows and rocky flats touched by the greenness of summer. Finally it drew to a stop before a small depot in the town of Blackfoot.

The rails had been laid no farther northward, and inquiry by Rose revealed that only by means of a stagecoach could they proceed toward the area of the Yankee Fork and the town of Bonanza. The stage would not leave until the following morning—and then might not be able to accommodate them. Deborah, watching passengers mill about the railroad ticket counter, wondered if every passenger who had come to Blackfoot on the train was trying to get to the goldfields.

They spent the night in a tar-papered, two-story structure that proclaimed itself to be the Elite Hotel. The beds proved to be lumpy and their supper an offering of salt pork with boiled potatoes. The stage was scheduled to leave just after sunup, but they left the hotel and walked to the stage depot in the chilliness of dawn. Each carried a bulky suitcase and hoped that their trunk had been transferred to the stage depot by a bewhiskered individual to whom they paid two dollars for the task.

They managed to get seats on the stage, but only to a distant point called Challis. They were told that a different stage line ran between Challis and the twin towns of Bonanza and Custer and that they might have to wait a day or more for passage beyond Challis.

From the moment the stagecoach wheels began to turn, and the dusty trail bent to a northwestward bearing, a sense of expectancy was upon Deborah. The morning was drenched in sunlight and clear. Ahead, a vast sage-strewn desert seemed to lead to a horizon dotted by great and wide-spaced buttes. There had been sufficient spring rain to bring bursts of wildflower color; an occasional antelope or deer watched the intruding stage and its passengers from a cautious distance. Often there was a flash of wings overhead as birds sought out their morning food. The song of a meadowlark challenged the rising sun.

But it was to something far beyond that Deborah's gaze and rapt attention turned. Far off, and seeming to be but a cloud bank on the horizon, was a distant upthrust of the land, the looming of a range of mountains whose higher peaks wore the white and shining snows of winter. She and Rose were sharing the inner seat of the coach with four men. Now Deborah thrust a finger toward the mountains and said aloud, "I wonder if it's possible that all of those mountains are in Idaho?"

All of the men turned to look at the eager-faced girl, but only one chose to comment. He was a stockily built fellow with a weather-seamed face and steady but squinting blue eyes. His clothing consisted of rough, knee-height boots; black woolen trousers held by sturdy suspenders; a red flannel shirt; and a worn hat that had once been gray and stylish. From beneath it, a shock of white but well-combed hair fell to the stranger's shoulders. His voice sounded in low and amused tones. "Miss, those mountains you're staring at are up around the diggings on the Lost River. We are headed up that way, but it'll take us a couple of days to get there. It's nigh onto a hundred miles. You're heading into some high country, all right. But it is just the beginning. Off westward is the Sawtooth country, sort of ringed about with high peaks. Beyond that there is range after range of mountains practically all the way up to Canada."

"We're going to Bonanza City," Deborah explained. "Is that in the mountains? Are there rivers? And woods?"

"Bonanza City, eh? That's in the Custer mining district up on the Yankee Fork of the Salmon River. Young lady, you had better believe Bonanza is in the mountains . . . so far up in the wilderness that it's said they use mountain goats to carry in the mail. And that river—the Salmon—you can see for yourself when this slow contrivance gets us to Challis."

There was a silence, broken only by the pounding hoofs and rattling harness of the team, as Deborah sorted out what he had told her. She would have asked him more, but when she again turned toward him he had fallen asleep with the battered hat over his face.

They stopped at a place called Hidden Springs to water the horses and to eat the lunches they had been warned to bring along. When the team had been changed at a wayside shack and corral, the coach got under way again. There was a shifting about of passengers, and Deborah and her mother were offered seats in the fresher air atop the coach. Deborah found herself seated next to the driver, a lanky individual with sandy-colored hair and a waxed moustache. He was also equipped with a colorful, mule skinner's array of commands and threats for the four horses. They were hitched in tandem, and the driver showed skill in maneuvering the fistful of reins.

She had closed her eyes against the brilliance of midafternoon when she was abruptly aware of a voice sounding behind her and of a hand touching her elbow.

"Miss Dexter," the deep voice said, "I don't suppose you would care to help an old codger break this blasted monotony by playing a game of cards."

She twisted about to face the speaker and then smiled. It was the fellow with a red shirt and intense blue eyes, the one who had seemed to know something of Bonanza City and of Idaho's array of mountains. Now he clutched a worn deck of cards, and his gaze seemed to be wistful. He was sitting on a tarped bedroll and had cleared the top of a suitcase for table space. Now he added, "If you wish, I can arrange a seat for you. Not the best, mind you. But as comfortable as this jolting chariot will allow."

Deborah glanced at her mother, seeking appraisal of the stranger's request, but Rose's face was emotionless. This was a decision Deborah was expected to make for herself. She mulled it over

77

for perhaps ten seconds, then with a half-daring and half-dubious smile she moved into position to be dealt a handful of cards. The driver glanced back and growled, "Iffen she's going to play cards with you, Sam, keep it simple—and straight. This rig ain't no gambling hall."

"Miss Dexter," the deep-voiced card player was saying, "I trust you know the intricacies and the matchless allure of the game of poker."

"It depends," Deborah replied guardedly. "Are you talking of draw poker, five-card stud, or a deal where one-eyed jacks are wild?" Her face was eager and yet unrevealing as she studied the cards he had dealt her. Her father had taught her to play poker during the lonely evenings on the Banner County homestead.

"I, myself, prefer a simple and friendly game of stud, miss, but you can change it if you wish— dealer's choice."

Ten minutes later Deborah was aware that the stranger's name was Sam Douglas, that he too was on the way to the valley of the Yankee Fork— and that his knowledge of poker was seemingly endless.

The game with this stranger wiled away many hours on the trip toward the ever-looming peaks marking the Lost River area. By the time they neared Challis, a bond of mutual respect had been forged between gambler Sam Douglas and herself. There was also a sense of future destiny asserting itself within Deborah Dexter. Someday . . . some-how their paths would cross again.

It was just short of noon when the stage rum-bled through a narrow rock gorge, crested a sage-brushed hill, and came alongside a small stream that led quickly downward. Although Rose had chosen to remain in the coach, Deborah was again seated beside the driver. Now she gazed ahead, and a small cry of excitement broke from her. Ahead was what seemed an immense valley, bordered by mountains and stretching from south to north. Through it was a broad silver band bordered by cottonwoods, by sprinklings of pine and fir, and by meadows created by the stream's overflowing.

The driver pulled on his reins and reached for a brake rigged to slow the stage's forward thrust. "Them buildings over on the hillside across the river is Challis settlement; it used to be called Station before there was a road up this way. It was a way station for packers who used mule trains to lug in supplies for forwarding to the gold diggings."

The one street of log and clapboard buildings held little interest for Deborah, but sight of the great river stirred her excitement. "That's the Salmon River, isn't it?" she asked.

"It sure is. Gets its start way up west in the mountains around the Stanley Basin and the Sawtooth Range and then flows east. Right here at Challis it bends north and heads toward a spot near Salmon City. Then it strikes into the darnedest canyon you can imagine. Keeps plowing west until it joins the Snake River over near the Oregon border. People call that part of the Salmon 'the river of no return.' That's because boats can go down it but can't come back up against the current. It's a wild one, this old Salmon River."

An hour later they crossed the river on a ferry

79

that cautiously worked its way to the far side near the straggling village. Deborah sat in utter wonder during the crossing. Never had she seen a river this wide and deep and fast-flowing. The sparkling clarity of the water was deceptive. When she assumed the water to be only a couple of feet deep, the driver scornfully told her that at that spot the river was deep enough to be far over her head. Twice she sighted great gray shadows flashing upstream and was told that they were oceangoing fish, the sturdy steelhead fighting their way upstream to spawning grounds. She stared in wonder at the mountain gateway from which the great river seemed to pour and then asked, "Is the Yankee Fork up that way? Will we be going into the canyon?"

"I don't think so, lady," the driver responded. "But you'd better ask someone else. Challis is the end of my run. Tomorrow about sunup I head back toward Blackfoot—and a mite of civilization."

Sam Douglas had thrust the deck of cards into his pocket and was getting his gear ready for unloading. He overheard the driver's assessment of Challis, and it brought from him a spirited reply. "Just what's wrong with Challis—other than it ain't so handy for you to get hold of a bottle of red-eye whiskey? This here Challis town is the gateway to a whale of a lot of Idaho's riches . . . gold . . . silver. For instance, take the towns over on the Yankee Fork . . . Custer . . . Bonanza City . . ."

"You take them, Sam. Damned if I want any part of that wilderness and cold and hip-high snow about ten months a year."

Sam Douglas disdained to reply and turned to

Deborah and Rose. "It'll be morning before the stage leaves for the beautiful Yankee Fork. However, there are safe and reasonably comfortable places to stay overnight in Challis."

"Will we reach Bonanza tomorrow?" Rose asked with weary anxiety.

"No. If we're lucky we will make it in about three days. It's some sixty miles. Mostly straight up one side of a mountain and down the opposite."

"Three days!" Deborah gasped. "You mean we will be in a bumpy old coach for seventy-two hours?"

"Naw! It ain't thataway at all. There are stage stations along the way that offer passable grub and sleeping quarters."

"And they will charge us a pretty penny, no doubt?" Rose asked.

Sam Douglas shrugged. "Nothing is for free along a stage route, ma'am. But you won't be robbed at the way stations, either."

"What are they like?" Deborah asked curiously.

"Most of them are simply cabins fixed up for taking care of stage drivers, passengers, and livestock. Two of the best on this Challis-to-Bonanza route are run by Miss Fannie Clark; they are known as Fannie's Upper Hole and Fannie's Lower Hole."

This revelation caused Debby Dexter to stare in silence at her mother, who quickly seemed to be scanning a distant horizon and oblivious of what was being said.

"Yes, sir, Miss Fannie knows her business," Douglas went on. She knows that the stage stops in the lowlands—in the protected hollows—are the moneymakers. She's made enough money to be buying and selling business lots in Custer and Bonanza City."

"Where I wish we were right now," Rose responded firmly.

They topped a high, jagged ridge and came into the remote valley of the Yankee Fork of the Salmon River near midafternoon on a day when not one cloud hovered above the sunlit mountains. The warmth of summer was about them, yet a wisp of wind stirred the tall pine and fir trees and nodded the flowers that grew in profusion along the dusty wagon trail they followed. They rounded a sharp curve, and abruptly Deborah caught her breath. Before them and sloping southward was a narrow, mountain-edged valley through which coursed a clear and fast-moving stream.

It seemed to the girl that the coach had swept her from a mountain wilderness into the busiest and most populated valley she had seen since leaving Ogden. In the foreground loomed a giant frame structure that seemed to climb a mountainside. From the structure belched smoke that rose and then drifted lazily eastward. Beyond, and down the valley was a continuation of streets and buildings that reached about as far as her gaze could encompass.

Sam Douglas noted the intentness of her survey, grinned, and then said, "There she blows, miss. The General Custer Mill—she's turned out millions of dollars' worth of gold and silver. The town hereabouts is called Custer also." He pointed. "Farther down the valley, beyond Jordan

Creek, is Bonanza City. It's about two miles from Custer. There's nigh onto five thousand people making a living from the mines."

Rose peered across the panorama, then spoke with a dubious tone. "I just hope we Dexters can make a living here."

"I never heard of anyone who was willing to work not finding some sort of job along the Yankee Fork." There was a bit of testiness about Sam Douglas' retort.

Within the hour, the stage drew to a stop in front of a slabsided building in Bonanza City. Sam Douglas had gotten off at Custer, so now the driver spoke up. "We're at the end o' the line, folks. Everybody out. This here gingerbreaded, two-story edy-fice is the Dodge Hotel. You'll be welcomed, but they don't like mud or booze on them plush carpets."

Presently Deborah was seated beside her mother on the one trunk they had brought. Behind them was the ornate doorway of the Dodge Hotel, and before them stretched a dusty street that seemed always busy with a variety of vehicles, men on horseback, and those afoot as they moved amid the business buildings of Bonanza City. Nearby, the Yankee Fork murmured protest of the boulders that impeded its way. Higher up, on the green slopes of the mountains, were the seemingly endless prospect holes left by gold seekers. Yet despite this plundering of nature, there was vast and tranquil beauty across this remote section of Idaho.

Rose Dexter glanced about worriedly. "If we go into that hotel it will cost us like sin. But we can't sit out here on the plank walk forever."

Deborah listened, then watched the approach of a small, energetic man wearing a white shirt and bowler hat. Quietly she asked her mother, "What was the name of the people Henry Carswell said we should look up?"

Rose quickly scanned a folded paper drawn from her purse. "The name Mr. Carswell mentioned was that of the Bill Trumble family."

Deborah nodded, then when the spry-stepping stranger was about to pass her on the sidewalk, she stood up to catch his attention. "Please, sir, can you tell us how to get in touch with the Trumble family? We're . . . we're strangers here."

The man's stare encompassed both Deborah's eager face and the luggage about the Dexters. "I would be glad to help, miss—if I could. My name is Charles Blair. I know just about every man, woman, and mule in Bonanza—but Trumble . . . Trumble. Hey, wait a jiffy. You couldn't mean Whispering Willie Trumble, could you?"

"We weren't told whether he whispers or shouts," Deborah answered, smiling. "A friend, back in Nebraska, told us to look up Bill Trumble. He said that Mr. Trumble could help us find lodging."

"Both the Dodge Hotel, right here, and the Blair House—which I happen to own—can provide lodging."

Rose got up from her seat on the trunk and faced the alert stranger. "Thank you for your time, sir, but we need to find the Trumbles. In all honesty, we've spent too much of our reserve funds already. We can't afford a high-class hotel."

"There may not be need to. Will Trumble had a cabin."

"Had?" Deborah repeated uneasily.

"Sure. He left about a month ago. Went to San Francisco to see some specialist about his throat. The cabin is empty. Not fancy, mind you. But it would offer shelter." He waited, studying their faces, then added, "I can show you the place, then have one of my men dray your trunk over to the cabin—if you decide to stay."

It was thus that the Dexters found their place to live in Bonanza City. The cabin proved to be one fair-sized room, to which was attached a log lean-to that served as kitchen, pantry, and as a storage shed for firewood. It was located beneath two tall fir trees a hundred yards from the Yankee Fork and where the somber hue of the forest met the expanse of meadowland on which the settlement stood.

They had been in the cabin less than half an hour when their first visitor knocked softly on the heavy plank of its door. Both Deborah and her mother moved in unison to open the door; then they stood in relieved amazement. Before them stood a middle-aged and robustly healthy woman wearing a sunbonnet and a gingham apron. Her dress was gray and dropped to the tops of sturdy, flat-heeled work shoes. She thrust out her hand in a friendly way. "I am Mrs. Jenner. Me and my man and our kids . . . we have three . . . live up the road a piece. My mister works at the big mill, the General Custer." She thrust a box covered with a white dish towel into Rose's arms. "You're likely too tired to fix supper. So here is what I could scrape up in a hurry." She glanced about the cabin, then added, "You will be needing some clean bedding too. I will see what I can find and send my daughter, Selma . . . she is going on thirteen—"

Overwhelmed by the gifts and the woman's flow of words, Rose managed to murmur aloud, "You're very kind and thoughtful. We didn't expect—"

"People around here try to take care of each other," Mrs. Jenner interrupted. "Who else would? It's a heap of weary miles to the outside world." As she moved as though to leave, her voice took on pride. "These Yankee Fork diggings may be way back in the hills and sort of hidden. But they're rich."

Deborah was staring out of the cabin's northward-facing window, watching sunset creep across the valley and touch the smoke of the General Custer Mill upstream. "Idaho!" she said at last. "Is it all as big and busy and challenging as this?" Her hand swept to encompass the entire scene.

"There's gold here, all right," their visitor said, smiling. "Silver too. It seems there is pay dirt all along the fork and up the mountains. But don't fall in love with Bonanza City and Custer. Not yet—not until you have spent a long, cold, and desperately isolated winter here." Mrs. Jenner's words grew brisk. "I've got to get back to the kids . . . and a venison roast I'm fixing. But mind you, come see the mister and me." She turned quickly and crossed the meadow, to be lost from sight behind screening bushes.

After a time the chill of high-country evening came on. They lighted a fire in the wood stove and took comfort in the warmth that circulated from the lean-to shed into the cabin. Later, when the promised bedding arrived in the arms of a tall, redheaded girl, they spread up the only bed. Rose and Deborah were tired, and sleep came easily to them this night.

"Mom, do you suppose a girl can do it? Find a place and dig for gold?" The words escaped Deborah in an excited burst as she snuggled deeper beneath two woolen blankets.

"Land of Goshen, Debbie. Gold. Gold and silver rainbows. And I suppose you'll just step across them to a tomorrow that won't have a single worry or care." Rose's voice was tired and fretful.

"But this *is* rich gold country, Mom. Perhaps I can—"

"Perhaps you can let me get some sleep, honey. Tomorrow we have to find out if we can keep using this cabin for a time and then get settled so I can look for work of some sort."

The words subdued Deborah and she remained awake but quiet. Moments later her mother's hand moved to grasp and hold hers. "I don't mean to be cross, Debbie," Rose said. "Come to think of it, I am glad we are here in an exciting place like this. At least one of your dreams is beginning to come true."

Hours later, when the morning sunlight was pouring through a window and they were cleaning and airing the cabin, Deborah noticed an envelope on a shelf. One end of the envelope had been torn away. It was addressed to Mr. William Trumble, Bonanza City, Idaho Territory. She would have ignored it had not her eye caught the return address. It read: Henry Carswell, Box Butte, Nebraska.

On sudden impulse Deborah picked up the envelope. Her mother had gone in search of water. Deborah stood for a time in indecision. Rose had taught her that it was almost indecent to read other people's mail. Yet this seemed a link with their past, with someone who had been their friend. Her curiosity was a consuming thing as she drew the folded sheet from its envelope and let her eyes scan it. Even before she had finished her reading, she uttered an excited cry and then opened the front door to peer out. Rose was approaching with a pail of water, so Deborah ran swiftly to meet her.

"Mom . . . listen, Mom. Guess what? This cabin we're staying in. It belongs to Mr. Carswell. And that isn't all! He owns a mine that William . . . or Bill . . . or Willie Trumble was working for him." She shoved the letter into Rose's hand, then grabbed the pail. "Read it, Mom. Maybe we can write to Mr. Carswell and keep this house." Her voice was rising in excitement. "And, Mom, if there really is a mine—a real honest-to-God gold mine—maybe you and I can—"

For once, Rose Dexter failed to scold her daughter for reading another person's letter. She was too busy studying Carswell's letter. Presently she said, "Why, this was written nearly two months ago. I wonder if that man of his, Trumble, ever wrote that he was leaving here . . . going to San Francisco."

"I don't know, Mom." Deborah was studying the small shack and the forested mountain slope rising behind it. "Mom, I hope Mr. Carswell lets us stay and . . . and that old Trumble stays in California."

"Honey, that's an awful thing to say about a sick person," Rose chided.

"I don't want him to be sick; I just want him to stay away. Then—if there really are gold diggings that Mr. Carswell owns—I bet he'd let us operate them."

Rose shook her head in dubious amazement. "And just what do we know about ores and rocks —or gold? Wouldn't we be a fine lot, looking for something we haven't even seen except in a coin or a ring. I just wish Mr. Carswell's property up here was a cafe . . . or a boardinghouse."

"Just the same," Deborah asserted firmly, "I am going to learn about mining. Who ever heard of a fortune being made out of fixing pie and coffee?"

"It's not a fortune I'm worried about," Rose responded tartly. "It's finding a way to make ends meet and keep a roof over our heads." She paused, then for a little time seemed lost in thought. Then she said slowly, "Debbie, maybe you hit the nail on the head. A pie and coffee shop. I'll wager there isn't a good one hereabouts. Now, let's see. That Mr. Blair—the man who said it would be all right for us to use the cabin. I will ask him whether it would make sense to start a little eating place. He should know; he's a businessman."

"I'll go with you to see him." Deborah's voice carried eagerness. "Perhaps he can tell us about Mr. Carswell's gold property—and what I will need to get it turning out—"

Rose threw her free arm in the air in frustration. Then she seized the water bucket and strode toward the cabin. Her voice, coming back over her shoulder, told of a decision. "All right, Miss Obstinate, go ahead and dig your gold. But just until cold weather comes—then back to school you go." Under her breath, Rose Dexter was telling herself hopefully: "Maybe the blasted diggings require big machinery and a lot of men. Then she can help me make pies—as a lady should!"

The next ten days brought several answers. First, the Dexters were assured that there was no reason why they should not continue to use the Trumble cabin—at least until Whispering Willie might return. A sampling of opinion among residents of Bonanza and Custer indicated that a small eating place would likely do well. Through the efforts of Charles Blair, a narrow building facing on the main street became available at reasonable rent. It would accommodate four tables and a long counter. Rose was able to work out terms for dishes and utensils with a variety store. Deborah painted a wooden sign to be nailed on a high post in front of the establishment. It bore the words PIE IN THE SKY. It was wedge-shaped, showing a steaming cup of coffee against a slice of crusty apple pie.

Rose's hope of the gold diggings owned by Carswell being too large for her daughter to tackle was quickly dashed. It was a sluicing operation a short way up Jordan Creek and consisted of a staked spot hardly larger than a fair-sized house. Upon a sandy bar at a bend of the creek sat a flume into which gravel and dark muck could be shoveled. This was washed down through a cleated sluicing box by water diverted from the creek. Deborah eyed the setup first with interest, and then with growing dismay. It was messy, cumbersome, and the water of the creek was icy cold. How could such a mud-making machine produce gold? If there was gold in the creek, why couldn't she see its shining magic? Or reach out and pluck nuggets from a shovelful of sand?

She sought out Charles Blair at his hotel. He was standing behind the registration counter. "Good morning, young lady. Your mother is a mighty fine cook. I just had breakfast at her place. It was already crowded. She needs help."

She ignored the hint and asked bluntly, "Mr. Blair, did Bill Trumble leave Bonanza, and take off for California, because his diggings up Jordan Creek are worthless?"

"I don't believe so," Blair said after carefully adding a column of figures. "What gave you that idea?"

"It's . . . it's such a ramshackle old thing. Just some rusted pipes, a sort of chute with cleats in it, and mud. Mud everywhere."

Blair laughed aloud. "You aren't very expert in mining, are you? Especially placer mining. That claim was a pretty fair producer when Whispering Willie Trumble was operating it. It's only a few skips and a jump from where a claim washed out over a hundred thousand dollars a year or so ago."

Lingering doubt and incomprehension were on Deborah's face as she said, "Do you know that the cabin where we're staying is owned by Henry Carswell, a man we knew back in Nebraska?"

"Your mother told me when she asked if she and you could continue using the cabin. I already knew that Whispering Willie Trumble was a hired hand for someone back East."

"And are we going to be able to keep the cabin?" Deborah asked anxiously.

"Sure. At least as far as folks hereabouts are concerned. Eventually it'll be up to that fellow Carswell, back in Nebraska. I advised your mother to get in touch with him."

Deborah listened and then asked abruptly, "Mr. Blair, what will I need to get started working that mud box and . . . and everything up there on Jordan Creek?"

He grinned in a wry but curious manner. "Young lady, what you are apt to need most you sure seem to have already. Persistence. The cussed stubbornness to grab a chance and hang on." He eyed her speculatively. "Beyond that . . . try finding someone who knows the craft and tricks of placer mining. And a little prayer or so might help."

She flashed him a smile of thanks and moved quickly toward the door, asking over her shoulder, "Who can you recommend hereabouts to teach me craft and tricks of prayer?"

When she had closed the door behind her, Charles Blair was lost for a few moments in contemplation. His mind seemed to have summed up a new and interesting possibility: *If that spunky girl stays in Idaho, the territory may be in for some excitement.*

Chapter 5

DEBORAH accompanied her mother to work the following morning. There seemed little doubt that the Pie in the Sky was destined to do a good business. Until midmorning there were tables and the counter to be reset and cleared, customers to be waited on, and an endless stream of dishes to be washed. It wasn't until after the noon lunch dishes were washed and stacked that the two Dexter women had time to sit down for a bite to eat and a breather. Deborah spoke, admiration warming her words. "Mom, this place is going to be a gold mine."

Rose smiled and leaned back. "It seems to be starting out well. But honey, does everything good in Idaho have to be a gold mine?"

"Oh, Mom—" Deborah answered ruefully.

"It's all right, Debbie. Now how about you going on home for the afternoon?"

The girl looked about. "But there's more to be done. Baking, for instance."

"I know. But I will need you most in the mornings. Besides, there is a woman coming in who wants me to try her out for permanent help."

Half an hour later, Deborah reached the cabin. She remained there only long enough to don clothing suitable for hiking and to retrieve a pair of work gloves that she guessed had been left by Whispering Willie. The sun was marking midafternoon when she strode through the busy settlement, followed the noisy course of the Yankee Fork, and then turned to follow the narrower and steeper Jordan Creek. Along the way she stopped twice to watch men shoveling sand and black mud into devices similar to the muddy and seemingly dilapidated rig on Willie Trumble's spot of creekfront.

The workingmen, most of whom were dressed in heavy, water-soaked clothing and dark, mud-smeared hats, seemed to be young, healthy, and busy. Upon her approach, each of them looked up and eyed her with curiosity. She greeted all of them, hoping someone would allow her to question him about what they were doing. Instead, they turned back to their work; there seemed to be an air of disapproval about them. It was as though she had entered a domain where women could be tolerated but not welcomed.

She took the hint and then remained silent as she passed three other sluicing operations. Soon she reached a bend in the creek. Here the banks were heavily brushed and for a hundred or so feet there were no claims of gold-seekers. The warmth of midafternoon clung about the valley; she noticed insects hovering above the stream's flow. Nearby, a blue jay took to wing and voiced his disapproval of her intrusion. She paused to listen—and then the song reached her ears. It was voiced in a strong but slightly off-key baritone that seemed to drift from a point screened by choke-cherry bushes.

> *Many a man is rocking another's child,*
> *When, alas, he thinks it's his own.*

She suppressed a giggle and awaited more words. When they came, they were in a language she surmised to be French. As they continued, she edged quietly through the bushes and came close to the water's edge. Stepping atop a rotted and fallen tree, she glanced along the stream as it cut its silver and sun-flecked way along a sizable and curving sandbar. She spotted the singer's enormous hat first, of incredibly tattered felt that shaded his face and dropped almost to his shoulders. His clothing was a ragged and mismatched assembly of work garments, below which were knee-high rubber boots.

He was peering into a beat-up and smoke-stained pan about a foot and a half in diameter. It was half full of water. Moments later he picked it up by the edge and moved it about. Water sloshed over its sides in a pattern that left a dark residue in the pan's bottom. Instinctively Deborah knew that the man was panning for gold. For a better view, she tiptoed higher onto the log—and it was her undoing. The rotted wood gave way beneath her feet with a resounding thud. She was thrown off balance and sharply forward. Then she was lying on the sandbar, her face only inches from the rush of Jordan Creek—and the stranger was laughing at her plight.

She lay still for a moment, gathering her wits and giving way to the anger building within her. The stupid oaf! Laughing when she might have broken an arm, or hit a big rock, or . . . She struggled to retrieve her straw hat and started to word a stinging rebuke, but then abruptly left it unspoken. The stranger had ceased laughing and had stepped close with an outstretched hand to help her to her feet.

She caught sight of his face as it was revealed for the first time below the ludicrously big hat. His eyes were brown and lively, set in a face that mingled concern and merriment. He swept the hat from his head and let it fall to the ground, and chestnut-hued hair tumbled almost to his shoulders. Except for a tiny moustache, he was clean-shaven. Deborah saw that he was young—about twenty-two.

"I hope you haven't hurt anything except your pride," he said.

"You still would have laughed," she accused.

He nodded. "Yes, I would have. That log, when it broke, sent you flying like a Fourth of July rocket. But luckily onto the sand. You aren't hurt, are you?"

"Probably not," Deborah conceded, and stared curiously at the pan he had been swishing. "Is that a real pan for gold? I never saw one before."

He squatted to pick it up and again slosh water expertly from its rim. "You named it," he said and grinned. "But this old pan is beaten and bent." He was silent for a moment as he picked small flecks from the small amount of black sand remaining in it. Then he wiped his hand on the grass and offered his hand to Deborah. "You must be new in these parts if you don't know gold-panning. And . . . and pardon me. My name is Lowell . . . Robert Lowell."

"I'm Deborah Dexter, from Nebraska. Back there we use pans for washing our faces and for kneading bread." She felt her resentment fading before his friendliness, and for the first time she smiled. "Is there much gold here?" she asked eagerly. Then before he could reply she also asked, "Do you own this patch of sand? Does the big mill buy your gold? How come you don't use one of those sluicing outfits? Could I learn to do that—work a pan for gold?"

Before answering, he waded into the stream and used the curved edge of the pan to dig deeply into underlying sand. When satisfied with the amount, he finished filling the pan with water. Then he waded ashore and thrust it into Deborah's hands. "Try it," he urged.

Moments later they were kneeling face to face on the sand bar, and Deborah was intent on mastering the circular motion with which the water and lighter sand were separated from the heavy particles, which sought the bottom of the pan.

"Gold is obstinate and elusive," Lowell explained. "It obeys only gravity . . . always seeking the bottom of everything. The pan. The creek. The very earth itself."

Deborah's gaze searched the pan and then lifted toward his face. Abruptly a strangely unfathomable sense of the stranger's closeness was upon her. His face was only inches from her and she was aware of his breathing and of the hands he had laid over hers to guide them in the circular movement of the pan. This, she thought, would be a pleasant way to spend quite a lot of time. Their eyes met, and she flushed. Something told her that Robert Lowell had read her thoughts.

She freed her hands of his, saying, "Let me try it alone; I may be getting the hang of it." When he was quiet, she sought to forestall any words he might speak. "I wish I knew all about sluicing," she went on. "There is a claim down this creek a piece that belongs to a man in Nebraska I know. There's a lot of old pine, a flume of some sort, and a lot of shoveled-up sand and dirt. I might—" Her words broke off. Lowell had again grasped the pan. Now he was pointing to a yellow and gleaming little object that had separated itself from the residue.

"Hold up," he commanded. "You've washed out a nugget. Not a big one . . . but the real thing." He reached into a nearby box and drew out a small and lidded glass jar. Then expertly he slid the particle of gold into it and replaced the lid. Then he handed it to Deborah.

She studied it breathlessly. "What is it worth?"

"Not a lot. Maybe five or six dollars."

She faced him, and now excitement parried the uneasiness born of his nearness. "You mean that gold . . . real gold . . . can be dug up and washed out that easy? Just like that?"

She started to hand the glass jar back to him, but he lifted a hand to push it back. "You keep it, Deborah. You panned it."

She stared into his face, now again close to her, and read the boyish enthusiasm—and something more—that lay across it. A laced pattern of sunlight fell through the trees and brush, and it seemed that the only sound along this portion of Jordan Creek was its expectant chuckle. Then Deborah's lips yielded to those of this man who so shortly before had aroused her anger. His hands lay gently on her shoulders.

She pushed him away, but not until she had savored the full tenderness of the kiss. "Thanks for the gold, Mr. . . . Mr. Lowell. Now I had best scoot for home."

"Yes, you should," he agreed, and there was a strange hoarseness to his tone. He waited until Deborah was a dozen feet from him and parting the boughs of a willow thicket before he called after her, "Be real careful if you try working the placer claim. It can be frustrating—and sometimes a bit dangerous."

She did not trust herself to speak again. Instead, she acknowledged his words by a wave of her hand. Then she sought out the trail by which she had approached the sandbar . . . and the first kiss that had ever aroused her like this. She realized that she was clutching the glass jar with a hand reddened by the cold water of the creek and yet sweating and trembling.

At home, she busied herself preparing a light supper for Rose and herself. Then a new and daring thought was upon her. Robert Lowell knows all about gold, she told herself. I can get him to teach me. She had already had a preliminary lesson.

The train of her thoughts was broken by sight of her mother walking tiredly toward her. And yet she knew that she would surely make another trip up Jordan Creek. The lure of gold would bring it about, but so would another compulsion—to look again into the face of Robert Lowell . . . hear his voice . . . and perhaps feel the touch of his hands.

Two weeks passed rapidly. Despite Deborah's daily trips to the post office, there was no answer to the letter she and Rose had sent to Henry Carswell. Business at the pie shop continued good and called for practically all of Rose's time and attention. Despite the work load, Rose insisted that Deborah have much of her afternoons free. "I'll have to manage without you once school starts," she told Deborah. Then she added with a shake of her head, "I suppose you'll spend every last minute prowling the gold diggings."

It was upon Deborah's tongue to tell Rose of the sandbar, to which she had already returned twice. Once Robert Lowell had not been there. On the other occasion he had shown her more of the rudiments of gold panning. There had been about him a reserve, almost a coolness that seemed to extend to everything except his thoroughness of instructing. He had listened to her words of thanks with a wry grin. "I just hope you know what you're letting yourself in for," he warned. "Panning the creeks is a risky and precarious way for a fellow—or especially a girl—to hack out a living. Too much time in these icy waters can lead to chilblains or rheumatiz."

And now, fourteen days after her first encounter with Lowell, Deborah asked her mother, "Can you for sure be home for supper tomorrow evening? There's someone I'd like to have come. To have you meet."

Rose peered intently at her daughter. "Of course I'll be there, Deborah. But . . . but who—"

"It is a man I met, Mom. His name is Robert Lowell, and he knows all about gold digging. And he's real nice too." Deborah was conscious of the close look Rose was giving her and of her own twinge of uneasiness. There was no sense of guilt, yet she had never felt just this way before.

"This man," Rose said in an even and unruffled

way, "he is young? You're attracted to him, Debbie?"

"How did you know that?"

"Because, honey, it wasn't a century ago that your father aroused my interest in the same way. Maybe you recall too that I found Bishop Stannard of more than passing interest."

"But I'm not in love, Mom."

Rose's response was a tender smile. Then abruptly she said, "Sakes alive, Deborah . . . I forgot to tell you. Know what? Mr. Carswell, Henry Carswell, is right here in town. He came in on the morning stage and is staying at the Blair House. Mr. Blair told me about it an hour ago." Rose pondered a moment and then asked, "Why can't we have Mr. Carswell over for supper tomorrow? After all, we're living in his house."

"Let's do that," Deborah agreed excitedly. "He can tell us all that has happened back in Box Butte. And . . . and I can find out about his placer claim. Whether Whispering Willie is really coming back to Bonanza. And whether Mr. Carswell will trust me to work that sluicing rig."

"Deborah . . . Deborah," Rose Dexter sighed. "When are you going to get this dream of a gold fortune out of your mind. You're a farm girl from Nebraska. You don't know one damned thing about working a gold claim. It's your father's side of you. Dreaming of a great fortune. A beautiful tomorrow. Of a rainbow beyond the hill."

The words brought a surge of anger in Deborah. "You're right, Mom. And I hope I am always like that—like my daddy. We're in Idaho. If my father were here he would go all out to carve a place . . . a future . . . a fortune for us. Well, he is dead and can't do it. But I am going to, Mom. Maybe I won't make a single dollar from gold. But someday this Territory of Idaho is going to pay me off. Idaho is going to know that Deborah Dexter and her mother are here."

Rose moved to take the angry girl into her arms. "Why are we shouting at each other, Debbie? All I want for you is happiness and schooling; and to never be hungry or homeless—or broke." She stroked Deborah's hair, then went on in a calmer way. "Well, right now," Rose said, "we'd better plan what to have for supper tomorrow evening. What would appeal to two hungry men, a saloonkeeper from Nebraska and a gold-digging Idahoan. Maybe trout. And steak."

"Just so there are a couple of your cream pies," Deborah said.

Deborah was out of bed just as dawn brought a flush of morning light to the Yankee Fork valley. Even before Rose left for the pie shop, the eager girl had given the cabin a thorough cleaning. They had fashioned dimity curtains for the two small windows. Now she rinsed out the curtains and pressed them carefully with a flat iron she heated atop the small stove. Later she searched the forest's edge for wildflowers and arranged them in a Mason jar.

Her mother promised to get word to Henry Carswell of their little dinner party, but it was up to Deborah to get in touch with flop-hatted Robert Lowell. Near midmorning she started toward Bonanza's small business district. After ordering steaks and some groceries, she looked about the street. Right then relief surged across her. It wouldn't be necessary for her to look for Robert Lowell at the sandbar. He was right across the street, standing in front of an assay office and caught up in conversation with its owner. Lowell was wearing the same old and soiled clothes, but he had removed the hat, and she was aware of his chestnut-hued hair and the way it was neatly combed; his face was animated, and his voice was lively.

She shifted her gaze, determined not to be caught gawking. She was an instant too late. Lowell spotted her and raised a hand in greeting. So did the assayer, an older man whom Deborah had waited on a few times at her mother's pie and coffee shop. Deborah stepped into the narrow, dusty street and came within easy calling distance. She spoke first to the assayer. "Good morning, sir. I hope the miners keep you real busy today."

He laughed and answered, "Good morning, Miss Dexter."

Deborah knew that her pulse had quickened as she spoke to the younger man. "Mr. Lowell, when you've finished your business, I have a question."

"Questions . . . questions." Lowell grinned, then said to the assayer, "She is full of questions. Wants to be a genuine gold prospector. Or a miner. Or a mogul."

After a few more words to the assayer, Robert Lowell also stepped into the street and came face to face with her. Before anything could be said, the approach of an ore wagon, drawn by a team of mules, caused them to get onto the plank sidewalk hurriedly.

Lowell's gaze encompassed her work clothes

and the rosy flush of her face. "Are you always up and about this early?" he demanded.

"Just . . . just when I have to get ready for a dinner party," she answered in confusion.

"A party," he repeated. "Is that your important question? How to give a party in the wilds of the Yankee Fork?"

"Can't you be serious for once?" she flared. "I don't need any gold panner to tell me how to arrange a dinner party."

"Then what in tarnation do you want to ask me?"

"Whether you would like to come. Be a guest at our home—my mother's and mine. Tonight. Say, eight o'clock." She waited to gather her wits and her words and then added, "We live in the cabin Whispering Trumble used to have. The man who owns it—Henry Carswell from Nebraska—is here in Bonanza and we're inviting him too."

Lowell stared at her speculatively. "You mean the Carswell who owns the placering claim that Whispering Willie used to work?"

"How did you find out about that?" she asked, gasping.

He reached out to capture and hold her hand. "First question deserves first answer. Deborah, I would be honored to come to dinner tonight. Lord, how long it has been since I tasted real home cooking. And I hear your mother is a whiz with a skillet."

"But I'll be doing most of the cooking," she said spiritedly.

He shook his head with a show of despair. "I suppose it's too late to beg off, to cancel out?"

She laughed aloud. "You're hooked, Mr. Lowell.

By your own words. And speaking of hooked, where on earth can I find someone to supply us with a batch of fresh trout? I am sure Mr. Carswell would love them."

"Just leave it to me, Deborah. How soon will you need them?"

She pointed a finger toward the market. "They are going to deliver some other things right after noon. If you could—"

"Worry no more. The elusive fish will be delivered along with your groceries."

"Are you sure you can catch them?" she persisted.

He turned to leave, then threw words over his shoulder. "Gold panning is my hobby, Miss Dexter. Fishing is the thing I do most and best."

Deborah stared after him, a certainty troubling and exciting her mind. If he had taken her in his arms, right there on Bonanza's main street, or had he kissed her, she surely could not have pushed him away—at least for a little while.

Rose came home from the pie shop an hour early, and their preparation of the meal was well under way. Rose glanced about the cleaned cabin with approval, then asked, "Debbie, just what are we going to wear? I know. I can iron the wrinkles out of that lavender dress I made in Ogden. The one that Bishop Stannard—" She cut her words off and glanced to see whether Deborah might have read more from them than Rose had intended to reveal.

"The bishop—you think of him often, don't you?" Deborah asked quietly.

"Yes, I do," Rose admitted. "And I think you

should know that Bishop Stannard plans to visit me, here in Bonanza, before winter sets in."

Deborah listened and then was very quiet for a time, lost in her own thoughts. In some way, the times when Robert Lowell's face had been close to hers, and his hands clasping hers, seemed now to lend new perspective to the possibility that her mother had found the Mormon churchman's offer of marriage attractive. Finally she said, "Mom, I know things can never again be as they were back in Banner County, when Daddy was alive. I've been lonely without him and know what you've gone through. If the bishop can bring you happiness, don't let me stand in your way."

"Time will tell, Debbie. I do appreciate your understanding," Rose answered. Then she reached into a bag she had brought home and handed an oblong box to Deborah.

Deborah opened the box to reveal a dress of pale yellow dimity, short-sleeved and belted. She held it to her with a gasp of delight. "Mom . . . oh, Mom . . . it is beautiful. Can I try it on now? And wear it tonight for our dinner?"

"Of course, silly. Why else would I have chosen today to give it to you? We can't have you wearing a black sateen shirt and a pair of overalls when Mr. Carswell and that gold panner of yours show up."

Deborah had slipped hurriedly into the dress and began to preen before a battered mirror hanging above the water pail and washbasin. "It fits, Mom. It really fits." She broke into a giggle. "Just wait until you see Robert's . . . Mr. Lowell's hat. The one he wears at work. I think it belonged to Paul Bunyon and that blue ox of his, Babe, chewed on it."

Rose laughed, then moved toward the lean-to and the cookstove. "Bring the washtub in, Debbie. We'll heat water for baths. Maybe mine will get rid of the Pie in the Sky smell."

Deborah was arranging and then rearranging their skimpy array of dishes and silverware on a pine-slab table, and darkness had descended into the valley when the hands of their clock reached seven forty-five. The odor of the food Rose was preparing permeated the cabin and sparked Deborah's hunger. She had just finished repolishing the chimney of the kerosene lamp when a knock sounded at the outer door. With eager anticipation she walked to the door and opened it. It was Henry Carswell standing in the light spilled by the lamp. Henry Carswell, looking exactly as though he had just stepped from his saloon in far-off Box Butte. He was wearing a dark suit, white shirt with stiff collar and flowing necktie, and holding his bowler hat in his hand.

"Mr. Carswell!" Deborah squealed. "Gosh, it's so good to see you again!" She stepped from the door and her arms encircled his neck. For a moment the grinning, middle-aged man held her tight, his cheek pressed to hers. Then he swept an approving gaze over her and said, "So it's that feisty kid again; by Godfrey, she's growing up. That dress—why can't Sears, Roebuck have something like it in their catalogue?"

Rose was waiting inside as they entered, and Carswell sniffed the air. Then he was firmly holding her hands. "Mrs. Dexter, why is it that any place we meet there's the smell of something great about to be popped from the oven?"

"Perhaps," Rose answered, blushing, "it is because this time Deborah and I are afraid you have in mind to dispossess us. We set up housekeeping here in the cabin you own."

"I think it is called 'claim-jumping' up here in Idaho," Carswell said. "And really I am grateful—"

Deborah failed to heed his further words. Again there had been a rapping on the door, soft and tentative. This time the lamp's rays revealed the smiling but almost anxious face of Robert Lowell. Deborah caught a sharply surprised breath as she swept her gaze downward from his neatly combed and parted hair. He had donned a suit of gray tweed and a green-tinted shirt and tie. Instinctively Deborah knew that the suit had not been worn for a long time and that Lowell was finding both it and his polished black boots more than a little uncomfortable.

For a while the gold seeker failed to utter a word. His gaze seemed caught by the sheen of her carefully brushed brown hair, by the lines of her new dress, and by the pulse throb she, herself, felt in her throat.

"Aren't you coming in?" she asked, almost in a whisper.

"Aren't you going to ask me to? Here." His hand came from behind him to reveal a fresh bouquet of wildflowers into which a dozen purple columbine had been carefully placed.

Both Rose and Carswell had been watching and waiting in silence. Now Rose moved closer, saying, "Debbie, are you going to let the young man stand outside all night?"

Deborah's hand sought Lowell's and drew him inside. Then she lifted the bouquet close to her face. "Thank you, Mr. . . . Mr. . . . Robert. Your bouquet is lovely. Now . . . Mom . . . Mr. Carswell . . . this is Robert Lowell. He wears a crazy hat and swishes a gold pan."

Rose offered her hand to Lowell; her smile urged him to feel at ease.

It wasn't until later, when the meal and the time of becoming acquainted were over, that Deborah had a chance to question Henry Carswell. He told her that the battles between the cattlemen and sheep association had quieted, and that her speech that night in Box Butte had helped to start the process. Then after a moment she asked, "Mr. Carswell, have you heard anything more of the missionaries—Nephi Oakes and Lemuel Froman?"

"That I have. They stopped by my home in Box Butte just last week. They were on their way to a new mission assignment in Ohio. They asked me to handle a little business for them in Nebraska."

A short silence ensued, in which Deborah realized that Robert Lowell was listening but had been left out of the conversation. Now she smiled at him, looked at her mother with a bit of grimness, and tossed a blunt question at Carswell. "Is that man Whispering Bill Trumble going to come back from California?"

Carswell studied her thoughtfully before answering. Then he said carefully, "He's not likely to. I had a letter from him. He is a pretty sick man. Throat cancer, I believe."

"What a pity," Rose said, sighing.

Robert Lowell stared at the tips of his boots, then said, "I didn't know him very well. But he was friendly . . . and had the reputation of being a good placering man and a square shooter."

Deborah, obviously shaken, came to her feet. For a time she was silent as her hands moved to rearrange blossoms in a vase. "He'd want the sluicing to go on. I am sure he would," she murmured. Then with a certain and decisive movement she again faced Carswell. "Henry," she began, and seemed unaware of speaking only his first name, "I know that you own the placering claim that Whispering Trumble was working. I have seen it . . . and studied every inch of it." Her words firmed almost to a defiant challenge. "We want to work that placer claim—Mr. Lowell and I. We want to lease it on a percentage basis."

The words brought Robert Lowell halfway from his seat, consternation tightening his face and widening his eyes. "God Almighty," he stammered, "wait a moment, girl. Who told you I would—"

Deborah turned toward him, her face flushed but with certainty in her voice. "Don't be stubborn, Robert. Of course you'll take charge—if Mr. Carswell makes a deal with us. It'll beat gold panning on a sandbar you don't even own . . . or ne'er-do-welling about every inch of Jordan Creek, and maybe the Yankee Fork."

Lowell listened, slumped back to the chair, and let a resigned grin break across his face. "You sure assume a lot, Deborah. And get right bossy. It'd be half fun—and half hell—to work that claim with you. But . . . you can't do it alone."

Rose got up from her chair, her face showing anger as she smoothed her lavender dress and then used agitated fingers to twist a locket at her throat. "Deborah, I am not going to listen to this nonsense." She walked toward the lean-to, from which there came an instant rattle of dishes.

Carswell watched her departure from the room, touched a match to the stub of his cigar, and then addressed Deborah. "You know, your mother is right. That sluicing claim hasn't made any money for me in three years. Just about breaks even. I will tell you where the opportunity and the money are in this camp. They're in feeding and housing the prospectors and the miners and the millhands. I want Rose to expand that pie place into a full-fledged restaurant. I intend to build a saloon and a boardinghouse . . . maybe a hotel for her to run."

Lowell had recovered enough to ask, "You mean you're going to settle in Bonanza or Custer?"

"Just during the summer. It's too cold for me up here in the high hills. Besides, I want to invest in land down around Blackfoot or Idaho Falls on the Snake River. The winters are a lot milder down there. Someday they're apt to irrigate a lot of that country with water from the Snake. Just about anything will grow thereabouts. I saw a patch of potatoes that—"

"You mean you'd farm?" Deborah asked, openmouthed.

"I said I would buy land. Get it ready for the farmers," Carswell countered. "With plenty of forage, that's bound to be a top livestock area too."

Deborah was standing behind a chair, her

hands firmly on its back. Carswell's appraisal of her mining ambitions had brought stubbornness into her face. Had she known it, her features at the moment resembled those of her father after a hailstorm had swept away his Banner County crop to leave him looking toward another year and another crop season with practically undaunted hope. Her words were carefully chosen as she looked unwaveringly at Carswell. "Then you don't think I have any business trying to dig gold . . . to operate that placering outfit that's just sitting idle on your claim?"

The saloonkeeper grinned wryly at her. "Deborah, it is likely that what I think won't cut one single bit of ice. Somewhere you picked up gold fever. If I refuse you a chance at my claim, you will just move on and look elsewhere. Maybe go gold panning to hell'n gone across a mountain. On some creek where snow gets ten feet deep in winter and the grizzly bears are looking for trouble in the summers." Carswell was silent for a few moments, savoring the fact that both Deborah and Lowell were watching and listening expectantly. Even Rose was quietly awaiting his words, for she was now standing in the doorway between the lean-to and the cabin.

"Now, Miss Dexter, just what sort of terms are you prepared to offer me for a lease on the placer claim?"

Her eyes became shrewdly appraising as they held to Carswell's face. "You already have a deal with Whispering Trumble, haven't you?"

"That arrangement will expire the first of September. It's one of the reasons I came up here to Bonanza." He shrugged and then added, "I don't know how I ever got tied into a gold-washing property in the first place."

It was Rose who answered, and her tone carried both doubt and resignation. "Because, Henry, you're a gambler. Willing to take a chance at anything that has even a small chance of turning a profit. A saloon. A potato farm in the desert. A few rusty pipes to get gold out of a creek—instead of earning it by hard work."

"You are right, Rose." Carswell laughed. "But don't try to tell me you won't be a convert to placer mining if and when your feisty girl washes a bit of high grade." Then he demanded of Deborah, "What are you going to offer for a lease? I have to leave here tomorrow, get back to Blackfoot. Let's talk turkey, Deborah."

She surprised him with the quickness and the confidence of her answer. "We want seventy percent of whatever mineral values we can produce— that is, up to fifty thousand dollars. After that, we want fifty percent—and an option to buy the claim."

"To buy for how much?" Carswell's words were blunt.

"For whatever three people, experienced mining men, say the claim is worth at that time."

Robert Lowell had been staring from one to the other of them. Now he ran a hand through his hair thoughtfully. "You're not going to get a fairer offer than that, sir."

"Are you prepared to put all this in writing?" Carswell asked.

"Are you prepared to sign it?" Lowell countered.

Carswell shrugged. "Guess I will have to. My

conscience would raise Old Ned if I sent this stubborn girl across the ranges to seek color." He waited, his face becoming serious. "There are a couple of stipulations, though."

"What?" Deborah asked.

"First, you've got to pay me ten dollars to seal the deal and make it legal. Second, it's no dice— and no contract, Miss Dexter, unless you agree that during winter months, from freeze-up to spring, you agree to get out of this crazy camp and go to a good school."

As he ended the words, the voices of both Rose and of Robert Lowell sounded. "She'll do it! I will see to that!"

Deborah spread her hands in a gesture of helplessness. "It is a conspiracy among . . . among all three of you. Well—did you really expect me to want to get by on a tenth-grade education?" She tossed the matter off as though determined, and then said, "We can have a lawyer draw up papers for the lease . . . tomorrow morning."

"Just be sure," Carswell snorted, "that you have that ten dollars to bind the deal."

It was Rose who surprised him. She turned momentarily toward a shelf. Then she thrust a couple of coins into his hand. "You've already got it." She smiled, and then to Deborah she said, "Don't get too joyous. It'll come out of your wages for helping at the pie shop."

For a moment embarrassment and confusion marked Carswell's face. Then he laughed and thrust the coins into his pocket. "Being as all of you are bound to stay here in the wilds, know what I'm going to use these ten dollars for? I am going to put ten more with it and buy a town lot in

one of those settlements along the Snake River—
down close to where summer spends the winter."

"I wonder," Deborah said, "what the missionaries, Mr. Oakes and Mr. Froman, would think of
our business deal."

"They would hope it works out well for you,
Deborah," Carswell assured her. "You will find
that young Mormons not only are spreaders of
their beliefs, they usually are shrewd businessmen."

"I want to write to them. Both of them. Can you
give me their address?"

Carswell nodded. "Sure I can. They'll be glad to
hear from you." He peered searchingly into Deborah's face, then added softly, "Especially . . . especially Lem Froman."

Rose Dexter listened, then turned to Robert
Lowell. "You have been pretty quiet through all
. . . all of my daughter's finagling. Mr. Lowell,
don't you have a feeling you're being roped into
something? Without hardly a say-so of your own?"

Lowell's face suddenly turned serious. He rose
and for a little time seemed to have his gaze on
something far off or long past. "Perhaps it is just
what I need . . . someone to give me a new sense of
direction. Maybe to reestablish goals that fell to
pieces—to shambles." He reached for Rose's hand
and squeezed it before moving to face Deborah.
"Will you . . . all of you . . . excuse me if I leave
now? I have enjoyed everything about this evening." For a moment his hand was on Deborah's
arm, and there was more than appreciation in his
eyes. Then Robert Lowell turned and abruptly left
the cabin.

"Deborah, he is real nice . . . but a bit strange," Rose murmured.

Carswell also was preparing to leave. "That young fellow—I would sure like to know where he was a year ago . . . or two . . . or even three," he murmured.

Chapter 6

O N THE same evening that Deborah and Rose Dexter served dinner to their guests, another meal was being put together in a small mountain clearing sixty miles southwest of Bonanza. The twilight had deepened almost to darkness as Jim and Mollie Plunkett guided their packtrain of twenty-two mules alongside a small stream. They had loaded the animals with food, supplies, and varied mining camp items at a trading post on the Union Pacific Railroad's line to Boise. Delivery would be made at a mine in the remote Thunder Mountain district north of the Yankee Fork.

The Plunketts had covered fifteen miles during a long day on the trail and were now nearing Galena Summit and the descent into Idaho's Stanley Basin. The trip was not a new experience for Jim and Mollie. Packing goods by mule back had been their livelihood for almost ten years. Once theirs had been one of several packtrains lugging goods into Bonanza and Custer; with the opening of roads for freight wagons and the stagecoach, their business had dwindled within the Yankee Fork towns. But there remained a need for their services at the mining camps to which roads had not yet been extended.

As Jim Plunkett unloaded the mules and prepared to let them graze on lush creekside grass, his wife rigged a small tent, laid out their bedroll, and gathered wood for a fire. She was a plump but strong woman of medium height. Life on the mountain trails had given Mollie unusual stamina; it had never caused her to lose her pleasant outlook upon life. She had acquired a personal interest in just about everyone in the remote mining camps. And hours spent leading or driving obstinate, sometimes balky mules had caused this merry-eyed woman to pick up . . . and polish . . . a collection of cursing words and phrases capable of searing the needles off a lofty Douglas fir.

It was the smell of strong coffee boiling above the campfire that told Jim Plunkett supper would soon be ready. He finished placing the packs in an orderly pile, picketed three mules from which he knew the others would not stray, and then knelt by the cold, swift-flowing stream to wash his hands and splash water against the rawness that a persistent swarm of black gnats had brought to his neck. He was a tall, almost gaunt man with slow and studied movements. Fifteen years before he had tried his luck as a prospector; luck had eluded Plunkett, and at his wife's suggestion they had bought a dozen mules and begun their business as packers. He seldom raised his voice, almost never laid a whip on an animal, and when things went wrong vented his frustration by mouthing a chew of tobacco.

But there was another side to Jim Plunkett. On the occasions when a fight was forced upon him, his deep gray eyes would turn cold, his face redden, and his long, dangling arms would come into play. It was told throughout the region that Plunkett could grasp a sizable adversary by the nape of the neck and send him spinning through a saloon doorway and into the street.

Just now there seemed only quiet gentleness about him. He looked about the camp, making sure that everything was safely in order for the night. Then he walked tiredly toward the campfire and his waiting wife.

She glanced up, then handed him a plate of food and a tin cup of coffee. As he settled onto a fallen tree, Mollie Plunkett studied his face and then said, "We've got to give it up . . . this packing business. Honey, we are just getting too old to be traipsing over these Sawtooth Mountains. Look at you. You're plumb beat. Besides, my bum leg is giving me fits again."

"What else can we do, Mollie?" he asked in a tired and concerned voice. "We've been packing in supplies so long it seems that the hind end of a mule is the only possible thing ahead of us."

"We could always get a little piece of land down along the Snake River and try raising fruit and chickens, Jim."

"Have you ever tried cleaning a chicken house? It's a stinking chore. And fruit trees would take several years to produce. We gotta have an income."

His wife smiled and then stroked his arm. Resignation had crept into her voice when she spoke. "I guess we'd best just admit it, Jim. We're mountain people . . . and crazy enough to prefer the country that gets all froze up—like those settlements of Bonanza and Custer, over on the Yankee Fork."

Jim wiped a biscuit across his empty plate and

emptied his second cup of coffee before answering. "What say we swing down to Bonanza City after we unload all this gear up on Thunder Mountain? They say the big Custer mill is operating again, and people are moving back into the district. Maybe I could get a job in the mill, at least for the winter."

"Whatever you think is best," Mollie agreed. "Likely I can get a job housekeeping at that hotel Charlie Blair operates."

"I don't know about that, Mollie. I wouldn't much cotton to having you make beds and empty chamber pots."

It was on Mollie Plunkett's lips to tell him that changing blankets and scouring thunder mugs would at least keep her out of the cold. Instead, her attention was caught by a sound from the nearby drove of mules. "Damn!" she said angrily. "I just knew it would happen! That was old Broken Ear letting us know there's trouble. There is a bear prowling about. And I hope to Christ it isn't a grizzly."

Before she was through speaking, Jim had come to his feet and lifted a heavy rifle. "Don't you worry, honey," he assured her. "If I don't see the prowlin' critter, probably a shot or two will scare him off. If I do spot him, you may have a nice bearskin robe to ease your rheumatism."

"You be careful, Jim. You hear? Be real careful." Then to the darkness and the forest she declared, "It's plain hell . . . this packing business . . . up here beyond the last speck of civilization." She was deeply concerned for the safety of her husband and the mules. But there was also sadness that in all likelihood this would be the last of the packing trips that had brought her and her husband to love and understanding and the reality of needing each other more than anything else in the world.

Exactly a week later, the Plunketts brought their twenty-two mules down the steep and crooked trail that drops from the Thunder Mountain mines to the narrow valley of the Yankee Fork. Save for their camping supplies and the raw skin of a large black bear, the packtrain was free of cargo. The mules sensed the end of the journey and pushed ahead. Presently they diverged onto a cutoff trail that would lead them along Jordan Creek. It was the same narrow way that Deborah Dexter had followed on the day when she had first sighted Robert Lowell on the sandbar.

The Plunketts and their mules passed that spot and hastened down the creek. They passed three claims where men were panning for gold. Then the Plunketts sighted something that caused them both to stare. At the claim where they had often seen Whispering Willie Trumble at work, two figures were bent above a length of heavy pipe. Both were clad in mud-smeared overalls and knee-length rubber boots. The head and face of the larger form was covered by a great flopping hat as he put reddened hands beneath the pipe and prepared for a back-spraining heave. At the other end, the smaller person also prepared to lift.

Mollie Plunkett spoke excitedly to her husband, "Jim! Look there! That is a *girl* trying to manhandle that big old pipe!"

The struggle with the pipe was unsuccessful,

and both Deborah and Lowell came wearily erect—to stare into the faces of the two strangers scarcely thirty feet away.

"You shouldn't be lifting anything that heavy," was Mollie Plunkett's greeting. "And how come old Whispering Willie ain't lending a hand?"

"He'd need a long arm," Deborah replied and laughed. "He's in California."

Mollie walked closer and peered into the girl's face, then said, "Don't mind us, child, we're just a couple of old busybodies . . . Jim and Mollie Plunkett." She waved a hand toward the halted mules, then added, "And all the little Plunketts."

There was a round of greetings as they got acquainted. Then presently Jim said in his slow drawl, "Mollie, why don't we hitch old Blunder to that pipe." He turned to Lowell to ask: "Have you got about twenty feet of heavy rope? Or a small cable would do. Then just show me and Blunder where you want the pipe."

Blunder proved to be both strong and cooperative; within ten minutes the pipe was in place. During its setting, both Mollie and Deborah had stood aside and watched. Deborah had learned that the Plunketts were bound for Bonanza looking for both old friends and any available job opportunities. Mollie had determined that these two "youngsters" were not claim jumpers but were tackling the formidable task of getting the sluicing operation into production.

Only when the Plunketts had been assured there were no other heavy pipes needing to be immediately moved did they prepare to continue toward Bonanza. Looking from Mollie's animated and cheerful face to Jim's calmer and wind-darkened features, Deborah suddenly hated to see them leave. These were people she could like, feel at ease with. Impulsively she wrote a few lines on a scrap of paper and handed it to Jim Plunkett. "You take this to the Pie in the Sky eating place in Bonanza. My mom runs it, and she's a real good cook. She'll fix you a nice meal—and this first one is on Robert and me." She waved off their thanks, then said, "If you decide to stay all winter, I'd sure like to work something out with you so we can use that Blunder mule."

"Yep." Mollie nodded. "And that old white bastard—" She cut off her words, waved in an embarrassed way, and prodded the last mule into motion. Moments later the packers and their animals were lost to view beyond a curve of the trail.

Within a week both Deborah and Rose Dexter were wondering how they had ever managed to exist along the Yankee Fork without the Plunketts. Mollie always seemed to be on hand at Rose's cafe when the work load was heaviest. With the sleeves of her calico dress rolled for action, she would tie into any work that needed doing. Jim showed up often at the sluicing claim on Jordan Creek. Both Deborah and Robert sensed that Jim was a tinkering genius, able to fix or improvise whenever a mechanical problem developed.

But these days of late summer were disappointing for Deborah. She had believed that once the sluicing equipment was in place and repaired, and water was washing shoveled sand along the riffle board, that gold would accumulate and that the operation would show a profit. It did not come about. Despite the long and tedious hours of work, the amount of fine gold accumulated was disappointingly small. Sometimes there would be an encouraging showing of the yellow metal, but this was erratic. There were hours when they seemed to draw a complete blank.

With each passing day Deborah grew thinner, tougher, and less apt to smile. There were other things weighing upon her mind too. Although he worked early and late, Robert Lowell had taken on a quietness that was almost taciturn. He was treating her as though she were a man, avoiding situations that might lead to physical contact or talk which could take a personal or romantic turn. To what extent this had been brought about by her mother, she could only guess. From the first, Rose had been lukewarm about the gold-placering claim; she had been outspoken in her opposition of Deborah spending so much time alone in the company of the young, enigmatic gold seeker.

September came with little improvement in production. On an evening when their work had been cut short by a heavy thunderstorm, Lowell called Deborah and Plunkett to his side. There was a mixture of discouragement and dogged tenacity on his face. "I think we're butting our heads against a stone wall." He turned to Deborah. "If you want, I'll continue as we are going until freeze-up. But I think we're going about this wrong."

"Have you any better idea?" she countered.

"Perhaps. But it is only a theory. Now look over there." Lowell waved his hand to indicate the stretch of streambank to the south side of Jordan

Creek. "There's a sort of dry gulch . . . see how the banks slope down. Sometime in the past, and probably for a few centuries, the creek flowed through it. Then something happened that forced the creek into its present channel."

Jim Plunkett studied the terrain and then scratched his head. "I see what you're getting at. There may be better gold digging in that old creekbed."

"So you two think we should get our rig set up over there," Deborah pondered.

Lowell squatted on the sand and let cold water flow about his fingers. "There is another possibility. We may be sluicing material that is too shallow in the creek. We aren't really touching the black sand that lies just above the rock strata. Gold has high specific gravity. It tends to want to return toward the center of the earth."

"Then we should be getting our muck farther down?" Deborah questioned.

"Possibly. But how? We would have to divert the entire flow of the creek. Other operators downstream would raise a real ruckus if we tried that."

"Then let's start moving our pipe and flume and riffle board tomorrow," Deborah said decisively.

"It won't be easy or simple," Jim Plunkett said studiedly. "First you'll have to make sure that the dry gulch is within the limits of your claim . . . or somehow get possession. Then how about water? Can we make it flow into the gulch by building a small diversion dam? But anyway, I won't be able to help you for two or three weeks. This time of year, me and Mollie always take a trip up into the

125

Stanley Basin and then down toward Ketchum. It's the best time of year for berries and fishing. It's our vacation. But we'll be back before the real cold sets in."

Deborah stared tiredly at the workings into which so much of their time and effort and hope had gone during the past weeks.

"Berries and fish . . . and always something new to look at and explore. Jim, right now I would give my share of this stubborn old riverfront to be heading out like that."

"You would?" Plunkett answered in surprise. "Then why don't you? I'd be pleased as Punch to have you along. Mollie would too."

Deborah heaved a sigh of resignation and spoke to Robert Lowell. "Wouldn't that be gratitude . . . my running off for a vacation just when you have all this moving to handle."

He grinned wryly and then told her, "You might as well trek along with Jim and Mollie. Before we move one pipe or timber there's a lot of paperwork and planning. Deborah, we will be lucky to have this cumbersome rig set up in the dry gulch by next June."

For nearly an hour after Plunkett had left for home, Deborah and Lowell lingered at the sluicing site. Both were reluctant to see so much labor and so many expectations come to naught. As darkness came on, Lowell, for the first time, walked with Deborah toward the Dexters' cabin. "You should know, Debbie," he said, "I am going to miss you."

She was aware, with quickened breath, that his rough, chapped hand was tight upon her own. "I could stay here, Robert."

"But you must not." His words were almost fierce. "I . . . I mean you should have the trip down to Ketchum."

Her eyes held level in their search of his face. "Is that the way you really want it?"

He stopped on the path, seemed to hesitate, and then let his arms gather her close. "Ever since that day on the sandbar I've wanted to do this. I didn't dare . . . as long as we had to work together every day. Debbie, what has happened? Have we fallen in love?"

Her pulse was pounding as she moved her lips close to his and murmured, "Would that be so terrible?"

"It would be a wonderful miracle . . . for me." He laid his lips upon hers, then held her at arm's length. Troubled words escaped him. "I have no right. Me . . . a tramp and a failure."

She started to lay her fingers on his lips to silence him. It seemed that only the twilight and his nearness and his acknowledgment of love were important.

"Hear me out," he urged. "Every impulse within me is to make love to you, but there is the need for decency—something I'm not noted for having. Damn it, Debbie, you're only about seventeen. And I am twenty-four."

"An old, old man," she mocked. If only he would be quiet and hold her tight again. The stirring within her had become almost a flame.

Robert Lowell broke free and put a couple of steps between them. In a strained, almost inaudible voice he said, "Go on home, Debbie, while I can still let you go. Tomorrow morning I have to face your mother, the Plunketts. Yes, and God Almighty—the mirror."

Deborah did not see him the next day, or the next. She did have a visit from Mollie Plunkett who was excited about the prospect of Deborah's company on the early autumn expedition to Stanley Basin and beyond. "Jim and I have it all planned. We'll each have a mule to ride and there will be two pack animals. Debbie, you can ride that old white son of a bitch we call Blunder." Mollie caught her breath and blushed. "Why can't I talk decent . . . properlike . . . instead of cursing? And in front of you, a lady!"

"I like you just the way you are, Mollie. Down to earth. Understanding. Helpful." She hesitated before asking, "Have you seen Robert?"

"Not hide nor hair of him. Likely he's taken a day or so off to traipse up to Thunder Mountain." Mollie scanned the girl's face and softened her voice. "You think a lot of that floppy-hatted prospector, don't you?"

"Mollie, maybe I am in love with him. I . . . I think I am."

Mollie heaved her bosom in understanding. "Likely you'll be sure when we get back from the trip. You'll have time and quiet to think things over. To make sure." She eyed Deborah and then added, "Jim says to tell you we will be heading out right after sunup tomorrow."

Even though Deborah had sensed the immensity of the Idaho mountain country as she made the stage trip from Blackfoot to Bonanza, a shock was in store for her. The pace at which they traveled on muleback was steady but leisurely as they ascended the land next to the Salmon River, threaded through heavy stands of timber, and finally came into the mountain-ringed Stanley Basin. The colors of autumn were everywhere now. The days held sunny and warm, yet both mornings and evenings of these shortening days were briskly chilly; at night the warmth of bedroll blankets warded off a coldness that hinted of impending winter.

The days of their travel took them into an almost uninhabited solitude. Rarely they would sight a prospector or other traveler. They stopped often, for the Plunketts delighted in pointing out vistas of far-off encircling peaks; dark, brooding forests that seemed to sweep to infinity; and the wild animals who held this as their domain. Fishing was excellent, and it seemed to Deborah that the bushes in many a mountain glen or ravine were literally festooned with chokecherries, mountain currants, and others that would provide the basis for jellies and jams.

They came, nearly a week later, into the lower and more gently sloping region, where the great mountains of the Sawtooth Range lie northward, and where folded and forested hills reach downward toward the valley of the Snake River. Open grasslands became more prevalent, although there were still mountain slopes from which creeks bent and dropped relentlessly.

And now Deborah and her companions began to encounter bands of sheep. Many of them were spread across the meadows and the open hillsides, with a fewer number grazing the timbered ridges. Other bands were on the move, following a well-defined but broad course toward the distant lowlands and then the desert country south of the Snake River. The Plunketts sometimes stopped to talk with the herders, for their years as packers had led to a sizable though widely scattered number of acquaintances and friends.

It was just short of noon on their seventh day out of Bonanza when they overtook an unusually large band of sheep. Deborah gave little heed as her mule rounded a point of timber and came abreast of two riders. When she looked up, she was scarcely twenty feet from the nearer herder. She stared unbelievingly at him, then gave a happy cry as she kicked the flanks of her mule and came closer to the now excited herder.

"Antonio—Antonio Onederra!" she yelled at him.

"You . . . you're Mizz Dexter," he managed to say, then dropped from his horse and rushed toward her. The girl shoved an eager hand toward the young Basque. "Antonio! What are you doing here? You look so much better. Healthy. Tanned."

He smiled delight, but she realized that as always he was unable to understand but very little of what she was saying.

"Mizz Dexter," he repeated, and clutched her hand to hold it tightly. He waved his free arm in a way that encompassed the long procession of grazing animals. "Tony's sheep," he said, and the words were proud and clear.

She dismounted from her mule to stand still and run an appraising gaze over him. He stood proudly erect and healthy.

Deborah was aware that Mollie and Jim Plunkett were almost at her side. Antonio had watched them too and now tried to form more English words. Then he turned to the second herder, who had been sitting quietly astride his horse. He was middle-aged, with dark hair and moustache and piercing gray eyes. A smile briefly touched his lips and he said, "Antonio asks that I translate. He wants you to stop for a bite of lunch with us. Also, he asked the names of your two friends and says to tell you that they are also welcome."

"Thank you, Mr. . . . Mr. . . ."

"Harding. Jeff Harding."

"Mr. Harding!" she gasped. "You're . . . you're the man who talked to my mother—back in Nebraska. And you sent the money for Antonio's train fare to Boise."

"It seems I get around." Jeff Harding chuckled. "Wherever sheepmen need me," he said quietly. Then he asked, "Where is your mother?"

"Back home in Bonanza, a town on the Yankee Fork of the Salmon River. We moved there from Ogden. My mother opened a little pie and coffee shop." She motioned Jim and Mollie Plunkett closer and introduced them, then volunteered, "We're on a sort of vacation trip down toward Ketchum."

A moment later Antonio Onederra spoke excitedly to Harding, who listened patiently and then told Deborah, "Antonio wants to know if you can head for Boise. Next week there is to be a Basque festival there. Antonio and I are leaving for Boise tomorrow. Antonio will take over again after the trailing crew gets this flock down to winter pasturing range."

"Where is that?" Deborah asked.

"Almost two hundred miles south of here, down on the desert and not far from the Nevada border. The sheep are wintered there, then brought back to these mountains for the summer."

Jim Plunkett had listened silently, but his searching gaze had covered Harding. Nor had Jim failed to notice the mahogany-handled pistols and the belt from which they hung. Now he asked bluntly, "Isn't it a bit unusual for you to be helping with a routine sheep drive, Mr. Harding? I have heard of you."

The words brought wariness to Jeff Harding; his response was brief and unrevealing. "Antonio is a new man in this Idaho country. The owners of this flock didn't want him to be alone if trouble developed."

Deborah thought, There has been trouble on this drive. But neither Antonio nor Harding are going to talk about it—not yet, anyway. It has to be over or they wouldn't be leaving the flock and heading for Boise.

Later, as they were munching cold sandwiches with strong coffee or icy water, Deborah asked Mollie about Boise.

"It's a nice town, and the capital of Idaho Territory," Mollie said. "It is in a big valley and right next to the Boise River. Not in the mountains, though they are close by. There are some real good stores; they carry things that you can't get anywhere else this side of Salt Lake City."

"I'd like to go there," Deborah said firmly. "I would like to see Boise, and all of the country from here to there."

Mollie turned to her husband, who smiled and nodded. "Debbie Dexter," Mollie said, "we're going to Boise. Late tomorrow should put us in Ketchum. Then we can catch the stage to Boise. I always wished I had a daughter I could take into the stores and pamper."

Both Antonio and Jeff Harding had been listening as they finished eating and began to pack up and prepare to move on. Now Deborah spoke to Harding. "Will you tell Antonio that we will go to Boise?"

"Likely he already knows. He is much better at understanding our language than at speaking it." Harding gestured Antonio to his side and began speaking to him in Basque. She listened as Harding and the Basque boy ended their exchange of words. Then the older man smiled at her and said, "Antonio wants to know if you will be at the Basque festival."

"I would like to. But we would need an invitation."

"Tony has invited you. And Deborah, I would like for you and the Plunketts to accept his invitation. Our sheep people need more of the understanding and goodwill of the Americans. And anybody in Boise can point you toward the festival events. Why not leave knowledge of your whereabouts with Ramon Echiverri at the Bank of Idaho?" Without further words, he signaled Antonio to get astride his horse; then without a backward glance they began to aid in getting their flock again on the move.

Both of the Plunketts slept much of the time on the stage ride outward from Ketchum. They had anticipated a long and jolting journey to the territory's capital, but found that the stage now connected with a train at Jerome. They had a smooth ride in a passenger coach and reached Boise at nine o'clock in the morning.

Deborah was surprised by the greenness of the valley and of the farmlands being carved out for irrigation from the river. To the north and east stood high and verdant hills. She sensed that beyond them lay the vastness of Idaho's mountains and woodlands. When she faced westward, there were more mountains, but these were more distant, beyond a broad expanse of the Boise River Valley. The day was warm, with an intensity of sunlight that caused her eyes to narrow. Heat waves already shimmered off a butte on the southern horizon. It seemed to Deborah that the broad expanse of sky, almost cloudless, was the deepest blue she had ever seen.

Plunkett left his wife and Deborah in the waiting room of the train station and took off afoot down the broad avenue leading eastward. He returned about an hour later, driving a gentle gray mare hitched to a two-wheeled buggy. He climbed down from the rig, joined the women, and began picking up their luggage.

The house where Jim had found rooms for them was a large, frame structure, boxlike and painted white. The ceilings were high, and each room was large. Deborah's had a brass bed, a wooden rocking chair, and a dresser with brass pulls on the drawers and an ornately framed mirror. There was also a commode with a water pitcher and a washbasin, and a white dresser scarf with embroidered pink roses. It was the most spacious room in which she had ever slept; it seemed to accentuate the bigness of Boise Valley, the looming mountains, and this place of which she had so long dreamed—Idaho Territory. She moved to an open window, where an errant breeze was stirring white lace curtains. Plainly in view was a building that Jim Plunkett said was the territorial capitol. Excitement stirred within her. "Just imagine . . . me, Deborah Dexter, in Boise. Right where all of the laws are made."

The reflective mood lasted only until her head touched a clean, white pillowcase, and she reveled in the rest offered by a real mattress. She slept soundly.

Peeking sunlight awakened her. She yawned, stretched, and then snuggled again under the quilt. Abruptly a thought struck her, tearing the last remnant of sleep from her eyes. What would it be like to have Robert Lowell in this bed beside me? What if his hand were to reach out and draw me closer? What if—

She slid quickly from the bed, dashed cold water on her face and hands, and then brushed vigorously at her tumbled brown hair. The activity brought full realization of the day ahead and its possibilities. She donned a crisp gingham dress from which Mollie had ironed every crease. She was ready to explore Boise. And yet . . . deep within her mind was the thought of Lowell, his floppy hat, his intense gaze, the feel of his lips upon hers.

Shortly after the lunch hour, while the Plunketts were relaxing in their room, Deborah happened across the assay office. She stood entranced by a large window in which were displayed more pieces of ore and mineral samples than she had ever realized could exist. Peering through the glass, she could see shelves lining the walls of a large room. Upon each shelf were mineral samples ranging from less than an inch in diameter to pieces larger than a dinner plate and standing several inches high. They were identified with names she had never heard, and she repeated them to herself. Antimony. Cobalt. Bentonite. Monazite. Across the plate-glass window was a gold-lettered sign reading FRANK WENTWORTH AND COMPANY, GEOLOGISTS AND MINERAL ANALYSTS.

When she entered, she came abreast of special cases enclosed in glass and designed so that sunlight from a window fell on the contents. Then she noticed a card that read GEMSTONES. The rainbow of color thrown back by the stones seemed something out of a fairy tale, for she was staring at sapphires, rubies, garnets, and opals. There were also the green of two-toned quartz plasma and the firelike glow of clear rock crystals. Her eyes roamed the collection, resting finally on a pale blue stone.

Instantly she was startled by a voice from close behind her. "That is an unusual water agate. I happened to find it in the lava around Squaw Butte, maybe forty miles from here."

The voice had caused her to turn; now she was facing a middle-aged man whose hair was almost snow white but carefully cut and brushed. His face was browned and rugged and yet sensitive, and laughter lurked in the blue eyes with which he was studying her.

"I didn't mean to startle you," he began. "But that blue stone is one of my favorites. I am Frank Wentworth, itinerant geologist and seeker after nature's treasures. I own this place—when it doesn't own me." He grinned easily, and asked, "And you are . . . ?"

"Deborah Dexter," she replied. "I am visiting in Boise. I live in Bonanza. That is on the Yankee Fork, way east of here."

"I've been there often, Miss Dexter. The mineral stratas there are quite rich . . . and often complex and baffling."

"They have baffled me," she said and her discouragement with the Jordan Creek placer claim tugged at her face. Then suddenly she was telling him of the placer claim and its equipment, of her journey to Idaho, and of the Mormon missionaries, Nephi Oakes and Lemuel Froman.

"Froman . . . Froman . . . he wasn't by any chance from Idaho, was he?"

"Yes, he was. I think he was from the farming country, down closer to Utah."

"Then I'm sure I know the family. Just last week I had a letter from Lemuel's father. He was inquiring about prospects for a lawyer here in Boise. It seems his son has a law education and is thinking of opening an office, or working for a law firm, here."

"Lemuel never mentioned law schooling to me."

"Probably not, Miss Dexter. Young Mormon missionaries give out a lot more information about their church and the Book of Mormon than they do about their personal lives."

Chapter 7

DEBORAH and the Plunketts left their rooming house at midmorning and were walking toward the riverbank spot where the Basques were gathering for the second day of their weekend fete. They had chosen an open stretch of grassy meadow with just enough trees to offer shade when the heat of midday would come on. Already campfires had been kindled and lighted; the smoke rose in blue-tinged and indolent spirals. Off to one side a group of men and older boys had chosen sides and were straining and shouting in a tug-of-war. Other people, in the colorful costumes of their homeland, stood about visiting.

As she made her way through the crowd, Deborah was sure that the festivities had drawn people not only from Boise but also from remote ranges such as that on which Antonio Onederra kept watch over his band of sheep. She nodded and smiled toward a group of middle-aged people who watched her arrival and that of the Plunketts. The Basques smiled politely in return, but there was a reserve about them for those of different descent and ways.

Near the area's center was a warehouselike building with walls of carved stone. She was nearing the structure when she first sighted Antonio. He was wearing a light gray jacket, dark and sturdy trousers, and a knitted blue beret, set now at a jaunty angle. Instead of his heavy boots, his feet were thrust into rope-soled *espadrilles*. Another man had used his bare palm to smash a ball against the stone wall, and as the ball rebounded, Antonio leaped sideways and thrust out his hand to send the ball speeding back to the wall.

"It's a *pelota* ball," Jim Plunkett explained. "They are just practicing. Debbie, you ought to see it when a few experts really get to playing. They use their bare hands like clubs."

As if he had sensed their approach, Antonio turned and looked straight toward Deborah. Then, motioning for a companion to take his place, Antonio turned and sped toward her. "Mizz Dexter! You are here—in Boise. You and . . . and how you say the name? Now I remember," and his lips formed a word: "Plunchett."

"That is close enough," Deborah said and laughed. "Before long you'll be calling them Mollie and Jim, as I do." She swept a gaze over the growing crowd, then added, in slow and clear words, "Antonio, we are friends. Now you should call me Deborah. Not Miss Dexter." He smiled but did not speak. Yet she was sure that he had understood and when alone would practice her name.

They were joined in a short while by two men and a woman. It was the tall and reserved Jeff Harding who performed introductions. "This is Mr. and Mrs. Ramon Echiverri, Deborah. Tony has spoken so highly of you that they insisted on meeting you and making sure you enjoy the fete."

Both of the Echiverris were of robust build. Ramon stood slightly over five and a half feet. He had removed his hat, revealing dark hair with a sprinkling of gray. The gaze of his dark eyes was direct and steady. There was an intangible air of self-assurance and authority about him. His wife, though deep-bosomed and plump, stood erect. Her complexion had been darkened by much time outdoors, yet it was singularly clear. She had borne children and known hardships, but she was both proud and content. Instinctively, Deborah knew that this couple were leaders and advisers of their people. Nor was she surprised that both spoke English well, although there were the lingering tones of their Basque heritage.

Ramon Echiverri spoke with calm dignity, welcoming the visitors and then saying to Deborah, "Both Antonio and Jeff Harding have told us how you and your mother cared for Antonio when he was badly beaten. We Basques are grateful, for Antonio is one of our fine young men. Mingle with us and enjoy our festival." He indicated for Jim Plunkett to accompany him, saying, "I hear you are a packer. Many times those of your calling have aided our herders, bringing letters and medicines and supplies to the camps."

"Come. You must keep me company while we finish preparing the meal," Mrs. Echiverri urged Deborah and Mollie, and guided them toward one of the cooking fires and a blue-checked cloth spread on the grass.

Later, when the men had gathered about the lunch cloths, goatskin wine vessels were brought out, but she was surprised at how sparingly the Basques drank the wine. It was used mostly in good-spirited and jesting toasts. From a little distance came the music of a *txisto,* a woodwind instrument she had never seen before. Then, in Basque, a priest worded a prayer of thanksgiving.

When it had ended, Deborah leaned close to Jim Plunkett and whispered, "I wonder if any of the Basque people are Mormons."

"I never heard of such a thing. They are Catholics and have been for centuries. They are deeply spiritual and have a lasting steadfastness for their Catholic faith."

The food was passed about. Deborah was delighted with its variety and delicious quality. Mountain trout with sweet peppers. Roasted and fried chickens, seasoned with wild sage. *Garbanzos,* large peas, cooked to tenderness. Corn bread. Cakes cooked in honey. And again goatskin flasks of sour wine to bring about the guttural and approving syllables so many of those present had learned in Guernica, their beloved city in the Pyrenees Mountains.

After the meal, there was a lull while food leftovers were put away, the dishes cleared, and some of the older participants settled for a nap. As if in respect for the sleepers, the children moved across the meadow, almost out of hearing, and settled into a game of tag.

Later came the planned entertainment for both young and old. It started with a high-kick contest and then the Dance of the Warriors. In this a dozen young men, clad in white, with red sashes and colorful berets, gave an exciting exhibition of acrobatic skill as they tossed one of their number high above their heads. There were also wood-chopping contests, after which the girls, wearing traditional Basque skirts and blouses, performed intricate rope-skipping rituals.

Finally came the great event of the day, a *pelota* game between two teams that had long been rivals. The skill of the players in driving the ball and countering the drives of others brought the entire crowd to its feet with loud cheers, jeers, and laughter. Antonio did not participate in the contest but stood ready as a substitute. Deborah realized he was utterly engrossed in the game. When it was over and the winners had been crowned, she started to walk toward him. Abruptly she stopped. From out of the crowd had stepped a girl of perhaps fifteen, her full blue skirt set off by a white blouse, a velvet bodice of darker blue, and the *zapi* head scarf, also of white, which Deborah had noticed was part of the traditional Basque costume. The girl's face was pleased but carried a blush as she came abreast of Antonio and halted. Then she lifted a small carved figure and spoke rapidly in Basque. Deborah knew that this was some sort of award, but deeper instinct told her that this young Basque girl considered Antonio Onederra also to be a prize.

The sun was nearing the serrated ridge westward and people were leaving the festival area when Debbie finished thanking the Echiverris and sought out Jeff Harding.

"Will you be returning with Antonio to his band of sheep?" she asked.

He shook his head somewhat ruefully. "It isn't necessary. I go wherever I am needed. Arizona or California or perhaps back to Nebraska or Wyoming."

Deborah studied him intently, then blurted, "My mother says you are a sort of lawman, Mr. Harding. An enforcer for the sheep ranchers of the West. Isn't that awfully dangerous?"

"Yes . . . sometimes there is danger. I have

learned to expect it, and I have ways of dealing with situations before they become really explosive. A few Basque families own their flocks and the grazing lands, and the number increases from year to year. Slowly." Harding was quiet as he gave thought to his words. Then he continued, "Maybe the biggest problem is lack of a steady and stabilized market for the wool clip. But that situation isn't limited to the Basques. All Idaho lamb and wool producers are caught in what seems near to a conspiracy. A few men manipulate the markets to their own advantage. Perhaps worse is that the woolen mills are mostly in the Midwest and along the Eastern Seaboard. The lamb-processing plants are centered in Chicago. Freight rates are high—in some cases ruinous."

Deborah's gaze held to his face as she commented, "You are devoted to the sheep growers, aren't you."

"They pay my wages," he said easily and shrugged. "But beyond that I have found sheepmen . . . and almost all ranchers . . . to be honest and hardworking, worthy of a better deal than they are getting."

Jeff Harding turned from her, noting that the Plunketts were approaching for a word of farewell. Then, in a voice that was low but full of concern, he said, "Deborah Dexter, don't settle for a shack in a mining camp, a plodding miner, and a houseful of kids—at least not too soon."

They left Boise the next morning, retracing their way by railroad and stagecoach to Ketchum. They retrieved their riding and packmules and headed back to Bonanza. They plodded steadily ahead over Galena Summit, through the Stanley Basin, and down the Salmon River toward its merging with the Yankee Fork. They had been gone almost three weeks. The ageless sorcery of autumn had brought deeper colors to the mountain foliage and had sprinkled the higher peaks with fresh snow. Winter would soon be at hand, and the settlements of Custer and Bonanza would settle into a semihibernation brought on by snowy isolation and the periods of searing cold.

For much of Deborah's trip homeward, she was quiet, even pensive.

She mulled over her conversation with Jeff Harding: *Maybe the biggest problem is lack of a steady and stabilized market for the wool clip. . . . A few men manipulate the markets to their own advantage . . .* From time to time, others had mentioned economic, even political corruption in the West to her. Why do people talk to me about such things? Deborah murmured to herself. As though I might do something about prices and politics . . . and God knows what else. How? I'm just seventeen years old and my mother runs a little pie shop in a mining camp. Memory of her father caused her to jerk erect. Wasn't she Tom Dexter's daughter? A wonderful and inspiring man, always sure that things were bound to work out if one but had faith in the future.

Suddenly Deborah could view her father's optimism and faith in a new and more revealing way: Daddy was hopeful. But more than that, he was always planning ahead, doing the things that were needed to achieve those high hopes. Likely, even though I try hard, there will be no way I can help the sheepmen get fairer prices . . . at least until— Abruptly her thoughts gathered into a single resolution: I've got to finish high school, then find a college. It will take four years or perhaps five.

It was well after dark on the day that Deborah and the Plunketts returned to Bonanza that Rose Dexter sought out her daughter. They had eaten a light meal during which Deborah had spoken excitedly of her time in Boise. Rose listened politely, but her thoughts seemed elsewhere. Finally she started a fire in the kitchen stove to warm the cabin. Then, almost defensively, she spoke out. "Deborah, I hardly know how to tell you. I am going to sell my restaurant business and leave Bonanza. Real soon."

"Why, Mother?"

"Because I am going to be married in October—to Bishop Stannard." When her daughter failed to reply immediately, Rose continued. "Joshua . . . Bishop Stannard . . . was here for two weeks; he came a couple of days after you and the Plunketts left. I hoped he and I could tell you together, but he had to return to Ogden."

Deborah keep her gaze steady on Rose's face. Then she asked, "Mom, are you a Mormon now?"

"Not yet, honey; I have to take instruction." Then with rising tension in her voice she asked, "Can't you understand? Why don't you say something . . . at least wish me well?"

"Mom . . . Mom. Give me time to realize this—and what it means to my future."

"The bishop and I talked about that. He thinks you should finish high school this winter in Salt Lake City and then enroll at the University of

Utah. That way you and I would be closer together."

Unfathomable resentment swelled in Deborah and showed in her eyes. "What about my having a say-so? You know that I have always wanted to live in Idaho. We've been here only a few weeks, but already I have friends and . . . and a placering claim."

"And a young fellow who is altogether too interested in you—at your age." Rose's lips were quivering between sorrow and rage.

For a second or so a searingly angry response was on the girl's tongue, but she remained silent. "Mom," she said finally and reached out to pull Rose near, "you have every right to get married. It is just that I want the best . . . want so much . . . for you. Bishop Stannard has one wife that we know of. And perhaps others. Some Mormons have—"

Rose lifted a quieting hand. "I know, Debbie. Joshua has been truthful with me. His first wife, somewhat older than I, is an invalid, a consumptive. The bishop provides a home for her down in Saint George, Utah. It's warmer and drier there." Rose hesitated, then drew a deep and bolstering breath. "Now—about his other wife. She is young, in her midtwenties. Her husband was a nephew of the bishop but was killed in a blasting accident. Bishop Stannard followed a suggestion of the Church and married her. To provide a home for her and her small child."

"Does he sleep with her?" Deborah asked, and the words were almost brutal.

"That is a matter among the bishop and me and

Almighty God," Rose replied, and she clamped her teeth over her lip.

"Then it is all settled," Deborah said tiredly. "When do you expect to leave?"

"Just as soon as you can get ready to go with me—and we can find a buyer for the pie shop."

"You don't give me much time or much choice, do you?" Deborah sighed bitterly. After a silence of a full minute, she spoke in a more controlled way. "Mom, why don't you lease the pie shop to Mollie Plunkett on a percentage deal? She would probably do well at it. At least she is honest; I'm sure of that."

"I just might do that. I'll talk to her and her husband. Now about you, Debbie."

"Yes, Mom, about me. I am not going to give you an answer tonight. I am too tired and mixed up. It has to be my decision. It is my life and my future. I can stay here in Bonanza. I can go with you to Utah. And perhaps I could even get a job in Boise." As she finished, Deborah Dexter knew what must come before her decision. She must again feel the arms of Robert Lowell about her and the ecstasy of his lips pressing hers. Yet also within her mind was her resolve to finish high school and then go to college. Could she do these things *and* marry Robert and bear his children?

For a time Rose watched her daughter in a troubled way, then she spoke. "Debbie, I hope you will learn to like Bishop Stannard—though I doubt you ever will. You will always have a tendency to see men, and judge them, in the light of what your father meant to you. But he is dead now. Neither of us can let his memory dominate our lives."

Suddenly Deborah flung herself into a chair,

dropped her head to the kitchen table, and gave way to uncontrollable sobs. Between them she said brokenly, "Mom, I miss him so. But I . . . I love you too, Mom. And now you're going away."

Rose started to reply, to say that Deborah would be going with her and that things would be no different between them. But she knew truthfully that things would never be quite the same. To her daughter she would be the wife of a Mormon bishop—one of three wives—instead of the widow of Tom Dexter, the man of hopes and dreams. So now she merely laid a comforting hand on Deborah's shoulder. Then recalling something, she walked across the room and picked up an unopened letter.

"Honey, this came for you nearly a week ago. I know you've been expecting it. It is from one of the Mormon missionaries . . . the older one, Nephi Oakes."

Deborah used a fist to wipe tears from her cheeks, then tore open the envelope.

Dear Deborah:

Elder Lemuel Froman and I received your welcome letter quite some time ago and were delighted to learn that you and Mrs. Dexter are now situated in Bonanza, Idaho Territory, and are in good health. Our delay in answering was caused by several new circumstances. We traveled widely through northern Ohio, carrying the Mormon message to both farm and city dwellers. The response has been gratifying, and surely the Lord has blessed our efforts.

Lemuel Froman asked me to let you know

he will write as quickly as possible. He is presently en route to Salt Lake City, having completed his tenure as a missionary. I believe he plans to take additional university work and become a member of the legal profession. As his parents reside in Idaho, you may see Lemuel before I do. The Church has sent me another coworker to replace him. I will miss Lemuel, for he was good-natured and devoted to our Church and its expansion.

You will note that I am now in the little city of Lorain. It is situated on the shore of Lake Erie, some twenty-five miles west of Cleveland. For the foreseeable future I will be busy establishing a stake—you would call it a branch—of our Church of Jesus Christ of Latter-day Saints.

There is a possibility that Lorain may become my permanent home, for there is a young lady here who has promised to marry me. Also, there is a business opportunity that intrigues me. It has to do with the wool industry. Would you believe that Ohio is one of the greatest producers of sheep and their fleeces?

Deborah, I hope that the Lord will soon put it in your mind and heart to become one of us Mormons, to accept and cherish the doctrines that we Latter-day Saints hold and know to be divine.

Do remember me to your fine and courageous mother.

Obediently yours,

Nephi Oakes

As Deborah refolded the letter and slid it into the envelope, she said thoughtfully, "The part about Lemuel . . . Lemuel Froman . . . tallies with something I heard in Boise—that his family is already inquiring about any openings in law firms or how best to set up a practice."

Rose tilted her head and smiled speculatively. "You know, honey, it always seemed to me that Lemuel Froman liked you quite a lot. Perhaps if—"

"Oh, Mom, quit imagining things. Do you know what I was to the missionaries? Just someone they hoped to convert to their Church. I don't think either one of them ever noticed how my hair was combed or what kind of dress I chose to wear." She waited, her face tightening in determination, and then said in low-spoken but forceful words, "I'll tell you who notices—Robert does. Robert Lowell. And, Mom, I am going to see him tomorrow . . . if he's still around."

"He is. You can just bet he is. And what do we know about him?" Rose was bristling. "Has he ever told you anything of his family? Of where he came from? What he expects to become?"

"I never asked him," Deborah defended. "Mom, you want me to approve of your marrying a Mormon bishop. Even say I should live with you both. But you can't see anything good in Robert, someone who has helped me at the gold claim and has never asked for a cent's pay. All you seem to think about is how no good he is and . . . and that probably he wants to start me in a life of sin." Anger was causing the girl's eyes to flash and her bosom to heave as she went on. "Maybe I will go to Salt

Lake City or Boise. But I'm not going to sneak out of Bonanza without seeing Robert."

Rose turned and looked out of a window in evident despair and defeat. "Why are we at each other's throat like this? Debbie, I just want the best for you, don't want to see you hurt or see you lose that wonderful belief that the future is yours to grasp. Yes . . . see your young man. Only your own decision will seem of any importance to you now."

Deborah awakened early the following morning. A chill had crept into the cabin, and outside there was the deep murmur of wind sweeping through the pine and fir boughs. Rose was still asleep in the adjoining room and did not waken as Deborah threw more wood on the banked fire and stirred the embers. She noticed that instead of the usual morning brightness the light outside was dull, almost sullen. If there is a storm behind this, she thought, it may mean the beginning of winter.

She washed her face and hands with cold water at the bench, and then combed her hair. The lean-to kitchen was warming; she moved into it to don heavy clothing, then busied herself preparing toast and hot tea. Her mind searched the meaning of the weather. What would this valley of the Yankee Fork be like when the streams became frozen and snow lay high within the forest and against the walls of the buildings? She had heard that during winter the temperature sometimes plunged far below zero. Surely much of the work must come to a halt under such conditions. Bonanza and Custer might be cut off from the rest of the world for days at a time. Even the mines . . . Abruptly she knew that today—this very morning—she must visit the placering claim. Her help might be needed if a storm was brewing.

Minutes later Rose was out of bed, dressed, and preparing to leave for the pie shop. There was a cheery calmness about her now.

"I'll have a busy day," Rose surmised. "Weather such as this brings a crowd in for coffee and a warm snack."

Before Deborah could do more than smile and nod, there was a firm knocking at the front door. Rose opened it to reveal Mollie Plunkett. She was wearing a cap with earflaps and a tan coat lined with sheep fleece. Her face was reddened by the wind but held a good-natured grin. She was holding the reins of a mule, and the animal wore a work harness.

Rose shivered in the whipping wind. "Come on in, Mollie. Hurry before this wind blows every stick of our fire right up the stovepipe."

"Close the damned door while I tie this mule to a tree," Mollie advised, and then added, "Tell Debbie to hurry and get into some work duds—and some long-handled underwear might be a good idea."

Minutes later the three women were drinking tea as Mollie explained. "Bob Lowell came by last evening, pretty late. He's uneasy that a storm is headed this way that may drop a lot of snow. He asked Jim to bring a mule to help move the rest of the sluicing gear into that dry gulch. But Jim can't this morning. And blast it, neither can I. There's a couple of fellows here from Challis who want to deal for our packmules. Now, Debbie, bein' as Jim and me have to meet those buyers, maybe you can take old Blunder outside to your sluicing claim . . . to help out a bit."

Deborah glanced toward her mother, expecting disapproval. Instead, Rose nodded in agreement. It was as though she realized she must accept the inevitable, that nothing she could say would shield her child from what another meeting with Robert Lowell might portend.

"It is your gold claim—and your life, Deborah," she said firmly. "Take the mule down. But, mind you, if a big storm blows in, you scoot for home." Rose put on a coat, tied a heavy scarf about her head, then nodded to Mollie Plunkett. "Why don't you walk as far as the pie shop with me, Mollie? It's on your way home."

Half an hour later, Deborah reached the placer site on Jordan Creek. She was leading Blunder and wearing heavy walking boots, a pair of patched overalls, and a heavy mackinaw. The tempo and chill of the wind had brought a flush to her face and some numbness to her fingers. She sighted Lowell, who was kneeling on the sand near the stream's edge and working with a pipe wrench to disconnect two steel bands that held a length of flume in place. The bolts had long since rusted; now Lowell's face was tense and his arms were straining. For moments she watched him in silence, knowing he was unaware of her presence. She was directly behind him and close enough to hear his heaving breath when the threads of the rusted bolts failed to yield.

Suddenly his voice sounded aloud. She stood silent, awed and mystified. What Robert Lowell said bore no relationship to the stubborn bolt or the job on which he was working.

"All right," he said, "I can't prove it! Perhaps I never can! Lacey, you lied—just as you lied about the ruptured spleen and the sutures and—" As though her presence, her silence, and her bated breath had alerted his senses, Robert Lowell wheeled about to look angrily into Deborah's face.

"What are you doing here—slipping up on me like this?"

"I wasn't slipping up," Deborah protested. "I just brought old Blunder for you to use. You wanted him, didn't you?"

Lowell was regaining his poise; his voice returned to normal. "I'm sorry, Deborah. You were lucky to get home from Boise before this wind hit us; there is snow behind it. Plenty of snow."

"What on earth were you talking about? Spleen? Sutures? Lacey?"

His face darkened and he seemed to fight for self-control. Finally he managed an uneasy laugh. "Oh, I was just talking about something from a book I'm reading. It seemed to make pulling on that wrench easier."

She looked directly into his eyes and smiled— and was absolutely certain that he was lying to her.

Their combined strength, pulling on the wrench, loosened the nut and allowed the flume to be freed. For the next hour they worked together, moving the final pieces of equipment to the new location in the dry gulch. It was a job they could not have accomplished but for the strength and pulling skill of Blunder.

They finished the task shortly after noon, then sought out a spot where heavy brush broke the intensity and chill of the wind. Lowell started to sit down on a well-grassed spot, then said, "Wait a minute. I have something that will help warm our insides." He disappeared toward the pile of equipment and returned with a metal bucket. It was filled with sawdust, into which he dug. Presently he pulled out a half-gallon Mason jar. Then a tin cup came into view and he dumped its sawdust content to the ground.

"Coffee," he said jubilantly. "Hot coffee! I learned the trick from a prospector up on Thunder Mountain." He poured a cupful and handed it to her. "Someone else is looking for a spot out of the wind," he said, and they watched the mule, Blunder, stop nearby and turn with his rump to the wind.

Deborah sipped eagerly and then handed the cup to him.

He reached for it and their hands touched. He took a quick swallow and then set the cup on the grass and said, "Debbie, I missed you . . . thought of you every day you were away."

"I am glad," she murmured. "Bob, I missed you too." The words gave way to a contented sigh as he drew her down beside him on the grass. "Hold me . . . hold me tight," she whispered, and at that moment was aware of the cold dampness of the first snowflake lighting on her upturned face. But she thought only of his nearness as he kissed her cheek and then sought her mouth.

"Debbie, I need you," he whispered. "God, how I need you." She pressed closer, knowing the ecstasy of his touch as fingers unfastened her coat and sought out a button of her blouse. I want you, Robert, her mind tolled. Come to me . . . here in the brush and the storm.

It was just when he moved again, coming to claim her, that a deafening roar sounded and the valley of Jordan Creek seemed to shudder. There was a sound of fright, a flash of white and fast-moving frenzy, and then a snapping sound as though a small branch had been broken. Instantly Deborah screamed with pain then lay writhing on the ground. "Oh, God! What happened? Robert, what is the matter?"

He had come swiftly to his feet and looked about when he answered. "It was the mule. Someone nearby on the creek set off a blasting charge. A big one. That damned mule spooked and ran."

"But my leg," she gasped. "I . . . I'm sure it's broken."

He knelt quickly beside her and she felt the cautious touch of his fingers.

"It's your left leg, just above the ankle, isn't it?" he asked.

Deborah nodded and then tried to struggle onto her elbow so she could look down. A gasp of pain escaped her and she fell weakly back. She listened as Robert spoke decisive words.

"It's broken, all right. In his fright, that damned mule must have stepped on you."

There was firm authority in Lowell's voice as he looked about, realizing that the ground was already whitening with snow. "That bone will have to be splinted and then set. But first I've got to get you out of here, take you home where it is warm. Debbie, if I catch that mule and then lift you onto him, can you hang on while I lead him up to your cabin?"

"Maybe I can," she answered, panting. "I'll

try." She smiled at him and added, "I'm sorry, Robert. Sorry it happened just when—"

He bent over and touched his lips to her forehead. "So am I. But you know what, Debbie? Maybe that mule has better sense than either of us."

All she remembered of the slow trek homeward in the worsening storm was snowfall that obscured her sight, a series of shocking pain thrusts as her foot touched the flanks of the mule, and the encouraging words that Lowell kept uttering. As they came into the cabin yard, the door flew open and her mother ran toward them, heedless of not having a coat or scarf. Her eyes swept the white torment of Deborah's face and she quickly turned to Lowell. "What on earth happened?" she asked in alarm.

"It was an accident, ma'am. The mule stepped on her leg. It is broken just above the ankle." Lowell was easing the painracked girl cautiously from the mule's back and preparing to carry her.

"If you will open the door, Mrs. Dexter, I'll carry her inside out of this storm."

Rose moved quickly to clear the way and said over her shoulder, "Lay her on the bed and I will warm a blanket."

Robert Lowell turned to Rose. "Is there somewhere you can get the mule in shelter? I'll be looking up some pieces of board we can cut and use for splints. I will need you when we put them on."

There was a small log stable at the forest's edge behind the cabin. By the time Rose had gotten Blunder inside it and had taken off the harness, she realized the intensity of the storm. Snow already lay two inches deep across the clearing; objects only a few steps away were becoming indistinct through the falling whiteness. She closed the stable door, drew her coat about her, and hurried back to the cabin. Inside, she thrust her hands for a few minutes close to the warmth of the stove. Then she moved to the bedside. Lowell was already there; on one side of the bed were sturdy sticks for splints. He had cut away part of the leg of Deborah's overall and removed the lacing from her boot. Now he was carefully drawing the boot from her foot. Despite his careful maneuvering, a quick breath of pain sometimes escaped Deborah.

"Just hang on, Debbie," he encouraged her. "This splinting won't take long."

Rose looked on in concern as the boot and then a stocking slid from the foot. She lit a kerosene lamp and moved it near. "Isn't the break going to have to be set? Shouldn't I go for a doctor?"

Robert shook his head. Grimness lay across his face after he stared briefly out the window. "Just now," he answered reluctantly, "the only doctor in the valley is up at Custer, two miles away. The snow will be a foot deep before you could get there and back. Besides, he is supposed to stay within a half hour's call of the big Custer mill."

"I'll just rest until tomorrow." Deborah's voice was almost a whisper. "Mom, stay here with me." She was quiet a moment and then added, "And you stay too, Robert. Inside. Out of the snow and cold."

Rose motioned Lowell into the kitchen lean-to, then asked in a worried undertone, "Can we do that, Mr. Lowell . . . let it wait until tomorrow?"

He faced her and there was challenge and determination about him as he answered, "It could be several days before this storm clears or we can get a doctor."

Rose's hand moved in a gesture of despair. "My God—no. She might get bone infection or . . . or become a cripple. Robert, what on earth can we do?"

For a time he stared at her with calm directness. Then, using her first name for the first time he said, "Rose, I believe I can set her leg. I have seen it done. Even helped a doctor once. The break seems to be a simple fracture."

"Can she endure the pain?"

"I am sure she can. The worst part will be pulling the bones into position, but that will take only a few seconds. Now . . . would you trust me to try to set the break?"

She nodded consent. "What other choice do we have? And you seem to know something of how it is done. Yes—go ahead. But I will want a doctor to look at the leg as quickly as possible."

"And I would want that also," he agreed. "Let's tell Deborah and get on with it. I'll need your help. And either a pain killer or a drink of straight whiskey will help to ease her through it." Lowell removed his coat, rolled up his sleeves, and said briskly, "Let's get some water boiling. We can use that and some lye soap to give the leg a thorough washing—both before and after."

Deborah overheard him. "You know, Robert," she said, "you sound just like a real doctor."

He turned from her, and she did not see the strange cast of his face. But she did hear his answer, spoken in a way that seemed to vent pent-up emotions. "Doctor! Forget that crazy idea, Deborah."

It was afternoon of the second day before the storm passed. In its wake was a mantle of snow measuring just under sixteen inches. No sooner had the cloud cover drifted eastward than the temperature began to plunge. Before morning it would touch below zero in the valley of the Yankee Fork.

Despite the weather conditions, there was a rap on the door as night began coming on. Rose went to the door and opened it slightly to peer out. Then she let out a welcoming cry. Standing in the yard were the two well-bundled forms of Jim and Mollie Plunkett. They stamped snow from their boots and entered. Jim went to the kitchen table and set down a canvas bag.

"We got real worried," Mollie explained. "The storm came on so quick we—" She broke off as she caught sight of Deborah lying on the bed covered by a blanket and of Robert Lowell. "What ails you, honey?" she asked Deborah. "Got the croup?"

"She has a broken leg. The mule stepped on it," Lowell explained. "He's out back in the stable now."

"Did you have a doctor for that leg?" Mollie demanded anxiously.

"The nearest one is in Custer . . . and the road is probably blocked," Lowell said.

"Nope. Old Doc Webster is down at Rose's pie shack right now. I saw him there a few minutes ago." She turned to her husband. "Jim, you shag up there and fetch that old sawbones."

Twenty-seven minutes later Jim Plunkett again came through the doorway, followed by an elderly and hump-shouldered man with a well-trimmed white moustache and matching Van Dyke beard.

"This is Doc Webster," Jim Plunkett announced, and then winked at Deborah. "You're in luck, gal. Doc is sober. When he's bellyin' up to the bar he couldn't doctor a ruptured duck. When he's sober . . . he's almighty handy with pills or one of them gadgets they call a scalpel."

The doctor grunted his disgust, nodded to those assembled, and then turned to Deborah. There was silence as Dr. Webster examined the fractured leg. "You're a lucky lady," he said finally. "A day or so from now you'll be up and around—using a crutch, of course."

Rose asked fretfully, "Aren't you going to set that leg—make sure it is done skillfully?"

The doctor turned and for a moment glared at her. Then he demanded, "Just who in thunderation set and splinted that fracture?" It wasn't until both Deborah and her mother had pointed toward Robert Lowell that he flushed, then said uneasily, "I hope I didn't botch the job too badly. I saw a doctor set a similar break once."

"You saw it done—just once?" Dr. Webster glared.

"Well . . . well . . . yes."

"And you're the damnedest liar that ever came into the Yankee Fork!" the doctor roared. Then he thrust an accusing finger against Lowell's chest. "No one," he continued, "could do a job like this without knowledge and skill and practice. To set that type of break, using the closed-reduction method, ain't a blacksmith's job. And it ain't done by ordinary prospectors. Now . . . out with it, son. What medical school—"

Robert Lowell's face had whitened; his eyes became those of a caged and prodded animal. "Damn it, sir, I told you!" He flung his arm in a gesture that encompassed all those within the room. "I told all of you!" Suddenly he rose, grabbed his coat from a nail, and plunged into the outer darkness and the deepening cold.

A week later the road between Challis and the Yankee Fork settlements was sufficiently cleared for freight wagons and the mail and passenger stage to get through. The storm was followed by a period of warm and sunny days, although the nights remained cold enough for a layer of ice to form on the water pails within the kitchens of Bonanza and Custer.

Within two days of Dr. Webster's visit, Deborah could move about the cabin on a crutch that Jim Plunkett fashioned for her. Her mother was gone much of the time, spending long hours at the cafe as she explained to Mollie Plunkett every facet of the cafe's operation. There was an aura about Rose Dexter akin to dreaminess; the time was shortening before Stannard would again arrive in Bonanza to accompany her back to Ogden . . . and the wedding that would follow.

Several times each day Deborah found herself standing at the cabin window, hoping that Robert Lowell might appear in the snowy yard. Why had he so angrily lied to her and to Dr. Webster about his past, his source of medical skill? She had been given only one hint of his whereabouts since his hasty departure under the doctor's questioning. The following day he had appeared at the cabin where Jim and Mollie Plunkett had settled for the winter.

"He was dressed for the trail and had a pair of snowshoes swung over his shoulder," Jim explained to Deborah. "He seemed calm enough, but there was a strangeness about that young fellow. His face was drawn. . . . I could have sworn he hadn't slept a wink."

"But didn't he mention me?" Deborah was close to tears.

"He just said, 'Tell Deborah that our paths are bound to meet—someday.' And he asked me to give you this." Jim Plunkett handed her a small black box and then quickly left the cabin.

She opened it and with trembling fingers folded back two layers of red tissue paper. A small cry of joy escaped her. Within the box was a flat piece of gold that had been hammered into oval shape. There was a small hole near the top so that a chain could be attached. Her eyes scanned the shining metal and her mind grasped the significance of lines etched upon it. Robert Lowell had re-created her sprawled form as she had lain beside Jordan Creek when the rotten log had broken and thrown her at his feet. In miniature letters, she read: *I fell for you too. Rbt. L.*

She clutched the medallion to her face. Then the tears came.

She fell into a tired sleep that lasted until darkness gathered over the valley, until her mother finished the long day's work at the pie shop and walked home. Presently Rose lighted a lamp; believing Deborah to still be asleep, she prepared to throw a comforter over her. Her movement was halted as Deborah sat up. "Mom," she said huskily, "I have made up my mind. I will go with you to Ogden when you and the bishop leave. I want to be there when you are married. And I want to go to school."

Rose sat down on the bed and drew the girl close. "I am so glad, Deborah. I have prayed you would decide to continue in school."

A hint of her usual mischievous self marked Debbie's reply. "Did you pray as a Methodist—or as a Mormon?"

"You're a nosey brat," Rose laughed. "Let's just say I prayed as a mother. I have an idea it's pretty much the same regardless of faith or creed." She waited briefly and then added, "Are you positive you want to leave Bonanza?"

"Yes—at least for a while. Until spring." Deborah raised the small box and its golden burden and explained that it was Robert's parting gift. "I loved him, Mom. He's the only man—except Daddy—I ever loved."

"I was just beginning to like him myself, Deborah. I think there is more to him than either of us realize."

Rose went to the kitchen and began heating water for tea. Then she came back to Deborah's side. "Guess what? Two men you know came into Bonanza today: Bishop Stannard . . . and our landlord, Henry Carswell."

"I would love to see Mr. Carswell," Deborah said, beaming, and then added politely, "and, of course, Bishop Stannard too."

"You will. Both of them are staying at the Blair House. The bishop will be calling on us tomorrow evening. Likely Carswell will show up before that; he was right concerned when I explained about your broken leg." Rose went to the kitchen and returned with two cups of steaming tea. As she handed one to her daughter, she said, "Honey, there are times I can't figure out Carswell. He is a fine businessman, hardheaded and sometimes sort of ruthless. Yet inside he's really gentle, concerned with people and their rights. Look how he defended those Mormon missionaries even when their preaching was aimed at cutting into his saloon business in Box Butte."

"I know," Deborah agreed. "He's also the sort of man people look to for leadership—and can trust." As she uttered the words, she thought of a startling possibility. For a moment she almost told Rose of the idea, but merely said, "I wonder if Mr. Carswell ever got hold of the farmland he wants down around Blackfoot?"

Her question was answered just after midmorning the following day. Henry Carswell, wearing the inevitable gray business suit and black bowler hat, stepped gingerly around a couple of muddy spots and entered the yard. They exchanged happy greetings, then sought out the warm sunshine on the front step and sat down. Deborah told him in detail of the recent developments in her life, and then Carswell volunteered news of his own.

"Like you and your mother," he said, grinning, "I've kicked the last bit of Nebraska dust from my boots. I sold out and cleared out; I'm a full-fledged Idaho citizen now, holding clear title to about four hundred acres of land upriver from Blackfoot.

And a bit more a hundred miles farther west along the Snake."

She turned to look squarely into his face in an oddly challenging way. "I am glad to hear about it, Henry. It will help. Will it ever help."

"Help what?" he demanded in bewilderment.

"Help to make you the governor of Idaho—when we become a full-fledged state."

"You're crazy, kid!" Carswell yelled and came to his feet in an agitated yet expectant way. "I am no politician. Likely there aren't twenty people between here and Boise who know me."

"They will." She smiled.

PART
TWO

Chapter 8

IN THE third week of May 1894, Deborah Dexter was awarded a degree by the University of Utah at Salt Lake City. She had finished both her final year of high school and her freshman college courses in a single year.

The students had elected to hold their commencement ceremonies outside. As Deborah walked to the reserved seating section, she breathed the coolness of the midmorning air and then glanced about. To her left the peaks of the Wasatch Range rose sharply. There were sloping stands of timber and large areas of green rangeland marking the escarpment where the great valley of the Salt Lake commenced. She could glimpse the lake, reflecting an immense reach of sunlight before becoming lost in a westward haze. Closer westward and much lower than the campus, Salt Lake City lay in great rectangular blocks and wide streets. Sunlight touched the dome of the state capitol, the oval dome of the tabernacle, and the spires of the temple.

As the strains of "Pomp and Circumstance" faded and a dignitary of the Mormon Church began the invocation, she looked curiously toward the bunting-draped stand. There were robed members of the faculty seated there, and off to one side a group of Church officials. She caught sight of Bishop Joshua Stannard, now her stepfather. Immediately she felt a keen sense of disappointment that her mother could not be here on this occasion. She recalled the last time she had been seen Rose Dexter Stannard—and the almost unbelievable circumstances under which it had taken place.

During her freshman year at the college she shared a room with another girl at a strictly supervised residence near the campus. Her persistent refusal to become one of the Latter-day Saints had brought a coolness between her and Bishop Stannard. There had also been several stormy sessions with her mother, who now was firmly indoctrinated into the Mormon faith. When Deborah was able to secure part-time work at the cafeteria, her parents had not objected strenuously to her moving out.

To this student residence, on a moonless night in November 1890, had come two middle-aged members of the Church. "We are here at Bishop Stannard's request, Miss Dexter, to accompany you to your parents' residence in Ogden. It concerns your mother."

"My mother!" Deborah repeated and paled. "Is . . . is she ill? Has there been an accident?"

"We only know that you are wanted at home. But please hurry; there is little time."

It was nearing two o'clock in the morning when Deborah reached the Stannard home in a quiet, residential part of Ogden.

Bishop Joshua Stannard opened the door. "Come in, Deborah," he urged in a low voice.

She stepped into the dimly lighted hall and searched her stepfather's face. It was tired and taut and stern, yet a resolute firmness burned in his deep-set eyes.

"Bishop, what happened? What is wrong?"

He led her toward a small study as he answered, "Your mother is waiting for you. She will explain, Deborah." He opened a door to reveal the room that served as his study. Deborah was conscious of walls lined with bookshelves, of a blaze flickering in a stone-manteled fireplace—and of her mother, sitting erect but white-faced and unsmiling behind the polished desk. An unknown fear grasped Deborah as she sped around the desk and threw her arms about Rose. "Oh! You had me so worried, Mom. Coming here. This time of night." As she lifted her head, she saw that the bishop had seated himself on a straight-backed chair and was clasping and unclasping his hands.

Rose Dexter Stannard continued to cling to her daughter's hand. Words broke from her, almost in a whisper. "Deborah, I am going to have to go away. Before morning. I won't see you for a long, long time." Rose's voice broke as she turned to her husband. "Joshua, you tell her. I . . . I can't."

"Sit down, daughter," the bishop said. His voice was shaken.

Deborah seated herself on the desk's edge with her arm firmly about her mother. This was the first time Bishop Stannard had ever called her *daughter*.

He gazed at her with a measure of pleading in his eyes, then began, "Your mother has told you of my other marriages. To the woman I married when I was quite young, and to the young widow whom I gave the protection of my home and my name."

"Yes, I know," Deborah murmured.

"You are aware also that earlier in the year our Church abolished plural marriage."

She nodded. The official end of polygamy had long been a topic of conversation and heated debate on campus. "How does all of this concern my mother?" she demanded impatiently. "Why is she having to leave her home? Without warning? In the middle of the night?"

Rose lifted her head to say firmly, "Because if I don't leave, men will take Joshua away. Before tomorrow's sun sets he will be jailed. Branded as a polygamist. Hounded. Ruined." Rose came unsteadily to her feet. "Debbie, I can't let that happen. I am going away. There is a place somewhere in the mountains where men of Mormon faith can conceal their second and third wives. It's . . . called a *sealed village*."

The impact of her mother's words held Deborah silent for a long time. Then anger—deep and furious anger—flushed her face and darkened her eyes as she faced the bishop.

"Why does my mother have to be the one to suffer? To be dragged away in the night to a hideout in the wilderness? How about your other wives . . . those you had before Mom fell for you and your . . . your Mormonism?"

Stannard lifted a hand. "Please hear me out, Deborah. I now have but two wives. My first died three months ago. As for the other, Abrigal, only a few years older than you, she cannot undertake a journey to our designated place of safety." He fell silent, and it was Rose who explained.

"She has a young son, only four years old, from her first marriage—to the young man who was

172

killed. And, Deborah, there is another reason—she is far along in pregnancy."

"By my stepfather?"

"Yes," Stannard said without hesitation. "She will bear my child. Deborah, try to understand. I am a churchman, following the divine precepts of our founders, Joseph Smith and Brigham Young. We hold that plural marriages are sanctioned by Almighty God."

Deborah stared at him with anger and pity. Then she said, "But not sanctioned or held legal by the government of Utah—or the federal agents who are baying on your trail."

A rustle of applause across the assembled crowd brought her mind back to the reality of the graduation scene. She again stared at her stepfather as he sat on the speakers' stand. My mother has been away for four years, she reflected, yet he sits up there as though only the furtherance of Mormonism is of any importance to him.

She scanned the section of seats given over to parents and visitors. At least there were two people who would seek her out after the ceremonies. Both Mollie and Jim Plunkett had arrived in Salt Lake City the previous day, determined to watch her receive one of the first degrees the University of Utah would present to a young woman majoring in business administration.

But it wasn't the Plunketts who came to her first after the recessional. A young couple picked their way through the crowd to approach her. At first glance she took them for strangers. Then abruptly her eyes widened and a small, glad cry escaped her. "Antonio! Antonio Onederra—how wonderful!" She grasped the hand of the smiling young Basque, noting the correctness of his dark suit, white shirt, and hand-loomed tie. At the same time she studied the young woman beside him, wearing a woolen dress of mint green, a matching beret, and spotless white shoes.

"And this—" Deborah said excitedly. "Now I remember! You're the young lady who presented Antonio with the award. At the fete back in Boise."

"You are right, Miss Dexter," Onederra answered. "Now she is my wife, Narcisa." There was still the musical Basque cadence of the words, but they were precise and clearly spoken.

"Antonio! You have learned English. How well you speak it."

Vast pride rode the young Basque's response. "She, my wife, helped me to learn. Another helped. The owner whose flocks I tended until only last February."

Deborah offered her hand to the young woman, who accepted it with timidity and grace. "And now where are you living? Surely Antonio doesn't make you share a tent and a campfire with him."

"I would gladly do that . . . just to be with Antonio. But he planned better things. We now have some rented ground, a small house, and sheep. Sheep of our very own."

"Only a small band, less than two hundred head," Antonio explained. "And we have what you call a . . . a mortgage."

"At the bank in Boise," Deborah said.

He shook his head. "That may come later, when I am naturalized and a landowner. Our mortgage

174

is held by a friend of the Basque people. One you know—Jeff Harding."

Deborah became aware of the Plunketts, who had broken from the thinning crowd and now stood near to offer their congratulations. "Mollie . . . Jim . . ." she said, waving them to her, "of course you remember Antonio Onederra. You met him at the Basque festival. And this is his wife, Narcisa."

The group exchanged pleasantries, and then Antonio announced that he and Narcisa were to become parents.

Deborah's eyes worked their way along Antonio's young wife, noting for the first time the revealing lines of pregnancy. She gathered the young wife's hands into her own. "I am so happy for you; be sure to let me know when your baby is born."

"She will have good care among our friends in Boise," Antonio spoke up reassuringly. "Our baby is going to be strong. A strong Basque—but an American too."

"What're your plans now, Debbie?" Mollie asked.

"I don't really know. If I were smart I would have some sort of job lined up; instead, I stand here with a piece of paper that says I'm through college—and I haven't the faintest idea what comes next."

Antonio had listened quietly, and now eagerness came into his face. He spoke briefly to his wife in Basque. Then somewhat hesitantly he said to Deborah, "We would be happy . . . if you could go with us . . . to Pocatello."

"You live up there? Near Pocatello?"

"No, Miss Dexter. But we are going there to-morrow. There is to be a spring meeting of the sheepmen of Idaho. It will last three days. Many Basque people will be there. Your friends. They would welcome you. If you could come it would make me glad. And my wife. And Jeff Harding—he says to me last week: Try to bring the young lady and her mother."

Deborah shook her head in perplexity. "I don't know, Antonio. My mother is a long way off; I haven't seen her for four years. And I have to look for a way of making a living." She knew that work would not be easily available at the university and that she would not become part of Bishop Stannard's household or derive her livelihood from him.

"Tell me where you will stay tonight," she suggested. "In the morning—after I have had time to think—I will let you know. I'm happy and honored that you invited me."

When the Basque couple had left, Mollie Plunkett spoke firmly. "Debbie, up in our room at the hotel we've been saving a letter addressed to you—from someone you haven't heard from in a goddamn long time."

Deborah's head lifted as she caught her breath.

At last they were in the Plunketts' room at the Hotel Utah, and the letter was laid in her hand. It was in a brown envelope, addressed in a clear, free-flowing hand and bearing the postmark of Spokane, Washington. It was postmarked nearly three weeks earlier and had no return address. She broke the seal, noting that the Plunketts had

176

slipped out of the room. She unfolded the single white sheet enclosed:

Dear Deborah,

Hopefully the Plunketts can give this to you on the day you don a robe and mortarboard. It has been a long time.

I hope the leg was well set and has given you little trouble. You were wise to go to college; I know how much it can mean. Yes, Deborah, I have decided to tell you. I was a medical student, in my fourth year, at the University of Washington. I was unable to finish and serve my internship. Nor will I be able to, for college officials and the State Medical Board have decreed otherwise. I won't tell you it doesn't hurt to be banished. Especially when with sufficient proof on my part of certain events it never would have happened. Whenever I see someone ill or injured and am not allowed to assist, I cannot but feel cheated.

But enough of that. What good would come of rehashing a closed and locked and probably forgotten case—or is the word "injustice"?

I have not returned to the Yankee Fork valley since you left. I was afraid I might find you there—and I'm sure no mule could keep me from your smile . . . your arms . . . you.

I have had means of indirectly knowing your whereabouts and of your fine progress at the university. And now you have graduated. My congratulations. I hope you will remember me and the sandbars of Jordan Creek when you see the small gift I have asked Jim and Mollie to place in your hands.

We may meet someday, but I would prefer that for the present you do not try to locate me.

And remember, for a time you were, for me, the best and loveliest part of Idaho. Make all of your tomorrows memorable; it will be easy with your unquenchable faith in each future day and year.

The wanderer,

Robert Lowell

As she scanned the final lines, and dropped the letter atop a table, Deborah wiped tears from her eyes. "Robert," she murmured, "you wonderful . . . stubborn . . . proud fool. As if any school matter would have made one bit of difference to me."

The Plunketts had reentered the room, and now Jim opened a closet door and pulled out a package. It was about a foot square, several inches high, and securely wrapped and tied. "We mustn't forget to give our gal this," he mumbled awkwardly, cutting the string with his pocketknife. "It is what Bob mentioned in the letter."

When the wrappings were thrown back, the sound of their excitement filled the room. It was a carving of a mule in pink-veined alabaster—and the mule was undeniably Blunder, who had broken her leg during the storm years ago at Jordan Creek.

Deborah Dexter took the carving into her arms and moved to a window. Her hand drew back a brocaded drape, then for a long while her eyes searched the lights of Salt Lake City. Yet her mind was probing things far away. Then she said, "Thank you . . . both of you . . . for making my graduation day perfect. Now I have decided. I'm going back to Idaho. No, not to Bonanza, for it would be too empty. Tomorrow I am going to Pocatello with Antonio Onederra and his wife. When I was in Nebraska years ago I just knew that in Idaho I might find the sort of happiness and the future my father always talked about. I am closer to Idaho now. Somehow now I belong to it and it to me." She picked up the letter and thrust it inside her blouse, close to the pounded gold locket she had worn since she left Bonanza.

The meeting of Idaho sheepmen, held early in June in Pocatello, brought together a large segment of the industry. Hopefully, means could be found to deal with an assortment of vexing and threatening problems. There was the constant problem of range disputes with the cattlemen; all too often it flared into hatred and violence. There had been instances during the past year when sheepmen had found their flocks, or portions of them, destroyed and the herders in lonely spots injured or killed. The cattlemen were prone to pass off such depredations as the work of Indians. In a few instances this was true, for the plight of the remaining Indians had become desperate.

There was also the matter of dealing with others whose influence was growing: the Mormons who were establishing more and more farming communities; the timber barons, who claimed immense areas north of the Clearwater River;

the railroad companies, whose power was derived largely from federal land grants; and the mining interests, whose influence came from the rich mineral deposits they exploited.

Years earlier, at the Basque festival in Boise, Jeff Harding, the thoughtful protector of the sheepmen, had touched briefly upon another problem facing the lamb and wool producers. As Deborah listened to speakers at the meeting, the conversation with Harding came frequently to her mind. He had told her of the sheepmen's lack of a steady and stabilized market for the wool clip and of how a few men manipulated the market to their own advantage. He had mentioned too the disadvantage brought about by lack of western woolen mills, by the long and expensive rail haul of wool to the spinning mills east of the Mississippi River.

Why do I concern myself about this? Deborah thought. And just what am I doing in Pocatello? I don't own a single acre of land or one sheep. Other than Antonio Onederra and his wife, I don't know another sheep rancher.

I'm searching for something, she reflected, something I can do to keep me in Idaho and give me a feeling of belonging. Idaho became a state four years ago. Big things are bound to happen. Fortunes will be made.

Within her a spark was kindling.

Her reverie was broken by the sound of a speaker being introduced. Two men had appeared at the speaker's stand. The older man she had met in Boise—the Basque leader, Ramon Echiverri. The other she recognized even before his name was spoken. Lemuel Froman! The Mormon missionary. Only now Echiverri was introducing him as a fine, young Boise attorney-at-law. Froman would address the gathering on acquiring grazing leases on Idaho lands.

Lemuel Froman placed a sheet of paper on the stand, then let his gaze sweep the audience. Then he saw Deborah. He smiled his recognition and bowed almost imperceptibly. He began his talk, and Deborah listened at first with somewhat disinterested politeness and with hope he would soon finish and she could greet him.

Within a few minutes she found herself caught up in what Froman was saying and his manner of speaking. The talk was simply worded and entirely practical. Yet as this young attorney spoke, his voice and his phrasing caused an attentive quietness to hover across the room. He is a born orator and yet a trained one, Deborah told herself. His way with words . . . his logic and his persuasion. Not all of those come from law training. They result from those months and years he spent pleading the cause of Mormonism. She studied Froman's form and face. He was clad in a dark brown business suit and a stiff, white shirt with high collar and a flowing necktie. His beard and hair were neatly combed; she noted with surprise that already there was a touch of gray at his temples and a maturity he had not had when last they met. Something has happened to him, she mused. He can't be more than twenty-five. Something is aging him rapidly. Too rapidly. Her mind went back to the hectic days in Box Butte and the manner in which he and Nephi Oakes had faced an ugly mob. His face had been as intense then as now, but youth and exuberance had clung as an

aura about him. He's too serious, she thought. It's
. . . it's as though he is driven.

The speech ended and drew generous applause.
Soon he walked to Deborah's side, and now excitement was written across his face. "Deborah—Deborah Dexter," he said. "It seems impossible . . .
just a fine impossibility . . . that I should find you
here—at a sheepmen's convention in Pocatello!"

As she answered, she was acutely aware that
her hand was lying in his firm grasp, and that his
steady gaze held unyieldingly to her face . . . with
a touch of wistfulness about it.

She was positive he had been about to mention
her mother and that he had stopped because he
was aware that Rose Dexter had become Rose
Stannard, the wife of Bishop Joshua Stannard—
and even now was a "sealed wife," hidden somewhere in a mountain-ringed wilderness. Deborah
chose to ease the moment for him. "I have just
graduated from the University of Utah."

"Congratulations, Deborah. I hope you let
Nephi know of what you have accomplished. He
was very interested in your future." Froman hesitated and then added, "He had high hopes of your
someday turning to our faith . . . becoming one in
spirit and purpose with the Latter-day Saints."

Deborah said firmly, "Lemuel, I have not seen
fit to become a Mormon, even though my mother
did. I keep asking myself whether she was right
or wrong. God knows what she may be going
through."

He listened in silence, his face troubled. "Deborah, your mother married a Mormon. Perhaps . . .
to a degree . . . out of loneliness, but surely because she loved the bishop. Mormon women en-

dure much. But don't mistake their motives. Our Church is sacred to them."

Deborah wanted to cry out in anger, to tell him of the fear and the near panic on Rose Stannard's face the night she had been spirited away to become a sealed wife. Instead she asked, "And how about you? Or do promising young lawyers have time for such things as marriage and setting up housekeeping?"

His lips tightened and he seemed to choose his words carefully. "Yes, Deborah, I have been married for almost three years. My wife is tall . . . blond . . . very pretty. She likes to entertain and to arrange fashion shows." He fell momentarily silent, then brightened. "We have a daughter, who is learning to talk now. We named her Janice. You would love her." Lemuel's voice had picked up in tempo and excitement. "And Nephi Oakes is also married. He is now in the spinning-mill business in Lorain, Ohio.

"Deborah, I have to meet two men for lunch. I think you know one of them, or know of him. Jeff Harding."

"How well I remember Mr. Harding. I met him in Boise, before I moved to Salt Lake City."

His next words were hesitant, almost as though they would arouse her disapproval or her anger. "Deborah, will you have dinner with me this evening?" He watched for a hint of her reply, then added hurriedly, "My wife and Janice aren't with me on this trip; the child is rather young for traveling."

Her smile put him at ease, then she said, "Lemuel, I would enjoy having dinner with you. We have so much to recall and talk over." Within her a small voice was telling her that this was the first time she had been invited to dine alone with a married man. She said, "I am staying at the Caribou Hotel."

"Good." He grinned. "My quarters are only a block from there. I will call for you just before eight o'clock." She nodded agreement and would have said more, but as her gaze moved about the almost-deserted meeting room she saw a tall, lithe man standing near the door. Instantly she recognized him as Jeff Harding and knew that he was waiting to greet her. She walked toward him and offered her hand. "I am glad you are here, Mr. Harding."

"I wouldn't dare not be." He laughed. "Not after threatening Antonio with all sorts of dire consequences if he failed to bring you back with him from Salt Lake City." His eyes moved over her in an assessing way. "You are indeed a young woman now, Deborah. And you went back to school. What are your plans now?" he asked.

"I am looking for work," she said bluntly. "Not necessarily a position. Just a job. I don't suppose you know any sheepman who needs a bookkeeper—or a not-so-great cook."

"Offhand I don't. Besides, young lady, you are now overqualified for either job." He walked with her from the building into the glare of sunlight. "The trouble remains pretty much as I told you in Boise. Politics and some damned raw dealing make it impossible for the sheepmen of Idaho to get a fair break. If only the wool growers could be sure of a steady market . . . at a figure that would allow them a fair profit." He shrugged his shoulders. "Maybe someday it will happen; but I guess that just now it is too much to ask."

Deborah had listened quietly; now she said, "Jeff, perhaps things will improve for the sheepmen if they sort of take things in their own hands."

"Like what? Our ranchers have precious little to say up at the statehouse in Boise."

"But we could change that," she said firmly.

There was an eagerness about her that caused Jeff Harding to peer more closely at her and to say, "For heaven's sake, get your dander up more often—you're pretty as sunset when you do."

She grinned appreciation of his remark; then suddenly she was telling this tall, quiet lawman of her interest in politics and that she believed she had found the man who would be an honest governor of Idaho, that she expected to work to elect him, and that she had told him of her plans. "Don't you want to know his name?" she teased.

"Not as much as I want to know how in holy heavens you expect to gather a few thousand votes for him."

Her reply startled him. "I need your help for that. Yours and the Basque people. And the miners. And maybe a lot of the Mormon farmers."

Jeff Harding's face took on both curiosity and disbelief. "Damn it all," he snapped, "who is this wonder man you're so sure of?"

She laughed aloud. "It is Henry Carswell. You'll remember him from Nebraska. Mr. Carswell is honest . . . and compassionate. He is a successful businessman. And he knows how to handle people. And now he is a resident of Idaho. He owns properties up at Bonanza and Custer, on the Yankee Fork, and he's bought a lot of land around Blackfoot. He laid out and started a whole new irrigated potato-growing district."

Harding said slowly, "I know about that potato-growing venture and that a man named Carswell heads it. But I didn't know it was the same Carswell who owned about half of Box Butte. But aren't you biting off more than you can chew? Politics is a closely knit and organized part of every aspect of business and wealth here in Idaho."

Deborah looked up and down the street. Her gaze rested presently on the Union Pacific depot. "I'll tell you what, Jeff," she said. "There is a lunchroom at the depot. If you will take me there for something to eat—out of this scorching sunlight—I'll tell you how I think we can get a campaign started. With your help, of course."

"Come along," he answered, and he placed his hand on her elbow. "I wouldn't miss hearing this for the world. Besides, I am hungry too."

When they had eaten and the coolness of the dining room had driven most of the flush from her face, Deborah said, "I have had a long time to puzzle over the wool-marketing problem of Antonio and of the other sheepmen. And you know what? It was just this morning, at the convention, that an idea struck me, one I should have looked into a long while ago."

Harding studied her as he lifted a glass of iced tea, then set it down. "You mean like persuading your Henry Carswell to become a sheepman as well as governor?" Irony and a tinge of bitterness rode the remark.

"I mean nothing of the kind . . . and I may have a lot more sensible idea."

186

"I am listening," he said in a more subdued way.

She told him then of the letter in which Nephi Oakes had revealed his plans to go into the spinning-mill business in Lorain, Ohio, and of Lemuel Froman's news that Oakes had done just that. "Suppose," Deborah speculated aloud, "that I write to Mr. Oakes to see if he could use a considerable quantity of Idaho-grown wool." Then she fell silent. "Likely the freight rates would eat up any profit."

Jeff Harding leaned forward, his eyes shrewd and interested. "Not necessarily. There are a great many grades and qualities of wool, Deborah, just as there are many breeds of sheep that produce them."

"Then you think I should write to Nephi Oakes?"

"It certainly wouldn't do any harm." He was silent, then added, "We could do even better. How about my getting together a selection of our best wool samples? We could send it to your man in Ohio along with the letter." Harding again lifted his glass. "Here's hoping we have luck. If we do, I suppose you will insist that every sheepman vote for Henry Carswell at the next election," he teased.

But Deborah grew pensive. "No, Jeff," she replied. "I don't want to buy votes. But I hope the sheep ranchers will have an opportunity to help choose their state officials." Then she brightened. About her again was the trust in the future that had been her father's legacy.

She skipped the afternoon session of the sheep growers' meeting and spent much of her time

187

penning a long and thoughtful letter to Nephi Oakes. When it was finished, she laid it aside to be included with the parcel of wool samples that Jeff Harding had offered to supply. After a time she noticed that the shadows of evening were lengthening. Soon she would need to bathe and to dress for the dinner to which Lemuel Froman had asked her.

Abruptly a thought was upon her. What would her reaction be if tonight Lemuel Froman were to put his arms about her and kiss her? But then she remembered Robert Lowell and the breathtaking wonder of being near him. The touch of his hands. The intentness of his gaze. The expectant wonder of something about to happen.

Something bittersweet and almost unbearable caused her to open a suitcase, search out Lowell's letter, and read it again. If only . . .

She forced her thoughts back to the present. Tomorrow the convention would end. Then what? She must find work . . . a place to live . . . a specific direction for her future. She knew she would remain in Idaho. But what could she do there?

A rap at her door told her she had given too much time to her reverie. Lemuel Froman had come to escort her to dinner. She touched her hair into order, ran her tongue over dry lips, and threw a light jacket about her. Well . . . tomorrow would likely take care of its own problems.

They walked through the small lobby of the hotel and onto the sidewalk. The last vestiges of twilight were fading, and the few streetlamps cast a friendly glow. Above this was a vast canopy of stars. There was also the scent of lilacs and the chirping of crickets. They had walked but a few steps when Lemuel stopped before a hitching rail.

"This is a rented team and rig," he said indicating two iron-gray horses and a highly polished buggy. "I got them from a livery stable."

"But that is extravagant," Deborah protested. "Couldn't we have just walked to the restaurant? It cannot be more than a block or so."

He untied the hitch rein and then helped her to the red leather seat of the buggy. She noticed that he now had the shyness she remembered so well from their Nebraska encounters. He had discarded the somber business suit of the attorney and was wearing a light gray jacket and a pale blue shirt with matching tie.

"Where I would like to take you, Deborah, is somewhat farther. There is an inn alongside the road to Blackfoot; it is a little more than three miles from here. Their food is said to be excellent. Especially their specialty, smoked sturgeon. Have you ever eaten sturgeon?"

She shook her head. "I only know it is some kind of seafood, Lemuel."

"Not exactly. The Snake River runs close by, and sturgeon move up and down it and the Columbia River all the way to the sea. Sturgeon have been caught weighing up to a thousand pounds."

As the hooves of their team beat a lively trot, they talked of the events of the convention. "I thought your talk was among the best," she told him.

"That is pleasant to hear—though doubtful." He grinned. "But if you like to listen to a born speaker—a spellbinder—you should hear a fellow by the name of Borah. William E. Borah. He's an attorney who came here from Kansas last year. Listening to him plead a case can send chills up and down your spine. He could say, 'Pass the butter, please' and his voice would demand the words be set to music—or engraved on a monument.''

"Nobody is or was that good a speaker, except possibly Daniel Webster." She laughed. Then suddenly she was serious. "Lemuel, you are trying to help the Basque people and other ranchers with legal matters. It makes us partners in a way." Then she was telling him of her talk with Jeff Harding and of their hope that through Nephi Oakes a market might be established for a part of the Idaho wool clip.

Froman nodded his head in encouragement, then said, "Nephi may be able to help or point you to a market; he is becoming a hardheaded and successful businessman as well as one of the leaders of our Church in the Midwest."

It was the first mention Lemuel Froman had made of his Mormonism, and she asked curiously, "You married a Mormon girl?"

"Yes, I grew up with her." His tone was suddenly noncommittal, almost wary.

"Tell me about your little girl," Deborah said, sensing she had touched an area of which he did not wish to speak.

His face softened, as did his voice. "She is our only child and believes that she owns her Daddy. She already likes for me to read to her and to tuck her in bed—the little blue-eyed, chestnut-haired vixen!"

A bittersweet thought flashed through Deborah's mind: If I had stayed in Bonanza . . . if lightning hadn't spooked that white mule—maybe now I would have a little girl or a boy.

Two hours later, after they had acclaimed the sturgeon and were lingering at a table with red and white checked linens and subdued candlelight, Deborah gave a determined sigh and asked, "Lemuel, in your travels through Idaho . . . or elsewhere . . . have you ever come across a man named Robert Lowell?" When he remained momentarily silent, she added quickly, "He is about your age; perhaps a little older. He has a moustache . . . wears mostly old tattered prospector's clothes . . . and sings a lot."

"Is that all?" Lemuel asked softly.

"Except that I . . . I know he went to medical school."

Froman reached out to touch her hand. "And except that you were—and perhaps still are—in love with him."

"Is it that obvious?" she asked.

"Your eyes are too honest for keeping secrets, Debbie. No I have never met your Robert Lowell. But someday I would like to." He studied her pensiveness, then added, "Debbie, Mormons love to dance. Tonight the convention committee has rented a hall for a sheepmen's ball. Would you like to attend—with me?"

"Attend a dance with a married Mormon," she chided him gaily. "After he has wined and dined me! How daring, Lemuel. But I am glad you asked; somehow tonight seems made for dancing."

"Just remember," he replied severely, "you were the one who partook of wine. You don't have to answer to the Church—yet."

He took her back to the hotel after a series of waltzes and other dance steps had stolen much of their night. As they stood at last in the dim light of the lobby, she was aware that his face looked young and animated and expectant. He gathered her hands into his and bent close. For long moments she sensed a struggle within him—desire battling with the barrier of his creed and his marriage. She knew that if he were to crush her to him and seek her lips, she would not resist. Suddenly he moved to hold her almost at arm's length. "Damn a marriage with nothing left," he grated. "How much does the Almighty expect even a churchman to endure?"

She felt his lips, carefully repressed, brush her cheek. "Good night, Deborah," he whispered, breathing heavily. "You have made my evening memorable."

"I had so much fun, too," she said as he turned toward the outer door. Then she stood rigidly still. Into her mind had come a saying of her mother's. It seemed to sum up her evening, her days on a Yankee Fork sandbar, and her life—Often a bridesmaid, but never a bride.

She was awakened the next morning by the sun climbing above a next-door building and rudely flooding her pillow with brightness. She rose, brushed her hair, and chose a skirt and blouse suitable for traveling. Even as she began packing, she was unsure of where she would go. Likely her most prudent course would be to journey back to Bonanza. While still trying to decide, she made her way to the hotel's restaurant.

"You are not an early riser," a voice accused

her as she slipped into a chair beside a window. She looked up, startled, full into the face of Jeff Harding as he towered above her.

"I went to the dance and stayed late," she confessed.

"So I've already heard, Deborah. I need not ask if you enjoyed the evening."

She motioned him into the chair opposite her. "I would buy you coffee and—"

"Thank you . . . no. I've had several cups as I waited for you."

"You waited so long for me?" she asked, puzzled.

"Yes, and you may be glad I did, young lady; I have a job prospect to discuss with you."

"You mean like counting sheep?" Her words were facetious, but eagerness widened her eyes.

"There is more to it than that. The officers of the Sheepmen's Association asked me to talk to you. There's a job. But it may be only temporary, and the pay sure won't buy diamonds."

"Will it pay for room and board?" she countered.

"That and a bit more. Deborah, you would be running a small office in Boise. Your main job would be different all right—something like writing indictments."

She shook her head. "You need a lawyer for that."

"Not really. Now listen while I try to explain. Just about every confidence man and crook in Idaho consider the ranchers—both cattlemen and sheep growers—as fair prey. And among the worst vultures are some who appear to be Honest Abes. What you would be doing is this: Every time a

rancher is bilked or fleeced, our association wants
to know the full details of the transaction. Then
letters will be sent to livestock men statewide describing the crook and his methods."

"But how would I know all that?"

"By our people reporting it to you—in utmost
confidence, of course. Most ranchers can read and
write, or at least their wives can. The others can
send information by word of mouth. And, by the
way, you will be dealing much of the time with the
Basques."

"Who have a language I can't even begin to understand," Deborah pointed out.

"But they have a spokesman who writes darned
good English. You know him—Ramon Echiverri."

"I believe I would like that," she said. "At least
to give it a try. If anything comes of my letters and
the wool samples we send to Nephi Oakes in Ohio,
that might fit into this job."

"Or vice versa." Harding nodded, then grinned
wryly, adding, "for all of which you are offered
sixty dollars a month. Deborah, it isn't much of a
job for a business major with a university degree."

Her decision was swift. "Mr. Harding, I will
take the job. When should I report?"

He drew a chained watch from his vest pocket
and studied it. "There is a train for Boise in two
hours. I am leaving on it. Can you?"

She drew a white napkin across her lips and
stood up. "Only if you can get my baggage to the
train depot on time," she challenged.

Chapter 9

I T WAS ten days before a suitable office was found for Deborah in Boise. Only Ramon Echiverri's wide acquaintance in the small city enabled them to seek out quarters within the association's slender budget. There were two well-lighted rooms on the second floor of a red brick building. The location was four blocks from the capitol building and just out of what was termed the high-rent district.

Access to the rooms was mainly by means of an inside stairway and hall, but there was also a series of wooden steps along the building's side, with a door leading into the smaller of the two office rooms. There was a carpet of intricate rose design in the larger room. The furniture was sparse and mostly homemade, but there was one cowhide chair, secured at an auction.

Bound for her first full day of work, Deborah walked toward the office when the sun was an hour high on a warm morning in mid-June. As always when she was in Boise, she strode leisurely, letting her eyes drink in the clearness of the atmosphere and the allure of the surrounding mountains. Closer at hand was the greenness of lawns and shrubs and trees nourished by a system of irrigation ditches supplied by the Boise River. This is going to be a beautiful city if some care is given to its planning, she reflected. She recalled what had been told her of the climate—how the Boise

Valley, protected by high mountains and with weather patterns influenced by the warm Humboldt Current of the Pacific Ocean, had few bitterly cold winter days. Also, the nearness of snowy mountain peaks caused the nights to cool after hot summer days. Deborah sensed that something would come about. She had first noticed it upon her arrival in the city—the feeling of coming home, that it was meant for her to be here in this busy capital city of Idaho, that here she would surely put down roots and remain for a long time.

After purchasing her office supplies, she sought out the town library, obtained several books on the history and geography of Idaho and the Pacific Northwest, and began to familiarize herself with the names and descriptions of towns and their surrounding areas. Ramon Echiverri came to the office twice that week; from him she learned the names and addresses of most of the Basque sheepmen of the state. She pinpointed their locations on a huge wall map. At first she wondered when Jeff Harding would show up with more instructions, but Echiverri informed her that business affairs had taken Harding to Nevada for at least three weeks. Her best contact with the outside world seemed to be the *Daily Statesman;* from it she began to clip every item dealing with the lamb and wool industry, and she sifted through several years of its back issues at the library. Then she began to write a summary of each instance where sheep owners or herders had come into harm's way.

Her first direct word from a wool grower in trouble arrived in the morning mail of her twelfth day. It had been written with a blunt pencil on portions of a soiled paper bag. Although there were misspelled words, the gist of the complaint was clear. The writer identified himself as Tom Roberts, of Muldoon, Idaho. Roberts had ordered both sheep medicines and shearing supplies from a circular mailed to him by the Nampuh Distributing Company of Boise. He had enclosed $63.80 in full payment and had received a package nearly a month later. It contained only about half of the medicines, and the other supplies were but poor imitations of the tools the circular had described and pictured. His letters of complaint to the company had brought no response. Lately he had had a letter, addressed to the company, returned and marked NO LONGER AT THIS LOCATION. Roberts asked if the association could help him.

Pleased at last to have something definite to work on, Deborah swung into action. She first penned a letter to Roberts, assuring him that the association would do its best to seek redress for him. She assured him she would advise him further as quickly as possible. She then copied his complaint, and using a letterpress, prepared copies to be mailed to every association member. But she did so with the uneasy feeling that the damage had already been done. Likely Nampuh Distributing Company had picked clean those on its "sucker list" and had swiftly moved on or dissolved the business.

Her fears were justified. The following day, after mailing the copies of Roberts' complaint, she closed the office and set out on foot to find Nampuh Distributing Company—its circular had given its address. An hour later she was standing on the porch of a shabby residence in the northeast corner of the city. When she rapped at the door a heavy, middle-aged woman appeared and stared out. "What do you want?" she demanded.

"I am sorry to disturb you," Deborah apologized. "Is the Nampuh Distributing Company located here?"

"Not anymore—thank God. They owe me nearly a month's rent for that basement they made a mess out of."

"Oh, they used to be located here? I have a letter that says so. If you know where the firm moved to and can tell me, it would help."

A freckled girl, evidently the woman's daughter, pushed the door open and crowded beside her mother. "Would you give me a half dollar if I tell you where them men went to?"

Deborah looked at her in amazement, then dug two coins from her purse. "Would you write their address down for me?"

The girl clutched the money and turned from the door. Presently she came back and handed Deborah a sizable piece of paper from a school notebook. "It's right there. I copied it from a card they gave me. They wanted me to forward any mail."

Deborah scanned the address with utter futility. It read: Joseph Bagley, General Delivery, Spokane, Washington.

"I suppose you know that Nampuh Distributing Company has cheated a lot of people," Deborah murmured.

"Hell, is that anything new in Idaho?" the woman screamed and slammed the door.

Within a week six more letters came detailing the devious dealings of Nampuh Distributing

Company. Deborah discussed each of them with Ramon Echiverri. Then she made a suggestion: Why not write again to all association members, this time suggesting that no orders be sent to mail-order companies until they had been investigated and approved by the association? Other correspondence was coming in now. There were complaints so varied as to prove that livestock men were prey for a variety of schemes. "Something has to be done to stop this robbery of honest, hardworking people," she told Ramon Echiverri.

He smiled at her in a half-hopeful, half-resigned way. "It will take time, Deborah. Our people have put up with such injustices countless times. At least we have made a beginning."

It was not her nature to remain downcast for very long, and two days after her visit to the distribution company's old location she again attacked the morning mail in a cool and reasonable frame of mind. Presently she came to an envelope that caused her face to brighten with expectancy. It was from Nephi Oakes and indicated he was now executive vice-president of Combined Spinning Mills in Lorain, Ohio. He came quickly to the point:

Deborah, your question as to whether we might be able to use Idaho wool has created considerable interest here. Also, thanks for sending the box of wool samples. Some of these are of a quality, fiber, and length that are not readily available from the growers of the Midwest. Under separate cover I am sending you full information. Probably we could

199

pursue this further if you can arrange to send larger samples of the types indicated.

As we see it, the foremost problem would be freight rates. They are somewhat prohibitive between Idaho and Ohio. But my suggestion is you first tell us the approximate quantities in which these specific types of clip might be available to us.

Is it possible that your association has someone familiar with grades, etc., who might come to Lorain for personal discussion of the matter?

Thank you for word of yourself and of the West. I am sure you will find ample use for your well-earned business degree if you choose to remain in Idaho. If you see Lemuel, be sure to give him my regards.

It would please me if Combined Spinning Mills of Lorain could be of service to you.

Most sincerely,

Nephi Oakes
Executive Vice-President

Her first impulse was to take the letter and go in search of Ramon Echiverri. She also calculated the days until Jeff Harding might return to Boise and she could break the news to him. She forced herself to remain at the office until midafternoon. Then she locked the door and hastened to her rooming house.

Reaching her room, she changed into an afternoon dress after washing the day's grime from her face and hands. Then again she was on her way, seeking out a street that would take her toward the Basque district and the Echiverri home. She had gone only two blocks when a sense of her whereabouts caused her to look about. She had come again to the window of Frank Wentworth's company, where she had once discussed gemstones with the genial Mr. Wentworth. Then, after she entered college, a correspondence had developed that over time became centered on the economics and politics of Idaho. Wentworth had encouraged her to look for a decent, honorable, and intelligent man to run for governor, and she had mentioned Henry Carswell's name. And, in fact, Carswell, at the Plunketts' encouragement, had visited Wentworth to discuss mineral rights to farmlands. But Wentworth was also able to assess him as a potential political leader.

Suddenly a man's voice sounded and she felt a restraining hand on her arm. She wheeled about in pleased surprise, to gaze into Wentworth's eager face.

"Deborah . . . Deborah Dexter from the Yankee Fork." He smiled and held his hat in his hand. "Just why are you passing my shop without so much as a howdy-do?"

"Mr. Wentworth, it is so good to see you again. It is just that I have to hurry over to the Basque district. It is important. I was telling myself I'd visit you tomorrow."

He fell into step beside her as they moved on. "Mind if I walk along?" When she smiled her pleasure, he studied her with a penetrating gaze. "You look older, Deborah . . . and somehow more . . . more . . . shall we say competent. But just as pretty as ever," he hastened to add, "and with more than a lick of common sense. I'm impressed with your record at the University of Utah.

"You know, a man by the name of Henry Carswell visited me two years ago. He asked about some legal aspects of mineral rights to farmlands and mentioned that you had suggested he call on me. But, Deborah, somehow I got the idea that you . . . and those friends of yours—Plunkett, isn't that the name?—wanted me to look this fellow over."

"And did you?" Deborah asked bluntly.

"Enough to realize that your friend Carswell is quite a capable and intelligent man."

"Yes, he is. Besides that, he knows how to run a profitable business and to gain other people's confidence and respect. What's more, Henry Carswell is just plain honest."

"And you remembered me writing that Idaho needs . . . desperately needs . . . political leaders with such qualities."

Deborah nodded, then added, "But you didn't just write *political leaders*, Mr. Wentworth. You wrote *governor!*"

"So I did," Wentworth acknowledged thoughtfully. "But what sort of following would this Henry Carswell have? It takes votes to win a nomination . . . and a heap more of them to win an election. Where will he get them?"

She was about to say that Carswell might have only her own support and that of the Plunketts. Instead, something akin to sheer inspiration changed her answer, and she asked, "Would the support of the Basque sheep people . . . and the other ranchers . . . and all the Mormons in Idaho

. . . and a good share of the miners . . . swing enough votes his way?"

He stopped in his tracks, seemed to do mental calculations, and then said with assurance, "Deborah, if we could deliver all that it would go one hell of a long way toward giving Idaho its first illustrious governor. How would you go about it?"

"I'm not at all sure—yet. Just the same, I'm going to talk to some people—to Ramon Echiverri, for one; I am on my way to his house now. And to Lem Froman. And to Charles Blair; he runs a hotel in Bonanza. Yes, and even to Bishop Stannard of the Mormons; he's my stepfather now." She was silent, then added, "And of course I can count on the Plunketts." She wanted to add the name of a whistling prospector called Robert Lowell but could not do so. Then she concluded, "Yes, Mr. Wentworth, there is even another man I may ask for help. He is a gambler. I met him a long time ago on a stage ride between Blackfoot and Challis. His name is Sam Douglas."

Frank Wentworth again swept his hat from his whitening hair. "Would you say that again?" he demanded. "You intend to stand there, Deborah, and tell me you know Sam Douglas? Child, how you get around!"

She laughed and then said accusingly, "You haven't asked why I happen to be in Boise, Mr. Wentworth."

"Deborah, there was no need. Boise is a small town; word of just about anything gets around in a hurry. Besides, I am handling some assay matters just now for your friend Ramon Echiverri."

"Then you already know of the new Sheepmen's

Association . . . how we are trying to protect members from fraud."

Wentworth answered gravely, "It is long overdue." He became quiet and studied her animated face. Then he added, "Come to see me, Deborah. But in the meantime, be careful. Some won't take kindly to what you . . . and the sheepmen . . . are attempting." He smiled and again tipped his hat. "Now, don't let me make you late for your visit to the Echiverris! I hear that Ramon's wife is the best Basque cook in Boise. They will invite you to supper. Take them up on it." He turned, waved, and retraced his steps toward his shop.

Deborah had thought to tell Wentworth of the letter from Nephi Oakes and the hope it might contain, but loyalty urged her to share the news first with Ramon Echiverri, and with Jeff Harding when he returned to Boise. I just wish Antonio Onederra didn't live so far from Boise, she thought. I'd love to see his face, and his wife's too, when I tell about the possibility of marketing wool in Ohio.

The thought caused her to recall the warning of Nephi Oakes that freight rates might be an insurmountable barrier to shipping wool to eastern points. She had heard of the high rates established by the Union Pacific Railroad because of its virtual monopoly of rail transportation through much of the West. She pondered alternatives. What if the wool could be sent to Ohio by way of those new railroads that had transcontinental lines across northern Idaho? The Northern Pacific. The Great Northern. But by what means could the wool be transported northward to stations on these routes? In describing Idaho, Wentworth had once written to her that the town of Lewiston, at the junction of the Snake and the Clearwater rivers, was an inland seaport. That freight vessels came to Lewiston from the Pacific Ocean by way of the Columbia and Snake rivers. It seemed a farfetched idea, but could wool be shipped from Lewiston by water to New Orleans?

Deep in such speculation, Deborah arrived at the large two-story home of the Echiverris. It stood on the banks of the Boise River and offered a boldly sweeping view of the mountains to the north and east. She had time only to tell them of Oakes' letter before she was urged to a heavily laden table. Besides Ramon and his wife there were three men at the table. All three looked to be Basque, while their trail-hardened bodies revealed that they probably were flock owners or herders. Although all of them spoke Basque, Deborah sensed that she was being accepted as a friend.

When the meal was finished, a strange-looking flagon of wine was used to fill the drinking cups. There was a pleasant odor and a tartness to the wine that caused Deborah's eyes to widen as the liquid sought her stomach.

Later the table was cleared, and Echiverri motioned for Deborah to sit beside him. He swept a hand that encompassed all those within the room. "Miss Dexter, I have told these men that you have an important letter. If you will read it out loud now, I will put it in the Basque language. Go slowly, please."

As Deborah began reading and Echiverri's voice filled the room, a silence came over those assembled. There was growing interest and then controlled eagerness and excitement. She finished the letter and then said to her translator, "It is the freight rates that bother me; what good is there having fine, marketable wool if railroad costs eat up all that the mill pays us?" Ramon spoke to his guests, and something akin to defeat replaced the hope on their faces. She hastened to speak again. "About the freight costs . . . I'm not giving up so quickly or so easily. There has to be a way to get your wool to Ohio—if it meets the needs and specifications of the mill at Lorain."

"We can find out." He scanned the technical sheet that Nephi Oakes had sent. "Jeff Harding should be back in Boise within ten days. But we won't wait for him to handle all this. Tomorrow we will start getting the samples together." Ramon smiled a bit tiredly and added, "At least by spreading the cost among us we can pay the freight on adequate samples. Your Mr. Oakes wants at least three hundred pounds each of six of the types we sent."

"Surely he will pay for it," Deborah said with concern.

"I am sure he will," Echiverri said, smiling. "But even if he shouldn't, the loss would be small compared to what the dealers here in Boise manage to steal from us."

Deborah stared at her letter again. "Mr. Oakes thinks we should send a representative to negotiate with his company if the shipment proves usable. Who could go?"

"There is none among us," Echiverri said regretfully. "I cannot leave my affairs here."

"How about Jeff Harding?"

Echiverri shook his head. "He would probably

be competent. But his going is out of the question. There are matters in Montana—" He broke off as though determined to reveal no more. For a time he spoke in Basque, letting his companions know the points under discussion. When one of them pointed toward Deborah, Echiverri said, "These men want to know why you can't go to Ohio as our representative. They pointed out that you are the paid secretary of the association."

"I couldn't," she protested. "I know nothing of wool grades and prices."

"But you could learn," Echiverri said quietly.

"Only in time. Even if I didn't have the office work to keep me busy, it would probably take a year for me to become knowledgeable."

"For this job, Deborah, I can show you all you need to know in about three weeks."

"And what of my office and my job in the meantime—while I'm traipsing off to Ohio for a month or so?"

"It should take you not more than two weeks at the most. While you are gone I can bring the mail of the association here. Perhaps answer the most pressing."

Gathering of the wool samples requested by Nephi Oakes proved a much longer process than Deborah had anticipated. Different lots were slow in reaching Boise from widely scattered parts of the state. They were then painstakingly studied and inspected by Ramon Echiverri and two of his most experienced friends. In two instances word was sent back to the producers to submit a second lot. It seemed to Deborah that these Basque sheepmen were demanding perfection of this first shipment to be forwarded to the mills in Ohio.

The days of summer wore into August as she continued sorting out the complaints of ranchers. Some of these proved to be only misunderstandings between the growers and reputable firms. In these instances she could usually arrange a satisfactory if not entirely friendly settlement. But the sprinkling of letters telling of fraud and deceit held her attention, for they had slowly fallen into a pattern. She began to surmise that only a handful of men were involved in these shady operations and that there were interrelationships among most of those involved. More frustrating and infuriating was her growing certainty that somehow men in Boise—men in the higher reaches of state government—were consciously overlooking or even participating in the covert operations.

She was studying a letter that seemed to confirm such a conspiracy as the shadows of an approaching Friday evening lengthened to engulf her office. An abrupt knocking at the door startled her and brought her to her feet. "Just a moment," she acknowledged, and then made sure that all revealing letters and documents were safely within her desk. Then she moved to the door and opened it. A gasp and a glad cry escaped her, for in the hallway stood tall and grinning Jim Plunkett and his beaming wife, whose arms were already outstretched.

"Mollie . . . Jim . . . come right in here," Deborah murmured and excitedly tried to hug both of them at once. "When did you get into town? Oh, Lord, it's good to see both of you."

Mollie Plunkett ran a loving but appraising eye over the girl. "Jim, doesn't she look pretty as hell, and businesslike too?" When her husband nodded agreement and as they sought out chairs, Mollie continued, "You know what, Debbie? This man of mine is in a dander to get up North . . . or at least most of the way to Canada. All I've heard all summer is, 'Mollie, let's get hold of Debbie Dexter and then go up on the Clearwater River.' It's just that Jim ain't satisfied unless he's chasing some rainbow over the next ridge."

Jim Plunkett looked at his wife with a self-satisfied smile. "Debbie," he drawled, "just ask my old woman who stayed up three nights in a row planning this year's sashay. She even learned to spell Orofino."

"That's a town up on the Clearwater River," Mollie explained.

"I know. It's a gold camp." Deborah's memory was delving into things written her long ago by Frank Wentworth. Then suddenly her mind was on a troubling letter she had thrust into a drawer. "Orofino," she repeated aloud. "That's only about forty miles from Lewiston."

"Forty-two miles, to be exact," Mollie revealed proudly. "Lewiston is where the Clearwater and Snake rivers join up. I heard that ships, big ocean-like ships, can come up the rivers to dock at Lewiston. Damn, Debbie, wouldn't it be fun to see that much water in one oversized creek?" She squirmed her broadness more comfortably into the chair and added, "We want you to go with us, honey."

Deborah closed her eyes, sighed, and then reluctantly shook her head. "I'm afraid not; I have this job, you know." She tried to concentrate on the duties of the day, but in her mind now were visions of cool streams, thrusting mountains, and the shadowy blue of tall forests. The day had been hot in Boise, and likely the approaching night would offer little relief. She remembered the coolness which evening brought to the valley of the Yankee Fork. *Maybe it is possible, just for a few days. The office work is well caught up; it will be at least three weeks before Mr. Echiverri has the wool shipments ready.* Deborah knew that her mind and her heart were seeking justification for something she longed to do, for going with her best friends to see the area of Idaho that had often been described to her as a wilderness wonderland.

An exciting thought swept over her. *Why not at least ask Ramon for a few days' vacation? Or would it exactly be a vacation? She could stop in Lewiston to ascertain whether shipping wool by the water route to New Orleans might be feasible. And there was the letter in that morning's mail.* She turned a questioning gaze upon the Plunketts. "If we went north to Lewiston . . . and to Orofino . . . wouldn't the stage take us through the town of Grangeville?" As if to answer her own question, Deborah rose and studied a large wall map of the state. "Yes, it would. Grangeville is about seventy-five miles from Lewiston."

After she had spoken, she grew thoughtful. *Is it possible?* she mused. *Or is there a mere chance that in so small a town as Grangeville I might get close to the source of much of our sheepmen's troubles?* But in her mind also was a remote but persistent warning. *I might be walking into danger . . . a lot of danger.*

The Plunketts had watched her in silence, but presently Mollie reached out to capture and hold her hand. "Honey, something is bothering you. If it is about money for the trip, Jim and I can—"

"No, Mollie, I have enough money." She moved about, making sure the office was in order and secure for the night. "When did you want to leave?"

"Probably Monday morning," Jim replied. "There is a stage leaving early Monday."

"Right now let's find a good restaurant where I can treat you to supper," Deborah said firmly. She thought a moment and then removed the letter from her desk and placed it in a beaded purse. Then she said, "If Ramon Echiverri agrees with me about something, I may very well be aboard that Monday stage with you." As they left the office she was pondering the coincidence—that the explosive letter now in her purse had arrived from a place called Grangeville on the same day that the Plunketts had arrived to urge her northward with them.

It was the stage ride up most of the length of Idaho that provided Deborah with an awesome overview of the state to which she had so long been attracted. Almost upon leaving Boise their route began climbing into an area of forested mountains. For the most part the road was a twisting and dusty way on which only their driver's skill kept the six horses, hitched two abreast in tandem, at a mile-consuming gait hour after hour. At times they crossed open, parklike areas, ablaze with the colors of late-summer flowers; then they traveled through dense and towering stands of yellow pine and Douglas fir. They forded innumerable small creeks that led dancing and clear water toward the river whose valley they continued to ascend. Often they were close beside the river; at other times they climbed a series of switchbacks that brought them to a dizzying height, where the river was a silver thread below them and the mountains seemed to reach almost across the world.

In the lower and damper areas where there were swales and beaver dams and lakes they were often watched by moose who lifted curious heads for a time and then resumed their search for water plants. On the higher ridges the brown splash of grazing elk was common; occasionally a bull elk would stand dominantly in the road, and care was taken to scare him off without arousing his anger. It seemed that deer were everywhere, as were smaller animals, who scurried for safety.

Deborah wiled away much of her time by trying to identify the many species of animals, birds, trees, and shrubs. Only when she was unsure would she turn to the Plunketts for help, knowing that their years in the mountains had well acquainted them with just about every plant and animal.

Finally they came to a stage station upon the edge of the westward-flowing Salmon River. The depth of its vast, canyonlike valley spoke of the time and force this great river had used to cut its way almost three hundred miles through the great mountain barrier that stretches northward through Idaho. Studying the alternating rapids and stretches of quietly flowing water, Deborah thought of the Salmon's beginning high in the remote Stanley Basin. What would it be like to traverse this river from the towns on the Yankee Fork . . . from Jordan Creek . . . to the place, now only a few miles distant, where the Salmon River would merge its swift flow with that of the even greater Snake River?

They remained overnight at a small hotel close to the river. From the small window of her room Deborah could see moonlight flinting on the restless water to create a view of almost ethereal beauty. At last the distant murmur of the stream and the cry of a night-flying bird lulled her into deep sleep. When she awakened, it was to know that now she had lost her heart completely to the allure of Idaho.

Two days later, at midmorning, the stage dropped Deborah and the Plunketts at a nondescript-appearing stage station and hotel in the town of Grangeville. Only Jim Plunkett had been here before; now he told them how the settlement of Grangeville was a natural and convenient gateway to the mines and camps of the Florence area. Florence, according to Jim, was probably the richest gold yielder in Idaho and could boast of a boot hill rivaling that of Tombstone, Arizona.

Deborah's first impression of Grangeville was its contrast with the beautiful valley in which it was located. A collection of clapboard and log structures, the settlement sprawled on the valley's south side. They had reached it by traversing the Buffalo Hump Mountains. Noting the wide levelness of the valley, its abundance of watering streams, and the abundant greenness of vegetation, she sensed that this might someday become a highly productive agricultural area.

During their trip northward Deborah had been reluctant to reveal to the Plunketts her reason for wanting to stop in this small frontierlike town.

Even though they were her best friends, likely they would consider her motives sketchy and without any real foundation. She, herself, knew she was playing a hunch.

Jim Plunkett's resourcefulness resulted in their finding a place to stay. The next northbound stage on which they could resume their journey would not arrive for two days. Plunkett, with his winning smile and drawl, explained all this to the proprietor of the most respectable of three rooming houses, and they were rented a small cabin and loaned enough bedding and linens to get them by.

When they had managed to wash off trail dust and get into clean clothing, Deborah knew the time had come for her to reveal the full—if slender—reason for their being in this small community.

"Jim . . . Mollie," she began as they sat on a planked front step and surveyed the serene loveliness of the timbered and stream-laced valley, "you are my most trusted friends . . . I can always count on you. I want to read something to you." She went inside the shack and returned with a letter, which she drew from its envelope. She held up the letter so they could see the few lines scrawled in pencil. Then she read aloud:

The Seketary—

Sheep herders asociation, etc.
By way of General Delevery
Boise, Idaho

If you really want the low down on how our statehouse is tied inter skinning stockmen LOOK INTER THE AFAIRS OF BLAIN

HALLIGAN WHO WANTS ALL THE LAND
JOININ HIS PLACE OVER NIGH
GRANGEVILLE.

The letter was unsigned . . . and carried the
postmark of Grangeville, Idaho.

"Jesus Christ! Have the slimy, thieving politicians got their grabhooks into stock growers too?"
Jim Plunkett exploded and came to his feet in a
fury-ridden way. "Isn't it enough that they screw
the miners and the Mormons?"

It was the first time Deborah had ever heard
such language from easygoing, mild-tongued Jim
Plunkett. She noted that for once even Mollie was
wide-eyed with stunned surprise.

"Now you know," Deborah said, "why we are
here . . . and the sort of thing I have to contend
with. For example, downright fraud has been
perpetrated against livestock men." Briefly, she
sketched for the Plunketts the affairs of the Nampuh Distributing Company and of Joseph Bagley's quick move to Spokane.

Mollie had regained her composure and listened
thoughtfully. "So, honey, you're here in Grangeville to find out if you can locate the man named
Blain Halligan . . . and see what he is up to."

"It is a little more complex than that, Mollie. I
doubt that the name Blain Halligan means anything to you; it didn't to me at first. Then I looked
into a directory of Idaho state government person-
nel. Blain Halligan is an assistant to our secretary of state. Supposedly he is in charge of all
matters concerning businesses and corporations
that use Idaho land, minerals, timber, and other
resources."

Jim Plunkett pursed his lips into a whistle.

"You're probing awfully close to the top, Deborah. Nobody could get much closer to the governor than that." His remark recalled the soberness with which Frank Wentworth had asked her to be careful.

Mollie Plunkett seemed to read the girl's unspoken thoughts, for she said uneasily, "We will help you all we can, Debbie; but you be all-fired careful. Just what are your plans?"

"I'm not sure myself. I want somehow to meet this Blain Halligan. Perhaps then some pieces of the puzzle may fall into place."

Meeting Blain Halligan proved far easier to achieve than Deborah had thought possible. She quickly learned at the town's general store that a trip of only six and a half miles into the valley's more meadowed section was needed to reach his ranch headquarters.

"You'll know his spread right away," the storekeeper volunteered. "Take the main road up north until you come to the corner of fancy post-and-rail fence. Then turn left and follow that fence down to just before it crosses the creek. The Halligan house is a big, rambling affair painted white and green; there's a lot of sheds and a new red barn . . . like back East. It is the fanciest place in these parts."

"Are we apt to find Mr. Halligan at home?" Deborah persisted.

"Almost certain to, young lady." The storekeeper scanned her curiously with watery blue eyes and asked, "Where do you folks hail from?"

Mollie Plunkett had been listening quietly but now cut in, "We're from Bonanza, down in the

Yankee Fork district. Just doing some sight-see-ing—mainly."

"Well, you will see something to open your eyes at Halligan's place. Just keeps getting bigger and fancier too."

"But with all that," Deborah asked demurely, "would Mr. Halligan have time to meet us?"

"I never heard of Halligan refusing to see a young woman, especially one with looks," the storekeeper replied. "Seeing as you're likely responsible folks, I'll let you drive my team and spring wagon up to Halligan's place."

When they had settled on an amount, the storekeeper said, "I thought at first, miss, you might be one of them couriers that sometimes bring messages to Mr. Halligan from his office in Boise."

"He must spend a lot of time in Boise, himself," Deborah ventured.

"Not so much. Hell—when did the governor's number two man have to keep a swivel chair warm?" He laughed knowingly, then turned to wait upon another customer.

It was somewhat after midmorning of the following day when Deborah and the Plunketts reached the well-constructed post-and-rail fence and followed it westward. They crested a gently sloping hill and then stared across a sprawling reach of meadow. There were cross fences, less fancy than the one their road followed; they divided the grassland into smaller pastures that Deborah judged to contain about forty acres each. In the closest one were about twenty horses; farther on were blocky and uniformly colored black cattle, at least a hundred head.

Mollie Plunkett straightened on her seat and

swore gently under her breath. "God Almighty, there must be good money in ranching up here—or in bein' one of the governor's buddies. Debbie, those horses are Morgans—blooded stock."

"And the cattle," Deborah commented. "They are Angus, black Aberdeen Angus."

Jim Plunkett squinted toward buildings breaking into view as the road curved. "Nobody up here in the panhandle has made enough money out of ranching to put together an outfit like this. Either mining money has gone into this place, or some railroad mogul like Jay Gould had a hand in it."

Suspicion and anger were building within Deborah. "Perhaps neither, Jim. Couldn't anybody have a ranch . . . and cattle . . . and horses like this if they were allowed to defraud, or downright steal from, people spread all across Idaho? Or perhaps a lot of the Pacific Northwest?"

They fell silent, had gone another mile, and were approaching a gate when Deborah first noted a lone horseman. He was off to one side in the cattle pasture but was riding at an angle that would intercept them at the gate, and was standing beside the gate when Jim drew their team to a halt. The horse from which he had dismounted first caught Deborah's attention. It was a bay mare with small ears that were attentively forward. It had wide-set eyes. Occasionally she tossed her head and lashed out with her long tail against the indignities of a hovering fly. Deborah sensed it would be a joy to ride this spirited animal. Moments passed and then the sound of the stranger's voice caused her to turn her full attention to him. He had removed a dark hat and was wiping his brow with a white linen handkerchief.

She judged him to be in his late thirties, a man of medium height, with black hair and a profile that seemed to Deborah almost that of a Grecian statue. His words were meant for all three of them, but his eyes, steel gray and direct, seemed to hold to Deborah's face with something like ironic amusement.

"Can I assist you?" he asked. "We don't often see strangers traveling our access road." He paused, then added, "Especially strangers driving our esteemed storekeeper's rig."

With a quick sidewise glance to Deborah, Mollie answered. "We're the Plunketts, from Bonanza down on the Yankee Fork. We deal in livestock. Heard you have some of the best in Idaho." She thrust an identifying finger. "This is my husband, Jim Plunkett . . . and this is our Deborah. We won't be buying any of your fine Morgans, seeings as how mostly we deal with those balky jackasses called mules. But we'd sure admire to see your Morgan mares—and if you don't mind—to look at your cattle."

"How do you know they are mine?" the stranger challenged.

Mollie grinned disarmingly. "Christ, young man, anyone with a lick of sense would realize that you are Blain Halligan himself."

During Mollie's disarming words, Deborah had continued silent. Two thoughts had forced themselves into her mind. Mollie had deliberately indicated that Deborah was a Plunkett, her daughter and Jim's. But more unsettling was the vague but persistent interest that this man sparked within her. What would it be like to have such a man lead her onto a dance floor, or walk beside her on a summer night? What would the flash of those intense eyes mean? Or that well-chiseled face bending in nearness to seek her lips? Had she gone crazy? If indeed this man were Blain Halligan, he would represent most of what she had come to despise. Greed. A lust for money at the expense of anyone, anywhere. An utter lack of compassion. I must somehow trap him, she told herself. I must hate him. I must, above all else, find a way to stop his preying on the decent people of our association. But another thought persisted: *He will. be hard to deal with—the handsome, thieving rascal.*

Abruptly the stranger smiled, then patted the mare who had nuzzled his arm. "Yes, I'll admit to being Blain Halligan . . . and this little mare is Barbary . . . as in Barbary Coast." He pointed to the buildings that loomed through spaced timber a half mile distant. "Why don't you folks follow me to the yard up there? There's shade and water for your team. Then likely the cook can scare us something for lunch."

Jim Plunkett studied Halligan, weighing both the sincerity and possible motive for the invitation. But it was Mollie who heaved a vast sigh, then accepted by saying, "Just wait until I get back to Bonanza and tell folks I was invited to eat with a real gentleman, likely the richest rancher in Idaho."

Halligan's response was a derisive laugh as he moved to open the gate and wave them through. "I am afraid your assessment of my wealth is badly overstated, Mrs. Plunkett. There are men in Idaho whose worth is many times greater than mine. Would you believe that at the present time the forests—the timber resources—of this state,

220

other than the part under federal ownership, are held by ten men or less?"

"What a despicable situation," Deborah flared.

Halligan swung into the saddle, reined his mare toward the buildings, then studied her face as he said, "I hardly believe any one of the fortunate ten would consider it so despicable, Miss Plunkett."

There was something in the way he accented the name Plunkett that brought a tinge of uneasiness to Deborah. Had there been mockery . . . or disbelief . . . or irony in his tone? She quickly asked, "Are there many ranches in this valley, or hereabouts?"

"Not yet," he answered, shaking his head. "The area has been little known or scarcely settled except for the gold and silver mines. People are just now beginning to realize the potential for ranching, and even for farming. There is abundant rainfall, rich soil, and rather mild winters; even fruit orchards would do well."

Little more was said on the way to the ranch yard, and Deborah gave her attention to a herd of black cows through which they drove. The grazing animals, fat, sleek, and well-proportioned, lifted their heads to watch curiously. Most of them had calves by their sides, large enough to indicate they would become yearlings in early spring. Sight of them swept Deborah's memory back to her childhood on the Banner County homestead. How carefully her father had nurtured his calves. He had told Deborah of their homestead as he saw it in his mind's eager eye. Cattle. Horses. Abundant hay meadows. Mature orchards.

Pensive bitterness touched Deborah's face. Why

couldn't her father live to see his dreams materialize? She lifted her eyes toward the nearby Morgan mare and her rider. What justice was there in a decent man like Tom Dexter dying by lightning, while a man such as Blain Halligan used dishonest means to build a magnificent ranch?

A sixth sense warned Deborah that Halligan was watching her in a silent and penetrating way. She met his gaze with an almost hostile one just as he smiled faintly and spoke.

"Deborah . . . may I call you that—just Deborah?" At her grudging nod he went on. "You know, just by watching you a bit I have learned a couple of things."

"Oh?" she murmured.

"Yes, I am sure I have. First, Deborah, you are an attractive young woman when your features take on a natural glow of enjoying life." Before she could comment he added, "Also, I am pretty certain that you don't like me one bit."

"Perhaps," she evaded the comment, "you're just seeing my realization of how hungry I have become; it seems a long way out from Grangeville."

Halligan remained quiet the couple of minutes it took them to reach the ranch yard. Then he waved toward the house as he assisted Mollie and then Deborah from the wagon. "Let's go in and harass my cook into dishing out something special."

While waiting the cook's summons, they sat in wrought-iron chairs on the veranda and sipped cold drinks. Deborah was glad that Jim Plunkett had managed to get Halligan into a discussion of the Florence mining district. She knew that this meal would but postpone the inevitable moment when she must thrust at Blain Halligan the questions that had been forming ever since she left Boise.

Two hours later, after they had enjoyed a meal of garden vegetables, excellent beef, and cold fruit dessert, Halligan asked, "Would you like to see our holding barn and corral for mares with young colts?"

Mollie said, "Jim, stay with me; I'd like a catnap, and I think you would too." There was more that her tone implied: *Stay here. Let Deborah handle it. She is old enough to take care of herself.*

In the barn there was the aroma of hay and that of horseflesh. Deborah ran caressing fingers over the silky and white-starred forehead of the youngest colt. "They are beautiful. So young and cuddly."

"Don't misjudge these colts," he warned. "Already they have strength and endurance that would amaze you. They are true Morgans—the best."

There was pride in his voice, pride that seemed to Deborah to stem from his yearning to acquire and hold the very best . . . to show the world that Blain Halligan was a man of wealth and prestige. Didn't she herself aspire to exactly the same thing? But I'll get them honestly, she thought. I will never build on the misfortunes . . . of those I can cheat.

Her right arm lay across the gate of a stall, and she was aware that his hand had moved to capture hers. Within her was quick forewarning that she must utter the accusations that would rouse his anger and hatred. Reluctance caused her to move to another stall; then, as though sparring for time, she asked, "Why do you call your saddle mare Barbary? As in Barbary Coast, you said?"

He looked squarely into her face. When words spilled from him they carried intensity and the smoldering of long-pent-up fires. "Because," he said, "that is what I am myself—Barbary Coast. I always will be." He flung an arm about the neck of the mare within the stall, as though seeking to prove possession. "I was born on San Francisco's Barbary Coast. Fathered by a Corsican sea captain who seduced the daughter of an Irish miner and then deserted her when he returned home. My mother raised me by mopping floors in bawdyhouses and sleazy restaurants. Her one obsession was that I go to school. Get to be somebody. I went to college, all right, when I was all of five years older than the other students. We had moved to Seattle, and there was the University of Washington. I managed to enroll and—" Halligan paused as Deborah caught a quick and excited breath.

"You went to the University of Washington?"

"I even graduated—in business."

"I don't suppose," she began doubtfully. "No, it wouldn't be possible."

"What?" he demanded curiously.

"That you knew him in college—a man named Robert Lowell."

He was silent so long that she was sure his reply would be negative. Instead, he furrowed his brow. "Likely it wasn't the same Robert Lowell, but was he in premedical classes?"

"Yes . . . yes," she answered urgently. "Was he in your classes . . . or did he graduate with you?"

"No, Deborah, I never knew him. Yet I remember there was a scandal at the university at the time. A student named Robert Lowell was practically forced to leave. It created quite a ruckus." Halligan studied her face and added, "This is very important to you, isn't it?"

She sensed that to lie or to be overly evasive would defeat the possibility of his revealing more. Her answer carried both truth and some revelation of her inner turmoil. She told him of Robert Lowell in Bonanza and of his disappearance. "The worst part is, Mr. Halligan," she concluded, "I have no idea where he is. He is so much like a wounded animal that wants to be alone with its pain."

Blain Halligan was studying her face and her words. "You were in love with Robert Lowell, weren't you?"

There was a clear steadiness in her reply. "Yes. I loved him; perhaps I still do."

He led the way until they stood outside in the sunlight. Then he asked abruptly, "Deborah, is that why you came here . . . and brought Mr. and Mrs. Plunkett with you?" A mirthless smile touched his face. "I knew from the first that they are not your parents. They were much too obvious in pretending that they are." When she did not instantly answer, he went on. "I have the distinct . . . and somehow distasteful . . . impression there is something you want from me."

She knew that the time for masquerade was over, that she must identify herself and then speak the words that would match them against each other. She paused, aware of the doubt and the curiosity on his face. Oh, damn it, she thought, if only I had a chance to rouse decency and compassion within him. They're hidden within him; I know they are.

Then she heard herself saying in an emotionless tone, "Mr. Halligan, you are right; I have been a pretender. My full name is Deborah Dexter. I am the secretary of the new Sheepmen's Association in Boise."

Bleakness crept over his face, seeming to center in his narrowing eyes. "Now we're getting somewhere, Miss Dexter. What do you want from me?"

She knew she must hurry her words and strive to remain calm, yet there was a catch in her voice. "Mr. Halligan, I wanted to meet a man so callous . . . so dishonest . . . and so bereft of decency that he would use a place of trust in state government to help defraud . . . and to steal from . . . the ranchers of his own state."

Blain Halligan, almost frozen with anger, asked, "Are you through? Is that all?"

"No, it isn't. Tell me just one thing: What sort of crookedness is the former Nampuh Distributing Company—and your henchman, Joseph Bagley— about to foist upon decent sheep and cattle growers now?"

By the darkening of his face, she knew that her thrust had struck home, that somehow Blain Halligan was aware of, if not a party to, the sneaky and unlawful manipulations of the missing Bagley.

Blain Halligan seemed to control himself and his words by grasping a corral railing with a grasp that whitened his knuckles. Then he snarled through gritted teeth, "Do yourself a favor, Miss Deborah Dexter—and me one too. Round up your

226

precious, simpleminded Plunketts and get the hell off my property."

She stepped an inch or two closer to him, and when she lifted a troubled but defiant face, the afternoon sunlight spelled out both the anger and the hurt within her. "Why?" she demanded. "Whatever caused you to get yourself and your statehouse position into such corruption?"

For a little while his self-control seemed to desert him. He waved a fisted hand that seemed to encompass the ranch and the valley. "To hell with your pious talk of purity and honesty. I told you I grew up on the Barbary Coast. You survived by grabbing . . . yes, by stealing, if you will, whatever you could get hold of without landing in prison. You liked my horses and my cattle and my land. Could I have gotten them by working as a miner or a lumberjack? Not in a million years. Now get the hell out of here and out of my business—and stay out."

She turned white, but anger seared her face. She drew a gold piece from her pocket and thrust it at him. "This is for our food. We will be off your land within half an hour—unless you've stolen the entire valley."

His foot moved to boot the coin contemptuously back toward her. "You will need that when the sheepmen's association is done for and you are out of a job—damn soon."

She turned, leaving the gold piece untouched in the yard. Then she flashed a challenging and somehow deadly smile toward him. "Before that, Mr. Halligan, there will be a new—and honest—man in the governor's chair."

His unbelieving laugh followed her as she

turned toward the ranch house to get the Plunketts. Her one desire was to get quickly beyond the holdings—and the mocking eyes—of a man with whom she was surely destined to do battle. She only regretted that she had not learned more of Robert Lowell and the incident for which he had been banned from a future in medicine.

Chapter 10

THEY LEFT Grangeville early the following day; almost immediately a softly persistent rain began falling. Deborah sat quietly within the coach, watching a passing panorama of meadows and forests. She had been told of the world of greenery created on Idaho's narrow northern panhandle by heavy rains sweeping in from the Pacific Coast. The variety and height of coniferous timber often caused her to gasp in delight. Surely this was one of nature's favored areas, where dreams could come true and empires be created.

For the final miles of their journey into the Clearwater River Valley and downstream to the town of Lewiston, she and the Plunketts had the inside of the coach to themselves, for the driver, bundled in rainwear, sat resolutely atop the rig.

Deborah's mood had turned serious and a little introspective as darkness came on and the stage rattled steadily ahead. At last she said, doubtingly, "You know, I wasn't very smart the way I handled things with Blain Halligan; I've an idea all I accomplished was to make a powerful enemy . . . and put him on his guard."

Mollie offered a reassuring hand but waited for her husband to speak.

"Debbie, I am glad you brought that up," Jim Plunkett began thoughtfully. "You are going to be in for a scrap, a big and nasty one." He stopped a moment and then went on. "But likely you foresaw trouble when you took on the job with the sheepmen."

Deborah nodded as she murmured, "Maybe I am in over my head. Right now Blain Halligan seems sort of invincible—damn him."

"Deborah," Jim answered, "has anyone told you that somehow you have become pretty powerful yourself? Mollie and I have heard a few comments tossed about. Right now you have the sheepmen and a lot of other livestock men pulling for you. If only others in Idaho could get behind you—"

The words brought Deborah alert and she said, "Not behind me really. But if the mine workers and the farmers—" She broke off and then said, almost explosively, "We can do it. But I will need help. Your help and that of others. We can stop Blain Halligan and others like him right in their slimy tracks. We can—by putting Henry Carswell into the governor's chair in Boise."

Her enthusiasm and conviction at that moment were overpowering.

"Let's give it a try," Jim said, grinning. Then he asked, "But what can I do?"

It was his wife who spoke up. "I'll tell you what, Jim Plunkett. You and me likely know at least five hundred people. It comes from our traipsing over half of Idaho when we were packers. I'm meeting one hell of a lot of others in that pie and coffee shop I took over from Debbie's ma. If this girl has spunk enough to try putting Mr. Carswell into the Idaho statehouse, we for damned sure are going to spread the word to every voter within fifty miles of the Yankee Fork towns."

"But we'd need the farmers down along the Snake River, clean from Idaho Falls to Oregon," Deborah surmised.

"Then go after them," Mollie said with a grin. "Use that Mormon fellow. That missionary turned lawyer you've known so long. What's his name?"

"You . . . you mean Lemuel Froman?"

"Sure she does," Jim nodded with satisfaction. "Most of the Snake River Valley farmers—and those elsewhere in Idaho—are Mormons. You'd better believe they are ready for a change. For twenty years they've been smarting and outraged by the tricks of Boise politicians to keep them from voting."

"It might work," Deborah said. "But you know what we really need on our side?"

"A jugful of goddamned good luck," Mollie said with a sigh.

"Something even harder to come by. An orator. A spellbinder. A man who travels all of Idaho."

There was half a minute of silence before a roar of laughter broke from Jim Plunkett. "Debbie, honey, you've just described him . . . to a tee."

Both Deborah and Mollie glanced at him in an expectant and curious way.

"Sam Douglas—good old foxy Sam," Jim said.

"Oh, Christ," Mollie said with a moan.

Deborah was silent as she recalled the man—he was red-shirted and aboard the stage from Blackfoot to Challis. A poker dealer and player with blue and inscrutable eyes.

For a moment she was about to acknowledge having met Sam Douglas. But was the time yet opportune? After all, good poker players never divulge all their potential strategy. She gazed at Plunkett with unrevealing eyes and nodded. "It sounds as though your Mr. Douglas might be useful. Does he often get to Boise?"

"Old Sam is everywhere often," Mollie said.

"When you see him, ask him to drop in on me in Boise—at the office."

"Likely he'll do it right away," Jim observed.

"There ain't no doubt. Not one damned bit of doubt," Mollie said, pursing her lips in an unrevealing but ominous way.

During their conversation the stage had come cautiously down a hill, and now the lights of Lewiston loomed ahead. The rain had ceased, and interludes of moonlight sifted through low-hanging clouds. Suddenly a cry of wonder broke from Deborah and she peered more closely into the night. "There is water out there . . . that I can't begin to see across. Look!"

Both of the Plunketts stared toward where she was pointing. Then Jim said, "It must be the Clearwater River; it's a whopper up here close to Lewiston. This is where it joins up with the Snake River."

"You mean we're just about where the big boats come into Idaho from the ocean?" Deborah marveled.

The stage was on a street along which both lights and buildings led toward the center of the town. Then five minutes later the stage drew to a stop in front of a large building that Deborah realized was a combination hotel, eating place, saloon,

232

and stage station. As she alighted from the stage she again caught sight of the broad expanse of water. It made shimmering reflections of the streetlights and the rays spilling from windows and doors. A thrill of excitement swept over her as she murmured, "Why we are right on the riverbank. It can't be more than a hundred feet away."

They managed to awaken a sleepy hotel clerk and arrange for rooms. Deborah was soon sound asleep.

Nine hours later Mollie awakened her. "Honey, you're gonna see something special when you peek out the window. Take a look."

Deborah's hand swept aside a heavy curtain and she peered out. Her eyes widened, and the last vestiges of sleep deserted her. For a moment it seemed that she was looking out to sea. Before her was the wide reach of the Clearwater River she had glimpsed the previous night. Perhaps half a mile downstream it blended into even greater water. Beyond its confluence with the Snake River, the vast and sunlighted stream reached westward as far as her eyes could reach. Far on the opposite shore were buildings and streets.

Mollie noticed her study of them and nodded. "Over there, across the Snake, that's Clarkston . . . in Washington State."

"Lewiston and Clarkston," Deborah repeated as she savored the view. "What a tribute to those intrepid voyagers Lewis and Clark." Her pulse quickened as she surveyed the activity of this great inland waterway. Two great ships, larger than any watercraft she had ever seen, lay alongside docks that extended into the river. Other vessels went about their work of moving lumber and grain and ore. Upstream on the Clearwater River she could see a vast basin filled with logs awaiting handling by the sawmills.

And this is but a beginning, Deborah silently told herself. These towns are bursting with activity and opportunity. For a moment she wished that her father and her mother could see the grandeur spread out before her. Thoughts of her parents—both now out of her life—saddened her, and she wept.

Mollie Plunkett stood patiently near and waited for her friend's tears to cease. Then Mollie asked quietly, "Honey, how about you and me doing a bit of sight-seeing? Likely there are stores here that carry things you don't see in Bonanza or even Boise."

Deborah agreed to accompany Mollie but remembered that she herself was in Lewiston for two purposes: to inquire discreetly about the whereabouts of a crook named Joseph Bagley and to check out the feasibility of a portion of Idaho's wool clip being loaded aboard ships here in Lewiston for an all-water journey to New Orleans. Could such arrangements conceivably have rates lower than those set by the railroads serving the mountainous West?

Her day along the streets and in the stores of Lewiston proved fruitless in obtaining any word of Joseph Bagley. The name drew only a blank or negative response whenever she or Mollie asked. Further discouragement came when she inquired at the shipping offices of the Columbia Navigation and Forwarding Company about the all-water route. She spoke with one of the firm's officials, an elderly man with white hair and beard. "We could offer satisfactory rates only to such West Coast cities as San Francisco and Los Angeles," he said. "But shipments beyond those points have the time-consuming and hazardous route by way of Cape Horn. It is really too bad that work on a canal across Panama had to stop when that Frenchman de Lesseps went bankrupt a few years ago."

With growing frustration, Deborah commented, "I don't suppose the railroads that go eastward from up here in northern Idaho would offer us any better chances or more reasonable rates."

"I'm afraid not, Miss Dexter. The rates of the Northern Pacific and the Great Northern are about as steep as those quoted by the Oregon Short Lines people down around Boise."

He handed her a card. "Keep this, Miss Dexter; we would be happy to handle shipments along the Pacific Coast."

"Thank you." She smiled. "I guess all I am going to achieve here in Lewiston is a shoreside view of more water than I ever laid eyes on before." She hesitated, seeing the kindliness of his face. "But it was really worthwhile coming here. This is beautiful country, Colonel Sanderson."

He nodded agreement and then asked, "How would you like to take a day-long boat trip up the Clearwater River? Up to the place where the North Fork merges with the stream coming in from the East? It is quite historic. Lewis and Clark camped there nearly a century ago, in 1805.

It is where they built rafts and dugout canoes to carry them on down to the Pacific shores."

"I would like that. I surely would," Deborah responded eagerly. Then she shrugged her regret. "But I can't. I have two friends . . . an elderly couple . . . here with me."

"Come now," he reproved. "Surely your friends can find enough to keep them occupied here in Lewiston for one day." He wrote rapidly on a slip of cardboard. "Take this. It will provide free transportation for you. If any questions are asked, tell the boatmen that Colonel Sanderson gave you the pass—to induce you and your Sheepmen's Association to remember us and our services." He smiled broadly. "And, Miss Dexter, enjoy yourself. You are too young to worry so."

The boat by which she traveled upstream the next morning was a no-frills launch used by the transportation company to move men and supplies. It had steam power and moved with slow certainty through the water. Its decks were heavily laden with boxes of foodstuffs, medical supplies, machine parts, and other necessities for the upstream mining camps. Every few miles it put to shore to discharge freight, passengers, and a mail sack or so.

But it was the river, the Clearwater, that fascinated Deborah. She sensed that so large and powerful a river must drain an immensity of forested slopes and alpine meadows. Except where disturbed by manmade devices, it flowed clear and cold, its ripples reflecting the sunlight as countless gems. At a point well above Lewiston, Deborah sighted Indians busy netting the largest fish she had ever seen. A crewman of the launch explained that both salmon and steelhead were caught here and smoked for winter use by the tribesmen.

Presently the launch ceased its forward movement and stood rocking in the river's swift current. Deborah looked about, then realized that a sizable mass of logs, being driven downstream, was temporarily utilizing the stream's deep channel. The size and length of the logs amazed Deborah. Then something that Mollie had said raced through her mind: "It's a shame that we Idahoans have allowed less than a dozen men—timber moguls—to grab control of most of the forests of this state—and for less than a dollar an acre."

Now Deborah Dexter's eyes narrowed. Tumultuous thoughts raced through her mind; her lips moved in unspoken words. "I have fifty dollars with me that I'm not going to need to get back to Boise. It isn't much—but I'm going to invest it—in timberland."

She again studied the floating logs. "I . . . I never realized they grew so long and so unblemished. Not twisty, like cottonwood and willows." She failed to realize that in her zest her voice had strengthened and now drifted clearly across the forward deck. "There is nothing like it in Nebraska . . . or around Ogden . . . or even down in the Yankee Fork country, around Bonanza."

As she uttered the final words, she became aware that others were listening. A couple of deckhands were laughing. Another man turned, startled. She glanced toward him—and full into the face most deeply imprinted in her memory, that of Robert Lowell.

Both her recognition and her surprise were

237

complete. She straightened, wide-eyed and almost unbelieving. His clothing was much the same as what he had worn during their days along Jordan Creek. The brown of his startled eyes was exactly as she remembered, yet something in his face told of the passing years. His moustache seemed that of a more mature man; there was a single streak of graying hair, almost lost in the chestnut-hued mass that tumbled to his shoulders.

His words came first as he gasped, "My God, Deborah . . . what are you doing here?"

She was conscious of his moving toward her, bending his head to look into her face, and gathering her hands into his own. For an instant she closed her eyes, savoring the excitement of his nearness. She sensed that only the presence of others on the deck deterred him from putting his arms about her. She backed a bit from him, smiled at his bewilderment, and said, "Why do I always find you way up a stream? And, Robert Lowell, if you think I was trailing you—you're wrong. At least this time."

His hand lifted to touch a blown strand of her dark hair and tuck it behind her ear. "Deborah," he said in almost a whispered tone, "you have changed. There is a quality of sureness about you. But you are still so appealing . . . so lovely."

"Robert, do you live near here? Are you still looking for gold?" He nodded indifferently. "A man has to keep his hand at something that provides a dollar. Some of the richest gold and silver stratas of Idaho are strung out along this Clearwater River."

238

"Why didn't you write to me?" she whispered urgently.

"I did write—several months ago."

"Just one letter—when I graduated," she accused. Then she added, "I looked for more letters, Robert. Wanted them and needed them." Her tone revealed more than her words.

The long-remembered remoteness came again to his face. "Deborah . . . Deborah," he murmured. "You didn't need a shiftless, roving prospector."

She moved so that the searching of her eyes bore down upon his face. "Perhaps, Robert Lowell, you don't need me . . . haven't since the day of that snowstorm . . ."

"Stop it!" he said. Then his face became a playground of warmth and yearning. "How long are you going to be here—along the Clearwater?" he asked.

She told him of the things that had brought her northward from Boise. "I believe this boat returns to Lewiston in late afternoon," she concluded with regret. Then, "How far up the river do you live?"

"Only about three miles, where this launch makes its last stops and turns around. There are a few cabins and some gold-placering activity in the river canyon. Lately there has been talk that some development company plans to lay out a regular townsite and call it Orofino."

Her eyes again swept the immensity of forested hills above the Clearwater valley. "I wish I had time to stay," she said, "really to get into the forest—maybe to find a grove I could buy

239

and call my own. And," she added almost wistfully, "to learn what sort of person you have become, Robert. What you do. How you live. Your plans and goals and dreams." Impulsively she turned, drew him to her, and rested her cheek tenderly against his. "It . . . it just isn't fair. To find you and have to leave within a few hours." She told him of the Plunketts awaiting her in Lewiston.

He drew her to the boat's rail, pointed toward the shore, and then spoke with full candor. "If staying here—with me—for a while is something you want as much as I want you, Deborah, why not? I have a cabin. Not fancy, but reasonably warm and comfortable. And private."

Before she answered she surveyed the beauty and the tranquillity of the river and the valley. Somewhere on shore chimney smoke was rising to drift lazily across the water and bring to her its fresh and acrid scent. Off to starboard an insect-seeking trout lunged from the water and then dropped back to create a mighty spray. The chugging of the launch's engine seemed very loud and insistent. So, suddenly, did the beating of Deborah's heart. Her hand reached up to smooth his hair; her eyes were clear and peaceful as she said, in tones only he could hear, "Let's write a note to the Plunketts. You and me together. Then Robert, take me ashore with you." She was silent a little while, noting the tenderness of his face.

Robert Lowell's cabin, less than a stone's throw from the edge of the Clearwater, had been built of hand-hewn logs and odds and ends of sawed lumber. At one end was a fireplace built of carefully chosen river boulders. There was only a single room, with two windows set to allow the breezes of summer to drift through the structure. They approached it when the sun was scarcely an hour beyond noon. There were two white pine trees in the yard; between them Robert had placed a handmade table that took advantage of the shade. Deborah hastened to it and sat down, letting her hand seek out and hold his.

He drew her closer, then asked, "Would it be fitting for me to carry you across the threshold?"

"Later I want you to, Robert. When darkness comes on. Right now I just want to see so much of this lovely valley and its river." She let her gaze roam the high, forested horizon and then asked, "Wouldn't it be fun . . . if we had horses . . . to ride up onto that high ridge and look across half of Idaho?"

"Your wish is my command, Miss Dexter," he said with an elaborate bow. Then he pointed to animals grazing in a nearby meadow. "It so happens that the livestock belong to me. Want to help me fetch the horses? There are two we can ride."

By way of an angling trail, they came to the top of the ridge an hour and a half later. The Clearwater River was now a silver band far below them, while far off to the south they could see a series of peaks that jutted their rocks and a little remaining snow toward the sky. In between lay an infinity of rolling hills with the purple smokiness of woodland distances.

"If only I could own part of that . . . the timberlands," Deborah said with a sigh. "It is beautiful, and it is bound to become valuable."

"There is no reason you can't, sweetheart. Listen . . . I had a reason for bringing you to this spot. Look over there to the left. See that gap through the ridges . . . how it sort of leads into an immense valley?" He hesitated, studying the awe of her face. "Deborah, whoever gets control of that gap, of a couple of hundred acres, is bound to have a fortune within his grasp."

"Why?" she asked quickly. "Is there such fine timber up there?"

"No. But there is something a lot better. That gap guards and controls the only potential access to well over thirty thousand acres of prime timberland. Douglas fir and white pine, with a lot of red cedar in the lower spots."

"My God," she gasped. "What would my father have thought of all this?"

"From what you have told me of him, likely he would have said, 'Debbie, didn't I always say there was a rainbow ahead for you,' " Robert Lowell replied.

"Why haven't you bought or sewed up all those acres in the gap?" she asked, her voice laden with wonder and incomprehension.

"Because, Debbie, I don't feel the urge or the desire to own the mountains. I just want to enjoy them . . . hide in them . . . perhaps still licking my wounds." He shrugged, then his voice became practical. "Besides, where would Robert Lowell get hold of two hundred dollars or more? I placer a dollar and spend a dollar. What the hell else matters?"

Deborah straightened and then clasped a hand

firmly over his mouth. "Listen to me, Robert. On the way up here I had to look up a man named Blain Halligan. Do you remember him?" A controlled flicker of interest crossed his face, but Lowell remained quiet as she said, "Blain Halligan is a . . . a bastard. But I found out something. He knows something he isn't telling. About your years at the University of Washington Medical School and the charges that were brought against you. I've an idea that a reopening of the case, with evidence forced out of some people, would clear you and your name. You will need money for that, likely quite a bit of money." She laid a hand on each of his cheeks and forced him to look into her steady brown eyes. "Robert, you big lug, don't you understand that I love you? That I want only the best for you?" She heaved an excited sigh, then plunged on. "Oh, damn it, Mr. Lowell, I've wanted you so long . . . to have you hold me tight . . . make love to me. But after that—after tonight at your cabin—you and I are going to do something else. We are going to buy those two hundred acres in the gap."

He plunged a hand into his pocket and pulled out a small collection of coins. "With what?" he demanded. "With these . . . less than five dollars?"

"Yes," she said firmly, "we will use that. Every penny you have. And put with it fifty dollars I brought from Boise for emergency money. And I am sure the Plunketts will lend me two or three hundred dollars until I can get my hands on that much."

He silenced her with a firm kiss and then said,

grinning, "Damn, but you can be a persuasive woman—and an irresistible one."

Deborah eyed him beguilingly. "Do you tell all of your women that?" She was unprepared for the way in which her bantering words caused Robert Lowell to flinch and for a moment to recoil from her.

"Deborah, what is it you see in me?" he asked presently. "You have accomplished so much while I seem to fritter away the years. Aren't there other men whom—?"

She rose and stood beside her saddled horse. As he helped her to mount, her arm was momentarily tight about him, and the feel of his taut, well-muscled body roused a long-dormant flame. "Rob," she said, and realized how few times she had used the shorter name, "there is no one else . . . and there never has been. Let's go home to your cabin; you have a pretty hungry female on your hands."

Later, when they had prepared a simple but satisfying meal, they sat at a plank table with a kerosene lamp casting its glow upon them. For quite a time they were content to sit looking into each other's face, listening to each other's voice, and linking their hands in mutual endearment. Time wore on, and the last vestiges of day faded into a moonless and quiet night. At last they rose and moved together toward the narrow but well-blanketed cot.

Then suddenly his arms were about her, pushing her backward. His lips were hard and demanding as they crushed upon hers. "Debbie . . .

Debbie," he murmured, "I have thought so often of you. Wanted you near like this."

She was conscious of his hand moving about to cradle her breast and of her own thighs responding to the miracle of his nearness. Moments later their clothing had been flung aside. She felt but little heeded the roughness of the woolen blanket.

"Robert, my own," she whispered, "take me. Take me now. I love you so."

For a time there was the closeness . . . the magic . . . the inevitable. Then quiet filled the cabin on the Clearwater as they slept, her head upon his shoulder and his arms yielding utter contentment.

In the full sunlight of morning, Deborah was the first to awaken. For a time she mulled the thought of getting quietly out of bed and preparing hot tea. But the stirring of the cold ashes within the stove would surely waken him. She nestled close, then drew a quick breath as his nakedness again sought her out.

Another hour passed before she again awakened—and knew that someone had stepped onto the outer porch and was already working the homemade latch. She sat in bewildered alarm, clutching the blanket against her breasts and belly. The door swung open. For an instant she was moving her lips to call aloud to Robert Lowell. Then all that was revealed by the spilled light from the doorway sealed her lips in silent and unbelieving shock.

A girl had come into the room and was staring toward the bed. She was of medium height, quite young, and obviously an Indian. And she was large with the final month of pregnancy.

Deborah glanced toward the man sharing the bed with her, but Lowell was still sleeping. His face seemed that of a tired and peaceful child.

Slowly Deborah came to her feet, throwing aside the blanket and clutching her skirt and blouse. Any second now this placid-faced and quiet Indian girl would surely cry out or speak aloud. And a certainty was crashing upon Deborah Dexter, numbing her mind and tearing the last remnants of sleep from her face. This quiet and watchful Indian girl was no stranger to Robert Lowell's cabin. She seemed a part of it and of his life. No doubt remained. *The child that she would soon bear had been fathered by the man in whose arms Deborah had so eagerly spent the night.*

At the moment, there was no anger about her . . . only a numbness that something like this could be, forming a yet unfathomable barrier to the future for which she longed and searched.

Deborah began quietly putting on her clothing; the eyes of the dusky-faced girl were inscrutable upon her, although this stranger remained with her back to the door through which she had entered. The girl was barefooted. About her forehead was a beaded band, below which black and unruly tresses fell midway down her back. She showed no animosity, only a curiosity encompassing every move Deborah made.

When Deborah bent close beside the bed to retrieve a shoe, Robert stirred and opened his eyes. At first he did not see the quiet intruder by the door, and his hand moved as though to encircle Deborah and draw her onto the bed beside him.

She moved quickly away, then spoke aloud for the first time. "Perhaps you had better get up. We have company." The words were low-spoken and seemingly unconcerned.

He rose on his elbow and glanced about. Then he said, almost savagely, "Willow Bud! What in hell are you doing here?"

His tone caused the Indian girl to stiffen slightly, and concern tightened the contours of her face. She answered in a voice that was low but filled the cabin, "My brother, Beaver Paw, said I should return to you; the fish curing is over, and I am no longer needed."

Lowell sat up in bed, glanced momentarily at Deborah, then started to wave the pregnant girl from the cabin.

"Let her stay!" Deborah's words came as a quick intercession. "This is *her* home—not mine."

In tense silence they both finished putting on their clothing. Deborah walked to the door, and the pregnant girl moved aside. Outside there was a small, clear stream. Deborah walked to it and lifted cold handfuls of water to her face, then worked to smooth and arrange her hair. Robert had followed closely behind her, and presently he spoke. "Debbie, I suppose this means the end of the trail for the two of us." When she did not immediately answer, he went on, "Can't you understand? I thought I had lost you . . . would never see you again. And she . . . Willow Bud . . . was here. She is Nez Percé, and I know her people; sometimes I tend their wounds and illnesses. It . . . it just happened between me and Willow Bud.

247

Just as it happened with you and me a long time ago in Bonanza. And again last night. God Almighty, Deborah, try to understand."

Her reply startled him as she asked, "Robert, answer me one thing—honestly. Have you any remaining desire to finish medical school? To become a doctor? Or are you contented to live like this—a ne'er-do-well? A squawman?"

"What chance have I got?" he said. "Nobody gets a fair shake if the powers-that-be are against him."

She heard him out and then shook her head. "I suppose I ought to be furious, Robert . . . coming here and then finding that all the time I've been second to another woman. One who likely doesn't even know you have been to medical school . . . that you are capable of accomplishing so much."

Her words roused ire within him and he flared, "Damn it, Deborah, I am what I am—and perhaps I like it that way. I don't have your sureness that tomorrow everything is going to be wonderful and shining with opportunity." He stormed back into the cabin. Deborah quickly followed him.

When she answered, there was both pity and a growing conviction in her voice. "I don't believe you really want to become a doctor, or even put out the effort it would take." Silence fell across the room. The Nez Percé girl looked from one to the other in a quiet and uncomprehending way. Then quietly she backed through the doorway, closed it, and was gone.

"I suppose, Deborah," Lowell said after a time, "you want me to take you back to catch the boat to Lewiston."

She stood quietly at the room's only window, her gaze encompassing the river valley and the upward-rising tiers of forest that receded to the far-off horizon. Something of its vastness and its challenge fashioned her response. "No, I am not going to dash madly back to Lewiston and then to Boise. You and I have some things to do. First, we are going to find a different place for me to stay a night or so. Robert Lowell, you and I are going to buy those two hundred acres in the gap, put our own lock on access to those thousands of acres. Before some railroad or timber mogul does it. I'm positive I can raise the money to handle it."

Lowell had been standing, but now he sank onto a bench and stared at her. "It beats hell," he muttered, "how cold and calculating you are."

His words caused her eyes to flash angrily. "Was I—last night, Robert? Was I cold and calculating when I came to you?" She paused, then continued thoughtfully, "It will take time . . . probably quite a lot of time . . . for me to know what is left in my heart for you. Right now it seems there is nothing but an aching emptiness . . . and a lot of revulsion."

"But you don't intend to let that interfere with business," he said.

Deborah bit back a stinging reply, then said, almost as though she were talking to an unruly child, "Whether we ever sleep together again has nothing to do with throwing away a possible chance to make a lot of money. Perhaps for both of us to become wealthy."

"Jesus Christ, Deborah!" he exclaimed, "what sort of person are you?" There was both astonishment and admiration in his voice. "First you find

out I'm going to father a half-breed; then you offer
to help me make a million dollars or so."

"I can't see how one has so much to do with the
other," she chided.

Chapter 11

Four days later, Deborah and the Plunketts arrived back in Boise. Their trip homeward had been uneventful but tiring. In her purse Deborah carried both a receipt for two hundred twenty-five dollars and a bill of sale attesting that two hundred acres of timberland had passed into the joint possession of Robert Lowell and herself. Knowledge of their success in arranging the purchase was a satisfying thing, but as the stage made its way southward from Lewiston the girl's quiet and preoccupied manner caused Jim Plunkett to comment to his wife when they were alone at a rest stop.

"It beats me, Mollie. When Debbie riled up that scoundrel, Blain Halligan, and got us all tossed off his ranch, she was bubblin' and happy. Now she engineers a big timber grab and turns quiet as a mouse." He ran his fingers through his hair thoughtfully, then added, "Likely she's planning some way to pile up a million bucks."

Mollie had studied Deborah Dexter with the perceptive and penetrating mind of a woman. Now she answered, with a bit of scorn for a man's blindness, "Plunkett, damned if you'll ever begin to understand women folks. Something happened up there on the Clearwater River. Something went wrong. Debbie ain't ready or wanting to talk about it, but I'd guess that true love isn't so true

251

just now between her and that here-today-gone-tomorrow Lowell."

The Plunketts remained only one day in Boise, then said regretful good-byes and began their journey back to Bonanza.

A sense of loneliness descended on Deborah with their departure. She rose early the following morning and walked to work. Soon she began sorting and opening the letters that had accumulated in her absence. One envelope caught her attention; it carried the name and return address of the Oregon Short Lines Railroad. It contained only an advertisement featuring a small map of the railroad's trackage and its tie-in with the transcontinental Union Pacific system. She scanned it, at first with indifference and then more closely. Then a thought came to her on how this vast railroad network was dependent on areas dominated by Mormons. Deborah rose and scanned a larger map in her office showing the routes of the entire Union Pacific Railroad. A thought was developing in her mind, vague but already laden with possibility. She sat down again and drummed her fingers thoughtfully. Her thoughts slowly took on the dimensions of a plan.

It was nearly noon when a light rapping on the door caused her to rise to open it. Ramon Echiverri entered and looked about the room in a relieved way. "I'm glad you are back safely, Deborah. There was an attempt to break into this office night before last."

"Was anything taken?" she asked anxiously.

"No. Luckily the building owner happened along. The prowler got away before the owner got a good look at him." Echiverri shook his head, then brightened. "A letter came while you were gone. From that Mr. Oakes at the spinning mills back East. They can use three large shipments of our Idaho wool this season. Want the first one right away. And, Deborah, they insist that we send someone there to represent us in contract negotiations."

The news brought a flush of delight to her, but it quickly vanished. "What good will it do, Ramon? I failed to find a means of securing freight rates we can live with." She hesitated, then smiled quickly toward the door. Another man had come into the office and had stood listening. It was Henry Carswell, clad in the inevitable business suit and necktie and holding his bowler hat. "You're a hard one to catch up with, Deborah Dexter," he complained with a smile.

She ran to welcome him with a glad hug. "It is about time the future governor of Idaho called upon me."

"Don't count too much on that—at least for a few years."

"Why?" she asked sharply. "Surely you aren't getting cold feet." She led him forward, meaning to introduce him to Ramon.

"Mr. Echiverri and I have already met," Carswell explained. "You don't think I would let a constituency like the Basque people go unnoticed, do you?"

"But . . . but if you're not going to run for office—" Deborah began.

Carswell smiled in amusement, then said, "Hold on. I did not say that. It's just that I am not trying for the governorship this term. I talked it over with a smart young lawyer here in Boise. His name is Borah . . . William E. Borah. He showed me a lot surer way of helping the farmers and the laboring classes—by being elected secretary of state."

Deborah was silent, but her mind instantly fastened on some salient facts. Idaho's secretary of state. As such Carswell would replace the individual to whom Blain Halligan had easy and questionable access. Might Henry Carswell, honest and aggressive, be the one to commence the downfall of the man who had helped loot the government of Idaho to build a magnificent ranch just beyond Grangeville?

She was still pondering the possibility when Carswell's brisk voice sounded a question. "From what I overheard, Deborah, I gather you're having a problem with the robberlike rates of the Union Pacific Railroad?"

She nodded and then answered in a troubled way. "A woolen mill in Ohio wants to contract for much of the Idaho clip on a regular basis. But we can't afford to send even one carload East."

Henry Carswell lifted his chin and seemed to concentrate on a ceiling water stain. Moments passed in utter silence. Then he spoke.

"Deborah, don't be so sure. Just maybe there is a way of getting cheap freight to Ohio for at least one load." He paused, shifting his gaze between the waiting girl and Ramon Echiverri, and evidently enjoying what he was about to disclose. It came as a question. "Debbie, do you remember how you got out here? Away from Nebraska?"

"Of course I do. In an emigrant car . . . chockfull of our belongings and a cow. And some chickens. And Antonio Onederra. And both of the Mormon missionaries."

"Right," Carswell answered, and then added with clipped and precise words, "Trains run both ways. Carry freight both ways. Who says that an emigrant car can't pull out of Boise loaded with the belongings of someone who's had a bellyful of Idaho and wants the softer climes of Ohio?"

"Wool is personal property until it is sold," Ramon Echiverri said softly, and his eyes were aglow with excited purpose.

The audacity of what Henry Carswell was proposing brought a burst of laughter from Deborah. "Let's try it," she agreed. "But first I think we should have someone who understands such things read the railroad regulations about shipments—I think they are called tariffs. I know just the lawyer to do it for us: Lemuel Froman." She did not add aloud that another idea was brewing within her mind, one in which Froman, formerly a missionary of the Church of Jesus Christ of Latter-day Saints, might be of even greater service.

Henry Carswell had also been thinking, and now he said, "We will need someone to act as our disgruntled emigrant wanting only to get back to Ohio."

Echiverri nodded gravely. "Such a person should not be hard to find. Farming hasn't paid very good hereabouts lately."

"He would have to be trustworthy . . . and a convincing sort," Deborah put in.

"I have thought of that also," Echiverri agreed, then added, "Why can't we have two men heading out for Ohio in the emigrant car? One a farmer."

"And the other?" Carswell asked.

A soft smile tugged at Echiverri's lean face, and he said, "I think our second emigrant should be Jeff Harding. I think we could persuade him to delay his other business for a while."

"God Almighty, yes. Just the man." Carswell grinned.

At eleven o'clock the following morning Deborah entered the law offices of Lemuel Froman and his associates in downtown Boise. An elderly woman in a white blouse and a long serge skirt stared at her critically and then showed her to the door of Froman's office.

Froman had been working at a desk cluttered with lawbooks and legal-looking documents. Now he rose and moved toward Deborah.

At first sight of his face she was startled. There was a strained tiredness about him that seemed to add years to his age. Something has happened since that night we danced together in Pocatello, her mind whispered. And she remembered the desperation of the words he had spoken then: *Damn a marriage with nothing left.*

"Lemuel," she greeted him, "you must be a very busy person, with little rest." Her words were an effort to mask her shock.

"Deborah, it is nice of you to look me up." He held her in a cautious way and led her to a chair beside his desk, then said, "Don't tell me that you too have legal problems."

"I do . . . and I suspect you will find them quite unusual. Lemuel, is it legal—and within the scope of railroad regulations—to send an emigrant car eastward over the Union Pacific Railroad?"

He jerked upright and looked shocked. "Deborah—not that. Surely not that. You want to return to Nebraska?"

She smiled at his dismay, then outlined the plan that Henry Carswell had conceived. The sheer audacity of it caused Froman to lean forward, eagerness dispelling some of his haggard appearance. Presently he said, "Debbie, you're exciting to have around. Something unusual always seems to happen wherever Deborah Dexter takes a hand." He paused, then in a more businesslike manner went on, "Unless the railroad tariffs specifically prohibit eastbound movement of emigrant cars, likely you can get away with it—at least once or twice. You can bet the railroad people will hurry to plug such a loophole . . . if it exists."

"I hope to goodness a loophole can be found," she said. "We have . . . somehow . . . to get a first substantial wool shipment to Nephi Oakes; he's helped us too much to let it fail now."

"Let me look into this. Today, Debbie. And come to think of it we may have an answer about the legality of the shipment right away. A friend of mine, a very fine attorney, has been involved in a case concerning freight tariffs. His name is Bill Borah. William E. Borah, to be exact."

"I have heard of him," she nodded.

"And you'll hear more; someday Bill Borah is going to have a big job in Washington. Maybe even as President." He waited, then timidity tinged his voice as he asked, "Debbie, how about having lunch with me? And . . . and thanks for not mentioning that just now my face looks like warmed-over death."

She looked at him with the direct and clear honesty he had come to know so well. "Lemuel, of course I noticed, but lately my own mirror doesn't seem to reflect so much of a dewy-eyed young dreamer."

"My mother used to say, Deborah, that sooner or later life breaks everyone's heart. Perhaps to keep us humble." A sigh escaped him, then he rose, moved near, and clutched her hand. "Deborah, my wife has left me. Without warning. Without a good-bye."

"She—a Mormon woman did that?" she answered unbelievingly.

He nodded and then murmured, "At least I have our child . . . my daughter, Janice. I have learned that my wife is in Sacramento, California, living with a construction engineer."

"Where is Janice now?"

"During the day I leave her with a motherly woman who lives near us. After work I pick her up and . . . and . . . I try to—"

His words were cut short as Deborah came to her feet and spoke words that were almost fierce. "Stop it, Lemuel! Stop torturing yourself! Right now I am taking you to lunch. It is my turn to buy. And Lemuel, if I meet you after work, can I go with you when you pick up Janice?"

Midmorning two days later a messenger came to Deborah's office and delivered a plain-appearing envelope, addressed to her and carefully sealed with wax. It contained a letter that read:

Dear Miss Dexter:
Mr. Borah has confirmed my opinion that no
258

legal or regulatory reason *presently* exists
that would prohibit your making shipments
to Lorain, Ohio, in the manner Mr. Carswell
suggested. I suggest that this be done as
quickly as possible and in a circumspect manner. It is doubtful the opportunity will exist
much beyond the first or, at best, second shipment.

                    Respectfully,

                    Lemuel Froman, attorney-at-law

To the single page was clipped a smaller memo
sheet bearing the neat but somewhat stilted hand-
writing of Froman:

Deborah,
My daughter, Janice, and I plan to have dinner at home this evening—about 8:00 P.M., if I
can bring things together in the kitchen.
Would you join us? Unless I hear otherwise,
we'll set an extra plate—and hope.

                    Lemuel

P.S. I am excited about your unique shipping
venture.

Deborah reread both messages and then
leaned back to stare out toward mountains rapidly attaining the varied hues of autumn. She
would tell Ramon Echiverri the good news about
sending an emigrant car eastward. Preliminary
plans had already been laid for assembling the
shipment and those who would accompany it.
Knowing the resourcefulness of the Basque sheep-

men and of Jeff Harding, she felt confident the emigrant car would be en route to Ohio within three or four days. But then what?

As she probed the dilemma, part of her mind was intent also on the plea of Lemuel Froman that she come to his home for an evening meal with him and his daughter. She knew she would go. Since her return from the Clearwater River and the night with Robert Lowell, a restlessness had been growing in her. It seemed lately to make her living quarters lonely and confining.

After a few minutes she thought of another reason to visit attorney Lemuel Froman. The thought had been born when she had studied the large map of the Union Pacific's routes and the surprisingly large Mormon territory through which they ran. She was aware of the respect in which Froman was held by the Mormons of Idaho. Were not these same churchmen populous and regular patrons of the railroad? Part of the railroad's routes passed through Utah, the center of the Mormon empire. She had little doubt that Nephi Oakes, although residing in Ohio, still could exert influence within the Church. Her eyes widened as the final facet dropped into place. Bishop Joshua Stannard! Her stepfather . . . husband of the mother Deborah had not seen for so long.

There was a pleased and purposeful smile on Deborah's face as she prepared to take the news of the emigrant-car venture to Ramon Echiverri. There was also the small beginning of a ruthlessness—the seed of which had been sown when a Nez Percé girl let light and realization into the cabin of Robert Lowell near the far-off Clearwater River.

She found Ramon Echiverri and his wife harvesting plump, red tomatoes in the rear of his home near the Boise River. They greeted her and then led the way to an immense cottonwood tree beneath which a bench had been placed in the shade. "Ramon," she said then, "we have it—the lawyers' opinion that we are not breaking the law, or railroad rules, by sending the emigrant car to Ohio."

"Good, Deborah. Now we must work fast. Get it loaded and ready, with our very best bales of this year's clip."

"How soon can we be ready, Ramon? I am so anxious."

"We all are. One of our people works in the railroad yards; he is sure he can have such a car set out for us on a couple of hours' notice. Quite a few of them have been coming into Boise and Caldwell lately."

"But how many days?" she persisted.

"I would say three days at the most. Our friend Jeff Harding will arrive here tomorrow afternoon; we have already found a middle-aged farmer who will load a small amount of household goods. Now . . . how about you?" he asked. "Can you be ready to catch the passenger train eastward a day or so after our shipment leaves Boise?"

"But Ramon . . . wait," she objected. "I just came back from a trip to Lewiston. Work at the association has been stacking up."

"Of course it has. But right now, Deborah, the most important thing is negotiating the contract with your friend at the mill in Ohio."

"But the association has so little cash. Should I,

or anyone, use it for travel? Perhaps by mail we can—"

"Not all details could be handled well by mail. It is slow and sometimes uncertain. If need be, we can use the proceeds from this first shipment for the contract expenses. You will go, won't you? It means—if we get a contract—that some of our people will be able to pay off mortgages."

"Sure I'll go. How could I refuse when you put it that way?" Deborah answered. "But about the permanent freight arrangements?"

"You will work something out . . . just as you thought of using the emigrant car. Our members have great confidence in you."

She was about to shake her head in concern over the future, but two things caused her to refrain: the confidence on the faces of the Echiverris, and the idea pent up within her. She clasped their hands and said, "I will get a railroad ticket right away."

She was close to her office when she realized it was noon and she was hungry. She noticed also that she was half a block from the office of Frank Wentworth, the mining engineer. She firmed her chin and thought, Maybe it ain't ladylike, but I am going to ask Mr. Wentworth to have lunch with me.

At that moment Wentworth came out of his office and looked directly at her. "Deborah Dexter," he said with relief, "what a pleasure to see you again. And I hope you have not had lunch. Otherwise I will have to meet a friend who is a professor of Greek mythology and listen for an hour to his interpretations."

Deborah merely grinned and said, "What are we waiting for, Mr. Wentworth? I'm hungry."

A short walk downtown brought them to a brownstone building opposite the Idaho State Capitol Building and the Ada County Courthouse. "There is a restaurant inside that I believe you will enjoy," Wentworth explained. "It is mostly for politicians—and those who hope to influence state officials. Perhaps you had better get acquainted with the place—and the patrons. Aren't you planning to make your friend Henry Carswell the governor?"

She shook her head. "Not for a while at least. Henry decided against it himself. It seems that a lawyer named Bill Borah advised him to wait, but to run for secretary of state in the next election."

They followed a formally clad waiter to a table and were seated before Wentworth spoke again. Then he said, "Henry Carswell got expert advice if it came from Bill Borah; no one else in this state is as knowledgeable concerning political trends and power."

Deborah had picked up a menu, but abruptly she let it drop to the white damask tablecloth. The waiter had reappeared—and following him to a nearby table was a man wearing a dark and well-cut business suit, a man she had last seen far northward in towering rage, the chief confidant of Idaho's present secretary of state—Blain Halligan!

He looked toward her in the same second and their gazes locked. For a moment there seemed a hint of recognition on Halligan's face, but he masked it well and offered a small bow, plus a wave of greeting to Frank Wentworth. The assayer acknowledged it and then said softly to Deborah, "Somehow I get the idea that you and Mr. Halligan have met before—and clashed."

"He is despicable. A scoundrel and a thieving crook," Deborah murmured.

"Granted," Wentworth said.

Speaking softly, Deborah told Wentworth of the plan to ship wool to Ohio using an emigrant car and of the plan's evident—if temporary—legality.

Wentworth smiled his satisfaction, then gazed at her for quite a while. "Deborah, do you realize that more and more you are building a power basis in this state? And . . . by the way . . . didn't you just get back from the Clearwater River country?"

"Yes, I did. And the Plunketts were up there with me. I invested in about two hundred acres of timberland."

"In a few years that could net you a tidy sum. Where is it?"

She told him of how the land commanded access to what seemed an unexplored wilderness of virgin forest.

"My God, Debbie Dexter," he murmured in amazement, "who advised you?"

She hesitated, then answered, "A friend of mine." She was about to withdraw into silence, but she had an urgent need to talk to someone who surely would understand. "Mr. Wentworth, you might as well know. I really went North in hopes of finding a man I was once in love with, over in Bonanza. Who I believed was still the only man alive for me."

"And you found him?" Wentworth encouraged in a whisper.

264

"Yes . . . living as a shiftless squawman. Just because he was expelled from medical school. He could have been a brilliant physician or surgeon." She lifted troubled eyes, then added, "It is too late. Now he has a Nez Percé girl large with child."

"That doesn't necessarily condemn him to oblivion, Deborah. Where did he attend medical school?"

"In Seattle. At the university." She glanced toward Blain Halligan, who was conversing with an older man. "Blain Halligan knows something about it. More than he is willing to tell. He went to the same school."

Wentworth's face had grown thoughtful as he asked, "Debbie, how old is your young friend, the squawman?"

"I'm not sure. I would say about twenty-seven."

Wentworth seemed engrossed in mental calculations before he spoke. "Deborah, perhaps I can throw a wee bit of light on all this. Blain Halligan was at the University of Washington about six years before your friend would have been admitted to medical school. But are you aware that there was another Halligan—a younger brother—in medical school? Probably at the same time your friend was there. As I recall, his name was Lacey Halligan. He practiced medicine over in Caldwell for a few months. Then he dropped out of sight."

Her face grew tense, and the glass she lifted trembled a little. "Do you suppose we can somehow pry into the school records of both Lacey Halligan and my friend? His name is Robert Lowell."

"It shouldn't be too formidable a task. But, young lady, does it all mean that much to you?"

She nodded her certainty, then confided, "I don't know which I want, really. To clear Robert's record—or to have something to help me nail Blain Halligan's hide to the wall. He is in league with an organizer of companies that try to steal our livestock men blind. He threatened to see that the Sheepmen's Association gets disbanded and me out of a job."

"Halligan has some powerful connections," Wentworth said seriously, "but so have you. There is trouble ahead. I'm concerned that you will not use the same no-holds-barred tactics that Blain Halligan uses."

"Don't be deceived, Mr. Wentworth. I didn't come to Idaho, or go to work for the association, with any intention of running away when things get rough."

"Then I know just the man to send out to the university at Seattle to do some quiet sleuthing."

"Who?" she asked.

"A fellow you know—at least you told me you know him—Sam Douglas."

"The gambler?" Deborah exclaimed. "Good Lord, how many hats does he wear? The Plunketts say he is a spellbinding orator. When I first came to Idaho and met him, I was assured he is a gambler. Now am I to believe he is also a detective?"

"He is good at whatever requires adroit handling and a bit of . . . what shall we call it—firm persuasion?"

"I hope that making use of his persuasion doesn't entirely empty my purse," Deborah answered cautiously.

"I doubt it will; Sam Douglas owes me a good turn, and I will remind him of it when he presents his bill."

"Now I must get back to the office," Deborah said, "to clear things up before I leave for Ohio. Besides, this evening I am having dinner with Lemuel Froman and his little daughter."

After Deborah had hastened off, Wentworth remained at the table in thoughtful silence. I don't like what all this is doing, he thought. It has been such a little time since she was fresh and eager. Today there was too much responsibility and desperation about her . . . and a hint it may harden into utter ruthlessness. *By God, Lem Froman could likely prevent that from happening. His wife isn't the kind who will come back to him. If Froman has a lick of sense he had better climb out of his isolated, embittered Mormon shell and make love to Deborah—about the most ambitious young woman in Idaho.*

Chapter 12

THREE DAYS later, Deborah left Boise on an east-bound train just as darkness fell. The emigrant car had rolled out of Boise the previous morning; aboard it was a baled shipment of the best wool that Ramon Echiverri and his Basque friends had been able to select. In the car also was a disenchanted Idaho homesteader and enough of his goods to lend credence to this being an emigrant car entitled to special freight rates.

Unobtrusively, the second man who would accompany the wool shipment had also boarded the car before dawn. Jeff Harding had with him only a tarped bedroll, a black leather suitcase with a couple of changes of clothing, and the pair of holstered pistols that were becoming widely known. So far they had seldom been used, but little doubt remained that they represented trouble for those who engaged in the folly of destroying sheep and the men who herded or owned them. Now they would protect the shipment that well could be the best hope of Idaho wool growers.

Deborah had planned her schedule with both certainty and hope. Above all else she must be in Lorain, Ohio, within a few hours of the arrival of the emigrant car. But regardless of this she intended to have a full day in Ogden, Utah. An entire summer had passed since her graduation from the university in Salt Lake City; during this time she had received but one letter from Bishop Joshua Stannard, her stepfather. Enclosed with it were two pages written in pencil by her mother. Deborah realized at once that one or two pages had been removed from her mother's message and surmised these missing lines had told more of Rose Dexter Stannard's whereabouts and life than either the bishop or other Mormon churchmen in authority cared to have known or possibly made public.

Ramon Echiverri had insisted she make the journey in comfort, going so far as to purchase her round-trip ticket himself. Never before had she traveled in a railroad sleeping car or eaten meals in a dining car. For a time she watched the lights of small stations and towns slip by and listened to what seemed the loneliness of the whistle's wail. Her will was firm as she contemplated her stay-over in Ogden. She would be meeting with her stepfather, and the encounter was apt to be far from pleasant. Somehow—before her return to Boise—she intended to see her mother and the place where she had been spirited.

She thought of another and more reasonable request she would make of Bishop Stannard, of his fellow Church officials, and likely of Wilford Woodruff, the president and prophet of the Mormon Church.

The train came into the station at Ogden shortly after dawn. Deborah went outside and hailed a cab. She had decided to arrive at Bishop Stannard's home unannounced. Likely she would need every advantage in dealing with him; perhaps the element of surprise might prove helpful.

As the buggy traveled the streets of Ogden, Deborah noted the rapid and orderly growth of this second largest of Utah's cities. As always, the mountains of the Wasatch Range stood close and steep at the settlement's eastern edge; but now myriad trees, touched by autumnal colors, lent a pleasant glow of color across Ogden. Presently she gazed southward toward Salt Lake City, knowing that the place of her college years was only thirty miles distant. She had friends there with whom she longed to visit; yet the need for being in Ohio on time precluded any hope of her visiting the city and the university.

The cab pulled up before the large, gabled home of her stepfather. Deborah walked up a flagstone walk and lifted the door knocker. The door was opened partway, and Deborah gazed into the surprised and inquiring face of a dark-haired young woman who appeared scarcely older than herself.

"Good morning," Deborah managed to say politely, "I am looking for Bishop Joshua Stannard."

The two women stood scanning each other, Deborah seeing a woman clad in a wrinkled gingham dress who obviously had not yet had time to make herself presentable. Pulling at her apron was a bright-curled boy of perhaps four. Deborah was aware that the woman resented her. Now the young woman spoke.

"Bishop Stannard is not here at the moment; perhaps you can come back later?"

"It would be difficult. You see, I am just passing through Ogden and have little time. I am Deborah

Dexter, from Boise—and the bishop is my stepfather."

As the name sounded, the young woman stiffened and her face paled. "You're—" she murmured. "You mean you are—?"

"Yes, I am . . . the daughter of the bishop's other wife." As the young mother's face began to crumple, Deborah reached out to touch her hand reassuringly. "Please don't worry . . . or cry. I am not here to cause trouble." She reached out to pick up the little boy. "What is his name?" she asked.

"His name is Daniel, but we call him Danny." The woman waited, then said tentatively, "Perhaps you should come in and wait for Bishop Stannard. He should be back from the pharmacy any minute." She ushered Deborah into a semidark front parlor, then called an older woman from somewhere farther back in the house. "Sarah, please look after the child. I have company."

When they were alone and seated on a huge, leather-covered couch, the young woman spoke in a more assured way. "I don't believe I told you my name, Deborah. I am Abrigal."

"Yes, I already knew. You were widowed when quite young, and Bishop Stannard offered you and your first child a home."

There was a heavy step in the hallway and Bishop Stannard, clad in a dark suit and a ruffled white shirt and flowing tie, stood staring down at them. Deborah noticed that he had aged considerably and grown much heavier. After rather stilted introductions, his young wife hastened from the room.

Bishop Stannard closed a heavy door behind

her, then seated himself stiffly on a chair facing the couch. She became conscious of the bishop's gaze upon her. "I am traveling, Bishop," she said finally. "I'm going to Lorain, Ohio, on business. I must catch the eastbound train from San Francisco tomorrow morning."

"To Lorain," he nodded. "Then you will no doubt see my friend Nephi Oakes—if you attend our services in the church there."

She came to the point with an abruptness that was neither resentful nor laden with personal warmth. "Bishop Stannard, you must surely wonder why I have come here. Are you surprised that I should be here to ask a favor of you?"

His face became guarded, but he merely said, "Go on, Deborah. But if it is money . . . I must warn you immediately—"

Deborah's face flushed at his presumption. Despite her every intention of keeping the peace, she flared, "Listen, Bishop. I would never take one red cent from you. Nor have I need to."

His face told of his satisfaction in having angered her. "My, my, child, you always have been a spitfire. But what can I do for you?"

She told him then, in a rush of words, of her position and responsibilities with the Idaho Sheepmen's Association and of the possibility of wool contracts with the spinning mills headed by Nephi Oakes. "I am going to Lorain with a select shipment. Such contracts can mean untold improvement of conditions for our ranchers . . . the producers."

Stannard was now leaning forward, intent on her every word. "Deborah," he said studiedly, "you must have come a long way—in a business

272

sense—in a short time. You are to be congratulated. But what is it you wish of me?"

"Two things. Just two," she shot back. "First, the freight rates charged by the railroads on eastbound wool shipments are ruinous. Downright robbery. The contracts with Mr. Oakes will do us no good unless we can find a way to lessen shipping costs."

"But I am not a railroad official."

"Of course you aren't. But you *are* a high officer of the most powerful force in this part of the West. Many of your Church people in Idaho, and no doubt in Utah and elsewhere, are farmers and ranchers. Wool producers. They also would benefit from reasonable freight rates; perhaps our association could benefit them in other ways."

Bishop Stannard rose, paced the floor, and then drew close to look into her now animated face. "Just what is it you propose I do?"

Her gaze locked with his, and momentarily she showed the aggressive hardness that had disturbed assayer Frank Wentworth. "What I want is just this," she said firmly. "Take this matter before the higher officials of the Mormon Church—all the way to the Council of Twelve Apostles if need be."

He turned, faced a window and seemed to study the boughs of a blue spruce. "The point you make is that the Church should bring pressure upon the railroad, seeking a rate reduction. Perhaps, Deborah, the idea has merit, but I will have to study it at length."

"Which won't do a bit of good, Bishop. Either we get speedy rate relief, or much of the wool-producing West is headed for bankruptcy. How much deep thought does it take to realize that?" She paused, her voice becoming thoughtful as she went on. "I am not asking you to do this by yourself. Already I have talked to the leaders of the Basque people and asked their help. I am going to ask others. Nephi Oakes. Lemuel Froman. Even a powerful farmowner I know in Idaho. I'm sure you have heard of him . . . Henry Carswell."

He nodded. "I remember meeting him once when you lived in the town of Bonanza. A capable, forceful man."

"Yes . . . and he will probably be Idaho's next secretary of state."

"Do you realize," Stannard persisted, "that the Union Pacific Railroad officials in Omaha will be hard to deal with in this matter?"

She rose and walked to stand beside him at the window. Then she said with certainty, "I also know that you can be persuasive—and that the hierarchy of your Church wields almost unbelievable power in this part of the West."

He smiled for the first time as he answered, "Deborah, perhaps you overrate us. I wish our voices could be heard more loudly and with less bias in Washington—at the White House and in Congress."

"That day will come . . . now that the Church has—" She broke off, not adding that the abolition of polygamy would aid the Mormon cause.

"At any rate, I will mention the matter to my superiors in Salt Lake City; I have to attend a meeting tomorrow."

"Will you, Bishop Stannard? The Church could help us—and their own causes. How soon do you suppose we can have an answer?"

"I have no idea, Deborah; sometimes it takes months for such things. At other times some sort of heavenly miracle seems to work and we have a solution within a week or so." Stannard's face was tired but not unkind as he faced her again. "You said you had two reasons for wanting to see me. I believe I already sense the second one. But . . . but go ahead."

"I won't take long," she reassured him, and then asked abruptly, "Where is my mother?"

The churchman recoiled sharply, his look becoming stony. "Deborah, I am not at liberty to reveal that. I can assure you that she is well."

"The hell she is!" Deborah shouted, and knew that she was close to tears. "What have you and your Mormon cohorts done with her—*to* her? Many weeks ago I got a short letter. The only one since she was dragged away in the night what seemed like ages ago. The letter had been opened and parts of it deleted. It told me nothing. All that was left was a hint she still is in her right mind. That and a couple of Mormon platitudes."

"Deborah . . . daughter . . . can't you take my word that she is well and happy?"

"But still a prisoner of sorts in a sealed-off place somewhere in the wilderness. And why, Bishop Stannard, why? Well I'll tell you why—so that you still can have two wives. So that you can maintain a wife and create children here in Ogden, yet have my mother's heart and soul and body when you tire of your younger woman."

He drew back an arm and for a moment it seemed he would strike her. Then he said, "Deborah, it is best you leave this house. I can tell you no more. I have been sworn to secrecy."

"So I am to leave, learning nothing of the one person I love above all others—my mother? All right, Bishop. I will go—quickly. But this I promise you: I am going to find my mother if I have to move heaven and hell to do so. If it takes the rest of my life." She stopped, breathed heavily, and strode toward the hall. Then she turned, defeat seeming to close about her. "I suppose," she murmured, "that I may as well forget about any help from your Church people in getting freight-rate reductions."

He rubbed his forehead as though trying to ease vast perplexity and pain, then he reassured her. "Daughter, that is another matter. A business matter. I will send a letter to you at Boise when I learn if progress can be made with the railroad."

She moved into the hallway, then stood torn and somehow reluctant to leave him thus. A moment later she stepped again into the parlor, to lay both of her trembling hands on his arms. "Bishop, why does it have to be like this between us? With the specter of my mother always keeping us at each other's throat?" When he lifted a whitened face, she kissed him on the cheek. When she again sought the hallway, he did not follow her. She moved to let herself out of the house, but a voice halted her. Abrigal Stannard was standing close by and extending a hand in which was a slip of paper. She said, "Here is the recipe I promised you. The one for blueberry muffins. Let me show you to the door, Deborah."

Somewhat bewildered, Deborah would have spoken of the slip of paper, but Abrigal's hand had lifted in a slight but silencing gesture. So instead

Deborah said, "Thank you, Abrigal, for making me feel so much at ease. Your children must be a joy. Perhaps someday—" She touched the young mother's cheek in an understanding way and left the house.

At the nearest street corner she found a cab. She settled into the seat with eager curiosity prodding her, but it wasn't until the vehicle was a full three blocks from the Stannard house that she unfolded the slip of paper in her hand. It read:

"Try the Greys River valley in Wyoming. Somewhere beyond a settlement called Afton."

She exhaled a breath so excited the driver glanced at her with curiosity. "Please don't mind me." Deborah forced her voice to seem casual. "I've just been given a wonderful . . . wonderful recipe."

Presently the driver said, "The Stannards are right good people. It is too bad about that oldest boy of theirs."

Deborah took a little while to respond, for her mind was reeling with the excitement of what the note revealed. At last she held in her hand a clue as to Rose Dexter's whereabouts.

The driver spoke again. "But it's likely the lad is better off at that place in Salt Lake City. Likely Mrs. Stannard told you about the boy, Peter. He was a rather small tyke and she was already a widow—had been for nigh onto a year—when the bishop married her and provided a home for her and the boy. Bishop Stannard did it *even though*

277

the boy was blind. Yes, ma'am . . . lost his sight in the same accident that killed his father."

Deborah could contain her curiosity no longer. Words of urgency escaped her. "My God—how awful. And I never heard about it. What . . . what happened?"

The driver reined his horse to a slower gait. "Ma'am, my name is Stover—Cliff Stover. I used to farm a bit up near Brigham City, north of here. That is where it happened. Abrigal was married to a young fellow named Ben Moffitt. When their boy came along, Ben was crazy about him; used to take him everywhere as soon as the little fellow could toddle. That day Ben was working in a rocky piece of land along the foothills. He wanted to plant a peach orchard and was blasting stone so he could cart it away. Something went God-awful wrong. A charge of black powder exploded while Ben was tamping it into a drill hole. The boy must have been beside him, for when Ben was killed, his son took part of the pure hell in his face." The driver paused and shuddered, then went on. "It was a young neighbor who found them; his name was Nephi Oakes, and his folks had a farm right close to mine. Nephi was hunting rabbits and heard the little tad's screams."

Deborah was breathing heavily, spellbound. Now she asked, "Do you mean the Nephi Oakes who became a Church missionary . . . and later moved to Ohio?"

The driver asked in a surprised voice, "Do you know Nephi?"

"Yes. I've known him for many years. But the little boy?" Deborah urged. "Are they sure he is permanently blinded? And why did his mother

278

and Bishop Stannard send him off to an institution in Salt Lake City? Many blind children live pretty normal lives at home."

"I've heard that a couple of doctors hold that the youngster's sight is gone for good; another one isn't so sure. Now, about the Stannards. Abrigal has a child now by the bishop, and likely he wouldn't leave her the time for caring for a blind one. Besides, there are some who say Bishop Stannard can't bear to have that sightless youngster around. Somehow Stannard blames himself for what happened. He was the one who suggested Ben Moffitt blast the rocks away for an orchard —he even furnished the powder."

Even before the talkative driver had finished, Deborah Dexter felt an urging and a conviction she knew she would be unable to deny. Somehow she was going to see Abrigal Stannard's blind child. She had not the slightest idea how she would greet the child, or what she might be able to do for him. She hastened to ask the driver, "Is there any way I could get to Salt Lake City today? And then return in time to catch the eastbound train from San Francisco in the morning?"

He stared at her unbelievingly. "You mean, ma'am, that—"

"Yes. I want to see him . . . the little blind boy. You see—in a way he is related to me." She did not add that she hoped also, upon reaching Ohio, to give Nephi Oakes firsthand information.

"So you're the lad's kin. Lady, you go ahead to Salt Lake City. It's about an hour's ride. In the morning, I will have your baggage at the Union

Pacific depot. Holy Jerusalem—wait until I tell my wife about this!"

The following day, as the Union Pacific Railroad's fastest passenger train carried her eastward across the loneliness of Wyoming, Deborah spent much of her time curled up on her seat in the sleeping car. Just now she had little desire for the company of other passengers or to even scan the passing panorama of desert and rangeland.

She recalled her brief meeting with eight-year-old Peter Moffitt. She found him easily through the University of Utah's hospital. Two facts aided her: She was a graduate of the school, and, more important now, a stepdaughter of Bishop Joshua Stannard. She scarcely heeded the facts that the bishop was not aware of her coming to Salt Lake City and had not given her permission to see Abrigal's son.

The elderly matron of a home for blind children escorted Deborah into a well-lighted, second-story room of an older brownstone in sight of the Mormon Tabernacle. Peter was standing alone in the room, his hands clutching a windowsill and his face uplifted to the warmth of the afternoon sun. The matron stood near the door and said quietly, "Peter, there is a lady here to see you."

He turned, then eagerly spoke one word: "Mama?"

Deborah dropped on her knees beside him, letting her hands touch his arms. He was tall and held himself proudly. "No, Peter. I am not your mother. My name is Deborah . . . Deborah Dexter. I am your stepsister."

As the Pullman wheels clicked off the miles to Ohio, Deborah thought: *Greys River valley . . . Somewhere beyond . . . Afton.* Her mother.

Deborah examined a map of the region. Close to the Idaho border was Star Valley, a narrow section of country surrounded by mountains. Within the valley was the settlement of Afton. Farther north was an irregular and somewhat curving line that marked the course of the Snake River from its birthplace in Yellowstone National Park, down through Jackson Hole and finally westward into Idaho. Another notation on the map caused her interest to increase—a stream coming from the southeast to join the Snake River almost at the Idaho border. *Greys River.*

When she descended from the Pullman in Lorain at noon of the third day, both Nephi Oakes and Jeff Harding were awaiting her on the platform. Excitement clutched her. It had been several years since she had last seen Nephi Oakes.

"Welcome to town, Deborah," Nephi said, smiling. "We have made reservations for you in a hotel I believe you will enjoy."

"Nephi, how thoughtful of you." She gazed appraisingly at him. "You look better fed and more successful than the Mormon missionary who rode west from Nebraska with us."

Before he could respond, the second man awaiting her stepped forward, holding a dusty stockmen's hat in his hand. His height caused her to peer upward into a weathertanned face highlighted by a moustache and by gray eyes that were friendly but seemed ever to move, as though seeking out the unusual or the dangerous.

"Jeff, how relieved I am to see you got here safely. Is the shipment—"

Jeff Harding touched her arm reassuringly. "Every pound of wool is safe in the best storeroom of Mr. Oakes' spinning mill."

Deborah nodded, but then an exciting certainty entered her mind. Jeff Harding seemed ever on the move as he fulfilled his duties with western sheep growers. Doubtless he had covered about every mile of Idaho—and very close to Idaho's eastern border lay Star Valley and the town of Afton and Greys River, in Wyoming. Right then she would have asked him about those places, but she remained silent. She had always liked and trusted Nephi Oakes. But he was even now a high-ranking Mormon who in all likelihood knew more than he would ever tell of the mysterious village of secluded wives.

Deborah Dexter and Jeff Harding remained in Lorain for the better part of five days. The mill could use the Idaho wool. When the contract was negotiated, Deborah was pleased to have Harding's opinion that it was equitable and would prove a boon to the Idaho wool growers. However, an ominous but vital clause was inserted: The contract would be valid only if freight rates could be secured from the railroads that would make the wool shipments both feasible and profitable.

"There may be some delay to see that lower rates will make them more money in the long run," Jeff Harding explained. "Use of an eastbound emigrant car is just a stopgap. We'll have to find another way."

"Our company will work for reasonable tariffs," Oakes assured them. "We want your Idaho wool. We need it."

Deborah revealed the plan she had broached to Bishop Stannard for help from the top leaders of the Mormon Church.

Nephi Oakes listened and then stared at her almost in disbelief. "You asked Stannard to do that? I have heard . . . that you and he haven't gotten along well."

"Sometimes I hate his . . . his guts," Deborah conceded. "But I have to admit that as my stepfather he has been pretty sensible and even agreeable—save in one terribly important respect."

Nephi Oakes sighed regretfully. "Yes, Deborah, I know how deeply you must be concerned. Hopefully before long—"

Deborah knew that Oakes was trying to urge patience and restraint, but that he would not violate the confidence of another Church official. She changed the subject by saying, "Nephi, I went to visit Abrigal Stannard's little boy—the one you found after that terrible accident."

"You did?" he asked with eager surprise. "You saw him in Salt Lake City?"

"Yes, after talking to his mother, I had a great need to see him. He is a fine young fellow."

"So was his father, Ben Moffitt. Tell me, Deborah, how does he seem to be adjusting to blindness? Did he seem resentful or rebellious?"

"Not in the least," she reassured him. "He seems to be just a normal . . . and very lovable

283

boy." She paused, remembering Peter's intense face turned to catch the light. "Nephi, has all medical help been exhausted? Is he really apt to remain blind forever?"

Deborah knew that her return to Boise must be delayed. She had vowed to see her mother. As she darkened her hotel room and crawled into bed that night the enormous task of reaching Rose Dexter Stannard caused her to shiver in nervous anticipation of what might lie ahead.

With their business finished in Lorain, Deborah Dexter and Jeff Harding took an alternate route, via the Burlington Lines, to Omaha. They chose to cross the farmlands of the Midwest by daylight, for Deborah wanted to see both the Mississippi and Missouri rivers and the verdant crops and orchards and meadows of this area. But her mind kept turning to the venture she had determined to undertake.

They transferred to a Union Pacific train at Omaha and were heading west at express-train speed. They were sitting in a comfortably appointed parlor car when Harding picked up a railroad timetable and said, "Deborah, before dawn we'll pass through Box Butte; soon after sunup we will come into Cheyenne."

Thought of Box Butte and its nearness to her childhood home in Banner County brought her mind quickly to her father, to the times they had delighted in being with each other, to his perpetual sureness that better days must lie just over a horizon of tomorrows, and to the small, barbed-wire-fenced bit of Nebraska homestead land in which he now was buried. She longed to visit his grave, to see her past . . .

Deborah heaved a reluctant but decisive sigh. She could not live in the past; but she could live the spirit of her father's hope. Suddenly she was aware that the time had come. She must now reveal to Jeff Harding her resolve to make an even longer and surely more hazardous trip—into Wyoming's Star Valley and the sealed Mormon village on Greys River.

"Jeff, have you ever been in a place called Star Valley in Wyoming, to a town named Afton?"

"Just once, Deborah. It is Mormon country. Good meadows and spectacular mountain scenery. There is a lot of wilderness up there. And some of the law is still carried in a gun there."

Deborah seemed to absorb every word in silence. Then she asked, "There is a river besides the Snake, isn't there? Greys River?"

"Yes," he said, nodding, "I rode past the spot where it comes into the Snake. Almost utter and isolated wilderness." Harding paused; when he spoke again, both his eyes and his voice were searching. "But why, Deborah? There is something behind these questions . . . something that's troubling you."

Deborah told him of her plan to find her mother, then handed him the few lines slipped to her by Abrigal Stannard.

Harding grew thoughtful. "I've heard of such sealed villages, Deborah; but in all my travels I have never stumbled onto one."

She stared at him, but his words caused no lessening of her determination to find Rose Stannard,

the third wife of a bishop of the Church of Jesus
Christ of Latter-day Saints.

"Jeff, I must tell you. I won't be returning to
Boise with you. Perhaps I won't get there for a
week or even a month. *Somehow* I am going to
find and get into that town of . . . of deceived and
imprisoned women. I am getting off this train at
Ogden and—"

"God in heaven," Jeff Harding said in worried
awe, "I don't believe anything I or anyone else can
say will stop you."

"Nothing at all, Jeff."

Harding looked about the car, making sure they
would not be overheard. Then he dropped his voice
into a murmur of urgency. "First, get this straight
—with not one damned bit of stubborn objection.
You'll head toward Greys River, all right—but *I*
will be right along with you. It will be risky and
maybe impossible for two of us to get to that
hideaway. By yourself, Debbie, it could be sui-
cidal."

She smiled, half relief and half sarcasm. "Talk
of *my* being stubborn. Jeff Harding, I would be
wasting my breath to say I am going to try it
alone."

"You always did catch on quick," he said,
smiling. "Now: Your idea of striking north from
Ogden ain't worth a hoot. You would be in Mormon country all the way—and watched long before you got near to Star Valley." He glanced
again at the railroad timetable and a Union Pacific system map. "Have your gear packed and be
ready to get off this train at Rock Springs, Wyoming."

"But that would be a couple of hundred miles

from Ogden," she protested. "And an awfully long way from Star Valley."

"And likely a safer approach," Harding said. "Deborah, I know something of the mountain ranges of Wyoming. Greys River has to rise in high country west of the Green River Valley. There is a place up there called LaBarge Meadows. An old-timer who had trapped beaver told me about it once. It seems the Meadows are pretty far up on LaBarge Creek, a stream that dumps into the Green River. I remember his remarking that the Meadows were about at the top of a divide . . . that it wasn't more than a short mule ride to where water flowed westward, scurrying toward the Snake River drainage. I have an idea the water he spoke of might have been in creeks that join Greys River. If so, we might sneak in the back door to the Mormon hideout."

"I have money enough," she replied eagerly, "so we can buy a couple of horses . . . and supplies."

"I could manage that too," he assured her. "But a couple of other things sort of trouble me."

"Like what, Jeff?"

"Like the weather. We're well into September now, and a mountain storm could hit in the high country anytime. Dump a lot of snow."

"You think that is likely?" Deborah asked anxiously.

"It could happen. Sometimes, except for frost and a light touch, the weather stays open well into October."

"I am willing to take that chance—if you are," she said quickly. Then when he nodded, Deborah asked, "You say something else troubles you. What is it?"

For the first time since she had known him, Jeff Harding seemed ill at ease, even embarrassed. She studied him for a time, then when she spoke there was sureness in her words and her manner. "Jeff, you're thinking of us . . . traveling together and even having to share camps. An unmarried man and woman."

"We'd likely get along better . . . be safer . . . if people took it for granted you are my wife, Deborah. You know what busybodies, even prudes, people can be even out in the back country."

Deborah looked at him and then laughed softly. "Jeff Harding, are you by any chance suggesting that we get married?"

"My great God—no! What an idea—with me maybe twenty years older than you!"

She eyed him in an amused and somehow disturbing way, then voiced words both encouraging and firm. "Mr. Harding, it is fun to see you flustered; it never happened to me before. No, we won't get hitched. But why can't we just let people assume we are? That we're on a vacation and exploring trip up toward Yellowstone Park?"

Harding grinned both admiration and relief. "Debbie, I've never quite been able to figure you out. Probably never will be. Or would be—even if you were Mrs. Jeff Harding."

They laughed so loudly that a portly, middle-aged fellow who had been sleeping a few seats away roused up and glared his disapproval.

They had no way of knowing that many miles to the southwest, where the Green River leaves the Flaming Gorge and hurries toward the dinosaur fossil cliffs of Colorado, events were transpiring that would affect their plans and their lives.

Chapter 13

THE SUN was scarcely half an hour above a rock-
and sage-strewn ridge eastward when Matt
Warner left the cabin and strode to the water's
edge. Instinct and the time and place caused him
to sweep the horizon in all directions with a wary
and appraising gaze. The stream, shrunken now
and showing sandbars, was the Green River at the
spot known as Little Hole, a dozen miles downstream from the multihued and crag-guarded canyons that John Wesley Powell had named
Flaming Gorge. To the west was the forested rise
of the high Uinta Mountains. In other directions
were brush- and juniper-covered slopes, now
touched with the yellow and gold hues of autumn.
Above the small and windowless log cabin was a
lazy lift of woodsmoke, born of the fire with which
Warner had prepared an early breakfast.

Presently he squatted down, seized a handful of
sand, and began scouring grease and flapjack bits
from an iron skillet. When the task was completed, he rinsed the black skillet in the river's
flow. Then he dashed water onto his face and the
arms up which he had rolled the sleeves of a
checked flannel shirt. The strengthening sunlight
glinted from his sandy hair and touched eyes that
were brown and intense. When at last he rose to
his feet, he again searched the slopes and the river's canyon. He was just short of thirty years old,

of medium height, and marked by the litheness of one whose time had been spent outdoors and in the saddle.

When his gaze turned eastward down the river, he straightened abruptly. From beyond a willowed curve, two riders had appeared guiding their mounts along the opposite shore. He sensed that they had sighted him at almost the same instant; then reasoned that they had been able to see the smoke from his cabin chimney for at least a mile. They were not yet in hailing distance as Warner laid a hand on the .38-gauge revolver at his hip. As the riders came steadily on, a bit of grimness touched his face; with measured steps he strode to the cabin and through the doorway. Half a minute later he reappeared, and now a Winchester repeating rifle lay in his hand, with his finger within the trigger guard.

The riders reached a spot directly across the river and halted horses that were obviously tired. Both horsemen wore ranch garb and had rolled slickers forming small packs tied by leather thongs behind their saddles. They faced each other for a brief exchange of low-spoken words; then the bulkier of the two called aloud across the autumn-dwindled stream.

"Matt . . . Matt Warner . . . is that you?"

The scratchy ring of the words, together with what his eyes now revealed of the pair, caused Matt Warner's face to take on added caution and something akin to disgust. "Yeah, Britt, it's me. Who the hell did you expect, Porter Rockwell?"

"Not by a jugful; I'm keeping clear of that Mormon enforcer." There was evident irritation and resentment as Britt Fullmer spoke the words.

291

Then in milder tones he asked, "You wouldn't have a cup of coffee and maybe a sourdough biscuit for me and my partner?"

"It might depend on who you're riding with," Warner countered. He was scrutinizing the second horseman, a tall individual with shoulder-length black hair, who had not yet spoken.

"I'll vouch for him, Warner; he is one of our kind. Name is Decker—Squint Decker."

"Christ Almighty, no—not him!" Warner whispered to himself. Then after thinking over the situation he called across the stream, "Splash your way on over . . . and careful of that hole about fifteen feet upstream. It's deep." As he uttered the warning, he thought, Why don't I just let both of the bastards fall in and drown?

When their horses had brought them safely to the north bank, Britt Fullmer looked about with an air of satisfaction. "You've got a pretty likely-looking camp here, Warner. Don't suppose you would mind company for a month or so. We gave the slip to a posse down in Colorado, then rode like hell day and night. Swapped horses a couple of times with obliging ranchers . . . while they were asleep. Damn, it's good to be here." With the words Britt Fullmer started to swing from the saddle. He dropped again into the saddle as Matt Warner's voice, suddenly sharp and cold, cut through the morning air.

"Hold it, Britt—and you too, fellow." He was gazing with ill-concealed contempt at Squint Decker as he continued, "You ain't going to perch here. Now get me straight, both of you. There's a pot of coffee inside . . . and you can throw some breakfast together. I'll even allow a couple of hours for your horses to get a bellyful of grass. Then you're heading out—any damn direction you please." As he spoke, Warner had stepped back until both men were under the menace of his Winchester.

Shock and fury tore at Fullmer's face. "Who in double hell do you think you are, Warner? The last time I knew, this layout belonged to Butch Cassidy." His eyes roved the glade and the cabin as he asked, "Ain't Butch about?"

Warner did not answer at once. Instead his full attention had turned to Squint Decker and the manner in which the angular-faced rider's hand was edging toward a holstered weapon.

"Touch that and you'll hit the ground a dead man," Warner warned in words resembling steel chips.

"What in hell is eating you?" Britt Fullmer continued. "After our riding together—you and me."

"We never rode *together*," Warner corrected. "Both of us rode for Cassidy—and with him—but not together."

"You claiming to be pure and innocent? Better than me?"

"Nope. No better, Britt." Warner's eyes had narrowed with watchfulness and contempt as he added, "But maybe I am a damned sight more choosy about who I pal around with."

"Meaning what?" Fullmer bristled.

"Hell, Britt . . . do I have to spell it out for you? I don't like killers—especially like your pal, Squint, here. One who would gun down a boy who wasn't even toting a gun."

"You're a liar—a son-of-a-bitch liar!" Squint Decker's voice had become shrill with fury. His hand seemed about to claw toward the weapon at his side. "That kid was—"

"I know what he was," Warner said quickly. "He was a Mexican boy . . . about twelve years old. Word gets about, even here along the Green River."

"What I want to know," Britt Fullmer cut in, "is where I can find Cassidy. Butch is a friend of mine; he'll surer'n hell have your hide for trying to drive us off like dogs, Warner."

The rifle was still upon the two unwelcome riders as Warner answered, "I'll take my chances on that. Now . . . both of you just ease your way up that hillside quicklike. And get out of my sight." He waited until they had reined their horses to leave, then added, "You may find Cassidy in Rock Springs, but more likely up around Lander or the Jackson Hole country. He knows about the Mexican boy too."

Matt Warner spoke no more but watched intently as the two rode toward a ridge, crested it, and were out of sight. "Likely they will head for Montana," he told himself. "Try to winter with the Plummer outfit up there."

Just beyond the ridge, in a juniper grove, Squint Decker jerked his black gelding to a stop. "I've a mind to ride back there and put a slug through that fellow, Warner. Nobody orders me around."

Britt Fullmer drew alongside him and stared. Then he said, "Squint, you are more of a fool than I thought. Know what? You ride back there—or even try to sneak back—and Matt Warner will kill you."

"That's your say-so, Fullmer. You notice he

didn't do one damned thing when I called him a son-of-a-bitch."

"For which you ought to climb down and offer up a prayer. Warner could have wiped you out in two seconds . . . and maybe me too. Take my advice, Squint. Leave him alone. You don't even stack high enough in the saddle to succeed in shooting a man like Matt in the back. Why else would he be Butch Cassidy's right-hand man?"

Squint Decker was urging his horse ahead as he boasted, "Just for now, Britt. Just for now. But one of these days I'll meet up with Warner again and call his hand."

"Shit!" was Fullmer's reply. He rode morosely on toward the distant Wyoming border. About him there was a growing and gnawing regret. Teaming up with Squint Decker hadn't worked out very well, because Fullmer now found himself on the run and not comfortably far ahead of a Colorado posse. It had caused him to be denied a hiding place on the Green River by a man whose friendship he had counted on to help provide safety and shelter and grub until spring thaws would come . . . and with them his possible acceptance by the Wild Bunch and its mastermind, Butch Cassidy.

Chapter 14

At a livery stable in Rock Springs Jeff Harding and Deborah happened across information that helped to speed them on their way northward toward Greys River.

"We're heading north . . . up toward Yellowstone Park," Harding told the white-whiskered proprietor. "We'd hoped you might have some saddles and a pack animal for sale."

"Matter of fact, I do have. But just now I don't have horses you would want for the trip. Next week, though—"

Harding shook his head. "Sorry. That would be too late."

"Wait a minute, partner," the oldster hastened to say. "Suppose I could outfit you with gear and fix it so you could get horses a far piece up north, up by Big Piney? It so happens a stage line runs once a week to Big Piney. You'd be in luck, too; the stage leaves today, just after noon. I could see to getting your gear—if you buy it now—loaded onto that stage for you."

Thus it was that Deborah Dexter and Jeff Harding boarded the northbound stage. In Harding's pocket was a letter from the proprietor asking that a rancher, whose property was just outside Big Piney, supply them with horses. The proprietor's parting comment as he watched them climb aboard the stage brought a smile to their faces.

"Mister, watch out for them bear in the Yellowstone—and take care of that pretty daughter of yours."

The stagecoach run from Rock Springs to Big Piney was an all-daylight run, with its course largely up the eastern side of the Green River Valley. As the driver pointed off westward with his whip, they could already see the forested rise of the Salt River Range, source of Greys River.

They came into Big Piney as darkness of the second day was gathering. A light rain was falling, and the brilliant yellow of lowland trees spoke ominously of the nearness of oncoming winter. Deborah noted the size of the hamlet with concern—just a meager cluster of cabins strung along an already muddy street. Together with their riding gear they had bought a white canvas tent. Jeff Harding seemed to read her thoughts and said, "I'll see what kind of shelter is to be had."

What proved to be available was literally a godsend. Harding was allowed to spread his gear on the counter of a tiny trading post/post office. The loneliness of the owner's wife, and her great desire to talk to another woman, won Deborah a cot with blankets in a nearby bedroom.

The rain continued for two days and then cleared into sunshine and briskly cool air. Westward, the mountains had been touched with light snow and gleamed white and sentrylike. In search of the promised horses, Harding struck out afoot for the ranch mentioned by the liveryman in Rock Springs.

The hours dragged on. Still Jeff Harding had not returned.

Deborah's mind turned to her utter dependence on Harding. She had known him for several years. Or did she really know him? From Boise he went on his quiet and seemingly secretive way, performing his duties for the sheep ranchers of the West. Never had he spoken to her of his past, his parents, or the place of his upbringing. Her train of thought led to more facets of her relationship with him. With no other man would she have undertaken a mission such as theirs to this raw frontier country. But how would they react when they must be alone through days . . . and nights?

Harding reappeared shortly after noon, riding in from the southeast astride a sturdy and spirited roan mare. He was clutching a length of lariat rope that led to the halters of a gray gelding and a smaller black mare.

The following day they were riding westward when sunshine first struck the mountains looming ahead. They moved in single file, with Harding leading the way and the packhorse, named Babe, bringing up the rear. There was movement and sound along their course—the flash of a mountain jay, the lifted heads of distant but curious antelope, and the circling watchfulness of an eagle overhead. They had chosen to follow South Piney Creek, for they had heard that its headwaters could not be far from LaBarge Creek.

They stopped to prepare a midday meal at the beginning of a canyon where the course of the South Piney began a steep climb. The spot offered dry limbs of both pine and aspen that could easily be gathered for a small fire; there was ample green grass and the clear, rock-rippled water of the stream. They judged they had covered eighteen or twenty miles behind them; they had scant knowledge of the distance ahead to LaBarge Creek and Greys River.

Deborah was measuring water and coffee into a tin pail, and Jeff had knelt close to the creek to wash dust from his face when they first realized they were not alone in the small canyon. The first warning came as Harding's roan mare, named Pet, flung her head into watchful posture, let her ears move forward, and then gave a soft whinny. With almost a single movement, Harding was on his feet and reaching to pull a rifle from the saddle scabbard at the mare's side. Then with a wordless movement he cautioned Deborah to silence.

Thirty seconds went by; there were only the sounds of the crackling fire and the murmur of the creek. Then there was the sound of hoofbeats and a faint murmur of creaking leather. From around a rocky point and through a scattering of pine trees two horsemen broke into sight and stopped abruptly. Jeff Harding noticed first the cautiousness of the strangers; then he was staring at their mounts, horses in poor condition, and evidently having been pushed almost to the limit of endurance. Only desperate men would ride their mounts to the edge of destruction, Harding thought.

The bulkier of the newcomers spoke first. "Friend, how about pointing that rifle somewhere else? We mean you no harm."

It was the reaction of the second stranger, a man with sharply pointed face and continually narrowed eyes, that brought added caution to Harding. This is no casual meeting, he thought.

They've picked up our trail and followed us. Fresh horses could mean life or death to them. Our horses! His mind raced. First of all, they must not sense his suspicion. It was important that the two not ride on ahead of him and Deborah; ambush or surprise attack must be averted.

With one hand Harding lowered the rifle, but he was aware of the speed with which his other could draw the holstered six-gun at his side. And now he spoke almost indifferently. "Light down and rest your horses. I'm Harding—Jeff Harding. Up this way to study the sheep graze and do a bit of fishing." He waited to see if mention of his name would bring a reaction. It seemed momentarily that the thin-faced visitor was about to speak to his companion, but he did not, and instead had turned his squinting gaze upon Deborah as she stood above the campfire.

The bulkier of the intruders spoke again. "We could sure use some coffee. Grub too, if you've got it to spare. Me . . . my name is Whitley. Joe Whitley. My friend is plain old Hank."

Harding knew the man was lying, but he ignored the lie. "Tell you what, gents," he said in unconcerned tones. "My wife there and I are on our honeymoon. My map shows there's a meadow upstream a piece. Likely with beaver ponds. And fish. We're going to mosey on up there. Why don't you fellows finish fixing the coffee?" He turned to Deborah, asking, "How about leaving some bread and cold beef for Mr. Whitley and Hank?" As he spoke, Jeff Harding was picking up the reins of their three horses. Presently the strangers slid from their saddles, watching hungrily as Deborah unpacked the food and placed it on the grass beside the campfire. His eyes were cold and calculating as he noticed that both strangers had revolvers slung low at their sides. If they were to make a play for the weapons, he must be clear of the horses and able to draw instantly. The lean-faced one seemed on the verge of gunplay, then seemed to think better of it and tore wolfishly at the bread and meat.

They're on the dodge all right, Harding thought. And maybe haven't eaten for a day or so. He stared more carefully at the one called Hank and tried to remember . . . to remember . . .

Harding motioned Deborah to mount up and then quickly yielded the reins of the packhorse to her. But his gaze remained with endless caution upon the two at the campfire.

"Seems you're in one hell of a hurry to shove off," the one calling himself Whitley said sourly.

"Just be plenty sure you bring our coffee pail when you come on up to the meadow," Harding countered. With deliberately cautious but sure movements he urged Deborah's mount and his own into motion. As they rode clear of the campsite and into the screening trees his gaze remained on the pair beside the fire.

They were a quarter mile from the camp and had rounded an abutment of the canyon wall when Jeff Harding's eyes widened and a low whistle escaped him. Deborah glanced anxiously back, then asked, "Jeff . . . are you all right? What happened?"

He spurred his horse into a faster gait and said, "Let's get out of here quick; we're two of the luckiest people alive."

Seeing the grimness on his face she dug her

heels into the gray gelding's flanks while jerking at the reins of the packhorse.

"Deborah . . . that man—the sour-faced, narrow-eyed one. Now I'm *sure* I know who he is."

"He looks sneaky—and mean," she said.

"That isn't half of it. His name is Squint Decker. When I was close to Durango, Colorado, before they called me to Boise to go East with you, I heard about him. The lawmen were looking all over hell's half acre for him."

Deborah's face paled, but her voice kept steady as she asked, "Why? What was he wanted for?"

For an instant it seemed that Jeff was loath to tell her. Then with crisp words he said, "Squint Decker killed a young boy. A Mexican kid who wasn't carrying even a slingshot."

"Oh, my God . . . how awful."

"It's him, all right. But I don't know who the other one is."

Presently they were beyond the canyon and onto a grassy stretch of meadow; beyond this the forest thickened and climbed along steep mountain slopes. Jeff sensed that beyond the ridge they would come onto the course of LaBarge Creek. He turned to Deborah. "We've got to keep moving," he urged. "Those fellows won't linger long after they bolt down something to eat."

"Their horses were about done in," she commented.

"Which is all the more reason they want ours. Plus our gear, our grub, and our guns. They'll be trailing us night and day."

Deborah glanced in agitation back along the course they had come since getting free of the camp and their unwanted guests. "I sure hated to give those rascals our coffee . . . and our dinner."

Harding laughed ruefully as he sought out the easiest way to begin climbing the ridge. "Better to go hungry and get away from them, Debbie, than find ourselves stranded without horses and maybe even our hides."

Her face flushed with anger as she asked, "Isn't there any law around here? A sheriff? A United States marshal we can report them to?"

"Debbie, there's likely no law within fifty or sixty miles. Maybe farther." His voice was concerned and patient as he went on, "The Mormon settlements of Star Valley are a long way west of here, the other side of the entire Salt River Range of mountains. Besides, how welcome would we be if we went prowling into a Mormon settlement? No, Debbie . . . right now we've got one thing going for us: Our horses are fresh and in good shape. The ones Whitley and Decker are astride can't make very good time until they have rested a bit and got their bellies full of grass. We had best ride steady for a long time. At least until it is too dark to get about."

It was thus that this day they eluded the two desperate men whose trail had led from far south in Colorado to one of the hideouts of Butch Cassidy in Utah and then northward. As Jeff Harding, wise to the ways of outlaws, mulled the appearance of the fat rider and of Squint Decker, a pattern seemed to emerge. In all probability the two outlaws had not meant to ride westward along South Piney Creek and enter this area that would offer neither food nor an opportunity for a robbery. Likely, Harding reasoned, they were heading north along the Green River Valley to head out for the Jackson Hole country and then on into Montana. Somehow they cut our trail this morning and decided we would be easy prey for things they need badly. They won't give up easily.

For the ensuing hours, as the afternoon wore on and evening shadows lengthened, Jeff Harding and Deborah rode westward. After cresting the ridge and dropping swiftly along slopes with scattered timber, they came onto a larger stream that both of them surmised to be LaBarge Creek. They rested their mounts for a few minutes, then rode on. Deborah managed to paw into the packhorse's burden and assemble a dry sandwich as they rode. They washed it down with creek water and kept on their way.

Darkness came on as they ascended LaBarge Creek, but when Harding realized there was enough moonlight to enable them to move, they kept cautiously on their way along the creek. At last Harding seemed satisfied with their progress and rode cautiously into a darker spot of heavy timber a scant hundred feet from the creek. He looked about, noting the lie of the land. Then he peered at Deborah. "You're about beat. So are the horses. Let's make camp here. I'll try to find a level bit of grass where you can bed down, Deborah."

"I'd give my half of Idaho for some cooked food and hot coffee right now, Jeff. Can we start a fire?"

"It's best that we don't . . . at least until morning," he responded. Then he chuckled. "I never was told that you own half of Idaho. An heiress, eh?"

She grimaced as she slid gingerly from the gray gelding, named Dusty, and tried her footing on the grass. "Heiress . . . no. Damn fool . . . likely." And suddenly as they stood in the quiet of the night-enshrouded grove she was telling Jeff Harding of her trip to Lewiston with the Plunketts, of going up the Clearwater River, and of the means by which she and Robert Lowell had gained title to a stretch of timberland commanding the entryway to a veritable wilderness of pine and fir and spruce. Her words skirted the night spent at Lowell's riverside shack and the appearance of a pregnant Indian girl.

But Harding seemed to glean more from her story than she meant to reveal, for he said presently, "So you met Robert Lowell up there. Deborah, I have heard rumors that you are in love with him. Are you?" The searching directness of his tone demanded an answer.

"Jeff, I don't know. Honest to God . . . I don't know. Back in Bonanza I thought I couldn't live without Robert. Then he disappeared for a long time. I do know I get furious at him. He could be a fine surgeon; instead he seems to mire down in a sort of self-pity. And . . . and to prefer the life of a squawman."

Jeff Harding did not answer. Instead, he moved about securing the horses for the night and giving her a few minutes to herself. When he spread his own bedroll it was at least twenty-five feet from her. "Get some sleep, Deborah. I think that about noon tomorrow we'll come onto the upper part of Greys River. God knows what sort of wilderness we will have to make our way through."

She dropped off to sleep quickly, but not before

she peered about. Harding had positioned himself with skill—in a place where intruders would have to move close beside him to reach either her, the horses, or their precious gear.

It seemed only seconds before Harding awakened her, and for a few moments she was fearful that their resting place had been discovered. Then her gaze fastened on the crimson rays of breaking daylight to the east. She yawned sleepily and would have nestled deeper beneath her blankets, but he forestalled her. "We'd best be up and on our way; there may be slow going ahead." He pointed to a small fire of twigs almost concealed beneath two boulders he had carried from the creek. There was the smell of boiling coffee in the air, and a skillet sat close to the blaze. "Suppose you stir up some flapjacks or something while I get us saddled and most of the gear packed."

Deborah crawled from beneath the blankets, nodding approval; then at creekside she plunged her hands into water so cold it caused her to gasp as she sloshed it against her face. She was aware of Harding walking to an ascending bank of the creek and looking back for a time, as though hoping to glimpse anything moving along the course of the stream behind them. When he returned, his face was thoughtful, but he ate hungrily and drank black coffee still too hot for her to handle. Then he said, "Deborah, I don't like our situation. Two men likely trailing us . . . one of them a murderer. And what lies ahead? Sometime tomorrow we're apt to find ourselves within shouting distance of that hidden village of Mormon women. We have no idea how large it is, how many people—or guards—are there, or whether there is a fortification around it."

Jeff stopped her look of protest with an upraised hand. "I'm not suggesting we give up. If I had thought that best, I'd have said so before we left Big Piney. Debbie, I want you to understand that this is going to be damned difficult—and maybe dangerous." He strode to his waiting mare, unstrapped a packsack, and drew out a revolver. "Here, I want you to take this—and, by God, use it if you must."

When he laid it in her hand there was no protest. She turned it over gently with close scrutiny. "I know how to use this, Jeff. My father taught me back in Nebraska."

They packed the few breakfast utensils, threw water on the small fire, and within minutes were again riding single file along the sharply ascending stream.

It was midafternoon, and they had crossed a divide strewn with brush and scattered pine, when they came onto a stream pointing toward the northwest. As they followed it, they noted the way in which smaller streams and one sizable creek joined to swell the volume of swiftly moving water. Behind them the hills were looming higher, while ahead there appeared to be the solitude of a widening valley. Jeff Harding studied it and then said quietly, "We're on Greys River now and Snake River drainage instead of Green River. And I wish I knew just where those bastards Decker and Whitley are."

His words brought a stricken tightness to Deborah's face. Presently she asked, "Jeff, what if we are leading those two cutthroats into the Mormon settlement—and there happen to be only women there?"

His answer was worded to assuage her fear. "I wouldn't worry about that. From what I have heard, the Mormon sealed villages are pretty heavily guarded. Besides, those women aren't helpless; they know how to take care of themselves and their children."

"Children?" she repeated. It was the first time she had considered the possibility of people other than wives in such an isolated community. Vividly before her were the faces of two children, a four-year-old little girl named Janice Froman, and Peter Moffitt, so blind and yet utterly appealing at the age of eight. Her thoughts became a yearning to see and hold each of them, to bestow upon them the love and tenderness that seemed so lacking in her own life. Perhaps, she thought, I will never have a child of my own. She turned bleak eyes toward the grandeur of the forested valley. For once, the sureness of bright tomorrows so long ago instilled in her by Tom Dexter seemed nebulous and unsure. What if life were to continue only as a struggle and she were not destined to reach the ultimate goal . . . to call up the morning, when life would have security and happiness? Moments of quiet passed, and she became aware of the concern with which Jeff Harding was watching her.

"You are tired, Deborah," he said. "This trip. The uncertainty."

She roused and answered, "Don't worry about me, Jeff. Sometimes I let dreams carry me off in strange directions."

Again they rode—throughout the afternoon, the evening, and until encroaching darkness warned them to set up shelter for the night. The river was now large and flowing swiftly among the rocks of a gulch where Harding sensed it would be difficult for intruders to harm them.

They prepared a light breakfast in the chill of dawn. A wind had risen during the early-morning hours; full daylight revealed broken clouds scurrying up the valley and often obscuring the timbered slopes of mountains climbing sharply on either side.

"It could be snowing before evening," Harding warned. "We'd best get as far downstream as we can today. I have an idea we will be dropping into a canyon as these mountains pinch in. At least that would mean more shelter from a storm."

It was noon when they came to a large and clear creek dropping into the river from the northeast. Here, in a timbered grove near the water's edge, they came upon cold ashes within rocks that had been set to hold a cooking vessel. A dozen steps away was a sunken spot in the grass, marked by what had once been a cross crudely formed of pine sticks. There was also a small slab of hewn pine on which had been burned the years of birth and death—1853–1878—and the weathered and fading words—Sheep Creek. The name of the person buried here was fully obliterated.

They moved to the junction of the river and the creek, watered their horses, and allowed them to feed on the cured grass while they, themselves, ate a cold and sparse lunch. There was a quiet bleakness upon both Harding and Deborah, brought about by the forlorn grave, the lowering and sunless weather, and the uncertainty of their quest.

The snow began falling about two hours later, when they had covered what Jeff Harding surmised to be five miles after leaving Sheep Creek. The wind dropped somewhat, and at first large and feathery flakes tumbled from a leaden sky. They thickened, quickly whitening the ground and touching the somberness of the tall pines and spruce with festoons of white. Then within minutes the wind quickened again; the snow became a veiling whiteness through which it became increasingly difficult to see ahead. Darkness would come early on this storm-racked day, creating difficulty for anyone bent on traveling the practically virgin solitude through which the river moved relentlessly on its way.

At a signal from Harding, they stopped to swing from their saddles and shrug into heavier coats. As they remounted, Deborah glanced about with amazement. "Look how thick and heavy this snow is . . . already an inch deep." Uneasiness crept into her voice as she asked, "Jeff, how can we be sure of finding our way? Or of reaching some sort of shelter? By morning we could be stranded."

His reply was reassuring, although there was now concern across his usually calm face. "We can follow along the river, Debbie, although at times we are apt to be at water's edge and then maybe fifty feet above it and not on too sure footing. It's best we keep an eye open for a stand of timber that would provide a wind break and fuel for a fire. This is going to get worse . . . maybe a lot worse."

They had gone scarcely a quarter mile more and

come into a meadowed widening of the canyon when Jeff Harding drew his horse to an abrupt halt. "Look at this," he said. "A cornerpost and a fence, a buck-and-rail fence." Had they already come unchallenged to an enclosure about the mysterious Mormon village?

The curtain of snow changed for a time from an impenetrable blankness to a lessening fall that allowed his eyes to sweep a hundred yards ahead. There was only a log structure, built where a dark cluster of spruce trees broke into a clearing. Behind it was a small livestock shelter and the curve of a mound that was likely a cellar to store perishables for winter. There was no smoke lifting from the cabin's stone chimney, and no light thrust from the windows against the gloom of snow and waning daylight. But within the fence, and near to the cabin was a cow, a good-sized calf, and two horses who stood with heads lowered and their rumps against the wind. They urged their mounts along the fence, which seemed to border the river. Perhaps there might be a gate or other sign of occupancy.

They had gone less than a dozen lengths of the fence poles when suddenly a man was standing before them. In his hands was a rifle blocking their forward movement, while at his feet lay half a dozen steel beaver traps. It was impossible to guess his build, clad as he was in a greatcoat formed of what Harding knew to be bearhide. His face was largely hidden by a dark beard, and his eyes seemed suspicious. "Where in damnation did you two come from?" he challenged.

"We came from Big Piney, over in the Green River Valley," Deborah said. "Rode up LaBarge

Creek and then down this stream. It's Greys River, isn't it?"

The stranger turned toward Jeff Harding, as though loath to accept a woman's words or acknowledge her presence. "Where are you heading?"

Jeff's reply was bluntly worded but carried no hint of anger or fear. "We are headed for the Mormon village down the river—hoping to make it before we get snowed in."

"Are you Mormons?" the stranger demanded.

"No—we are not," Deborah answered.

The stranger shifted his rifle, then said coldly, "Then you are a couple of damned fools looking for more trouble than you can handle."

Deborah took a steadying breath and said, "My mother is a Mormon. She . . . she is in that concealed village." When the rifleman failed to answer, she asked with apparent anxiety, "There is such a village, isn't there?"

"Maybe there is and maybe there ain't. I've found out that a body stays healthy by not being too nosy—or blabbermouthed."

Harding looked about, his eyes encompassing the snowy valley, the storm, and the nearing of darkness. Then he said, "Would it make sense for us to try anything against you? Pass us through so we can try to reach some sort of shelter." When the stranger stood without moving, seeming to ponder the idea, Harding added, "No, we don't have any idea of harming you or your property, but there's a bit of warning I should give you: Two men are following us. They have been on our trail for perhaps seventy miles. One is wanted for murder in Colorado, and likely the other isn't much better."

"How come they ain't ketched you?" the stranger asked skeptically.

"Only because we have better and fresher horses—which means ~~you~~ had better look well to your stock for a day or so."

The revelation was acknowledged as the stranger finally lowered his rifle and spat his disgust into the snow. "Damn country is loaded with thieves and no-goods these days. About time for Jim Oldland to pull up stakes, gather his trappin's, and head out. Maybe to the Cascades . . . or Alaska."

Then he stepped back, leaving the way ahead clear. "You had best get on. We're in for one hell of a night, with maybe snow up to a horse's belly." He seemed to ponder and then said, almost cordially, "You can't make it to the Mormon cabins tonight. Not in this storm. It is down the canyon several miles and about ten creeks away. Tell you what. Just around the bend, maybe half a mile from the end of my fence, you'll find a cabin . . . just across the river, so you'll have to ford it. 'Twas built a long time ago by some fur trappers wintering up here for beaver pelts." They had nodded thanks and were moving anxiously off when he called after them. "Them two bastards trailing you—who did they gun down? A lawman?"

"No," Jeff Harding called back. "He bushwhacked a young sheep herder, a Mexican boy who never even got a chance to see him."

Distance and snow-filled air kept them from

hearing his reply. "Maybe there is a bounty, or I can help hang the sons of bitches."

The cabin was small, dirt-floored, and with evidence of pack rats and perhaps a skunk about. Yet no structure could have proved more welcome as Deborah and her companion sought it out in the gloom of that storm-swept night. There was no stove or fireplace, only a device built of heavy tin in which a fire could be built, with the smoke carried through a roof hole near the ridgepole. In nearby and sheltering timber was a makeshift corral of unpeeled poles lashed to several trees with rusted wire. Here their horses would be kept from wandering during the night, although there was no means of providing fodder.

That night was one of a fight for survival. The wind sweeping up the river canyon gained fierceness with late evening. It seemed to sift blown snow through a dozen or more of the old cabin's cracks and log spaces. Nor could the contrivance that passed for a stove do much to heat the drafty room. Both of them managed to get fitful bits of sleep under bedrolls thrown together for warmth. It was the nearest Deborah had slept to her companion and the first time she had felt his body against hers. But tonight only the creeping cold and the snow drifting into the room concerned them—that, and anxiety about the condition of their horses.

Long after midnight Deborah and Jeff fell asleep. In the first gray light, Deborah awakened. She realized two things: She was shaking with cold; the fire had burned out. Something seemed missing, too . . . the roaring of the wind and the constant touch of blown snow within the room.

Jeff awoke, struggled sleepily to his feet, threw twigs on the cold ashes, and touched a match to them. Even though the wind was down, it took an hour for an aura of warm comfort to spread across the cabin; the heat came only as Harding made trips into the outer night for armloads of wood. At last full daylight came. They prepared coffee and warmed chunks of bread by holding them close to the flames with pointed sticks.

Later, when the first warming rays of sunlight picked their way between two logs, they walked outside to gaze about. The wind was now but a subdued and cold pressure against their faces; overhead, white and broken clouds moved almost indolently. Often they obscured the forested slopes and snowclad peaks that loomed remotely aloft. It seemed that five inches of snow had fallen, but in open spots it had blown into knee-deep drifts. A certainty was upon Harding. The storm and drifted snow, together with the weakened condition of their pursuers' horses, would work to slow or stall them. Even now they might be afoot; it would doubtless take them a day or so to catch up.

Within two hours the day was warming rapidly, for much of the mellowness of Indian summer still clung to this valley of Greys River.

At midmorning they saddled the horses after allowing them to graze on grass the wind had swept free of snow. At last Harding worded the matter foremost in both of their minds. The Mormon cabins. Several miles . . . about ten creeks away.

315

"That sounds like about a two-hour ride," Jeff said studiedly. "Maybe a bit more in this snow."

Later, the shadows of riverbank trees told them that noon was at hand. They had ridden through a narrow, canyonlike stretch and abruptly came to where the river swung more to westward at the base of a towering rock ledge. Within another hundred feet the valley widened; heavy stands of timber came down to the edge of a meadow. There was also the reflected light from where the sunlight struck a waterfall. And across the clearing, half hidden by pine and spruce of magnificent height, smoke lifted in blue spirals from half a dozen chimneys—of cabins within a palisade of logs—and beyond a sturdily planked gate.

"Jeff," the girl breathed, "look how strong that . . . that wall is built. Like something out of the Indian wars, or *The Last of the Mohicans*."

"They mean business, all right," he said. "Nobody is apt to take them by surprise—not with a fortress like that. We must be where we've headed for, Debbie—the secret Mormon settlement."

They edged their horses ahead, coming into position that would bring them under scrutiny from anyone watching within the stockade. When no one seemed to appear, they rode closer. It wasn't until they turned to diverge from the dim, downstream trail, now but a winding whiteness of snow, that they were challenged. For a moment the heavy gate moved slightly ajar and a man stepped out. He stood for a little while appraising them. Presently his arm moved in a gesture that was meant to wave them on their way. Instead, Jeff Harding nudged his horse as though to draw closer to the clustered buildings. The reaction of the man by the gate was alert and immediate. His hand dropped to the handle of a holstered revolver and he strode with evident purpose toward them. As he neared, both Deborah and Harding scrutinized him. He was clad in black, homespun jacket and trousers and was wearing the broad-brimmed type of hat that Deborah had so often seen in the Utah farming and ranching country. He was obviously past middle age, with a weathered and stern face. When only a small distance separated them, he stopped, swept wary eyes across them, and asked, "Just what are you two doing here?"

"We are looking for my mother," Deborah said. "Her name is Rose Stannard. The wife of Bishop Joshua Stannard. She is here—is she not?"

She needed no more affirmation than the stunned blankness—and then the caution—that marked the guard's face.

"Who are you? How did you find this place?" There was mingled astonishment and anger riding his questions.

"We rode in from Rock Springs, then up through Big Piney and LaBarge Creek. Then down this river."

"You mean through the night and the storm?" He seemed incredulous.

"We spent last night in a deserted cabin, upriver quite a ways. A man who called himself Jim Oldland pointed us to it, just before it got dark."

"Well, stranger," the guard said firmly, "you had better keep right on downriver."

"You mean all the way to Star Valley?" Deborah challenged.

"I didn't say where. Just get out of this canyon—and forget what you saw here."

With growing anger and defiance, Deborah swung down from her saddle. "Listen, mister. I haven't ~~seen~~ my mother for several years. Don't know whether she is sick or dead or even out of her mind in this godforsaken place. Now, you can take me into your hideout of women, or shoot me. But here I stay until I either see my mother or have some answers."

Jeff Harding fortified her words as he said calmly, "What the lady says, goes; I'm here to back her hand."

For tense seconds it seemed that the guard would move to draw the weapon at his hip. Then in evident bewilderment he turned to face the stockade, and his hand lifted in a gesture that was clearly for help. The barricading doors swung open again and another figure emerged. Deborah caught her breath, for advancing toward them was a woman wearing a sunbonnet and a long, severely serviceable gray dress. In her hands was a rifle.

She came up beside the guard, swept searching eyes over the two intruders, then asked in a firm but well-modulated voice, "What is this all about? Speak up, you two."

Deborah angered at the repeated questioning. She heatedly repeated her intentions to the woman and told her of their freezing ordeal at the cabin the night before.

"We cannot give you the information you seek, or admit you within the stockade," the woman replied. "It is forbidden. Yet . . . God forbid that you perish in the cold and I be held responsible in His everlasting sight."

"We would bring you no harm, or break word

to anyone," Deborah said. "If you have a living mother, wouldn't you risk as much to see her . . . after the loneliness and uncertainty of years?"

The Mormon woman listened but did not reply. Instead she motioned the guard to walk with her beyond Deborah's hearing. After a brief discussion she returned and spoke. "It is beyond my power to admit you within our small community, even for a meal or a night's stay. The punishment for my doing so would be unthinkable. But your obstinacy fills us with vast anxiety. I have a suggestion, Miss . . . Miss—"

"Dexter . . . Deborah Dexter." When the woman nodded, Debbie added, "And my friend is Jeff Harding."

It seemed to Harding that the guard was startled at mention of his name, but his attention riveted on the woman, who was saying, "Tomorrow afternoon, or the following day, there will be men here, some of them our leaders. We can lay your request before them for a decision."

"And meanwhile we spend freezing nights right here, I suppose." Irony and baffled anger grew about Deborah.

"Child, would to our Precious Redeemer that I could tell you otherwise." She hesitated, then said swiftly, "Go back to the cabin and wait. If you need food, we can spare some things for you to take. You have my promise that someone will come there within two days with the decision—and perhaps with word of the one you seek."

Chapter 15

THEY RODE reluctantly back to the cabin and with few words between them prepared a meal from their fresh supplies. Although the day remained sunny, by midafternoon a chill was in the air and foretold a colder night. They tied up the horses and allowed them to graze about the clearing. They also found an abundance of dead wood, hacked it into convenient lengths, and stacked much of it inside the cabin. Later they mixed water with clay from the riverbank and worked it into the widest cracks of this structure that must be their shelter for at least another night.

In late afternoon the sun dropped behind a high westward ridge, and soon the cabin was enveloped in deepening shadows, while a bit to the north the sun still lighted a small clearing. It was Deborah who first saw the three deer move cautiously from the timber to begin feeding in the sunlight. All three were tawny does, fat from a mild autumn and ample vegetation. Occasionally one of the three would raise her head and look warily about. When the tranquillity of the scene brought a sigh of pleasure to Deborah, she called softly to Jeff and then pointed. His reaction was different. Quickly and silently, he lifted his rifle to his shoulder, and before Deborah could protest, a single shot reverberated from the canyon wall. One deer crumpled on the grass.

Darkness came an hour later. After a warming meal of roast venison, they sat on a bench that had long ago been fashioned from a split log. There was the cheery crackle of warming flames and the pleasant scent of Jeff Harding's pipe.

She was quiet for a time, her mind touched by the wonder of how little was needed to provide elemental security. A fire . . . enclosing walls . . . the knowledge of fresh meat hung in a nearby tree for curing . . . the companionship of a man. A silence ensued during which she knew the aura of well-being for what it was, a respite from tiredness and anxiety and a time of strengthening for what might lie ahead. Presently she asked, "Jeff, whatever possessed me to ask so much of you . . . to interrupt your job and your routine and your life to risk this dangerous business of trying to find my mother?"

He lay his brown and strong hand over hers; for a moment his face was the most revealing she had ever seen it. "Likely, Debbie, it is because in some ways we are two of a kind. Whether or not you realize it, you have almost incredible ambitions. You want a world that is perfect . . . by your standards. I do too. But where you use business means, I must use the tools of a lawman. Some say those of an enforcer. You want the ranchers to get a fair deal. By God, so do I—and it's my job to clean out those who would rob and murder and plunder." The seconds passed, and both watched embers changing from a flame's glow to the dull redness that precedes ashes.

They were content to sit for a time in silence, wondering what tomorrow might bring and what the eventual end of their quest would bring. After a time Harding rose to throw more wood on the fire. For a moment Deborah wondered if he would return to her side . . . or spread his bedroll at the room's further end. She realized little of the forces driving this lawman or his reaction to her presence and their aloneness. But she sensed the stirrings within herself and her own vulnerability; if Jeff Harding should take her into his arms—or his bed—she would respond gladly and with passion.

The fire was brightening when he rose and gazed toward her. "Deborah," he said, his voice strained, "I never before wanted a woman as I want you."

She raised her eyes to him with utter calm, although her breathing quickened. "Then why torture yourself, Jeff? I am not a dewy-eyed little schoolgirl—not anymore." Her hand reached out to him with tenderness and assurance.

After a while they slept. Deborah's last drowsy thought was of the strength and comfort of the well-muscled shoulder on which her head was nestled.

Later she awakened with startled suddenness. The fire had dwindled to a few ruby-tinged bits, allowing almost total darkness to envelop the room. She listened intently and for a few seconds there were only the sounds of Jeff's sleeping breath and the voice of the river protesting the rocks in its course. Then out of the night came a new and different sound, a distant wail such as she had never before heard. Her eyes widened and she tensed, for the cry carried a likeness to that of a woman in pain or terror. She started to waken Jeff Harding

322

but quickly broke off the effort. Now she knew! This was the lonesome and sorrowful and searching cry of a mountain lion. Probably far off, probably from a cat in search of prey or a mate. She turned and carefully tucked more of the bedding about Jeff, glad for his presence and the protection of the cabin walls. Then again she slept.

Minutes later the panther's scream sounded again, this time loud and seemingly fraught with terror. Instant pandemonium followed. Outside, there was the frightened squeal of the horses, a crash of breaking timbers, and a pounding of hooves that quickly died in the distance. The bedlam had brought Jeff to his feet, fully awake. "Oh, Christ, Deborah," he said in sudden realization, "the horses . . . all three of them . . . they've broken the corral poles. Panicked by a mountain lion."

He grabbed for his rifle, flung open the door and stepped outside. Thirty seconds later he was back; the starkness of his face and eyes drew the last vestige of sleep from Deborah. "Are they gone?" she asked, gasping.

He nodded, then grated, "More likely they're already a half mile up the valley; they could be miles from here soon, maybe headed back to the Big Piney country. They're gone."

They again fed the blaze of fire. When daylight came, they prepared coffee, and warmed chunks of bread with sharpened sticks. From time to time each of them glanced wordlessly at their gear and the saddles they had brought into the cabin. Finally, sunlight picked its way between two unchinked logs. They both walked outside and looked about.

Deborah spoke first, "It wouldn't be too far, would it, to walk up to that fenced place and ask the man . . . Jim Oldland . . . if he's seen our horses?"

"We can do it, but I have the feeling Oldland was happy to see us away from his place. Besides, Deborah, we'd be fools to leave our gear and supplies here unattended. We are apt to need every—"

"Then you go alone, up to Oldland's," Deborah insisted.

"No, by God," he snapped. "If those bastards trailing us get hold of our horses, they could show up here at any time. You'd be by yourself . . . and there are two of them."

She fell silent, knowing the folly of their becoming separated. Within her too was memory of the face of Squint Decker across the campfire back on South Piney Creek. He was capable of murdering a young boy. Would there be any limit to his ruthlessness?

The day warmed rapidly, and by noon there was scant snow left. There was little to do now except wait.

For long moments Deborah thought of Jeff Harding and of what had transpired between them the previous night. She felt no remorse, for it seemed that it was meant to be. But what now? In what direction might this changed relationship point her life? If they should escape their present plight, they must return to Boise and pick up the threads of their everyday lives. She sensed that there would be no marriage for her with this man, whose activities took him constantly across the West from one dangerous situation to another.

The routine of a home with wife and children would dull and perhaps destroy him. Within Jeff Harding sexual tumult could build to a crescendo. Yet she surmised that such urging did not come frequently, for his foremost passion was his work and the justice he hoped to help spread across the ranchlands. And what of the other men in her life? Lemuel Froman, dedicated to his Mormon faith and tortured by memory of a wife who had forsaken both their Church and himself. More mind-searing was her memory of Robert Lowell. She had hoped, for a time, after that night of mingled love and passion along the distant Clearwater River, that she had become pregnant and would bear his child.

Abruptly her bittersweet thoughts ended. From the riverbank, Jeff Harding had uttered a low-voiced word of warning. She looked quickly toward him in the moment he was raising his rifle. His eyes swept the entire perimeter of the valley, then fastened in a downstream position—along the way to the Mormon village. Deborah came quickly to her feet. Her first thought was of her pistol and how she had carelessly left it in the cabin. She started to move, but a quick gesture from Harding halted her.

Now there was a sound, the dull thud of horses' hooves, followed moments later by the creaking of saddle leather. Then from around a point of rocks and a clump of underbrush three riders came into sight. Momentarily Deborah scanned their mounts, hoping to see the horses that had escaped, but the approaching horses were none she had ever seen. Both she and Jeff waited as the riders neared. A gasp escaped her as she realized that astride one of the horses sat a woman. Wild hope sprang within Deborah—that she would see the face of her mother there. Then, almost in despair, she knew the woman to be the Mormon who had confronted her and Jeff outside the sealed village.

The three came steadily closer. And then a gasp escaped Deborah—a gasp that became a small, unbelieving cry. The larger man was now clearly within view—a man she knew to be a black-clad Mormon churchman, a man who was no stranger—Bishop Joshua Stannard, her stepfather. So intense was her gaze upon him that she failed to realize that the third rider was the somber guard who had first blocked their approach to the stockade.

As Deborah stood trancelike watching their nearing, Jeff Harding lowered his rifle. Then he lifted a hand that acknowledged their presence. Stannard and the guard returned the gesture, and the three rode steadily forward. Jeff walked slowly up from the water's edge and stood by Deborah's side.

When only a few feet separated them, Bishop Stannard drew his chestnut-hued gelding to a halt; the other two came abreast of him and also stopped. For a time the Mormon bishop's gaze lay in an unrevealing manner upon his stepdaughter. There was a slight pause, during which her face took on the old stubbornness and defiance.

Stannard's first words, spoken in his richly resonant voice, seemed almost conciliatory. "Well, Deborah . . . what now?"

Even before she could reply, Deborah was aware of the Mormon guard scanning the cabin, the broken corral, and the clearing. How long would it be before he realized their helplessness? She sought to hide such stark reality as she looked unswervingly into her stepfather's face. Then she said, "You ask *what now?* Bishop, surely you know that better than I."

Stannard shook his head, then his voice took on both perplexity and grimness. "So you have somehow found this place. I suppose that if you leave here you will not hesitate to reveal to our persecutors the location of our Mormon village."

"Why not?" she flared. "For my mother—and likely many other women—it is a prison . . . and . . . and a place of degradation and misery."

"Hush!" It was the voice of the Mormon woman, speaking now for the first time. "Young woman, you know so little whereof you speak. No woman has ever been brought into this valley by force or against her will. Nor have any of us been mistreated. We stay here willingly . . . gladly . . . determined to await the day when we can return to our homes and families within the security and protection of our beloved Church. Yes, miss, we are proud to be Mormon women. It is the host of federal agents, sent by a misguided government in Washington, who must someday answer to God for their harassment."

What sort of answer Deborah Dexter would have made, the woman was destined never to know. The soft whinny of Stannard's gelding froze Jeff Harding's face to alertness and caused him to whirl about. "Watch out," he snapped, "there are others out there!" His chin jutted toward where the first afternoon shadows were obscuring the canyon. He turned cold eyes and words toward the

Mormons. "Have you sent others—arranged to ambush us?"

The question was unanswered as the Mormon guard reined his horse to provide more protection for the older woman and Bishop Stannard. The guard spoke jerky and suspicious words. "Bishop, something is wrong here. These two may have set a trap . . . and maybe there are others with them. Look over there. Look around. There are no horses here."

"You're wrong as hell, both of you," Harding said quickly. "But there's trouble ahead. Take cover—all of you. And watch your horses."

Something in his voice, a sincerity and an urgency, caused all three Mormons to dismount. It seemed to Deborah that they moved with incredible speed as they positioned the horses to form token protection; weapons appeared in the hands of all three, and they listened silently as Deborah spoke in an almost pleading voice, "Our horses escaped last night. Men have been following us. Maybe they captured our horses. The men are dangerous. A murderer and—"

Her words broke off in a small cry of consternation. From out of the deepening timber shadows upstream four horsemen appeared. Two of them were astride mounts that Deborah and Jeff instantly recognized, their roan mare and gray gelding. For a moment all four of the nearing horsemen hesitated. They stopped, and one pulled a pack animal to a halt, then remained in the opening long enough for Harding to see that all three of the escaped animals had been captured. Warily, the four reined back into the timber. Harding turned to face the bishop and said, "If you want to leave now, we would understand. But I wouldn't advise it. These bastards—at least two of them—are desperate criminals. They trailed us here, all the way from the Green River Valley. One is a known murderer. Likely they've joined up somehow with others on the dodge."

During his words the Mormon guard had been studying him with deep concentration. Now the guard spoke decisively. "Bishop, I know who this man is—and we can trust him. Since yesterday I have been trying to place him. Now I know. He is Jeff Harding, the lawman who travels about for the sheepmen. In Idaho. In Utah. Over most of this western country."

Harding nodded briefly while continuing to search the grove into which the intruders had ridden. "What matters right now," Harding said, "is what we are going to do. If those four discover there are supplies . . . and horses . . . and guns . . . and women at your village, all hell is going to break loose." As his words ended, Harding jerked about, raised his rifle, and fired. "Get down. Take any cover you can. They're splitting up, trying to take us from any direction." He watched as a lone rider spurred quickly back into the timber.

Bishop Stannard had sprawled onto the grass, and now with his rifle swung toward the disappearing rider, he said, "There is no way they can continue down the river without showing themselves. This old cabin was built by trappers who made sure of no Indian surprises." He paused and looked at the older woman. "Sarah, wouldn't it be best for you and my daughter to stay inside the cabin? Do it now before those hell raisers get closer."

After Deborah and the Mormon woman had disappeared through the doorway, Stannard spoke to the guard. "Miles, we had best get set. None of those riders must get by us toward the village." He turned to Harding and added, "It is best, no doubt, that you protect the cabin . . . the women."

Jeff had observed the man's calm and judgment with satisfaction, so he replied, "Likely best I do just that." He edged into a more secluded spot and motioned for the bishop to join him. "From here we can pretty well put a stop to anyone riding downstream." He paused, watching the practiced stealth with which the guard was edging the Mormons' horses into a timbered place where they could be half hidden and tied.

Suddenly Stannard said, "Harding, you are a man whose ability and integrity are almost household words. Yet you join up with my stepdaughter, an erratic and headstrong girl. She could never have come to this place . . . and this dangerous situation . . . save for your aiding her."

"Headstrong, yes. Erratic, no. Stannard, whether or not you know it, Deborah Dexter is one of the most levelheaded and capable women I ever met. I came because I understand her obsession in wanting to see her mother. But above that I came hoping to protect her, for she would have ventured here in spite of you . . . and of me . . . and of hell's fire itself."

The words seemed to establish an understanding between them, and together they watched quietly as the sun dropped and twilight filled the valley. At last Jeff said, "If I know anything of Squint Decker and Whitley, they'll want to make their move as soon as they think darkness will hide them."

Presently the Bishop said, "I wish, Harding, that I had brought a heavier coat. It gets cold fast up this valley once the sun has deserted it."

"If you can hold this fort a little while, Bishop, there are a couple of saddle blankets in the cabin. I'll get—" Already Jeff was crawling, gun in hand, toward the low and shadowy structure. He was halfway to the door when the sudden fury of attack was upon them. From an upstream spot and from the slopes, above where they narrowed into a canyon, came the flash and roar of shots directed at the cabin. Instantly Harding knew it was an effort to ascertain the position of those around the cabin and to get them to waste shots. Harding crept ahead, his prevailing thought and fear now for the safety of the two women; the cabin walls were of heavy logs, but always there was a chance of a bullet entering cracks between logs and crashing inside.

He reached the door . . . and realized that it was partway open. "Debbie," he called in a muffled voice, "are you two all right in there?"

The Mormon woman answered, and Harding realized that she was squatted just within the doorway with a rifle in her hands as she said, "She is back farther. I told her to stay where there is a bit more protection . . . if she will just keep lying down." She might have said more, but again there was a rattle of shots across the darkness. This time there was one answering shot—Harding knew that it had been fired by the Mormon guard.

From across the river was the quick cry of a wounded man and the shrill and frightened neighing of a plunging horse. A slight relief shot through Harding. Perhaps now there might be only three attackers to contend with. But hope dimmed when from the direction of the commotion there was a red flash that sent a bullet smashing against the door within inches of Harding's head. Then quickly a rifle again blazed; Jeff realized it had been fired by Bishop Stannard to seal off the progress of at least one rider toward the downstream trail. It was followed by hoofbeats as the rider retreated into heavier timber. Harding peered toward the inner gloom of the cabin. "That bullet that smashed into the door. It was damned close. Were either of you—?"

This time Deborah answered, and he realized that she had come to her feet and moved close to the doorway. "I'm all right. Are you, Mrs. Towne?"

"I think so," the Mormon woman's voice sounded. Then she added quickly, "Bishop Stannard—do you suppose he is all right?"

"Only if he moved mighty quick after taking that shot," Harding said grimly. "They've poured a few bullets at the spot where his gun flashed. But you two—get down and stay down!" As he uttered the words, Harding listened. A new sound had come out of the darkness, the faint whisper of approaching footsteps. He came erect, with his back to the cabin wall. An instant later Harding moved with catlike speed and silence to the cabin's far end. Then there was the sound of shots as he saw a quickly looming form and knew that the stranger had seen him. But the shots had not come from this intruder; instead they had sounded from somewhere in front of the cabin. But now they were momentarily forgotten in another blazing duel as the creeping stranger spotted Harding and swung about to fire. But Harding's weapon spewed lead. The intruder was jolted backward, stood swaying for a moment, then crumpled silently to the ground.

Harding probed the darkness, but there was only gloom. He retrieved the gun from the fallen man's limp hand and plunged quickly through the doorway. It seemed, he thought, that the intruders would give up trying to bypass the cabin and continue downstream; instead, they would probably make a desperate frontal attack, to wipe out those in the cabin and those intent on guarding it.

Abruptly there was a sharp cry and a muffled oath from the cabin—and Harding knew that his moments of absence had enabled at least one of the attackers to gain entry. Harding jumped toward the doorway—and collided with another form. A surprised and furious squeal told him that he had come up against the burly figure of the man who had called himself Joe Whitley. Harding broke free, threw down the captured weapon, and swept a hand toward his own holster. Simultaneously a gun blazed within the room, and a numbing stinging sensation just inches below his groin told Harding that a bullet had torn through his leg.

At that moment his senses seemed entirely clear. A voice from outside told him that the Mormon woman was outside and had gotten off a shot. Now she warned, "Watch out, Bishop—he's after you!"

Harding's leg was giving way beneath his weight, although he struggled to remain upright. Now he knew that the others in the room were Whitley, Squint Decker . . . and Deborah. And then another form loomed through the doorway, his voice calling out, "Deborah—where?"

There was a slice of blinding light, a roar that seemed to engulf the room, and the stench of gunpowder. With it came the savage voice of Squint Decker: "Kill every livin' son-of-a-bitch!"

Jeff Harding was on his knees when he steadied to aim toward where Decker's gun had flashed. But as he did so, the heavy form of Joe Whitley came between the gun and its target. Whitley grunted in pain and then swung wildly about to dash toward the open doorway. The grim terror of the situation seared Jeff Harding's mind. He knew that he was bleeding, but it seemed of little import to him. Doubtless Squint Decker's shot had torn through the bishop and now he lay dead or unconscious upon the dirt floor. From outside came the sound of shots, but to Harding they seemed far off and somehow unreal.

His mind fastened upon Deborah; he was desperate to know if she was safe. He knew that Squint Decker would also be looking for her, now seeking only to kill.

The sound of Squint Decker's breathing at last revealed his position—that and the merest of shadows as he moved cautiously between Harding and a place where some light came between two logs. Harding slowly lifted his revolver . . . aimed . . . fired . . . and missed. Now there was a startled snarl as Decker wheeled about to take aim where Jeff's gun had flashed. There would not be time to move . . .

Even as Decker's arm lifted his weapon, another shot threw light and sound across the cabin. Harding watched it almost uncomprehendingly. Only one person could have fired it . . . accurately and at point-blank range, so effectively that the body of Squint Decker was lifeless as it crashed against the log wall, then sprawled close to the ashes of the burned-out fire.

"Deborah! My God, Deborah!" Harding managed to utter—and then blank clouds led him into unconsciousness.

Deborah moved in a half-dazed and aimless way toward the door and the outer darkness. She would have fired the gun again, had not two people quickly moved to her side. The Mormon woman reached her first, taking her into strong arms. With her was the Mormon guard.

Minutes later, in the glow of quickly lighted grass fagots, fully the carnage was revealed. Bishop Joshua Stannard lay dead, close to the doorway; a wound in his chest had stained the nearby earth. Then the lifeless form of Squint Decker. And then Jeff Harding, whose face was white, his eyes half closed, blood still seeping from the leg wound.

Deborah threw trembling hands over her eyes. "My God," she moaned, "what have I done? Killed a man. Caused the bishop to be shot. And . . . and now Jeff is—"

Warmth and light were in the cabin when, half an hour later, Jeff Harding stirred beneath the blanket that had been tucked about him. A soft moan escaped him and after a few minutes he opened his eyes. As realization returned, he struggled to sit up. The Mormon woman pushed him firmly down. "You just lie quiet; we don't want any more bleeding."

Jeff ceased the stirring, but his gaze roamed the dingy cabin, resting finally on Deborah as she stirred a small pot in which gruel was simmering. She laid the spoon aside and knelt at his side. "You are going to be all right, Jeff. We think the bullet passed through your leg." Then she told him of the results of the battle.

There was a silence between them as the Mormon woman came closer and again examined his wound. "Do you think you can ride a horse—after a bit—if we get you into the saddle?"

He moved very slightly, seeming to test his leg. "Probably I can. But where to?"

"Down to our village, of course; you will need much care."

A shudder ran through Deborah. "I don't know if I can bear it now—to see my mother and to tell her about the bishop."

"You must have meant more to him than either of us realized," Harding said, perplexed. "He was calling to you . . . trying to get to your side . . . when the bullet struck him down."

"I know," Deborah conceded in a tiredly broken way. "He was married to my mother, but God help me, his other wife, and young daughter, are waiting right now for his return to Ogden." She wept in the bitterness of despair.

Deborah stared for long moments into the glowing embers of the fire. For the first time in her life, the firelight seemed a thing of hopelessness and of dread. Had her dreams of Idaho . . . of the West . . . and of joyously calling up the morning been nothing but the siren of Fate leading to ultimate defeat and heartbreak?

After a time she lowered her head onto her arms and gave way to racking sobs. As her time of agony dragged on, she was scarcely aware of the Mormon woman moving to her side to ease an arm about her and press the windblown hair and grief-torn face to an ample and comforting shoulder.

Snow and wind, the onslaught of a new storm, were blasting through the canyon when the silent and troubled group of riders came within view of the Mormon village the following day. They had met Jim Oldland, who told them that he had found the last of the intruders—the man they knew as Whitley—dead.

Now the heavy plank gates of the village were unlocked and swung open. They rode inside and then drew to a stop in a small, well-grassed clearing around which several log structures were grouped.

Four men, none seeming younger than fifty years, came forward; presently they were joined by a dozen children and a scattering of rather plainly clad women. None among them spoke, seeming to await words of explanation and direction from Sarah Towne. In that small pause, Deborah swept eagerly searching eyes across the assembled women. A pang of disappointment and uneasiness crept over her: The face of Rose Dexter Stannard was not among those assembled.

Presently Sarah Towne spoke, her words quiet

and studied. "We have nothing to fear from the man and woman who are strangers among us. They helped prevent what might have been a serious attempt to harm or destroy us of the village." She paused, then almost reluctantly laid the lead rope of the body-carrying horse into the hands of the more sturdy of the old men. "Bishop Stannard was killed last night; we have brought his remains here. He died in defense of our little village and of those he loved. I ask to be the one to tell his widow, Rose . . . and to offer my prayers with her."

At mention of her mother's name, Deborah stared toward Sarah Towne. It was the first time Deborah's hopes had been confirmed: Rose Stannard was in this secluded settlement. This was what Deborah had longed for, and for which she had undertaken an arduous and dangerous journey. But now what could she say to her mother? Or . . . even more agonizing . . . what would Rose say to her?

And now the thoughtful eyes of Sarah Towne, seemingly a leader in this strange village, were upon her. "Climb off your horse, Deborah; you will be safely cared for by the sisters of our faith. I shall send for you to join me after a time."

"But . . . but my—"

"After a bit, Deborah. Give me a little time with her first." Sarah Towne turned to Harding. "The men will show you to quarters, Mr. Harding . . . and stable all of the horses." She peered up and down the canyon, assessing the heavy clouds and the wind's direction. Then she dismounted, handed the reins of her horse to an older boy, and spoke again, with something of finality. "Neither you nor Miss Dexter are in any way prisoners. Yet with what seems to be a heavy storm moving in, you'd be well advised to stay here, wait it out, and give your wound a chance to heal somewhat."

Jeff Harding stared at her with growing admiration and then said, "You know, Miss Sarah, I think you are incredible. To bear up as you do and to show such compassion . . . after the way we came here. Unannounced. Uninvited. Yes, and unwanted."

She flashed the broadest smile he had yet seen on her face. "Aren't we Mormons supposed to show compassion . . . or understanding . . . or mercy?"

The room to which Deborah was escorted was small but warm and clean. Upon the rough timbers of the floor were sizable hooked rugs, and a heavy quilt of patchwork design lay neatly upon the bed and spoke of hours of careful needlework. The window was small, but upon its narrow sill sat a glass jar of dried grasses and flowers that enhanced the design of the gaily figured muslin curtain. The woman who showed her to these quarters was young, clad in a serviceable gray dress, and obviously ill at ease. She stood silent and attentive as Deborah sank onto a homemade stool with a vast sigh of relief, smiled, and said, "Thank you for this wonderful bit of comfort; it seems ages ago that I was last in a real room . . . with a clean, warm bed."

The young woman smiled in a reserved but appreciative manner. "I am Anna . . . Anna Langley. I will call you when supper is ready."

As the young woman withdrew from the room,

Deborah breathed wonderment, as Jeff Harding had done earlier. How could it be that she—an unwanted and uninvited stranger and one who had rashly imperiled this settlement—could in return be offered comfort and security and perhaps great understanding?

Later, after she was brought hot water and washed, she listened to the tempo of wind searching along the eaves of the cabin and watched the increasing thickness of snow piling on the outer window ledge. Suddenly her eyelids drooped tiredly and her head nodded. There was an aura of well-being about her as she lay down and drew the patchwork quilt over her. Then she slept.

Two hours later a voice and a hand upon her shoulder awakened her. "Deborah, wake up. Your mother wants to see you now."

Deborah rose to her feet, momentarily rubbed her eyes, then searched the older woman's face questioningly. There was no clue as to whether she would be welcomed by Rose Stannard or coldly condemned for what her actions had brought about. She would know only when she stood in the presence of her mother, for the face of Sarah Towne was quiet . . . firm . . . unrevealing.

"You had best put on your coat. It isn't far, but the wind and snow are pretty bad." A minute later they left the room to face into heavy and screening snow. Deborah, without real sense of her whereabouts or direction, reached for Sarah Towne's hand; they walked ahead in silence, except for the deep resonance of wind sweeping through the pines and the spruce.

They had gone no more than fifty steps when

another log structure loomed before them. They mounted a tiny porch that was already mantled by several inches of snow, and then Mrs. Towne opened a door to let them inside.

Quickly there was a dampness across Deborah's face as particles of snow melted under the warmth of the cabin. She was heedless of them as she gazed about. Across the room and bending over a small table, Rose Stannard was touching a match to the wick of a kerosene lamp; when it smoked the glass chimney a bit, she used a dish towel to restore the luster. Her movements seemed protracted and unsure, as though she were striving for both time and control. When the lamp's yellow glow cast soft radiance across the room she turned slowly toward Deborah; in that same moment Sarah Towne left the room.

The lamplight seemed to lay across Rose Stannard's face in a revealing way. Deborah's first reaction was a hurried and somewhat disbelieving gasp of breath. This woman was older, quieter, and much thinner than Deborah remembered. Her hair was touched with gray; there were lines across her forehead and about her deep-set eyes. What has this place done to her? Deborah's mind questioned.

Deborah took an uncertain step forward, trying to read something from the face of the woman who had straightened, lifted her gaze, and was silently awaiting. "Mother, I am Deborah. Would you rather I leave?"

Rose's scrutiny seemed to become momentarily intense and searching. Then her face crumpled as quick steps brought her to the girl with outstretched arms. "Oh, Debbie . . . Debbie, child? Why did it have to happen this way?"

There was a fierceness and longing born of their long separation as Deborah's face pressed to that of Rose Stannard. "The bishop," Deborah murmured, "I had no idea he was within a hundred miles of this valley. God, Mom, if only I had stayed away, not let my obstinacy cause his death and . . . and . . ." The words dropped off as Rose Stannard's hand moved firmly to cover her daughter's mouth in a gently hushing manner.

"Deborah, stop. Don't condemn yourself. Sarah Towne has told me all that happened up there at the old cabin. Couldn't it have been God's will that you come into this valley just when you did?" Rose stepped back, to hold Deborah at arm's length and look hungrily into her face, then said, "You are grown up. I wondered so often about you." Her arm again encircled the girl and she added, "I see so much of your father in you. The same dogged persistence. Now! Take off your wraps while I fix some tea and a bite to eat."

Later, as they sat facing each other across the small table, Rose smiled tentatively and asked, "Debbie, have you found all that you expected to in Idaho? I've heard of your graduation from college and of your having a job with the Sheepmen's Association in Boise. Is it what you want . . . or makes you happy?"

"Mom, I don't know. Honest to God I don't. Everything seemed to be shaping up so well . . . until . . . until last night. Mom, last night during the attack upon our cabin I killed a man; maybe that—and the fact that the bishop, my own stepfa-

ther, was there and was killed because of me—"
She threw shaking hands to her face. "Mom, how
am I going to bear it or live with myself?" She
paused, then sobbed uncontrollably.

After she had composed herself, she asked,
"How about you, Mom? You won't stay here in
this hidden place any longer, will you? I want you
in Boise with me."

There was grief across Rose's face but also determination as she rose and refilled the teacups;
then, reseated, she sipped at the steaming tea in
silence. When at last she spoke, her words were
firm and assured. "Deborah, do you remember
those times in Nebraska when you so often said
that everything would be better in Idaho, when
like your father you were so positive that the
days ahead would yield success and peace and
joy?"

Deborah nodded numbly. "I hope that somehow
I may feel that way again. That someday—"

"You will, honey. You will. That hope was bred
into you by Tom Dexter, your father. I have an
idea you will never lose that faith and hope. But I
will never live in Boise."

"Mom, why?"

"Because, Debbie, I know for certain that I have
come closer to finding those golden tomorrows of
your father than you have—or perhaps ever will. I
have my friends and my faith. Yes, child, the faith
and the fortitude of our Church of Jesus Christ of
Latter-day Saints. I am a Mormon. Do you know
what that means, or how I cherish the God-given
revelations of our great, martyred leader, Joseph
Smith?"

"But where will you go? What sort of living can you provide for yourself?"

"The Church will find work for me." Rose Stannard braced her shoulders and lifted her chin with pride. "After all, Debbie, Bishop Stannard stood high in the Church councils . . . and I was his wife."

The following day sunlight broke through, but the chill of winter now hovered in the thin and dry mountain air. Brief services were held for Bishop Joshua Stannard. As they came to a close, Sarah Towne sought out Deborah. "There will be men here tomorrow from Afton. They will take Bishop Stannard's body with them to Afton and start it on its way to Ogden. It is best you go with them, Deborah. You will be given safe conduct."

"But . . . but my mother? And my friend, Mr. Harding?"

"Both will accompany you. Your mother believes she will be needed now with the bishop's family in Ogden. Mr. Harding declares he is fit to undertake the trip . . . and that he is going out of Greys River country just as he came in—with you journeying along with him."

"Mrs. Towne, now I realize how a remote and lonely village such as this can survive. It does so on the strength and good sense of people such as you." When Sarah Towne smiled quietly, Deborah went on. "But will it be safe for you and others here in this tiny settlement? Word may get out, and other thieves and . . ."

"We will be reinforced, Deborah, and constantly on guard. Besides, I am certain that

344

the need for sealed villages such as ours, born of misunderstanding and bigotry and desperation, will cease to be shortly, and we will be able to regain our rightful place in the Mormon cities and towns and farms."

Chapter 16

TWELVE DAYS later, Deborah Dexter returned to Boise. She traveled from Ogden alone, for during the grueling ride from Star Valley to Ogden Jeff Harding's wound had little chance to heal.

Deborah rose early on the morning after her arrival and prepared to walk the few blocks to her office. The day was overcast, with wind that surged through the streets, kicking up dust and stripping the few remaining leaves from the trees. Winter was definitely in the air in Boise; she surmised that before the end of the day snow might fall heavily across Idaho's mountains and this capital city.

Once at her desk, she placed a hand to her forehead and for a time closed her eyes. Just what had she accomplished by leaving the train at Rock Springs to seek out a wilderness valley, a hidden village, and a woman named Rose Dexter Stannard, whom she now realized would never forsake the teachings of Joseph Smith and Brigham Young?

She began sorting the mail. She had almost completed the task when an official-looking white envelope caught her attention. It bore the return address of William E. Borah, attorney-at-law, and was directed to her personal attention. She drew a deep breath, turned it over twice, and broke the seal. Her gaze darted over the lines:

Dear Miss Dexter:

Our mutual friend, attorney Lemuel Froman, has asked that I inform you of two actions that have been taken within the past few days by the officials of the Union Pacific Railroad Company.

First, they have forcibly brought to our attention the highly irregular manner in which the Sheepmen's Association used one of their emigrant freight cars for transporting a shipment of wool to Lorain, Ohio, classifying the contents as materials subject to lower freight rates. The railroad wants to make it absolutely clear that such a shipment will be neither accepted, waybilled, or tolerated in the future.

Second, all this becomes academic and unnecessary in view of another action by the railroad's Board of Directors. Upon the request and insistence of your association—and the demands of the officials of the Church of Jesus Christ of Latter-day Saints, at Salt Lake City, a new tariff is being prepared for shipment of wool and certain other farm and ranch commodities from this part of the West to points beyond the Missouri River. We do not yet have a copy of these tariffs, but it is our understanding that the rates will be reduced to a considerable degree.

Mr. Froman thinks we should get together as soon as possible to discuss this with you further. Let us know when this would be convenient.

Sincerely,

William E. Borah

347

She lifted her eyes, turning to look out upon the city and the mountains beyond. Someone must have presented the case of the sheepmen and other ranchers convincingly to the influential leaders of the Mormon Church. She knew it must have been Bishop Joshua Stannard, her own stepfather. Now he would never know of his success, nor would she be able to thank him.

She knew that she should immediately break the good news to Ramon Echiverri, Antonio Onederra, and others of the Basque community. But work, important work, awaited her right here in the office. Two of her letters were complaints by association members in the far western part of Idaho. Their content and their similarity caused anger to darken Deborah's face. Mail fraud was again being perpetrated against sheep ranchers— and the all-too-familiar pattern took her thoughts back to her first days as secretary and the nefarious mail operations of Joseph Bagley and the Nampuh Distributing Company. This time the offending company had put out a circular listing various supplies from Bearpaw Enterprises in Grangeville.

"Grangeville!" she said aloud. "Right in Blain Halligan's front yard!"

One other letter attracted her particular attention. It was in a soiled envelope and addressed in a labored, penciled scrawl; there was no return address. The post office cancellation circle read Bayhorse, Idaho, with a date now ten days past. She fingered the envelope with curiosity and then broke the seal. Inside there was a single sheet of blue-lined, school-type tablet paper. It read:

Sheepgrowers officers
Boise, Idaho

Sirs—

My name is Charley Irving and I run cattle
here in Custer County. Jim Plunkett is a
friend of mine and so is Mollie, his wife. They
thought as how I should write to you and Jim
said you make it hot for theiving fellers who
cheat sheep herders, Etc. through the mail. I
don't think much of sheep but mebbe you can
help me. There's an outfit up at Grangeville
that calls themselves the *Bearpaw Enter
Prizes* and send out a katalog to us cattle
ranchers. They are crooked bastards out to
skin us alive.

I ordered some vet supplies and put $18.00
in the letter. That was last August. Now I
have not got . . .

Abruptly Deborah sat upright, the letter
clutched in her hand. Her breath quickened. "My
God!" she muttered aloud. "Here is the answer!
Why haven't I seen it before? Now—if only Henry
Carswell is in town . . . or I can get him here
quickly!"

She glanced at the wall clock and noted its nearness to noon. Again studying the cattleman's letter, she saw the pattern of larceny and fraud that
had so long enraged her. She made a mental note
of the writer's name and then locked the letter in
her desk. Then she penned a quick note to Jim and
Mollie Plunkett, asking them to come right away.

She glanced about the office. She needed a telephone. She needed to call Ramon Echiverri and

Frank Wentworth . . . and Lemuel Froman. And letters must be written now to all association members; they must be given the heartening news of the impending freight reduction by the Union Pacific and of the certainty of contracts with the spinning mills in Lorain. And just as urgently, they must be alerted to the danger of becoming entangled with Bearpaw Enterprises, wheelers and dealers of Grangeville.

Deborah's mind reverted to the letter from rancher Charley Irving. Suddenly she was writing, the pencil flying in a vain attempt to keep up with her thoughts. Half an hour passed and she realized that it was well beyond lunchtime and she was hungry. If Frank Wentworth isn't out of town, she thought, he will be at the assay office, back from lunch. She rose, locked all confidential material in her desk, and put on her coat and gloves. Leaving the office, she carefully locked the door.

Outside, a full-blown snow storm was in progress, with wind searching the streets and playing a somber dirge among the naked boughs of trees that bordered the street. She leaned into the veiling whiteness with a feeling akin to joy. Winter had a way of exciting Deborah. It had been so on the lonely sweep of Nebraska prairie and during the storms that piled both snow and deep cold into the valley of the Yankee Fork. She noted that the wind was blowing from the north. It brought thoughts of how much deeper and lasting the snow cover would be in the high mountains and in the more northward reaches of Idaho. The trend of her thoughts carried into the Clearwater River country. How isolated at such a time must be the stream-side cabin of Robert Lowell. Would he still be there, accepting the endearments of a quiet-eyed Indian girl and nursing the hopelessness that had followed him from a medical school in Seattle to a mining venture on Jordan Creek and then to his seemingly self-imposed oblivion as a squawman?

She trudged ahead, her steps carrying her toward Wentworth's Assay Office. She was thinking now of something that had not been on her mind much since leaving the train at Rock Springs with Jeff Harding. Surely by now Sam Douglas must be back in Boise and finished with the bit of sleuthing she and Wentworth had asked that he undertake regarding Lowell's expulsion from medical school—and the part, if any, the brothers Halligan had played in bringing about his banishment.

On her way to Wentworth's, she stopped off at the telephone company and arranged for a phone to be installed in her office.

Engrossed in thought, she almost trudged past the entrance to Wentworth's shop. Suddenly an outthrust hand and a voice caused her to look up abruptly.

"Deborah! Is it really you? I was on my way to your office, hoping you had returned."

She peered at his dark but intense face, and her voice took on surprise. "Antonio . . . Antonio Onederra. But how come you're not out at the—"

"Deborah, haven't you heard?" he interrupted. "About Ramon Echiverri?"

"Heard what?" she said anxiously.

"He died last week. A very sudden heart attack. That is why I am in Boise. Mrs. Echiverri asked me to try to handle the duties of our Basque community and the Sheepmen's Association for a little while."

The sudden news caused tears to mingle with the dampness of snow on Deborah's face; her eyes took on desolation. "Oh, Tony, why? Why did it happen just when I have wonderful news for the Basques? For all sheep people?" She told him of the contract and the impending freight reduction.

Several minutes later, after saying good-bye to Antonio, Deborah entered Frank Wentworth's store and found him in his office. After bringing him up to date on her activities, the talk got down to politics . . . and corruption in high places . . . and to Henry Carswell as a candidate for secretary of state of Idaho.

"Politics in this state is a serious and sometimes vicious business, Deborah," Frank Wentworth said. "Just now it would take a *cause*—and a following—to enable Henry Carswell to make even a decent showing in the race for secretary of state."

"Mr. Wentworth, that is one reason why I am here. You know of the trouble our Sheepmen's Association had with the dishonesty and fraud of the Nampuh Distributing Company. I have reason to believe that the same individuals are now back in business as Bearpaw Enterprises, operating out of Grangeville. Also, a letter came in this morning with proof that the Bearpaw outfit is using mail fraud in dealing with all livestock men and farmers. Not just the sheepmen! But if Henry Carswell can prove this dishonesty and rid Idaho of such vultures, he will have political power—a means of becoming secretary of state. *And I can put the damning material in his hands—right now!"*

Wentworth had listened in rapt silence. Now he ran his fingers thoughtfully through his white hair. "I don't have to warn you that the wrongdoing may reach far beyond the Bearpaw operations. In fact—"

"In fact," she cut in, "it even now reaches into the statehouse—because of the corrupt practices and payoffs of men who are allowed to rob and ravish Idaho and its honest people. Such sleazy bastards as Blain Halligan . . . who has been entrusted with guarding many of our natural resources."

"Deborah, there is much truth in what you say," Wentworth said. "And you are treading on the edge of dangerous ground . . . perhaps a volcano." He assessed her face for a reaction, then grinned. "Nothing I could say would deter you, would it, young lady? So . . . where do we begin? Yes, I said *we*. Damn it, girl, you and your man Carswell can use help, even from an old man like me."

"First we get Henry Carswell into Boise, into your office or mine," Deborah said quickly. "Let him know what he is in for. The battle and maybe the ballots. Another starting place may be in my compiling a complete dossier on Halligan."

Deborah rode to the office the following day in a sleigh drawn by two coal-black horses who plodded the snowy streets with little difficulty. The snowfall began to slacken, and the lights of homes and businesses seemed to create a glow of brilliance. Many of the people were shoveling walks and visiting with neighbors while children tried out sleds and built forts. As the clouds became broken, sunlight broke through intermittently to reveal much of the whitened city and the lower foothills beyond. As the sleigh moved ahead to the tempo of the horses' trotting hooves and the clear tone of harness bells, people looked toward the rig and waved. Winter was upon Boise, with the promise of holidays for which the community would spend several weeks preparing.

As she called aloud to those along her route and for a time cheered on a dozen boys defending a snow fort, Deborah was suddenly aware of a new emotion. Boise was now her home; these people were her friends and neighbors, bound in a community spirit of togetherness. She sensed that more than ever Boise meant a place of putting down roots and of permanence for her.

Then abruptly a thought occurred to her. I want a house—of my own. Just as I want it and plan it. For me . . . and maybe for Peter Moffitt, the little blind boy, Abrigal Stannard's son. If only she will let me adopt him.

But, Deborah realized, money for such a house was a problem. She estimated it would cost ten thousand dollars, including land and expenses, for her new home. Where could she get that amount of money? Her income was just under a hundred dollars a month, and she had one hundred sixty-five dollars in savings.

She knew she must try. But when she went to the Boise City National Bank for a loan, she was politely but firmly refused—until she remembered to mention, at the last minute, her joint ownership of the two hundred acres of timberland on the

Clearwater River near Orofino. The loan officer promised to be in touch with her. Deborah had, she hoped, set in motion what she believed would be a brighter future . . . a new tomorrow.

She had come into the main hallway, and her office key was in her hand when she first glimpsed two men standing close beside her doorway. Her startled gaze swept them, a gasp escaped her, and she started quickly to turn away. In that moment both men sprang quietly forward, one on either side of her; quickly a hand was across her mouth to muffle the scream building within her. Her arms were jerked to her back, and the key was torn from her grasp. She struggled, turned, and aimed a hard kick at one assailant. It landed only inches below his groin and brought an angry grunt of pain. Her arms were wrenched again, sending pain into her shoulders. A short, vicious-looking club was now in the hand of the one she had kicked, and he whispered hoarsely, "Try that again, sister, and I'll knock your silly brains out."

She peered from one face to the other. Neither assailant was masked, and in the subdued hallway light she realized she had never seen either man before. Both were bearded and seemed middle-aged. Their clothing was identical: a black cap with the earflaps down and the bill pulled low, a plaid mackinaw, and dark-hued woolen pants. One man was heavily jowled; the face of the other was lean and just now twisted into a snarl, and his gloved hand was over her mouth with an almost choking hold. Within seconds the heavier-set individual had thrust her key into the office door, unlocked it, and moved quickly inside. Deborah was forced inside the room, and the door was pushed shut.

Abruptly one of the men spoke; his voice, though low-toned, was nasal and told of exertion. "All right, where is it? By God, tell us or we'll tear the whole place apart."

"She can't talk with your big mitt over her mouth." The deep voice of the other intruder was impatient and disgusted.

A surge of fury ran through Deborah, and she managed to get her lips momentarily free of the clawlike hand. "Who are you? What do you want?"

The thin-faced assailant swung her about so that her eyes were only inches from his own. "Never mind who we are. We know who you are, Miss Deborah Dexter . . . and what you are: the office lackey for a bunch of mischief-making sheepherders. Now—do we get the paper peaceful-like, or do we beat the hell out of you?"

When her eyes remained angrily on his face, he spoke again. "I'll give you about five seconds."

His hand was lifting the club when the heavier man spoke. "Hold it a bit, Lenny. Maybe she just doesn't know what we're here for." He pushed closer. "We want the paper that your snoop brought here from Seattle. The one that a squealing bitch turned over to that slippery bastard . . . Sam Douglas. Now, where is it? Tell us or there is hell going to break loose. Right here."

There was a short silence in which Deborah studied the faces before her, trying to imprint their every feature upon her memory. And there was something else—a muffled step of someone coming up the steps at the end of the outer hallway. She knew that she must create sound that would keep her attackers unaware of whoever was outside. "All right," she murmured hoarsely, "I'll show you. Just don't hit—" At her words the arms holding her were dropped . . . and she could move. Instantly she swung about, ducked beneath an arm attempting to again encircle her, and pulled with all her strength at the hallway door. It swung open—to reveal an overall-clad workman with a toolbelt around his waist and a box in his arms. Deborah thrust into the doorway, her hands snaking out to seize the box. Then she was lifting it from the arms of an astonished telephone installer—to hurtle it with all her force and fury into the face of the thin-faced intruder. It caught him unaware, smashing him backward and to his knees. Then her clenched fist raised. She would have struck the heavier man, who was reaching out toward her, but her effort was cut short by a new voice—that of Henry Carswell, now standing in the hall with a pistol in his hand. He pointed it toward the bulky assailant. "Get back in that room and keep your hands heavenward!" he snapped. Then he glanced toward the kneeling stranger, who was attempting to rise while wiping blood from his face. "Jesus, Deborah," Carswell said, "what was in that box—a sledgehammer?"

"Hell no," the installer said plaintively. "It was a wall telephone. What's going on?"

Deborah's chest was heaving with emotion and excitement. "These . . . these bastards broke in here. Into my office and tried to rob me."

Deborah turned to where the two would-be paper snatchers sat glowering under the menace of

Carswell's weapon. Her eyes narrowed and her face reddened with rage. "I don't know yet who you are, you two. Maybe the police will. But damn you, you can do something for me. Get word to the man who hired you—to Blain Halligan—that if he wants a fight he sure as damnation is going to get it. He came at me. Now it's my turn."

Chapter 17

At lunch two days later Deborah met for the first time William E. Borah, the brilliant young lawyer who would later spend thirty-three years as a United States senator and become nationally known as "Mr. Idaho." She had made her first telephone call from the office to Lemuel Froman, and while the operator was completing it, Deborah's mind reviewed the letter in which attorney Borah had suggested a personal meeting between herself and the two lawyers.

"Lemuel," she said after exchanging greetings, "I'm so excited about a letter I got from Mr. Borah—and what has happened about the freight rates on wool. Could we all get together soon, perhaps today?"

"Let me call you back, say in twenty minutes. I'll try to get hold of Bill Borah and arrange something. And, Debbie . . . welcome back to Boise. I missed you." There was excitement in his voice, and something within Deborah stirred to its challenge.

His call back revealed that Borah could meet them at twelve-thirty in the dining room of the Overland Hotel.

She walked into the lobby of the Overland Hotel at twelve-twenty-five. For years it had been one of Boise's leading hostelries, a favorite dining place of the town's businessmen and favored by visitors from out of state. She looked about the busy room, then chose a seat close to the open doors of the dining room. Within, there was an expanse of sturdy, ladder-backed chairs and tables covered with white linen. She noted also that the waiters were smartly clad in semiformal wear and that on each table was a small but tasteful bowl of fresh flowers.

Moments passed and then she glanced up. Coming toward her were the two lawyers. Lemuel Froman was dressed in a dark, pinstriped business suit, a white shirt, and a starched collar. The attire of the man accompanying him seemed somewhat more relaxed. He also wore a white shirt, but its collar was low and soft as it supported a dotted blue bow tie. His trousers, well creased above glossy black shoes, were of gray flannel; they were held up by a wide leather belt. His jacket was of a deeper gray and was now unbuttoned as its tail fell almost to his knees. Just below his belt was a watch fob sporting an insignia of the University of Kansas. In his hand was a modified, almost white "plantation" hat with a broad brim.

But it was William E. Borah's facial features that caught and held Deborah's attention as Froman introduced his companion. There was a forcefulness about Borah's face, radiating from a solid and determined chin and accentuated by steady but friendly eyes peering at her from beneath thick, dark brows. His hair was cut short, neatly trimmed and meticulously parted on the left side above a high forehead.

Now he was saying, in the richly resonant tones of an orator, "Miss Dexter, I have looked forward to meeting you; I must confess, though, that I had expected a somewhat older woman—and not such an attractive one."

The gathering of lunch patrons was now thickening, and they joined the movement into the dining room. Deborah became aware of the many who greeted William Borah . . . and the ingratiating charm but common sense of his replies. She had a quick realization: I want Lemuel as my lawyer; I know him and he is my friend. But when the stakes are high or the case is involved, I want William E. Borah as my lawyer also.

After a time, Lemuel Froman touched a damask napkin to his lips and pushed his chair a few inches from the table. He glanced about, and Deborah knew he was ascertaining who might be within listening distance. Obviously reassured, he said, "Deborah, the new Union Pacific tariff on wool and allied shipments to eastern points— those beyond the Missouri River—has been released. Both Mr. Borah and I received a copy yesterday. The rates are greatly to the advantage of the sheepmen."

Deborah expressed her immense satisfaction. Then she told them of the great help of high officials in the Mormon Church in pressuring the railroad, and of the critical intervention of her late stepfather, Bishop Joshua Stannard.

Later, when talk turned to her travels, Deborah mentioned the two hundred acres of timberland she had bought in northern Idaho, and that she had used it as collateral for a new house she was planning to build.

Lemuel Froman's eyes widened as he asked, "Your *what?*"

"My timberland. I guess I never thought to mention it to you. I have part interest in two hundred acres of good forestland near Orofino, up the Clearwater River from Lewiston. My land controls the only feasible access to several thousand acres of excellent timber. A friend of mine suggested I buy it."

"Miss Dexter—Deborah," William Borah said—"could you give me more specific description and location of the land?"

As she told him, Borah was quietly making notes, using a pencil and the back of an envelope drawn from his pocket. After she had finished, he stared thoughtfully into a distance that might encompass much of Idaho's virgin wilderness. "Deborah," he said at last, "I am glad this came up. I want to check these locations with something I have at the office. Meanwhile, I hope you will not put an encumbrance of any kind on this forestland without letting Lemuel and me examine the documents in advance. This may be vital to you."

Deborah leaned forward intrigued, "But why, Mr. Borah? Don't you believe I may have clear title?"

"There is little doubt that you have clear title. And you may have far more."

"What do you mean?" Her voice was uncomprehending.

Borah smiled somewhat hesitantly. "Perhaps I shouldn't be arousing your hopes. Not yet. But I can say this much: There is tremendous interest just now in our northern woodlands. Word is out that soon the federal government is likely to set aside vast reaches of timber country—in Idaho and elsewhere—as forest reserves to be administered by the Department of the Interior. It may happen within three years, and surely within five."

"But I have a deed. Ownership."

"So you do, Deborah. But only to your two hundred acres. Right now literally millions of acres of prime timber-producing land are up for grabs. The railroads already own vast sections. But they want more. Also, with midwestern timber-producing areas such as Minnesota and Michigan and Wisconsin beginning to show depletion, the big timber companies, the lumber mills, have been seeking to grab up the best forestlands of our Idaho mountains in the northern counties."

Satisfaction, together with excitement, marked Deborah's face. "At least we—Robert Lowell and I—have the only access to one large area. We can keep them out." In her eagerness, Deborah failed to note the startled look that came into Lemuel Froman's eyes at her mention of her co-owner's name.

"Don't assume that you can keep owners and interested operators out over a long time," Borah cautioned. "The companies and some individuals are powerful. Doubtless they will seek to invoke the right of eminent domain." He peered at her under gathered brows and smiled. Then he said, "That is a legal term, but I imagine you already know its meaning and purpose."

"I should understand it a little," Deborah laughed. "I had to give a report once on *Eminent Domain* in a class at the University."

"Where was that, Deborah?"

"At the University of Utah, in Salt Lake City."

"I attended KU, Kansas University, myself.

Then thought I would practice law in Seattle. But somehow I got stranded here in Boise with only fifteen dollars. I've never made enough to get out of town." Borah's eyes were sparkling.

"That stranding, as he calls it, was a fine break for the profession of law in Idaho," Froman spoke up and there was admiration in his voice.

"I am beginning to realize why," Deborah agreed, and then turned in perplexity to Borah. "So in reality I have no defense against sawmill men, railroads, and others crossing our land."

"Hardly that," Borah said with a laugh. "The proceedings of eminent domain aren't accomplished so readily."

"What he means," Froman cut in decisively, "is that a smart attorney can dredge up ways to delay the proceedings and the decision for a long time."

"For how long?" Deborah's tone was harshly practical.

"It depends on the circumstances and the nature of those involved," Borah explained. "In some cases it can mean only a short delay of a few weeks or months. In others, it can mean practically forever." He tugged at his watch fob, drew out a silver-plated timepiece, and said, "I have to run along now." He took Deborah's hand firmly. "This has been most enjoyable. And, Deborah, do remember to let me look over any bank collateral papers." He bowed, picked up his hat, and turned to leave the dining room.

Deborah watched him go and then said, "I like that man. There is something powerful about him and yet he is so down-to-earth."

"Bill Borah is smart," Froman said, "and he is fair. He can also be a ruthless trial attorney. But I don't believe he could be underhanded or take a bribe." Froman paused, glanced toward her, and said, "You look lovely, Deborah—and I have missed you."

"I am glad, Lemuel. And I am so anxious to see Janice."

He paused and then said, "Deborah, earlier you mentioned the name of Robert Lowell. Do you . . . or is there . . . ?"

She eyed him in a teasing way. "Do you mean is there a man?" When he failed to answer, her eyes grew strangely tender. "Yes, Lemuel, there is someone. Someone I want to take to my arms and my heart and my home—a young man who is only eight years old and who is blind. Lemuel, I want to—I must—adopt him. His mother is Abrigal Stannard. His name is Peter Moffitt."

"I know of the boy," Froman said in evident surprise. "During our years together as missionaries, Nephi Oakes spoke often of him and the tragedy that blinded the little fellow. But would his mother consent to an adoption?"

"I believe she might," Deborah responded. "I have met her and been in her home. She is now a widow with a young daughter to provide for. Besides, Peter has been in a school for the blind in Salt Lake City for some time."

"Wouldn't he be better off to remain there, Deborah?"

"I cannot believe that. What school can offer the love and the understanding and the comfort that—?" She broke off, appeal and emotion bringing tears to her eyes. Then she added hopefully, "There is another reason. It is possible that a delicate and very expensive operation might restore

Peter's sight, at least to some degree. I want to give him that chance."

Froman's face had taken on both awe and doubt as he said softly, "But Deborah, the boy is fully of Mormon faith . . . while . . . while—"

"While I am not," she finished for him. "Are love and understanding and compassion confined to those who are Latter-day Saints?"

Lemuel Froman flushed and swallowed hard. "You know I don't believe that. Deborah, am I an ogre just because of my faith? And you have overlooked one thing, something that is likely essential. It is highly unusual—almost unheard of—for the courts to award custody of a minor child to an unmarried person."

His words widened Deborah's eyes in shock. "Then you think—"

His hand moved out to capture and hold hers. "What I think, Debbie Dexter, is that you are the most unselfish and bighearted woman I have ever known." His voice became almost a whisper. "Debbie, there is a way, almost a miracle way, for you—for you and me—to open a new world for Peter, for my little Janice, and . . . and for ourselves. Will you marry me?"

The emotion of his appeal and its unexpectedness brought a gasp of surprise from her, and he hastened to say, "I have the right now to ask it, to let you know I love you. My wife has obtained a divorce . . . in California."

As she heard him out, Deborah had mixed emotions. There was a stirring within her that the touch of his hand, the sound of his voice, and the appeal of his quiet eyes had aroused ever since that first day on a vacant lot in far-off Box Butte,

Nebraska. She knew that within him was the power, if he should take her in his arms with tenderness, to arouse a desire for him . . . and to bear his children. But she was also certain that the abiding mistress of Lemuel Froman, the one to whom he would pay unyielding respect and homage, was the Mormon Church. If she failed to become a Mormon, there would always be a chasm separating them, and in time it would surely widen.

After these few moments of reverie, she looked into his face and said, "Listen to me. I am thrilled and I am proud. But also confused. I need time. Lemuel, give me that time and I will give you an honest answer."

He was wordless for a time, seeming content with her nearness and the honesty of her words. Then he said, "Of course you need time, Debbie— just as I need you, and Janice needs a mother. And surely just as young Peter Moffitt needs both of us. Don't make my hours . . . and days . . . of waiting very long."

Deborah awakened the following morning after a night of troubled sleep. Her first thought was of the things she must accomplish. A committee must quickly get the name of Henry Carswell before Idaho's voters as the logical choice for secretary of state. But first must come effective action against the insidious Bearpaw Enterprises and the power behind its scheming.

Deborah stirred uncomfortably in the bed, then realized that she had come down with a wretched cold. Presently she slept again—and the hours of the morning wore toward noon.

Later, a persistent knocking at the door awakened her. Her steps were unsteady as she made her way to the hallway door and opened it—to give forth a small cry of relief and of joy. Between two suitcases and wearing a bearskin coat stood Mollie Plunkett, her plump face wreathed in a grin.

"Mollie, Oh, Mollie—get me to the toilet fast as hell."

Later, when Mollie had guided her back to the room and tucked her back in bed, Deborah asked, "Where is Jim? Is he waiting downstairs?"

"Not this time, honey. Plunkett had to stay in Bonanza to help a new mine pick out and buy some ore hauling mules. People seem to think that only Jim knows anything about mules." Mollie was pushing Deborah back in bed with one firm hand and using the other to search through her handbag. "Debbie Dexter, damn it, you stay covered and quiet. I'm going to rub your chest with bear fat ointment."

"It stinks," Deborah grimaced.

"What if it does? It'll relieve that congestion and your sniffles."

"But I am going to the office, Mollie. I have to."

"All you have to do is use your brains, stay in that bed and start getting well. Hell's fire, honey, you ain't lost one bit of that stubbornness." Mollie unbuttoned the girl's nightgown and scooped up the ointment. Presently she was rubbing and as firm fingers moved across Deborah's breasts the girl reddened with embarrassment.

"Christ alive," Mollie fretted, "don't tense up so. You've not got anything that any other woman doesn't have—except maybe they are a bit prettier. Some nice pointers instead of saggers."

Deborah broke into a gale of laughter and then presently asked, "Mollie, where did you learn to massage that way?"

"I don't know. Maybe from milking cows or rubbing Jim's back after a long day in the saddle." She buttoned the nightgown, then said, "Now, child, you go back to sleep. We'll talk when you wake up."

Deborah snuggled deeper into the warmth of the bed. Now that Mollie was by her side the cold and sniffles already seemed better. For a little while she tried sleepily to make her mind put in order the things she must do, the decisions she must make. But languor stole over her, her eyelids closed and her breath took on the evenness of sleep.

When she awakened, most of the day had passed and the shadows of evening were encroaching upon the room. Presently her gaze centered upon Mollie Plunkett who was sitting beside a small table and reading the *Idaho Daily Statesman* in the subdued light from a lamp.

"You have let me sleep all day, Mollie," she fretted.

"Well, you feel better, don't you?"

Deborah made movements as though to climb out of bed. "I have to get down to the office. My work—"

"Your work will be there when you feel better. Dammit, Debbie, stay in that bed and keep covered. And by the way, that young man Antonio— you know, the Basque one—stopped by while you slept. I told him you were laid up for a while. Later he came back with these." Mollie was pointing toward an arrangement of pink and white carnations. "He said tell you he would keep an eye on the office—him and Mrs. Itchy Verry."

"You mean Mrs. Echiverri, bless her soul." Deborah yawned widely, then she said, "I'm hungry. Awfully hungry."

"I was waiting for you to say that," Mollie nodded, and rose to her feet. She moved toward the door and then turned to add, "Don't you dast climb out of that bed, Deborah—except maybe to use a chamber pot."

She was back five minutes later, with a clean linen cloth folded across her arm and a tray in her hands. Deborah was eyeing her in surprise when she explained, "Your landlady said I should fix a bite for us here rather than look for a take-out restaurant. She says for me to stay here with you and look after you; she has a spare room I can use."

Deborah shook her head in wonder, then she said softly, "Mollie Plunkett, the Good Lord sure had my needs and my comfort in mind when he sent you and Jim my way, down along Jordan Creek back there in Bonanza." She took a sip of steaming tea, smiled into the older woman's face and spoke again. "Mollie, why don't you and Jim move to Boise? The winters aren't anywhere as severe as they are up there along the Yankee Fork. Besides, I need both of you around. I am about ready to build a home here; there can be either separate rooms or . . . or even a small house just for you and Jim."

Mollie's breath quickened to a pronounced heaving of her hefty bosom. "Christ, honey, you sure are a fine persuader. The fact is that Jim and I already have a move to Boise in mind, just as soon as we can sell out and close up in Bonanza. But there is something you must understand. Jim and me will buy our own place here. Plunkett and I are independent as hogs on ice. We got that way roaming the mountains with mule trains when we was packers. Deborah, we know you love us, but by Gadfrey, you gotta be free to live your own life. Someday some man is bound to sweep you right off those restless feet of yours."

"I am off them right now," Deborah answered fretfully. "And there are a dozen things I should be doing." She tugged the blankets more tightly about her shoulders, dabbed a handkerchief at her watering eyes and muttered crossly, "Here I am stuck in bed with a wretched cold. Everything will have to wait, Mollie. Every confounded thing."

Chapter 18

MOLLIE cared for her that day, but there were problems and events not destined to wait. Some of them Deborah had herself brought about. Her activities had been wide in scope and touched many people; now developments would come about that would not be altered by her stay in bed.

Later that same evening Mollie awakened her. "Guess who's waiting in the parlor and won't budge until I let him talk to you?"

Deborah blinked drowsily, attempted to clear her scratchy throat, and then answered gloomily, "The way I feel, I don't believe I even care."

Mollie was holding slippers and a robe. "Does the presence of a widely known Idaho gambler stir your pulse?"

"You mean—?" Deborah said with widening eyes.

"I sure do. Old Sam Douglas is waiting."

Mollie left, to return quickly with Sam Douglas following. As he came in, Deborah ran quickly appraising eyes over him. How little he seemed to have changed since that day, on a stage moving northward out of Blackfoot, when he had spoken of the matchless allure of a game called poker. There were still the deeply weathered face, the intense blue eyes, and the locks of white hair.

When Mollie had left the room, Sam Douglas said, "Deborah, I hate to barge in like this when you're not feeling well, but it is important that I tell you what happened in Seattle."

Deborah dabbed a handkerchief to her nose and said, "I already know that you mailed something important. Two thugs broke into my office and tried to make me hand it over—something I didn't even have."

Douglas grinned and replied, "Henry Carswell has already told me about that fracas." Douglas paused, ran a searching hand through his thatch of white hair, and said, "What your rude visitors were after is safely in my pocket. I have had a copy made to leave with you, and I suggest you get it into a safe or bank vault. Deborah, your friend Robert Lowell was taken for quite a ride out there in Washington. He was made the victim, the fall guy—"

"You mean—?"

"Blain Halligan did attend the university in Seattle. So did his younger brother, Lacey . . . a few years after Blain left the school. In fact, Lacey was a classmate of Robert Lowell and they took some medical classes together."

"I already know about that, pretty much," Deborah said. "But what else?"

"Lacey Halligan was a sharp surgical student and made good grades. He also liked to live high . . . like renting a yacht for weekends on Puget Sound. He got pretty badly in debt to some Seattle loan sharks. When they made things unpleasant, Lacey tried to get quite a lot more money from Blain. That didn't work, and Lacey was in a real squeeze. And that was when one of his creditors came up with quite an idea."

"I think I'm beginning to understand . . . just a little," Deborah nodded. "Go on."

"A certain character named Dutch Gammage had come down from Yukon Territory with a potful of money. Maybe more. He was bankrolling the loan shark—and he also had been sowing wild oats in just about every one of Alaska's coastal towns." Douglas paused, studied the wall, and said, "I'll try to make it short—and delicate. A young 'lady' showed up from the frozen Northland, on the trail of Dutch Gammage . . . with fire in her eyes . . . and claiming she was already a month or so pregnant with his child. The loan shark put Gammage in touch with Lacey Halligan. Some none-too-subtle suggestions were made as to how Lacey could square his debts—and he agreed to perform an illegal and pretty risky abortion."

"Do you have proof of all this?" Deborah demanded excitedly.

"It is all in my pocket, in black and white. Deborah, I got hold of a fellow who was an intermediary between the loan shark and Lacey Halligan. I sifted out some things that sort of . . . well . . . enabled me to tighten the screws and get him to talk. Lacey did the job, all right. I even have the young woman's name."

"But how about Robert? If he was not mixed up in all this, how did he get blamed . . . expelled from the university?"

"Deborah, that is where it gets a bit weird. I know what took place, but I don't have the proof—yet. That's why I want to spend a few more days in Seattle—and get someone else to talk. But I wanted to have your say-so before I did more. It all costs money to pry loose, you know."

"Sam, I want you to go back to Seattle to wrap this up. And I want Mollie Plunkett to hear every word of this. Would you call her in and then re-peat what you have told me?"

"Yeah, Debbie. But there's a little more to tell."

"I know that. And I want Mollie to hear that too."

After Molly came in, Douglas summarized what he had disclosed of Lacey Halligan's complicity in the Seattle affair. Then he continued: "Even be-fore performing the operation, Lacey was looking for a scapegoat, and he found one right handily. He knew that Robert Lowell was hard pressed for school funds and looking for reasonable quarters. And wouldn't you know it? Bighearted friend that he was to Lowell, could he do less than offer him some quarters he just happened to have avail-able?—those in which the abortion had been per-formed. Lowell gratefully moved in. Two days later he was startled to have a young woman call upon him, insisting that he perform an abortion upon her—and the police broke in while she was pleading her cause. She promptly told the lawmen that *Robert Lowell* had performed such an opera-tion on a friend of hers. Two weeks later Lowell was kicked out of the medical school. And there you have it, Deborah."

Later that same evening, and as Deborah slept, a group of men came one by one into the Overland Hotel and made their way to a room on one of the upper floors. Had she known of their meeting, her curiosity and excitement would have demanded

375

an explanation. Those who laid their coats and hats on the bed and gathered around a table were there for a purpose Deborah had herself established, that of starting a campaign to nominate Henry Carswell as a candidate for secretary of state of Idaho. Among those present were Carswell himself, Sam Douglas and Jeff Harding, Antonio Onederra, Frank Wentworth, and Jim Plunkett.

Sam Douglas spoke first. "I think we are here to size up a way to do some overdue housecleaning at the Capitol building. First, though, I ought to tell you I visited Deborah Dexter this evening; she is laid up with a cold. Which maybe is good because it keeps her away from here. I'll let Henry—Mr. Henry Carswell—explain, seeing as he asked for this auspicious get-together."

Carswell looked from face to face and grinned a bit sheepishly. Then as he began to speak, his words and tone seemed to take on authority. "I think you all know the trouble the sheepmen and now the cattlemen of Idaho have been having with fake supply outfits. Deborah has sure had her hands full, but she has found out a few things, one being that the thieving rascals have access to private information—and actually to protection—through Blain Halligan, the deputy to the secretary of state, from up at Grangeville."

Carswell paused, and Frank Wentworth spoke up. "What Mr. Carswell hasn't told you is that Deborah and I think Henry Carswell can be nominated and elected secretary of state at the fall election. We are here to get this effort off the ground. Henry, you are willing to make a run at it?"

Carswell studied them one by one and then replied, "I am, if you men are willing to back my hand. Besides, Deborah already has a plan as to where we should start."

"Like where?" It was the first time Jeff Harding had said a word.

In terse, businesslike terms Carswell told them of Bearpaw Enterprises at Grangeville and its fleecing of livestock growers. Then he added, "Deborah and I talked this over. We believe that if somehow we can clean out this Bearpaw and its festering corruption—and let all of Idaho know we've done it—we can count on a stack of votes. I know that down in my part of the state, along the Snake River west of Idaho Falls, farmers will back us for a cleanup."

"A lot of miners feel the same way," Jim Plunkett commented. Then he asked, "Should we talk to Deborah again?"

Frank Wentworth shook his head. "It is time for action, not more talk. I don't think that plucky girl should know any more about this until we can tell her that Bearpaw Enterprises is out of business. For good and under any name."

Henry Carswell nodded. "I am ready to join a sort of cleanup committee and head for Grangeville."

"All of you should know something first," Wentworth cautioned. "Grangeville is the home and the stronghold of Blain Halligan. No doubt he is a crook, using his office to protect his interest in Bearpaw Enterprises. He is pretty ruthless . . . maybe dangerous . . . and will be on guard."

"All the more reason for Deborah Dexter not knowing what we're up to," Carswell said. "She would get herself up to Grangeville come hell or high water to help wipe out Bearpaw and take a swipe at Halligan."

Antonio Onederra had taken in every word but not spoken. Now he said softly, "She has done great things for our association. I will go to Grangeville with you, Mr. Carswell."

"I don't think so," Jeff Harding said calmly. "Tony, you have a wife and now also a son to look after. It seems to me this is a job for single men— like me." Harding came to his feet and walked a bit restlessly about the room. Then he faced them again. "Don't think I am trying to take charge, but I have been in such spots before. Just part of my job. Usually three men can accomplish as much as a crowd." He turned to Carswell. "So how about you and me—"

"Now you wait one mule-braying minute!" It was Jim Plunkett, now on his feet. "You ain't leaving me out. No, sir! I've knowed Debbie about as long as just about any of you, except maybe Mr. Carswell here. I'm surer than hell going to be one of the fiddlers when that Bearpaw outfit dances its last tune. Otherwise Mollie—that's my wife—"

"All right, Plunkett. All right," Harding said, laughing. "You've convinced me. So it'll be you and Mr. Carswell and me heading upstate."

"And I get left out in the cold," Wentworth snapped.

"Not by a damned sight," Henry Carswell answered firmly. "We need someone right here in Boise keeping an eye on the activities of the secretary of state and zeroing in on the Bureau of Natural Resources. That is Blain Halligan's department."

378

"And his means of building quite an empire," Wentworth said angrily. "Well, okay . . . if it has to be that way."

"Thank you, Frank," Harding answered. "Now, one more thing. It would be a dead giveaway if Halligan or the Bearpaw people found out we all got into Grangeville together. Let's take our separate ways, getting there at different times."

Sam Douglas lifted a face that held disappointment. "I was looking forward to being one of those chosen for the fracas. I tell you what: I have to make another trip to Seattle. How about me just happening through Grangeville on the way?"

Harding studied the gambler's face. "You might just do that. It never hurts to have an ace in the hole, does it?"

"How in blazes should I know?" Douglas asked. "I'm just an innocent old gambler."

It was another two days before Mollie consented to Deborah's leaving her rooming house and returning to the office. During that time she had two more visitors. Mrs. Echiverri, Ramon's widow, came by.

"How did you find out I have been ill?" Deborah asked.

"I think everyone knows, especially your Basque friends. But it was our man Jeff Harding who told me. He was up here to see you . . . remember?" Mollie Plunkett had told her that Jeff Harding had brought flowers but refused to let Deborah be awakened; he had left without her seeing him.

Now Deborah said, "But that was two days ago. Why hasn't he come back?"

"Because, Deborah, he is not in Boise. Yesterday he left in quite a hurry. Said he might be gone a week or ten days."

"But where did he go? He shouldn't be traipsing around like that. Not yet. He has been in the hospital in Salt Lake City."

The older woman nodded calmly. "Deborah, Jeff Harding doesn't ask anyone's permission to travel."

"Well, I will just have to wait until he shows up, won't I?" Sensing that Mrs. Echiverri's eyes were steady upon her, she asked, "And how is Tony—Antonio Onederra? Is he out of town too?"

"No. He is busy today helping get wool ready for shipping east on the railroad. Then he has to go back to his ranch and his wife and son. But he will be back shortly."

The Basque widow had hardly left the rooming house when Mollie escorted Frank Wentworth into the small sitting room just off Deborah's bedroom. Then she sought out her patient. Deborah moved through the doorway and yelped with joy upon seeing the elderly assayer.

When they were both seated, he said, "Sam Douglas dropped by my shop before he left to go back to Seattle. He told me to keep an eye on you."

"You mean Sam has already taken off . . . left Boise?"

"Yesterday evening. And, oh, yes, Henry Carswell is out of town too."

"Isn't anyone left around?" she asked. "Jeff Harding left . . . and Tony Onederra is going home tonight. Now Henry Carswell is gone too. And . . . and Sam Douglas. On top of that, Jim Plunkett hasn't showed up either. Not a blasted

380

one of the Carswell for secretary of state committee seems to care whether we ever get organized and under way."

Wentworth took some time before answering. "Well, at least I am here, if that's any satisfaction." He smiled to himself. Evidently Deborah had no inkling of the plan to expose Blain Halligan and Bearpaw Enterprises and that Harding, Carswell, Douglas, and Jim Plunkett were headed toward Grangeville to set that plan in motion. He decided to change the subject.

"Deborah, about that two hundred acres of timberland you got hold of up near Orofino. Did you know there is suddenly a lot of interest in Idaho's northern woodlands?"

She nodded. "Mr. Borah, the attorney, mentioned it. Lemuel Froman and I had lunch with him a few days ago. He said lots of the forest is bound to be set aside for National Forest Reserves before long. And also that the big lumbering companies and the railroads are stepping up their timber buying."

"True. But did Borah mention the skulduggery that all this is bringing about?"

"Not really. He did caution me to let him review the papers before I make any kind of deal." Deborah's interest was deepening.

Wentworth seemed to ponder and then drew a long breath before speaking. "Deborah, you know that ever since the creation of the Territory in 1863 there have been deep problems. Too many scoundrels holding offices and too few statesmen or even honest men. Don't get me wrong. Things have improved a lot since Idaho achieved statehood. But that was only about four years ago. You don't root out imbedded political intrigue and rascality in so short a time. We both know it hasn't been entirely swept from certain statehouse offices. And surer 'n hell not from the Bureau of Natural Resources of the Idaho Department of State."

"And never will be as long as Blain Halligan remains the bureau chief," Deborah said tersely.

"I have a feeling that will change pretty drastically if our man, Henry Carswell, musters up enough votes."

But Deborah's eyes became suspicious. She studied Wentworth's face and said, "You know, I get the impression that you are holding something back from me. Somehow you seemed a bit secretive and evasive when I asked about the members of the Carswell committee." She snapped her fingers. "So they all left town—just like that. I think they have headed up toward Grangeville. Maybe for a surprise party at Bearpaw Enterprises."

Momentarily, a startled look was on Wentworth's face. Then he shrugged his shoulders. "Yes, they have gone to Grangeville. Jeff Harding. Carswell. And Sam Douglas and Jim Plunkett."

"But why didn't they wait? I wanted to go along. There may be a lot of trouble."

"Which is exactly why you were left here. That and the very good reason that you have been sick." Wentworth laid a reassuring hand on hers. "Let them handle it, Debbie. Just for once stay at home, get well, and await word of what happens."

"It will be unbearable to wait and to worry," she said, pouting.

The morning after Wentworth's visit, Deborah visited the Boise City National Bank and was told that her loan application, with her timber holdings as collateral, had been approved. In great joy, Deborah then consulted an architect and real-estate agents. My dream of a home, she thought, is coming true.

Deborah spent the next two days at the office, spending long hours in catching up on correspondence and other work that had piled up. Upon her return to the rooming house on the second evening, Mollie Plunkett, who had spent the day about town, was waiting for her. She was in high spirits. "Guess what, honey? Old Mollie has found a nice little house to rent. Just right for me and Jim. And later on we can buy it if we're of a mind to."

"That's wonderful, Mollie, but I will sure miss you." She hesitated and then asked, "When is Jim going to get over here from Bonanza?"

Mollie caught her breath. "Why, didn't I tell you? Plunkett stopped by while you was laid up in bed. He'd just gotten here to Boise that day. Saw me a while, then said he was heading north for a spell. On business."

Suddenly Deborah was sure that her friend was not revealing all she knew. But no purpose would be served by trying to force Mollie to say more. She knows, all right, she thought. She knows the men are up there at Grangeville and there may be trouble. Danger. Oh, God, what have I brought about? So short a time after I caused Jeff to be wounded and the bishop killed. Is this all I am ever to accomplish . . . bring misery and suffering and . . . and death to those about me? At that moment her dreams of tomorrow's rainbow and of calling up a glorious morning were the dimmest since she had sat beside Rose Dexter in Nebraska and gazed back toward her father's grave.

The following day was Friday. She went about her duties in a subdued way. She had just returned from lunch when the telephone rang. Unaccustomed to the sound, she jumped from her chair and ran toward the instrument. There was something of dread about her. What if it were Frank Wentworth calling? What if bad news had reached him from Grangeville? What if—? Her hand was trembling as she lifted the receiver and said softly, "Hello."

"Is that you, Deborah?" She recognized the voice instantly as that of Lemuel Froman.

"Deborah, are you all right? You sound . . . well, sort of faint. This is Lemuel."

"I know, Lemuel. I am all right."

"That is good. I . . . I mean it's good you feel better. I met Frank Wentworth and he told me of your having a cold. And you know what else? He had a great idea—that I take you out for dinner. Would you? Could you? Do you feel you are up to it?"

She laughed softly. "Lemuel, you know what? You sound just like a teenager asking for his first date." She was forming a mental picture of his face, touched with uncertainty and perspiration. "Lemuel, I think I would enjoy a restaurant dinner immensely."

"Then how about my calling for you about eight o'clock?"

"Fine, Lemuel. I will be ready . . . and hungry."

384

She replaced the receiver and leaned against the wall. At least this time it wasn't bad news. Then she was thinking of Lemuel Froman. After the lunch with William Borah, he had seemed calm and confident as he had urged her to marry him. But now, in asking for a dinner together, he had seemed boyish, hesitant, and utterly without confidence. She attributed his moods to the pressures of a broken marriage. Yet weren't there even greater pressures? Those of trying always to adhere to the precepts of Mormonism? Deborah walked back to her desk and began putting things away. On the way home she could mail the letters she had prepared. And it might just be early enough to pick out a new dress and wash and curl her hair. She had an air of expectation. Strangely, it seemed to drive away the last vestiges of her illness, and it drove from her mind . . . at least to a bearable extent . . . the thought of what might even now be taking place in Grangeville.

Half an hour later, she entered Boise's most expensive clothing store and let her gaze search over the evening dresses on display. Then she smiled excitedly. There was a dress of a style and hue she had never seen before. It was blue and rustled softly. Almost as though a breeze is rustling leaves beside a lake, she thought. In a dressing room, she removed her street clothes and stepped into the gown. "Why . . . why it is lovely," she said quietly. "This is the one I want." There were sleeves and a yoke of delicate lace, below which the dress fit snugly about her waist and then flared to drop within a few inches of the floor. She ran an exploring hand across its smoothness and smiled her delight. She knew that very little alteration would be required to make it fit perfectly.

It would be an hour before she could pick up her new dress. Right then she decided on a shopping spree. Gloves. Suitable shoes. And perhaps even a new cape. She had never before gone about buying clothing with such zest and sheer happiness. And why not have her hair cared for this time by a professional?

It was just before sundown when she climbed the steps of her rooming house, panting from her burden of bundles and from an exuberance she had not known for a long time. Mollie opened the door, and her eyes grew amazed. "Holy Jesus, Debbie! All that stuff—are you moving in or out?"

"I'm going to dress up. Really dress up to go out to dinner," Deborah bubbled. "Mollie, help me get dressed. I want to look nice tonight. I'm having dinner with Lemuel Froman. The lawyer. The one who was a Mormon missionary. The one who has an adorable little girl. And . . . and . . . Mollie, he wants me to marry him."

Mollie asked in a tender way, "And you want to do it, honey . . . to marry him?"

Deborah had placed the bundles on her bed. It was when she turned to answer that she caught sight of the letter lying on her bedside table. The reply she was forming for Mollie remained unworded as she picked up the envelope and scanned it with quickening breath. The return address read simply: R. Lowell, Orofino, Idaho.

Mollie, who was peering sharply at her, said, "It's a wonder you got it, addressed that way, just to Boise."

Deborah had broken the seal and withdrawn the folded single page. Then she was reading:

Dear Deborah,

I hope this reaches you soon and finds you in your usual good health. I am writing because of some things that have been going on up here that will no doubt have great effect on our forestlands.

Deborah, it is vital that I see you and explain right away, so I will leave for Boise day after tomorrow and should be there Monday. I will look you up at the wool growers' office.

I have so much to tell you . . . things best not put on paper.

Always,

Robert

Chapter 19

H ENRY CARSWELL was the first of the committee to reach Grangeville. He stepped from a northbound stage just as darkness was coming on. He looked about the snow-covered vista of forest and of distant mountains as the last rays of sunshine laid a rose-hued glow upon the frozen landscape and a town that at first seemed to Carswell to be in deep hibernation. Except for smoke rising from the chimneys of huddled buildings and the glow of a few lamps, there was no visible activity away from the livery stable.

He picked up his suitcase and walked toward an unpainted structure of boards over which slabs had been nailed to seal the cracks. A breeze was moving loose snow along the single business street, carrying a chill that caused Carswell to draw the collar of his mackinaw more closely about his throat. He had not encountered temperatures this low since a night long ago on the Yankee Fork. It's odd, he mused silently, it was because of Deborah Dexter that I had to endure this sort of weather, back in '89. Here I go again . . ."

Minutes later he felt considerably better. The sign on the door had: Branigan's Buffalo Chip. Beds and Grub. Walk in. After pushing inside, he dropped his luggage to the floor and looked about. There was a stone fireplace at the room's rear, and now the flames were intent on reducing a six-foot length of pine log to ashes. Off to its side was a counter, behind which were boxes for letters and keys; across the room, a door led into a smaller room. Half a dozen people were sitting on battered stools or standing with elbows propped on a polished bar. Behind it was a large but somewhat flawed mirror. Carswell eyed the bar and backbar momentarily. Then his eyes lifted—to a gilt-framed and six-foot-long portrait of the most enticing-looking nude he had ever gazed upon. She was reclining on a silken couch and facing the customers.

A stranger stirred from one of the saloon stools and came toward him.

"I take it you're looking for lodging," the middle-aged and heavily jowled stranger said in greeting.

Carswell tore his gaze from the painting and stamped snow onto burlap bags just inside the door. "You guessed it, Mr.—" His words carried expectancy for the other man to reveal his name.

"Branigan is the name. You can have your choice of three rooms; we don't get many over-nighters when it's this cold outside. Supper will be ready in about an hour." He handed Carswell a key. "If you take the downstairs room, there is a stove and firewood. And the room and supper and breakfast will set you back only a buck-fifty. Booze is extra, of course, but you'll have the company of Miriam."

"Miriam?" Carswell asked and swallowed hard.

"Sure. Miriam . . . the dame in the painting. After a belt or so of liquor, old Miriam is bound to make you feel sort of cozy all over."

Carswell grinned a bit uncertainly and strode to the counter to sign the register. It might be easy to let liquor dim one's wits at Branigan's hostelry, but he hadn't come to this icy panhandle of Idaho for pleasure. Right now might be an opportune time to begin seeking vital information. Somewhere around, and likely within a few miles, was a business about which he intended to learn a lot more. But common sense warned that inquiry about Bearpaw Enterprises must be made in a seemingly disinterested way.

When he had paid the overnight fee and was handed a worn leather key tag, Carswell said tentatively, "I might be staying over; I've some business that needs attending to here in Grangeville."

The words brought a grin and evident curiosity as the hotel owner asked, "What line of business are you in, Mr. Carswell?"

"You might say I'm a land dealer. Looking over places where people are bound to be coming in . . . people who will be looking for business buildings and places to live when the boom starts."

For a moment the proprietor of Branigan's Buffalo Chip was clearly startled. He stared at Carswell, started to ask a question, and then seemed to think better of his impulse. After a time he managed a knowing smile and said, "Ah, yes. Grangeville is indeed on the verge of rapid growth; perhaps, as you indicate, a boom." With what he evidently hoped was discretion, he added, "Why not have a drink—on the house—Mr. Carswell, while we get a fire started in your room? We always want satisfied patrons at the Buffalo Chip."

Henry Carswell nodded acceptance and strode toward the bar; he cautiously kept his suitcase close to his side. He found a vacant stool and asked the bartender for a Scotch and soda. As he awaited it he was conscious of curious glances from the few customers already in the saloon. Tomorrow he could rent a livery stable team and drive about the town. He was sure that by that time his purpose would be known to any interested party. Henry Carswell had come to Grangeville as the representative of big interests—and the forerunner of a boom that would surely outdo anything yet seen in Idaho's gold country. It shouldn't be hard to get directions to Bearpaw Enterprises.

Jim Plunkett's arrival in Grangeville was far less auspicious. He had ridden the same stage from Boise as Henry Carswell. But at a small logging operation a dozen miles south of the town, Jim had asked the driver to stop and let him off. He retrieved a straw valise from the baggage rack and stared after the stage as it carried Henry northward. He gained a meal and a cot upon which to sleep by telling the woods boss that he had been unable to pay his fare farther but was willing to wash pots and pans. When morning came, he dug into his bag and donned some of the most worn pants and checkered shirt that any miner had ever cast aside. By the time he had cleaned up after an early breakfasting crew, he knew that luck was playing his way. A wagon would leave for Grangeville at midmorning to pick up supplies; he was free to climb aboard and be on his way.

Jim had already decided the course he would take. He had lived so many years among roaming prospectors he was thoroughly familiar with their ways. They were a restless lot, roaming the West and the Idaho Mountains in a never-ending search of an elusive yellow metal. Most of the time they were broke or nearly so. Yet somehow they could scrape up enough for grub and gear to get them to the next rumored gold strike. In Grangeville, the citizenry would pay him scant heed. He would be just another itinerant seeker of gold dust, waiting for a partner to join him and for good weather to allow their trekking into the Buffalo Hump Mountains. If people should consider him eccentric, so much the better. A person can learn a lot, he reasoned, if the townspeople believe him incapable of understanding what is said in his presence.

There was one person in the town that Jim Plunkett hoped he would not encounter . . . not for a time at least. He was determined to keep his distance from a certain storekeeper with watery blue eyes—and a spring wagon and team of horses he had just last summer rented to the Plunketts and Deborah Dexter.

The logging camp teamster dropped Plunkett and his seedy-looking valise at almost the identical spot where on the previous night Henry Carswell had descended from the stage.

He picked up his meager luggage and stumbled a bit uncertainly into Branigan's Buffalo Chip. Moments later, after having carefully doled out the necessary five cents, he sat with a mug of beer and peered—with what he hoped was a semistupid air—about the saloon and into the adjoining lobby. There was no sign of Henry Carswell. A clock on the lobby wall was moving toward half-past one. Within a few hours another stage should be pulling into Grangeville from the south. Two men that, according to plan, he must pass off as total strangers would be aboard it.

He finished the beer and reluctantly spent another five cents for a refill. When the bartender handed it to him, Plunkett said dejectedly, "I don't suppose there's any chance a pick-and-shovel man could find work hereabouts."

The bartender laughed his dismay aloud. "Find work digging? With the ground frozen down practically to hell . . . and two feet of snow on the ground? You must be crazy, man!"

Plunkett managed to look rueful. "Doesn't do a body any harm to ask, does it?"

"I'll tell you what, old man," the bartender said with mixed contempt and pity, "Mr. Branigan owns this hotel, and he should be back soon. We have some water pipes that froze up last night. Maybe—"

"It would be right down my alley to thaw 'em out," Jim assured him.

The evening stage into Grangeville was delayed two hours by a road-blocking avalanche a dozen miles north of the Salmon River Canyon. When it finally halted in front of the Buffalo Chip, two well-bundled passengers reclaimed their bags and trudged tiredly into the lobby. The first to approach the fireplace and thrust out his chilled hands was Sam Douglas. Branigan came from behind his counter and extended his hand. "Sam Douglas . . . how are you? And what brings a gambler here in midwinter? Are you running from the law?"

Douglas grasped the offered hand and answered in a stentorian voice, "No lawmen are trailing me—yet, Branigan. But likely they will be if I don't pick up enough gold pieces and greenbacks to pay my badly delinquent bills."

The hotelkeeper did not respond, for he had swung about to face and study Jeff Harding, who was waiting quietly at the counter and peering with seeming indifference at the guest register. Harding had unbuttoned his heavy sheepskin coat, and now Branigan was staring at the badge of a United States marshal.

In a brusque voice Harding asked, "Can you provide me and my friend, Mr. Douglas, with rooms for a few days?"

Branigan nodded in a satisfied way. "Yes, sir, Mr.—"

"Harding. Jeff Harding."

Now Branigan's curiosity surged, and he inquired, "You're from Boise, aren't you? Even up here we have heard of you and your work as a lawman. I hope you don't mind if I ask if you are here on . . . on business?"

In reply, Jeff Harding drew a none-too-distinct picture from his pocket; it revealed a man of perhaps thirty years and with Mexican facial characteristics. "Have you seen this fellow hereabouts?" Jeff saw no reason to mention that the picture was of a man he knew to be serving ten to twenty years in the territorial prison at Yuma, Arizona. Instead he said decisively, "I'll find him . . . stay on his trail as long as I have to."

Harding had signed the register and picked up a key when the passing of a workman nearby caused him to glance up at a ragged and grimy-handed old codger laden with a hammer and a pipe wrench. Jeff Harding stared at him and then said to Sam Douglas, "They have down-and-outers even in Grangeville." Then both of them stared, without the least evident flicker of recognition, into the watchful and somewhat satisfied face of Jim Plunkett.

Henry Carswell's day had been busy. The snow that lay across the valley and the town had deterred him but little, for he had managed to rent both a sturdy team of gray geldings and a light sleigh, which the liveryman termed a cutter. Before noon Carswell had spent three hours driving about Grangeville and its immediate vicinity. Several times he stopped and talked with residents. None of them found out specifically the exact sort of property he was interested in buying, but word soon spread about town that the man obviously knew about a real-estate boom. It would soon come about as the result of a vast business deal not yet divulged.

He stopped for lunch at the only restaurant that offered competition to the Buffalo Chip. Even before he had finished a somewhat tough steak, men were drifting to his table with word of local land and buildings that just might be available. He jotted down the locations but courteously declined to have anyone accompany him on his afternoon survey.

It wasn't until late afternoon that he found Bearpaw Enterprises. One of the jottings in his small notebook led him down a snowy and secluded lane east of town. He came around a bend in the road and halted the gray team.

Ahead were two sets of buildings. The first consisted of a rundown log house and a barn whose center swayed with age and neglect. Only the location seemed to have merit; there was a buck-and-rail fence enclosing what he surmised to be three acres having a gentle southward slope and a sprinkling of tall spruce behind the buildings. It lay quiet and deserted, but the entrepreneur in Henry Carswell pictured the possibilities of the site.

Then his eyes fixed on the property just beyond. There was a fence of metal posts and heavy link that enclosed a sizable structure of milled lumber. This was neither a barn nor a house. There were no wagons or other rigs standing about it, but the front doors were large enough that any such vehicles could be taken inside. The trodden and wheel-crunched snow gave evidence of considerable traffic, and now smoke drifted from three chimneys. Instinct told Carswell that his search was nearly over. There was no sign. This was not the setup of a firm that depended on being known locally.

Carswell flipped a page of his notebook and again studied some notes, but these were older. It was a name he was seeking, one that had been given to him a long time ago by Deborah Dexter. He read a bit farther and then murmured, "Bagley; Joseph Bagley. That's the jasper she said skipped out and went to Spokane, the one who seemed to ramrod the Nampuh Distributing Company down in Boise." He pocketed the notebook and stared at the steel fence. "It's worth a try, even if it is a long shot," he murmured, and then he slapped his team into motion toward the gate he knew would be locked.

He reached it and hitched his horses to a steel post after he covertly slid the notebook beneath the leather of the cutter's seat. He strode to the securely locked gate. He shook the gate and stared at the front of the sprawling building, where there were two windows and a door. A full three minutes passed and he hung persistently about the gate. It is only when they consider me a damned nuisance—or perhaps a threat—that they are apt to show themselves, he reasoned.

Another minute passed and again he vigorously rattled the gate; its clanging was clearly audible across the enclosed yard. Now a man had stepped from the building's entrance and was walking with long and impatient strides toward him.

"You sure take a hell of a long time getting around to letting anyone in!" Carswell snapped. "I haven't got all day."

The sour-faced stranger seemed taken aback as he grasped the bars of the gate and stared through. Presently he said, "This gate is always locked. This is private property and nobody is allowed in unless the boss says so."

Henry Carswell decided on a bluff, and his voice took on greater crispness. "Then you just flag your ass back in there and tell Joe Bagley that Henry Carswell, from Blackfoot and Pocatello, is here to place an order." There was a moment of hesitation as the man beyond the gate showed perplexity and something akin to fear.

"You've come to the wrong place, mister; we don't sell anything. This ain't a store."

"Well who said it was?" Carswell seemed to

rage. "This is Bearpaw Enterprises, isn't it? I own farms down along the Snake River, and my tenants order from you." He made as though to turn away in disgust. "Christ, why waste my time!"

He was halfway to the sleigh when the nonplussed stranger called him back. "I guess . . . seeing as you're all the way from Pocatello . . . the boss wouldn't object. He's not here this afternoon." He thrust a key into the lock and swung the gate ajar just enough for Carswell to enter. With some trepidation the man hoping to become Idaho's secretary of state saw the gate closed and locked behind him.

As they trudged toward the front door, Carswell asked, "What's your name, son?" He had already ascertained that the man beside him was young, probably in his early thirties, and had a thin sort of face beneath a plaid cap with earflaps snugly down. He's a strong one, Carswell thought, sort of a dance-hall bouncer type. Suspicious . . . but not the world's most intelligent lackey.

"You just call me Lenny, if you need a name." He swung open a door and motioned for Carswell to enter. Then he asked, "What do you need?"

Carswell had anticipated the query; his answer was prompt and unhesitating. "Mostly I need poison to clean out the goddamned wolves and coyotes and badgers. Then I want to stock up on veterinary medicines." As he spoke, his eyes were sweeping the room. He had expected an office, with desks and chairs and boxes of correspondence and records. There was nothing of the sort. Instead, there was an assortment of nailing and banding and labeling material for cartons. Nearby was a can of paint, a brush, and a stencil.

398

Its lettering confirmed what he already knew. It read: BEARPAW ENTERPRISES, GRANGEVILLE, IDAHO.

There was an unpainted and scuffed-up door that clearly led into the building's larger portion. But it was closed. Carswell knew that he must get beyond that door. After a moment, he asked, "Don't you have someplace where a man can relieve his bladder?"

Lenny pointed to the door. "It's right inside there . . . the door to the left. Use the trough; it spills into a hole outside."

Henry pushed through the door . . . and his eyes widened. There were three men working here, nailing crates and boxes together, while stacked paper containers, pails, bottles, and small cardboard boxes evidently awaited packing in fine sawmill shavings and excelsior. He wanted to look about longer, but he knew that Lenny expected him back soon. Carswell stepped into the privy and used the trough; then he came out, again swept his gaze over the busy room, and rejoined Lenny, who was waiting to write down more of his order. "I'll need some calf-castrating tools, if you have them. Yes and half a dozen pairs of good sheep shears. Yeah, and I almost forgot, something for spavined horses and them with collar galls." He paused as though pondering whether his order was complete. But instead he was establishing one salient fact in his mind: Behind that crating room there had to be other space, where goods were stocked. Even worthless and fraudulent goods had to be manufactured—or concocted. But what he had to remember was the exact position of the big potbellied stove in the crating room . . . and how one leg had been replaced by a half-dozen bricks shoved beneath the stove's base.

He turned to the waiting Lenny. "That about does it, I guess. Figure up how much I owe you." He was drawing his wallet from his coat pocket when he added, "Get the order together and ship it to me at Pocatello. That's on the Union Pacific Railroad."

Ten minutes later he breathed easier; he was again outside the ominous fence, had put Bearpaw Enterprises behind him, and was driving briskly down the snow-packed road.

Back at Bearpaw Enterprises, Lenny walked to the labeling room after letting Carswell off the premises. He fingered almost seventy-five dollars in currency that had been given him in prepayment for goods to be shipped. He idly turned the pages of the receipt book from which he had torn a pencil-written acknowledgment of the money and handed it to Carswell. Abruptly he stopped and stared into space—and into the past. From the first, his visitor had seemed vaguely familiar. Now his mind was carrying him back. To a small office building. To a young woman who had torn herself from his grasp to seize a heavy box from a workman and to smash it against the face of the man who had been sent to pilfer the office. Yes, he acknowledged unwillingly to himself, that fellow who just drove away. Surer than hell, he was the one who barged into the room and shoved a gun into my ribs. Kept it there until the law came running. He lifted a sweated hand and wiped his forehead. His lips were drying, and he felt sick. "Oh, shit!" he gasped. "What am I gonna do? Letting him in here." For a time he mulled the idea of pocketing the cash and saying nothing. But he had passed out a receipt. "Besides, when the sly bastard went to the privy, some of our workers must have seen him. They'll be talking."

He looked at the clock and muttered, "Just a couple of hours 'til closing time. Then . . . damn it to hell . . . I've got to heist my butt over to the ranch and spill all of this." He glared at the pad on which he had listed Carswell's order. His face grew savage but smug. "Well, anyhow, that sneaky old fool is gonna get some of the worst medicines and tools Bearpaw can scrounge up."

Carswell returned to the Buffalo Chip in high spirits. Luck had been with him. His satisfaction heightened when he noticed both Sam Douglas and Jeff Harding had registered. Now, if only Jim Plunkett had managed to come unobtrusively into Grangeville.

He realized, however, that the stranger who called himself Lenny was not the one toward whom the attention and actions of the committee must be turned. Nor would the seemingly nebulous Joseph Bagley likely prove to be the ultimate power. It might be easy to put Bearpaw Enterprises out of business, at least for a while; but Carswell sensed that another, probably far more dangerous mission must be accomplished. The involvement of Blain Halligan must be searched out and brought to a halt. Otherwise, within a few weeks or months another Bearpaw or Nampuh type of swindle might spring up anywhere within Idaho. He was committed now, as were his three associates, to a final wiping out of these ventures that sought to swindle and literally rob livestock producers. He knew Deborah had seen clearly that in so doing he could achieve a statewide popularity that would likely sweep him into office as secretary of state. But to Henry Carswell there seemed an equally impelling reason for the risky effort. It would assure that Deborah Dexter would not try to take things into her own hands, for she would persist despite the odds, the tangle of intrigue and crooked politics, and the very real personal danger.

The first person Carswell's gaze encountered as he entered the Buffalo Chip and shrugged off a knee-length sheepskin coat was someone who had emerged from a back hallway of the building with an armful of fireplace wood. When he had stacked it neatly beside the hearth, he turned and looked up. For the first time, Carswell caught sight of a face bereft of its usual sandy moustache, a face that right now was showing surprise and the beginning of a grin—the face of Jim Plunkett, as he stood in the ill-assorted and worn clothing that marked him as a down-and-outer. He moved toward Carswell and said in an almost wheedling way, "I'll take care of your coat, mister. And your bags, if you left them outside. I'm the choreman here. The roustabout." Plunkett's eyes probed the room and assured him that at the moment they were the only ones in it. Then he whispered in a low and hurried voice, "Both Jeff and Douglas have got rooms upstairs. Me? I was put in a cubbyhole next to the kitchen. But I can get about . . . doing chores, you understand."

Aloud, Carswell replied, "I already have a room, old-timer. First one to the left downstairs. I could use some hot water in about fifteen minutes." He thrust a half dollar toward the seedy-looking man. "Don't forget—in about fifteen minutes . . . after I have a belt of liquor to thaw me out." They drew apart, both satisfied that they had appeared to be strangers when they met.

Carswell entered the saloon and looked quickly about. Both Jeff Harding and Sam Douglas were standing with one foot on the brass railing and evidencing satisfaction with the drinks in their hands. They glanced up, stared momentarily at him, and then appeared utterly disinterested. The room was crowded now, but as Carswell neared the bar, a group of men pushed back to make way for him. He judged that should he linger, more land and buildings would be offered for his inspection. He took a spot near Sam Douglas, ordered his usual Scotch, and after downing a third of it lifted his gaze to the still-intriguing Miriam. "You know, stranger," he said, turning to Douglas, "I used to have a saloon about like this back in Nebraska. If I'd have gotten hold of a picture like that to put up over my backbar, business would sure have picked up. I'd never have drifted out here to Idaho and gotten into the real-estate business."

Without blinking an eye, Sam Douglas took a tug at his beer and wiped his moustache. Then he answered, "Ah, yes, the lure of luscious Idaho pulchritude. Only a rare diamond flush, bestowed upon one at the proper time, can cause the pulse to race in greater ecstasy."

"I take it you're a gambling man," Carswell commented warily.

Douglas nodded. "And you are in real estate, also a gamble." He waited a bit and added, "It has been in my mind to invest in a bit of mother earth. Perhaps you could advise me."

"If you care to walk upstairs, to my room," Carswell offered, "I have some excellent brochures of Snake River properties. By the way, I am Henry Carswell, from Pocatello."

Douglas thrust out a hand. "And I am Sam Douglas." He indicated the man who had stood thoughtfully listening. "And this is my friend Jeff Harding. I am sure he would enjoy seeing the brochures also. But not until after supper . . . say, in an hour and a half."

Thus the three came together in privacy. They were joined presently by Jim Plunkett, who appeared at the door with a coal scuttle and ash shovel in hand. "If I need a quick excuse for being here," he grinned, "I'm doctoring the heating stove over yonder."

They lost no time coming to the urgent business at hand. Carswell sketched for them what he had encountered within the fence encircling Bearpaw Enterprises. "What I don't understand," he concluded, "is their not having any office . . . at least not that I saw. They have to have mail and records and such."

"You didn't see the entire insides of the building, did you?" Jeff Harding asked.

"No. But just the same, I have a feeling that there isn't any office. That the Bearpaw Enterprises records and papers—and likely their cash— are kept elsewhere."

"And you never saw hide nor hair of a Joseph Bagley either, did you?" Jim Plunkett asked.

"Not unless he was one of the fellows in that packing room."

404

"I have an idea," Jeff Harding said slowly, "that when we find out where the records are, that is where we should look for this Bagley fellow. And we may be surprised when we find out just who he is."

"Meaning maybe that Blain Halligan is him . . . that he wears two hats," Plunkett said.

"There is one thing we have to do," Jeff Harding said. "But we must act fast—within a day or so. We can't keep up this business of not working with each other very long. One of us is bound to blunder and let the cat out of the bag. Or someone will happen into town and bust our little conspiracy wide open."

"He is right," Carswell said. "I want to make another visit to Bearpaw's layout. Tomorrow night." He looked at Jeff Harding. "Two of us should accomplish as much as half a dozen. Jeff, I would like to have you with me."

At the words, Jim Plunkett grew thoughtful. "And what I would like to do is pay another visit to Blain Halligan's ranch home; I was there once before, a few months ago." He paused and looked speculatively at Sam Douglas. "Would the idea of trotting along with me be of interest?"

"I would not fancy sitting around here with all three of you out and about. Not even having anyone to play pinochle with," Douglas responded testily. "Of course I'd enjoy a peek at Halligan's retreat."

Jeff Harding said, "I hope each of you realize fully what we may be getting ourselves in for. It has been my experience that raids like these sometimes backfire—even when planned in every detail." He paused, ran thoughtful eyes over them, and continued. "Remember, there is a chance that we'll have to get out of town damned fast."

Henry Carswell combed his fingers through his hair. His gaze had grown somber as he paced the floor and then faced them. "It's not too late to call this expedition off; I wouldn't want any of you risking your necks just to put me in an office down at the statehouse in Boise."

"Hell's fire, Henry," Jim Plunkett said, "where did you get the idea we're up here snooping around just because you want to get into politics? How about the decision we made not to risk having Deborah Dexter trying to clean up that thieving Bearpaw bunch all by herself?"

"He is right," Jeff Harding said. "But it goes deeper than Deborah's battle. What chance will the cattlemen and sheep growers of Idaho have of getting the bloodsuckers off their backs unless we go through with this cleanup?" When they failed to answer, Harding spoke again, and this time there was a touch of anxiety in his voice. "When we split up—Henry and I to visit Bearpaw's warehouse, and Jim and Sam to attempt a call on Halligan—we will be cutting our forces in half . . . and doubling the risk to all concerned."

Sam Douglas came to his feet. Then he said, "Well, we know what has to be done. Now how about working out a few details and drifting apart? I think Branigan is chomping at the bit to have a go at me at poker."

"Before we go into them details," Plunkett spoke up, "how about deciding how we are going to get away from Grangeville after raising the hell we came here to raise?"

"I have thought about that," Carswell nodded. "What we need is to set a place outside of town to get together, say like an old swaybacked barn I know of. Then leave the rest to me." He told them where to find it.

Plunkett grunted, but it was evident his thoughts were elsewhere. Finally he said, "You know, we might have help from some of the natives if we knew which ones to approach. Not everyone hereabouts cottons to Blain Halligan. I recall it was a letter that Deborah got from someone soured on Halligan that first tipped her off to his shenanigans. That letter was sent from right here in Grangeville." Then he added, "Old Plunkett, the dim-witted prospector, is going to make a few inquiries come tomorrow morning."

"While you are at it," Carswell urged, "try to pry out what this confounded weather is going to be like by tomorrow night."

"It is likely to be snowing," Jeff Harding said quickly.

"How do you know?" Douglas demanded.

"Because it's beginning to snow right now," and Jeff pointed to a window across which a swirl of white was racing.

Contrary to Harding's prediction, the storm broke up before dawn after putting down only another inch of snow. Yet there was a gray sullenness about the morning. Members of the committee, realizing that this would likely be their last day in Grangeville, spent it in widely differing ways. Henry Carswell, scanning his notebook, found the name and address of the owner of the run-down log house and swaybacked barn. After half an hour of haggling, a deal was struck. Carswell counted out two hundred dollars in greenbacks. "This is good-faith money," he explained. "When you can turn over a paper showing you have clear title and can assign it to me, I will pay the balance."

"Hell, I can write that out right now. Sweet and simple," the owner protested. He was a middle-aged fellow who evidently desired to move to a warmer climate.

"Nope," Carswell parried, "you get a quitclaim deed filled out and sign it before a couple of witnesses. Then mail it to me at this address." He was writing rapidly on the back of a soiled envelope. "I'll leave a check with you now for the rest of the money—but it won't be any good until I get that deed."

"Do you want a receipt for this two hundred?"

Carswell eyed him shrewdly. "It's not necessary; you look like an honest man. But there are a couple of things I would like."

"Such as?"

"I want your permission to use the old house and barn for a day or so while I am here."

"No reason you can't." The owner shrugged indifferently.

Then Henry Carswell asked quietly but bluntly, "Is everybody around this town beholden to the rancher Blain Halligan—or in fear of him?" He paused, and then as though to justify the question, he added, "Whenever I mention looking over or possibly buying any of Halligan's holdings, people clam up. They seem scared."

The words seemed to flame resentment and anger in the other man's eyes. Then he blurted out,

"Halligan has his hooks into a fair slice of this valley—and quite a few people too—but he don't by a damn sight rule the whole roost. Me, I keep clear of him. Because . . . because I hate the man's guts."

Carswell fought to keep excitement out of his voice as he said, "If you care to mention the names of a few others who feel the same way you do, I likely can raise that good-faith money to, say, three hundred dollars. And don't worry, fellow; your name won't be revealed."

Minutes later, when Carswell left the owner thumbing greenbacks, he had three names firmly imprinted in his mind. He had not deemed it expedient to let the property owner write down the names.

Carswell lost no time seeking out Jim Plunkett, who was carrying ashes to a pile behind the Buffalo Chip. "Jim, we may have a real break . . . three local people who'd be glad to see Blain Halligan get his comeuppance. Is there any way you can manage to chat with them? I have their names."

Plunkett dumped ashes onto a growing pile. "Likely I can, Henry. I will be off duty until toward evening. What do you want me to ask?"

Carswell's eyes narrowed and he looked about. When assured no one else was near, he said, "I have a strong hunch that one of the three may have written that first letter to Deborah—the one that tied Blain Halligan into the old Nampuh Distributing Company and the skulduggery at the Idaho State Capitol."

"We haven't much time," Plunkett replied.

"Jeff Harding is uneasy. He thinks we may be tinkering with dynamite."

"And he sure could be right," Carswell agreed. "Something else: Get word to Jeff to meet me tonight, just after dark, at the swaybacked barn. I sort of own it now." Then he asked in a worried way, "Have you and Sam Douglas planned how you are going to get out to Halligan's ranch and manage to get inside the house?"

"Pretty well, we have, Henry." For a couple of minutes Jim Plunkett sketched a verbal picture of what he recalled of Blain Halligan's ranch and its house. "We are going to ride out there and yell that all hell has broken loose at the Bearpaw warehouse. But, mind you, that will be an hour *after* you and Jeff Harding make your call at the warehouse. We figure news like that will sure thin out Halligan's hands and send them scurrying. Then we can get down to business."

"But what if any of them recognize you . . . or Sam Douglas?"

"We're pretty sure they won't—at least at first. Not the way we'll be dressed and made up."

"Jim, be damned careful," Carswell said at last. "Something about this bothers me. I have learned that Halligan is probably at his ranch—and he isn't a fool."

"Just so he is fooled for a little while," Plunkett replied. Then he asked, "Just what time do you expect to get into Bearpaw? We'll need to time this thing."

"Don't start anyone riding toward the warehouse before nine o'clock. We should be out of it by then." Carswell wanted to utter more words of caution but said simply, "Remember, we meet on the stage road near the swaybacked barn."

It was already dark when the southbound stage, which had left Lewiston, on the Clearwater River, the previous day, drew up before the Buffalo Chip. The driver climbed down and opened the vehicle's door. There were only three passengers, huddled under an ancient buffalo robe.

"Everybody out," the driver said decisively. "This is Grangeville and we're at Branigan's Buffalo Chip. Inside yuh can get food and a bed. And if you're amind to, have a belt of liquor to unfreeze your innards."

"How soon do we take off again?" a portly passenger asked as he stirred and came to his feet.

"Not until daylight," the driver answered. "I reckon there'll be a lot of snowdrifts and slow going ahead."

Without further questions or protest the three retrieved their hand luggage and filed into the lobby. The driver unloaded some freight and then drove off into the stormy darkness to seek out a stable.

Inside, Jim Plunkett was adding logs to the fireplace blaze. The blast of cold air that entered with the stage passengers caused him to turn and look them over. The portly one he guessed to be a dry-goods salesman, while the second was a gray-haired woman whose features and clothing marked her as an Indian, likely a Nez Percé. But when Plunkett caught sight of the third passenger, his eyes widened and he caught an excited breath. He dropped two logs onto the brick of the hearth and stepped quickly forward to scan the passenger's face.

"God Almighty!" he said aloud and thrust out a hand. "You're Lowell . . . Robert Lowell."

Chapter 20

IN BOISE, on the evening that Deborah received
the short and unrevealing letter from Robert
Lowell, she read and reread it with mixed emotions. What possibly could have happened regarding their timberland that would cause Lowell
to write to her and then hasten toward Boise?
Things best not put on paper, he wrote. Was he
speaking in terms of business, or of certain memo-
ries shared only by the two of them? She sank
down on the bed's edge and handed the letter to
Mollie. "Why is it," she asked, "that any man has
a way of writing a page and not really telling you
anything?"

Mollie's eyes scanned the handwritten lines,
then in a practical voice she replied, "I think
it says quite a bit, Debbie. He is coming here.
Should arrive Monday. He wants to talk business
. . . and . . . maybe monkey business. You know
he was always addlepated about you."

Deborah reached out and drew the blue dress
from a box. "Now I will have the letter on my
mind. Tonight. At dinner—and afterward."

Mollie eyed the dress as Deborah held it against
herself. "That is too pretty a thing to buy and then
not use right away. Besides, Debbie, you wouldn't
solve one blasted thing by sitting here alone and
wondering about what hibernating Bob Lowell is

going to tell you." There was firmness and a bit of rancor in Mollie's words.

"You have never exactly approved of Robert, have you, Mollie?"

"No, by Jesus. Not since he skedaddled away from Bonanza and practically deserted you." Mollie hesitated, pursed her lips, and then plunged ahead. "Besides, you never told me what went sour that time you ran into Lowell up there on the Clearwater River. But you were hurt, honey. Hurt deep down."

Deborah looked up to search her friend's concerned face. Then she told Mollie of her night with Robert and of the Indian girl pregnant with his child.

Mollie had begun pacing the floor, but stopped to dab at her eyes with a handkerchief. Her voice took on frustration. "What burns my old saddle-warped butt, Debbie, is that this precious Mr. Robert Lowell has damn near broken your heart. Honey, Jim and me know you are something special . . . like the daughter we never had. So we don't want to see you get hurt. Are you really serious about this Mormon fellow, Lemuel Froman? Will you be happy and contented with him?"

"Mollie, he will treat me wonderfully well. I am sure of that. And he has the sweetest little girl."

Mollie threw her hands aloft. "Damn it to hell, Deborah—are you marrying him because of a cute young'un, or are you head over heels in love? So much that you can't bear to be away from him day or night? That's the kind of love you need . . . and deserve, honey."

As Deborah absorbed Mollie's troubled words, she realized that her innermost thoughts were not with Lemuel Froman, nor were they about the forthcoming visit of Robert Lowell. Instead, they were in the far-off Greys River valley of Wyoming, recalling the words of Jeff Harding: *I never before wanted a woman as I want you.* For long moments she was silent, recalling how she had told herself that Jeff was surely not of the marrying kind and that likely he seldom gave into the compulsive desire for a woman's nearness . . . her love . . . her body.

She turned to her companion, her voice trembling with emotion. "Mollie, were you ever torn in different directions?"

When no answer came, she continued, "I want to go out with Lemuel tonight. Dine. Dance. Maybe even drink a bit too much. I want to laugh and to forget work and troubles. Maybe then I'll know whether I'll grow to love him—and marry him." She drew a deep breath, then added, "All I know of Robert's visit is that we will have business to discuss. Something of what there was between us is tarnished—perhaps gone."

But Deborah's face, the wistfulness of it, and the softness of her eyes suddenly seemed to lend utter truth to Mollie Plunkett's intuition: There is someone else.

At exactly ten minutes before eight o'clock, Deborah's landlady told her that a gentleman was waiting in the parlor below. She took a final look at herself in the long mirror and smiled in a gaily pleased way; then she picked up her coat and turned to Mollie. "I can't remember your ever meeting Lemuel . . . and I want you to. Walk downstairs with me, please, Mollie."

415

Lemuel Froman was sitting somewhat stiffly on the edge of a leather chair. He was wearing a dark suit, a white, high-collared shirt, and a maroon-hued necktie. The gloss of his black shoes spoke of tedious brushing; he moved a pair of new gloves restlessly from one hand to the other. He rose as the two women approached him. He was clean-shaven now, and his face, to Deborah, seemed to speak of inner suffering.

After the introductions, Froman took Deborah's coat and held it for her to slip into. Now he said, "Your gown is lovely, Deborah. And . . . and it is nice to meet you, Mrs. Plunkett. I have heard of you often." His phrases were commonplace, but the richness of his trained voice seemed to lend sincerity.

Both Deborah and he were aware of Mollie's scrutiny. "Don't worry about Deborah," Lemuel assured her. "I'll have her home at a satisfactory hour."

His words caused an impish grin to leap into Mollie's plump face. "Hell's fire, young fellow," she said, "Debbie knows when to cut it for home. You just see that she doesn't get chilled." With the warning, Mollie turned and trudged back up the stairs.

Froman watched her go, then he murmured, "I'm quite sure that she doesn't approve of me."

In Deborah's mind was memory of the scathing words Mollie had used earlier in the evening to voice her opinion of Robert Lowell. "Lemuel, don't let it worry you," she replied. "I am not at all sure that Mollie would approve of anyone whom she feels might be courting me. She is wonderful to me. Like a mother. But overprotective." She

416

tucked her hand under his arm, and together they left the building and walked to the surrey awaiting them at the street's edge.

They drove through the chilly night to a restaurant which Deborah had never before visited. The structure was of peeled and varnished logs, set back in a grove of trees and with a yard lighted by mellow gas lamps.

Inside, there was warmth, subdued lighting, and the murmur of conversation. Near an enormous stone fireplace, music was being performed by a string quartet. There was a large room with well-spaced couches and chairs; its motif was of Idaho history, and there were paintings of the state's scenic spots. Two doors, wide and portiered, led into adjacent rooms. Through one, Deborah glimpsed an array of tables, each with white linen and a vase containing a single fresh-cut carnation. The second door, directly across the lobby, had its inner view discreetly cut off by large, folding screens, but the chant of a croupier and the whirring of a roulette wheel proclaimed its nature.

They were escorted to a table that Deborah felt certain was one of the choice ones of the dining room. It offered the coziness of a nearby fireplace and a view of the town's lighted streets through a large and uncurtained window. Gazing out, Deborah noted the way in which the light of a full moon seemed to lay across Boise and reveal the slopes of nearby mountains. She knew that in the higher country the snow was deep and that the temperature would plunge before morning.

She studied the menu, but for a little while this place of dining and enjoyment seemed oddly lonely and insignificant. It was through those austere northern mountains that four men had hastened on a mission that should have been her responsibility. The face of each came before her. Henry Carswell, cool and businesslike. Sam Douglas, with the calculated reserve of a seasoned gambler. Jim Plunkett, grinning and easygoing but keen-minded and persevering. And last of all, the quiet confidence and gentle understanding of Jeff Harding.

She looked up, to see that Lemuel Froman was watching her in a puzzled manner.

"Deborah, your mind was far away. I hope you are really hungry. What appeals to you?"

"The seafood assortment," she answered. She hesitated momentarily, then added, "But let me choose the wine. Do you mind?"

He stared at her in silence, and it took time for him to mask the shock and disapproval that lay across his face. Then he muttered, "Of course, if you really care for such—it is an alcoholic beverage, you know."

She remembered then. Remembered that according to his Mormon creed he must not indulge in drinks containing alcohol. Nor must he partake of coffee or tea. So she said quietly, "I am sorry, Lemuel. Your Church teachings . . . I forgot them." She turned to the waiter. "May I have a glass of fruit juice . . . or lemonade."

The meal proved to be delicious and they smiled often, talking of his law practice, of their first meeting in Nebraska, and of her school years in Salt Lake City. Yet the incident had somehow built a small but uncomfortable barrier between them. Finishing her seafood, Deborah would have liked a cup of coffee, but she did not mention it.

Presently they rose to dance on a sizable hardwood floor ringed by tables. The quartet broke into a Viennese waltz. He's a beautiful dancer, she thought, and let him lead her in the steps of the dance. Presently he leaned to place his lips close to her ear. "At least, Debbie, we Mormons are not denied the pleasure of music and dancing." She pressed his hand in response and they stayed on the floor in step to the plaintive strains of "Aura Lee."

"Did you know that this is a West Point class song, but called 'Army Blue'?" he asked.

"No. But isn't it lovely . . . and haunting. My mother used to tell me that her father marched to it during the Civil War."

"Your mother," he repeated. "She has become highly respected for her work among our women and children." Froman's tone conveyed somehow a silent reproach that Deborah had not chosen to become a Latter-day Saint.

When they were back at their table, Deborah looked about the dining room. More people were now seated and there was a pleasant hum of voices across the room. Presently her gaze rested on two men seated at a nearby table; she recognized both of them at once: Frank Wentworth, with his carefully brushed silver hair, and the younger and strangely dominant form of William E. Borah. They caught sight of her, waved, and then presently made their way beyond the screened door of the gaming room.

"I would like to go in there, Lemuel—if women are permitted to do so. I'd . . . I'd even like to wager a few dollars. I was too young to be allowed in the gambling halls at Bonanza and Custer."

Again he became hesitant and restrained. Clearly his impulse was to accompany her into the gambling room. But immediately it gave way to doubt and self-denial. "Go ahead. I will wait here for you."

The words sparked her anger. "Never mind, Lemuel. I guess such a pastime is forbidden by your Church. Damn it, Lemuel, when are you going to give yourself a break? Unwind and have the pleasures always denied you?"

"There are recreations far more spiritual and uplifting than drinking and gambling and—" he responded bitterly.

"Perhaps—but aside from dancing, we certainly have not tainted ourselves with them tonight, have we?"

His eyes took on both bafflement and disappointment. Then he asked, almost in a whisper, "Do we have to quarrel like this, Deborah? I wanted so much for you to enjoy yourself—and possibly consent to be my wife. I . . . I am in love with you, Debbie. Can't you realize it?" His face had become that of a hurt and anxious boy.

She reached across and laid her hand on his. "Thank you for trying to assure my having a wonderful evening, Lemuel. But hadn't we best face up to the hard facts and the truth? I could never be or become the type of wife you need."

"But Debbie, I love you. I think I have loved you for a long, long time."

"You think you do, probably because of your self-denial and your loneliness. But I am sure you would grow to despise me, to consider me a millstone about your neck."

"But I had planned for us to have a Temple wedding . . . in Salt Lake City."

"When I am not even a member of your Church? They would not permit me inside the door."

"All that would be required," he replied, "is for you to take indoctrination classes. Just for a few weeks."

She gazed at him as one would at a persistent but misunderstanding child. "Oh, Lemuel, don't you see what I am trying to say? I would never be a good Mormon. I am apathetic toward the very things that mean the most to you."

He looked aghast. "Our Church, God's realm on earth, means no more to you than that?"

"God is wherever you find him," Deborah answered patiently. "It is your Mormonism that leaves me apathetic. Lemuel, please try to understand me."

His face had whitened, and he whispered, "Deborah . . . we . . . we could overcome all that. You could learn—I would help—"

She braced herself against the hope she was shattering. "Lemuel, do I have to spell it out for you? For a growing multitude of people, Mormonism . . . is a satisfying, even an inspiring way of life. But I cannot embrace it. Now or ever. If I should marry you, you would grow to despise me."

"But what of Janice, my little girl . . . and of our plans for Peter, the blind boy?"

The words shook her, and Deborah knew she was close to tears. "Oh, God! Lemuel, no marriage can be built just on the needs and the love of children. We can't sacrifice them like that."

"Then I have my answer—the final, torturing answer?" Lemuel had folded his napkin and was rising from the table. His voice was harsh as he asked, "Would you like me to take you home?"

She touched his hand and then shook her head. "I would rather you didn't. It would only prolong our misery."

When he had stridden from the room, she sat for several minutes in a numbed sort of reverie. What a ghastly way of ending their dinner. Yet, she thought, it would have been even more unfair to keep him waiting or to marry him. Damn it, is this my role in life: to destroy the dreams and the ambitions of the men attracted to me?

She shrugged off the dismal thought. A waiter appeared and told her that Lemuel had already paid the dinner check, but that she could have an after-dinner drink, if she wanted. Her first impulse was to order one, then she shook her head. She left the table, crossed the dining room and the lobby. Then she stepped inside the gaming room.

When an overseeing employee approached, she smiled with more confidence than she felt. Then she asked, "Would you kindly tell Mr. Frank Wentworth that Miss Dexter would like to speak to him?"

Within seconds Wentworth was at her side. His gaze became one of concern as he asked softly, "What, what in the world is the matter, Deborah? You are ashen, as though you have seen ghosts or watched someone die." He was leading her toward his table. "Bill Borah had to leave a while ago. Sit down. Sit down and tell me about it, honey. First, though, can I order you a drink?"

For a moment she rested her head in her hands,

with her elbows on the table. Then she murmured, "I want to tell you. But not now . . . not here. Mr. Wentworth, can we do something crazy, you and I?"

"Like what?" he asked, reaching across to push an errant lock of her brown hair into place.

"Like our going and rousing out Mollie Plunkett, making her get dressed—and then going on down and beating on Mama Echiverri's door. Then I want to drink too much of Mama Echiverri's wine. Yes, damn it to hell, Frank, I want to get drunk. And cry my heart out."

Chapter 21

To HENRY CARSWELL and the other members of the committee, the arrival of Robert Lowell at the Buffalo Chip brought an entirely new facet to their situation. Scarcely an hour remained before they would put their plan into action.

It was Sam Douglas who spoke urgent words to Lowell after Jim Plunkett had broken the news of the Lowell's arrival.

"Young fellow," Douglas began, "you sure chose an odd time to show up here. There's likely to be one hell of a ruckus tonight, and unless you think as much of Deborah Dexter as she does of you, you should stay put here and keep your mouth shut." Douglas filled him in on the plan and its background.

"And I've got something else to tell you," Douglas continued, "so brace yourself. You recall that rap you took out in Seattle? When they kicked you out of medical school for allegedly performing an abortion?"

Lowell's face slackened in surprise and he grasped Sam Douglas' arm. "How come you know about that?" he demanded.

"Because Deborah Dexter sent me out there to find out. You were framed, boy. Framed by that nice, friendly classmate who actually wielded the knife—Lacey Halligan!"

His revelation caused Robert Lowell to step

backward with wide and almost disbelieving eyes. "Somehow I always had a hunch Lacey was mixed up in it. But to think he actually operated. Why, Douglas? Why?"

Douglas told him of Lacey's gambling debts. Then he added, "You know who is paying me to set you clean?"

Robert nodded. "Yes . . . I know. Deborah never gives up." His hands pressed his eyes, and he murmured, "Oh, God, Deborah . . . what have I done to you?"

Sam Douglas listened as though striving to piece together a puzzle. Then he said coldly, "Lowell, I don't know what you've done *to* her, but I sure as hell know what you can do *for* her: You can ride out with us tonight!"

After coordinating plans, the four members of the committee and Robert Lowell slipped out of Grangeville later that evening. They were aided by a chill wind and intermittent swirls of snow that kept the streets almost deserted.

Now Henry Carswell sought out Harding within a grove of white pine trees at Grangeville's north edge. Throughout his stay, Jeff Harding had been limping painfully from the wound he had received at Greys River. Now he came quietly to the side of the light sled and a team of restless gray geldings.

"I knew you sure aren't in shape to hike all the way out to the swaybacked barn . . . the way we had planned," Carswell said. "But here's what I figure. Likely our visit to Bearpaw won't take as long as Douglas and Plunkett and young Lowell will need out at Halligan's ranch. I worked it out with Sam. We will wait for the three of them at a creek crossing about two miles south on the Boise road. Jim says there is a sawmill setup quite a piece beyond that. With these horses, fresh and full-bellied, we ought to all make it to hell and gone out of Grangeville."

There were only the sounds of wind, the softly muffled hoofbeats, and the loneliness of the road as they drove through the night. There was no starlight and no way to accurately mark distance. Then they came to a bend in the road, and Carswell pulled the horses to a stop. "The old log house and swaybacked barn are maybe three hundred yards ahead," he said. "The Bearpaw layout is less than a quarter mile beyond it. I'm gonna ease this team and rig in behind the old barn; we can put the horses inside the barn."

"Then what?" Harding's voice was tense but quiet.

"Then we are on our own, you and me. Afoot."

Presently they came to the metal fence around Bearpaw Enterprises, approaching it in back of the sprawling building and well away from the locked gate. The snow had drifted deeply onto the lower ground. Peering about in the scant light they became aware that midway in the swale the fence crossed a large ditch, and within the snow-burdened ditch only some loosely hung pieces of sheet metal denied access to the inner yard and the building.

Carswell tugged at the rusted sheet metal, noting that it lifted a few inches above the snow. "You go first, Jeff. Sort of burrow through the drift. Then get up and keep your eyes peeled; it'll take me longer. I want to make sure we can scurry out this way one hell of a lot faster than we are getting in."

They squinted at the shadowy bulk of the building ahead and then spurted toward it. The rear wall was of roughly milled vertical timbers, with narrow strips covering the cracks. There was a heavily bolted, wide wagon door which apparently had not been used since the recent snowfalls. There was a single window well above the large door; to one side of the window a battered shutter was creaking in the wind. They stared cautiously about.

"Likely they have a night watchman," Jeff surmised aloud. "But on a cold, stormy night like this he's apt to keep close to the stove. Maybe look around the building every hour or so."

"Without a ladder, we can't even try to force that window," Carswell said. "Maybe we ought to get around to the front; that's where the rooms are I saw. And more windows."

"I don't think so," Jeff answered. "Henry, this rear end of the place is likely to be storage space." He walked to the corner of the building, turned, and for a time was lost to Carswell's sight. When Harding returned, there seemed a purpose about him and in his arms was an object Carswell immediately recognized.

"What are you going to do with a set of wagon doubletrees? Where'd you get them?" he whispered.

"From an old lumber-hauling wagon about buried in snow along that east wall. You see this?" Harding pointed to a metal hooking device at the end of one singletree. "If you can hoist me onto your shoulders, I probably can lift this doubletree and set the hook in the window frame. Then I can shinny up it and maybe work that window loose."

"You could fall and bust your ass too, Jeff. You limp enough now."

"You just get me up there, hand me the one end, and then see that you stand plumb still," Jeff instructed calmly.

Only two minutes later he had succeeded in imbedding the hook into the window's lower ledge and had scrambled upward to run cold, numbing hands along the window sash. The frame yielded stubbornly to his clutch, and he was able to get his fingers inside it. There was a sharp tearing sound as a metal latch gave way. Then unexpectedly the entire framed window was in his hand, and he was trying to hang onto the doubletree while lowering the window to an amazed Carswell.

Carswell grasped the window sash and cautiously leaned it against the building.

Harding drew himself painfully upward but at last straddled the opening. He unhooked the doubletree and lowered it. "Somehow I am going to pull you up here with this. But . . . make it quick. You're a heavy . . ."

Carswell grasped the doubletree and was working his way upward . . . hand over hand . . . foot over foot against the building's side.

Eventually both were able to reach the floor inside the building. Now darkness was their problem; they could only feel their way. They encountered stacked lumber, a wagon, and a wilderness of empty barrels. Once a board of the floor beneath them creaked loudly. They stopped to listen, but there was only the sound of the wind as it

428

searched the outer eaves and swept in the window opening behind them.

They reached a wall, and through an unlocked door came into what Carswell sensed was a smaller and less cluttered room. It seemed, as they felt about, to be only a storage area and a passage to the front of the building. They were edging through the gloom, seeking another doorway, when the sounds came to them—footsteps, in the room they were seeking. Then abruptly a door swung open. Lanternlight spilled about them; a heavily coated figure took a startled backward step. His voice tore through the shadowy room. "Boss! Get in here fast! The bastards have broken in!"

In that tense second, Carswell had glimpsed the startled face of the lanternbearer. It's Lenny, he thought. Damn—they're expecting us . . . maybe laid a trap.

Even as the thought seared his mind, Carswell was watching Jeff Harding move into action. His arm had gone about the startled youth's neck, and a hand was silencing further outcry as it pressed over Lenny's mouth. In an effort to break free, Lenny's arm lashed out, and the lantern, striking a wall, shattered and went out. But there was still light coming through the open doorway, light that revealed far more than Carswell wanted to see. The room ahead took on instant familiarity. On his first visit to Bearpaw he had approached from the privy to stand on the edge of this room. His gaze now encompassed the boxing and crating area—and the potbellied stove with cherry-hued flames beyond an isinglass door.

But now three men confronted him, their faces

grimly angry in the light of two kerosene lamps bracketed against the wall. In the hand of the nearest one was a revolver pointed toward the gut area of Jeff Harding.

"Get your hands up. Both of you. Spread against that wall." Carswell moved quickly to comply. But in that moment Harding twisted and was further shielded by the struggling Lenny. With speed that Carswell could scarcely comprehend, Lenny's arm was twisted upward and he cried out in pain and ceased to struggle. And in Harding's hand appeared a wicked-looking Colt revolver—now pointed at the man who had ordered their surrender.

Fury tore the nearest stranger's face . . . and suddenly Carswell stared at it with growing certainty. It was the face of a tall and well-featured man not yet middle-aged, with dark hair and a hint of Latin ancestry. Now there was no fear in his voice, only cold calculation as he spoke to Jeff Harding. "I don't know who you are, fellow. But just remember I can have half a dozen men here within a minute."

As the words ended, Carswell was sure of two things. He and Jeff had unexpectedly encountered the kingpin of Bearpaw Enterprises. This had to be Blain Halligan, himself—and he was boldly lying about having more men within call. But there was no denying that he was backed now by two hard-looking characters, both surely armed. Carswell shifted his gaze to Harding . . . and drew a quick breath. Carswell had never seen Jeff Harding's face as it now appeared in the pale yellow lamplight. His eyes were narrowed and cold; there seemed no emotion about him, only a deadliness of purpose. And now Jeff was speaking.

"Call your men—and you won't be alive to see them come through the doorway."

"Damn it . . . who are you?" Blain Halligan asked. "How come you to sneak into a man's legitimate place of business?"

A low and mirthless laugh came from Harding. *"Legitimate?* Sure I'll tell you. I am Jeff Harding, an employee of the sheepmen of the West."

Even as the words ended, Carswell was watching the two strangers who had stood close to Halligan. Now they were edging apart. Within seconds Harding could be under menace from three directions. Jeff had noticed it also. Now he said quietly, "Hold it, you two. I'd hate to have to shoot an eye out of either of you."

At that moment Carswell sensed that this was a standoff between Halligan and Jeff Harding, with his friend having the disadvantage because Lenny was in his grasp and able to push about. It can't last much longer, Carswell's mind flashed. Then he peered intently at the potbellied stove and he said aloud and almost sociably, "Jeff, we've made a mistake. None of these men appears to be Joseph Bagley . . . from Nampuh. He's the bastard we want. Maybe we ought to apologize and—wait 'til I spit out this tobacco chaw, and I'll explain." He glanced at the floor, seemed to look for a target spot, mouthed an imaginary quid, and stepped casually forward. Then his foot was a blur as it snaked forward to strike a brick holding one corner. He seemed to stumble, but his hand caught the stove's door latch and jerked it open.

431

Then his shoulder struck the huge stove and toppled it forward.

Hell seemed to break loose then. One of Halligan's men screamed a curse as a length of hot stovepipe crashed on him. He flung an arm upward, and in so doing knocked one of the kerosene lamps from its bracket. The chimney shattered and the glow vanished, leaving the room in semidarkness. There was a grunt from Lenny as he sought to break from Harding's grasp.

Carswell managed to regain his feet. He saw the sweep of Harding's revolver as it came down in a stunning blow to Lenny's head, then the mingled fury and disbelief with which Blain Halligan stood watching flames leap from the spilled stove coals to the paper and shavings and small boxes. Lenny's knees buckled and he slipped to the floor, half blocking the opening through which Jeff and Carswell had entered the room.

There were excited shouts and curses. An instant later Carswell felt a swish of air as a bullet sang past his left ear and plowed into the wall behind him. Then he saw that the man was positioning for another try. It never came, for his weapon fell to the floor as Jeff Harding shot it from his fingers. Halligan bent to retrieve the gun, but Carswell kicked it from him.

And now the flames were out of control, licking their way across the floor, leaping into the boxing material, and blackening the room with smoke and heat and ever-growing danger.

The guard from whose hand Harding had shot the pistol turned, holding his wrist, and hurried toward the door that led to the privy and the rooms in front. His companion had grabbed a bur-lap sack and was frantically beating at the flames.

"You sons-of-bitches," Blain Halligan said with cold fury, "I'll see that you pay for this. Hang maybe . . ." But the words trailed off as he gazed in hopeless bafflement at the room. Then he too lunged toward the doorway. Seeming to disregard his one remaining guard and the still unconscious Lenny, he attempted to close the door to trap those within the room.

Jeff Harding swung his weapon about. "Don't touch it, fellow." The words, emphasized by the cold menace of his revolver, stayed Halligan's hand.

Henry Carswell was coughing. "Let's get out of here, Jeff . . . damn quick. Out the front." He turned to the sack-flailing guard. "That ain't going to do one bit of good." He pointed at Lenny. "And you'd better drag your friend out with you —or watch him roast."

With fast but guarded movements, Harding and Carswell made for the front doorway. There was little doubt now: By sunrise Bearpaw Enterprises would be a charred mass.

Abruptly their way was blocked as Halligan swung about. For the first time a gun was in his hand. Carswell noted it and yelled, "Watch out, Jeff—he's gonna shoot!" At the warning, Harding tried to come into position for a hurried shot. He was slowed by Lenny, who was regaining con-sciousness and stumbling blindly about. Carswell swept the scene in utter desperation. No doubt re-mained. As soon as Harding was clear of the weaving Lenny and the guard who had been dragging him, Halligan would shoot—to kill. And the advantage was definitely his.

In a calm and easy voice, Carswell spoke directly to Blain Halligan. "Go ahead and shoot, you fool. Go ahead." His words caught Halligan off guard, and he listened as Carswell went on. "Do it, damn you, Halligan. Right away, for you won't be alive two minutes from now. Know why? We've three men waiting at that front door. *And one of them is Robert Lowell.*"

There was only a momentary delay as Halligan's face jerked more directly toward Carswell . . . and the hand holding the gun wavered. Without warning, Carswell sprang forward. His hand twisted Blain Halligan's wrist so the pistol was pointing upward. There was a shot as Halligan's trigger finger tightened, but the bullet crashed harmlessly into the ceiling, and the gun clattered to the floor. The delay had been enough. Jeff Harding had swung clear of Lenny and the guard. And now Harding's face carried something new— the deadliness of a man whose life has just been in jeopardy. "Move toward the door, Halligan," he snapped, "Now!"

Carswell picked the gun up. The room behind them had become an inferno of smoke and flames as Harding and Carswell edged toward the front door. There could be no retracing their steps to the back-wall window where less than ten minutes ago they had clambered into the building. The thought struck Carswell that likely the surging of wind through the open window would fan and spread the flames.

They reached the front door with the Bearpaw men crowded before them. Then Harding spoke.

"You will get out safe now—all of you. But get this straight. We're going outside first. Don't as much as stick a head out . . . any of you . . . for about half a minute." He motioned to Carswell to throw open the door. They shoved their way outside and pushed the door shut. Then they raced around the building's corner. They reached the ditch and the opening through which they had crawled into the yard, then plopped to their bellies in the snow and wiggled hastily toward escape. Now there was the sound of running footsteps, of furious oaths, and of men hoping somehow to search them out and destroy them.

Presently they reached the old barn and Harding asked, "How can we get back into town without maybe meeting up with others on the road we took here? Those flames at Bearpaw will be spotted and start half the town this way."

"I scouted another way out for us," Carswell answered. "There's another road—not much more than a trail—we can take to come onto the stage route to Boise about a mile south of Grangeville. It's an old mining road, rough and snow-drifted, but by being real careful we can get through."

They waited for fifteen minutes; twice there was the sound of men and horses passing swiftly toward Bearpaw. At last Carswell untied the horses; they took them outside and fastened the harness traces again to the sleigh. "I reckon it is now or never," Carswell said.

They eased the team past the old cabin, opened a barbed-wire gate, and came again onto the main road. Carswell urged the gray geldings into a fast trot, but before they could reach the crossroad half a dozen fast-moving riders loomed ahead, heading toward Bearpaw. He drew the sleigh to a halt and waited for the riders to come within hearing distance. Then he called, "Don't run us over. We've got to get to town to locate some Bearpaw people—to get word to Mr. Halligan that the place is burning down . . . likely to the ground."

The riders brought restless horses to a halt, and their front men stared searchingly at the sleigh and at Carswell. Then one of them said, "Sure! Now I know you . . . you're the fellow who's been looking at real estate the past couple of days."

"That's right," Carswell assured him blandly. "This gent and I"—he moved an elbow toward Harding—"drove out to see if there were many packrats at that place with the swayback barn and old log house. I bought it today." He eased the team firmly ahead. "I can't talk more right now— got to get word to the Bearpaw people!"

The riders moved on, and Carswell and Harding rode to the crossroad. Now time would be vital. They must reach the Boise stage road, find a secluded spot, and await the return of the three who had ridden toward the Halligan ranch.

At exactly the same moment that Henry Carswell had forced a pistol from Blain Halligan's grasp, a breathless and obviously shaken Sam Douglas spurred his mount up a snow-spotted lane several miles west of Grangeville. He came presently to a plank gate; it was closed, chained, and locked, denying access to the main house and outbuildings of Halligan's ranch. In Douglas' mind were the directions provided by Jim Plunkett, who with his wife and Deborah Dexter had visited this place months before. Only about three minutes had passed since Douglas had parted company with Plunkett and Robert Lowell. They had drawn their horses into seclusion well off the entrance lane and would await the outcome of Sam's agitated approach to the headquarters.

Now Douglas sounded an urgently demanding yell: "Hello the house!" He paused to listen, and when there was no answer from the quiet and darkened buildings, his voice took on impatience. "Hell! Ain't nobody looking after this outfit? Unlock the gate, you hear? I've gotta see my friend Blain Halligan right away! Got news for him! Important news!"

"Hold on and quiet down. Jesus Christ!" a voice sounded. "I'm coming. You trying to wake half of Idaho?"

"Then get it unlocked," Douglas demanded. "I asked you, is Blain here? It's urgent as hell."

The form of a sheepskin-coated man approached on the far side of the gate and looked up. "Who are you, anyhow?"

"My name is Judson . . . Joe Judson," Douglas lied glibly, then he added excitedly, "I've rode all the way out from town. There's big trouble at Bearpaw. I don't know what exactly, but they need ol' Blain and everyone else. You got horses stabled?"

"Sure—but—" the ranch employee answered uncertainly.

"Let me in and I'll help your hands get saddled. Damn it, man, shake a leg! Every minute counts!"

Under Douglas' fiery persuasion, the man dug in a pocket, pulled out a key, and opened the lock. Sam Douglas fought a grin as he noticed that the lock was left hanging by its hasp in the chain as the gate opened. His bluff had worked. And now he asked hurriedly, "How many men can you send?"

"Just four. Others are already in town." The ranch hand had turned as though to make toward the nearby barn.

"Then get all four out here. On the double, man." As he spoke, Douglas quickly made sure the hired hand's back was turned. Then with a single swift motion he lifted the padlock from the chain . . . and threw it mightily toward the distant white dimness of a snowdrift. Then he dropped from his horse and walked beside the employee. "Hold on," he exclaimed in seeming self-disgust, "I forgot. They especially want Joe Bagley over at Bearpaw."

The ranch hand stared at him through the darkness. "Bagley? Did you say Bagley? There ain't nobody hereabouts named that. Never heard of such."

· "Maybe I got the name wrong," Douglas said indifferently. Now he was certain of something he had been pondering ever since the arrival of the committee in Grangeville.

Within minutes four horsemen had been routed out of the bunkhouse and gathered at the open gate. Sam Douglas remounted his horse in evident urgency to lead them. "We gotta ride like the Devil was prodding us. Make straight for Bearpaw." He paused and then seemed disappointed as he added, "I may get behind you boys; I tired my horse getting out here. But keep going. I'll catch up." He glared at the only man afoot, the hand who had opened the gate. "Ain't you riding with us?"

"I've not been on a horse for ten years. Busted bones and sciatica." The employee was suddenly staring at the gate chair. "Besides, I gotta see where I dropped the goddamn padlock."

As the four ranch hands rode swiftly up the lane and away from headquarters, Sam Douglas was prominently among them. Questions were thrown at him, but he could say only that some sort of catastrophe had befallen Bearpaw. Only their hurried appearance there might help. Cautiously he reined his horse to become the rearmost rider. Two compelling thoughts were crowding on Sam Douglas. Surely Carswell and Jeff Harding would by now be clear of Bearpaw. And just as certainly there had to be a man other than the gatekeeper at Halligan's headquarters. When the four riders were well in front of him, Douglas swore angrily at his "slow" horse. Then unobtrusively he turned from the lane. A low call brought both Plunkett and Lowell to his side.

"We can get in," Douglas said simply. "There's an old ranch roustabout there—looking for a lock he ain't apt to find. We can handle him. Four others are hell bent to Bearpaw."

Wordless and cautious, the three rode out of the secluding gloom and approached the lane. It was just before they turned toward the ranch buildings that Jim Plunkett drew his mount sharply up and stared eastward. Then he pointed and murmured aloud, "Take a look over there, on the horizon. For a second I saw something on fire." As they watched it came again, the restless red glow. Then it was lost from view. Somewhere across the intervening miles, clouds had closed in.

"That would be about where Bearpaw is . . . or

was," Douglas said. "And I am sure praying Henry and Jeff are a long way from that spot by now."

They came within a hundred yards of the gate. Douglas halted the others in the darkness and then let his horse plod quietly to the gate. It was still ajar, and a couple of yards off to the left the old hand was walking back and forth. He looked up, saw Sam Douglas and strode to the gatepost.

"What are you doing back here?" he asked.

Douglas hacked an overly loud cough and then dropped from horse. "My horse just plumb gave out. Got another one here?"

"He sure don't look that tuckered." There was suspicion in the roustabout's voice now, and his hand moved nervously toward a coat pocket. "You . . . you tricked me—and got that damned lock."

Douglas moved casually closer. Almost imperceptible sounds told him of the close approach of Plunkett and Lowell. The ranch hand heard them too and glanced quickly up. With delicate movements, Sam touched the length of heavy chain and brought it within his grasp. He waited but a second . . . until the roustabout's head was turned. Then with calculated force Douglas swung the chain—and its heavy links caught the ranch hand just behind the ear. His knees buckled and he slid unconscious to the ground.

Plunkett began to unfasten his lariat rope. "Let's get him gagged and trussed up. Quick. We can toss him in the barn. Someone's bound to find him when a bunch of mad riders gets back here."

After they had stowed the roustabout in the barn, Sam Douglas said, "Jim, you've pretty well told us the room layout inside. Suppose you stay

440

out here. Keep an eye on our horses . . . and watch for anyone riding in." He drew a deep breath and turned to Lowell. "You and me are going into the house. What I'm looking for is some business books . . . records . . . correspondence. Carswell got the idea they aren't kept out at Bearpaw."

Lowell nodded, then murmured, "We've been lucky, getting rid of some of the hired hands. But when you yelled for the gate to be opened anyone within half a mile would have heard. There may be others . . . hid out and waiting for trouble."

"Then we will have to take the chance, son. Want me to go inside by myself?"

"Do I look that scared?" Lowell growled.

"You should. I sure am." Douglas was moving, toward the rear porch of the ranch house. "Keep close and ready for anything. I've a hunch we will stumble onto at least one bastard inside. Maybe that mysterious Joseph Bagley—and maybe someone you'll recognize." As Douglas' voice dropped to silence, his mind was again grasping at a nebulous but persistent thought: *Maybe one and one only make one.*.

Through an unlatched screen door they stepped onto an enclosed porch. It took only four steps for Sam Douglas to tread his way across the porch and come to the heavy wooden door of the main house. He was aware of Robert Lowell's nearness directly behind him as his own hand turned the doorknob. Off to one side, Robert Lowell could glimpse a tall, wide rick of stovewood.

As Sam Douglas started to open the door, Lowell spotted movement at the woodpile's far end. In instant desperation, his hands snaked out—to shove Douglas down and through the barely open

441

doorway. There was a flash, the loud sound of a shot and the rush of a bulky form toward them. Lowell sensed that the bullet had buried itself in either the floor or the door casing. In the next instant an arm thrust out to knock him away from the doorway, causing him to stumble to his knees. He grabbed one of his assailant's legs. Then Lowell's arm flailed about to seize either the gun or the arm holding it. The man above him struggled, lashed out a vicious kick, and then, trying to break free of Lowell's encircling arm, backed into the woodpile.

It seemed that the entire house was caving in upon Bob Lowell as the stacked wood crashed about both of them. Lowell lay for a few seconds panting . . . and knowing that he must be the first to rise and take command. He felt cautiously among the strewn sticks of wood. Then he encountered a hand of the man pinned down close by—a hand from which the gun had fallen. Cautiously he shoved wood aside and attempted to rise. Then abruptly he was listening. Sounds were coming from the kitchen, and lamplight was pouring from the room into which he had started to push Sam Douglas.

As Lowell rose, he was able to make out the man sprawled below him. It was a stranger, with fury on his face and with black, tangled hair. Already he too was frantically pawing for the dropped weapon. Before he could find it or come to his feet, Lowell put a sudden end to his efforts—by lifting one of the lengths of split wood and swinging it viciously against his attacker's head. The gun-wielder gasped as his head was smashed sideways. Then he lay unconscious among the debris.

442

Lowell turned and stared. Within the lighted room, now revealed as a large kitchen, Sam Douglas was on his feet. And another man was facing him . . . a man at whom Douglas was staring in a fascinated way. Neither was moving. Douglas was crouched, his hands at his sides, breathing heavily. He made no attempt to overpower the other man, who stood in stunned amazement. He was fully twenty years younger than Sam Douglas and of slender build. His eyes were deeply recessed and coal black in the uncertain glow of the lamp he was holding. There was a paleness about his face, and lines that spoke of either long illness or dissipation. Already he was prematurely bald, but the fringe of hair was russet-hued and sprinkled with white.

One thought formed in Robert Lowell's shocked and unbelieving mind: *Jesus . . . Lacey . . . you . . . you look older than the hills.*

And now the figure holding the lamp was speaking to Sam Douglas. "Who are you? Who let you in here? This . . . this is a private home. Blain Halligan's home. I . . . I could have you—"

"You could . . . but you won't, Lacey," Douglas answered. "We are here for a little talk with you and with Joe Bagley. Remember him? Bagley of the Nampuh Distributing Company?"

The words brought startled surprise into Lacey Halligan's eyes, but he quickly masked it. Then he said, "I haven't heard of Bagley for months. Not since Blain—" He broke stubbornly off as though sensing he might reveal too much. Also, his face had slackened and he was now staring at Robert Lowell.

"What's the matter?" Douglas growled. "Do

you see a ghost? Maybe a ghost from that lousy frame-up I found out about in Seattle?" There was almost unbearable tension within the room as the three stared at each other in hostile confrontation. Then Douglas inched to where his face was only inches from that of Lacey Halligan. "You know something else I've found out, fellow? There isn't any Joseph Bagley. Never was . . . and never will be. Blain—that sche..ing brother of yours—needed a front man for his thieving operations. He hand-picked you for the job."

Robert Lowell had watched and listened, his gaze taking on increased fury. He would have spoken but was deterred by a sound on the porch—that of wood being pushed about. He knew its significance and menace instantly—the gunman was regaining consciousness. And if he should find the revolver . . . Lowell swung about—and knew he was too late. The man he had knocked senseless was now just beyond the door on his hands and knees and peering into the kitchen. And in his hand he was lifting the revolver.

At that moment Sam Douglas saw him. Douglas' arm seemed a blur as it fell to his hip and fired the pistol drawn from his belt holster. The man near the open doorway seemed to be driven backward a little, then he slumped, thrashed out his last moment, and lay still.

"Get his gun," Douglas said in a dispassionate voice. "We may need it before we're out of this place."

As Lowell obeyed, Lacey Halligan was still watching him with something akin to incomprehension. His hand was shaking and he turned to place the lamp on a table.

"It has been a long time, Lacey," Robert Lowell murmured, and there was almost pity in his voice.

He might have said more, but suddenly the figure of Jim Plunkett loomed in the doorway. He peered first at the dead man and then at Douglas. "Do you need help, Sam? Them shots—"

"Just have the horses ready," Douglas responded. "We're about through here." He turned to Lacey Halligan. "Halligan, I am not going to play games or bluff. I have enough on you now to justify thirty years or so in the penitentiary. You know goddamn well that this is Robert Lowell . . . you framed him for a botched-up abortion you did yourself. He got kicked out of medical school."

"You're just guessing. That was years ago. No one is going to believe that sort of talk."

"I've got proof. Signed, sealed, and delivered. Now there's just one more thing you can do for us."

"What?" The one word came from Halligan with terror.

"You're going to show us where the Bearpaw records and correspondence are. Maybe some of the letters you signed with the name of Joseph Bagley—master swindler and brother of Idaho's most contemptible bureau chief."

"There aren't any papers here. Just some ranch stuff. It's out there . . . at the warehouse."

Douglas listened briefly. He knew he must act quickly. He stepped forward, grasped the flickering kerosene lamp, and shoved Lacey Halligan toward an inner door. "Get going . . . and don't try my patience." He waited as Halligan seemed mindful to resist, then he added coldly, "Lacey, I don't want to shoot you. I have already been

forced to kill one man tonight. Don't make yourself the second."

It was through a spacious living room and down
a hallway that they came to the ranch office. Halligan led the way, with Douglas close and watchful behind him. Robert Lowell brought up the
rear, and his gaze darted about, taking in the
magnificence of this home and looking for quick
escape routes to the outside.

In the office and on a desk, papers were scattered about. It was evident that even this evening
someone had been working here. On a shelf was
a row of cardboard file boxes. Lacey Halligan
walked past them and began pawing through papers on a recessed wall shelf. "I tell you this is a
ranch office," he murmured. "Cattle records. Feed
costs. Building information."

Robert Lowell stepped close to the desk and
lifted a ledger. As he did so, a slightly open drawer
caught his attention. He turned to call to Sam
Douglas—and the words froze on his lips. From beneath the shelved papers Lacey Halligan had
pulled a heavy and wickedly bladed knife. He
lunged toward Douglas, whose hands were bur-
dened with one of the cardboard boxes.

The box caught the full, slicing swing of Halligan's first thrust. Halligan snarled a baffled oath
and drew back for another stabbing attempt.
Then Robert Lowell was upon him, lashing out
with a kick of his heavy boot. It caught Lacey just
above the knee and threw him off balance. Then
with a rancor and hatred nurtured throughout
the years of his banishment, Lowell seemed to
have nothing but contempt for the knife and its
wielder. He kicked the knife brutally from Lac-

ey's grasp and pushed the panting man to the floor. Then Lowell fell to a position astride him and grasped Lacey's throat. "You miserable, conniving son-of-a-bitch, Halligan. Why? Why me? My life ruined . . . when medicine and surgery were all I ever wanted?" In despair he slapped Halligan's face . . . and again . . . until the slighter man lay white and cringing.

How long it might have continued no one was destined to know, for now Sam Douglas, busy pulling out the desk drawer, spoke up. "Better let him go, boy—before you too become a killer." He watched as Lowell got reluctantly to his feet, cold fury still about him. Then abruptly the sound of Douglas' voice changed. He had drawn a bulky checkbook from the drawer.

"By God, here it is, Robert! The gut stuff of Bearpaw. Hand me one of those file boxes. If it's full, dump it out. We're taking just what is in this drawer. It ought to be enough."

His words caused Lacey Halligan to stir in consternation and fright. "Blain will see you hang for this."

"Likely. Very likely," Sam Douglas nodded. "But a certain future secretary of state—and one hell of a lot of ranchers—will bless old Sam's memory." He took the empty file from Lowell and dumped the contents of two drawers into it. Then he stared at Lacey Halligan, who was struggling to a sitting position. "Just stay there and take it easy for five minutes or so. You understand, Lacey, it's better to be prudent than all shot up. Besides, I know how to get a few depositions from the Seattle gents about that abortion." He tucked the box under his arm, then motioning Robert

447

Lowell to keep close, Sam Douglas strode back down the hall, across the living room, through the kitchen, and onto the porch. For a second his gaze raked the body of the gunman lying against the spilled and scattered wood. In that short time Sam Douglas seemed older . . . tireder. Then he went into the darkness of the Halligan ranch yard to search out Jim Plunkett and the waiting horses. The gate was still open as they rode out, but Sam Douglas seemed unaware of time and of place or of the deepening cold of the night.

Despite their apprehension, they met no returning Halligan riders on the way back toward Grangeville. Almost an hour later they rode clear of a cluster of timber and saw the lights of town showing dimly through a snowfall. They halted their horses.

"We can skirt the settlement," Douglas reasoned aloud, "and come onto the Boise stage road tolerably close to where Carswell and Jeff Harding said they'd meet us with the team and sleigh."

"What about these horses we are riding?" Plunkett questioned uneasily. "The livery stable fellow will sure start looking for us if we don't return his horses and gear when we agreed to— before midnight."

Lowell had sat listening. Now he shook his head and spoke up. "How about the outfit Carswell hired to get about, the horses and sled? Is that all we're likely to have to get the five of us clear of Grangeville? Maybe with Halligan's riders—or even a posse—hot on our trail?"

"That bothers me too," Plunkett answered. "There is a telephone at that logging outfit down the road. Someone could phone ahead and ask that we be headed off."

"Then we will have to fight our way through," Douglas said. "And that sled is all the transportation we've got or are likely to have."

"Maybe not," Lowell answered thoughtfully. "Not if you two are willing to risk going back into Grangeville for a short time." Robert Lowell leaned closer, speaking urgently. "The stagecoach I came on . . . it's still in town. If . . . if I could persuade the driver, sort of bribe him to—" He seemed to ponder, and then shrugged dejectedly, before saying, "I'd better forget it. He would want more money than I'm carrying."

Douglas started to reply but remained silent as Jim Plunkett's voice took on urgency. "It might work, Lowell. But didn't he have other passengers . . . and maybe some mail?"

"Just two passengers," Lowell said, nodding. "And the mail sacks are safe in the post office. The next stage would pick up the passengers—a dry-goods salesman and a woman. An Indian who probably is in no hurry." He jerked impatiently at his bridle reins. "But why waste time? I don't have the money."

"Maybe not. But you sure have a fascinating idea," Douglas replied. "Now, me . . . I happen to have a couple of hundred dollars on me." He turned to Plunkett. "How about you, Jim?"

Plunkett grinned wryly. "Mollie keeps the money sock at our house. I talked her out of sixty dollars. It's yours if you need it. Just leave me a buck or so for tobacco."

"You fellows are talking big money," Lowell informed them. "Let me have fifty dollars. That ought to lure the stage driver out of his warm bed."

They rode, silent and watchful, toward the center of town. Few lights were burning now and a snowy chillness lay along the deserted streets. They turned a corner and approached Branigan's Buffalo Chip. Lights shone through windows of the hotel and saloon to reveal a dozen saddled horses at the hitching racks. Men came and went through the doors, and there was a din of excited conversation. They learned that the Bearpaw warehouse had been burned. From a shadowed distance, Douglas and his companions watched with growing concern. Among the horses were those on which four riders had left Halligan's ranch yard at the urgent insistence of Douglas himself. He turned to Lowell and Plunkett. "Something tells me we'd better hightail it out of here on the double. That crowd is nasty . . . and getting more so."

"But we need the stage," Lowell protested. "If only I knew where the driver bedded down."

"Hell, I can tell you that," Jim Plunkett spoke up softly. "Inside Branigan's Chip, on the first floor and way to the back is a big room with three beds. It's used by the stage drivers. And likely no one else. I swamped it out three or four times."

"Then," Lowell asked, "what if you two were to wait around here while I saunter into the saloon? There's a good chance nobody would recognize me, or figure me to be part of your group."

Douglas handed him some folded currency. "Take a fling at it, Robert. But be careful—and hurry. We haven't much time before meeting Harding and Carswell."

Lowell maintained a calm face but his heart was pounding as he sauntered down the length of street, skirted the tied saddle horses, and entered the Buffalo Chip. There were a dozen men inside and a buzz of angry voices.

Lowell was moving in a disinterested way toward the rear of the lobby and soon would be out of hearing range. Now he said aloud in an agitated way, "I've gotta see the stage driver. Right away. Damn it, I lost my turquoise ring coming down from Lewiston. It is worth a lot to me . . . sentimental reasons." He sensed that no one was really listening to him.

Lowell hurried down the darkened hallway and found what Jim Plunkett had assured him would be the sleeping room for the stage drivers. The door was unlocked, but a chair had been propped against the inner knob. He shook the door and managed to dislodge the chair; it clattered to the floor. He stepped inside and drew a breath of relief. A kerosene lamp was burning, with its wick turned down to cast but a dim glow. The driver who had brought him to Grangeville was alone in the room, and now he was sitting up in bed and staring sleepily at the intruder. The driver was still clad in heavy gray underwear, but now he stepped from the bed and fumbled for his pants.

Robert Lowell drew near to him and lost no time with preliminaries. "How would you like to make this? Just for a couple of hours' work?" He waved the currency close to the driver's face. "There is fifty dollars here, likely as much or more than a month's salary."

Sight of the money was fast driving away the last vestiges of sleep as the driver pulled up his suspenders. "You're not wanting me to break the law, are you? Hand over the U.S. mail sacks . . . or something like that?"

"Nothing of the kind," Lowell assured him. "I just want you to hitch up the stage right away, then haul me and two friends down the Boise road."

"I'd have to take on my passengers—and the mail sacks."

"There won't be time."

Lowell was still extending the wad of currency, and now avarice showed in the driver's face. "I could claim I took sick and was trying to reach a doctor I know toward McCall." He reached for the money.

When the driver had donned a heavy sheepskin coat and found his long rawhide whip, they left the Buffalo Chip through the back doorway. Minutes later they reached the anxiously waiting Plunkett and Douglas. With the stage driver riding double with Jim Plunkett, they made haste to the livery barn. The night hostler was nowhere about, and the harnessing and hitching of the stage horses took only five minutes.

Now, as the three climbed aboard the stage, the driver said with concern, "I've gotta go up to the post office and pick up the mail sack. Can't leave without it. I have a key. The mail's gotta go, or here I stay."

Jim Plunkett turned worriedly to his companions. "That means we have to ride this rig right smack past the Buffalo Chip; there's no other way to get to the post office. That mail sack is too heavy to pack by hand."

Sam Douglas had started to climb through the

open doorway of the stage, but now he stopped. "You boys get inside. I've an idea it would be better for me to ride up top with the driver for a spell."

Without protest, Plunkett stepped inside and took his place far to the left, where he could scan one side of the darkened street. He motioned for Robert Lowell to sit on the right side. The fact that Plunkett had taken the side giving the better view of the Buffalo Chip did not escape Lowell, but he remained quiet.

There were the sounds of harness rattle, of hoofbeats, and of the stage's lurching over ruts and snow as they broke into the street at a trotting pace. Within seconds the lighted windows of the Buffalo Chip came into view. Otherwise, the night was dark and quiet; the storm had stopped, and moonlight filtered through broken clouds. They reached the post office, just past the Buffalo Chip. The driver yielded the reins to Sam Douglas, climbed to the ground, and hastened to the building. Soon he was walking slowly back to the coach, dragging a bulky mail sack, when Sam Douglas, peering anxiously behind, saw the door of the Buffalo Chip open. A man started toward the hitchrack. Then abruptly he stopped and stared at the halted stagecoach. A startled yell escaped him, and he ran back into the Buffalo Chip.

"Let's haul that bag aboard—and get up here quick!" Douglas ordered the driver. "Take these reins . . . so we can get the hell out of here fast!"

But there was not enough time. Even as the driver's long whip snaked out to touch the restless team into motion, men were spilling from the Buffalo Chip into the street. A heavily coated form jumped into the street and seized the bridle of a lead-team horse; the team and coach slowed quickly to a halt. The quickly appraising gaze of Sam Douglas encompassed the scene. Most of the men who had poured from the Buffalo Chip remained onlookers along the plankwalk. Only three had come into the street to challenge the passing of the stage.

The driver, usually silent, was yelling now at the man who had grasped the bridle. "Let go of that mare!" he was saying. "You're interfering with the Lewiston-to-Boise stage and the United States mail! You hear me, you bastard—leggo of my team!"

Another form drew close to the stage, and a pistol was in his hand. Now he said to the one still hanging onto the bridle, "Let me handle this. You smoke them out, Lenny. Me . . . I'm going to hold right onto this bridle."

Despite the tension of the moment, Sam Douglas' mind grasped the implication of the name. *Lenny,* he repeated to himself. That's the one Carswell tricked into letting him inside the Bearpaw building.

A lot more was revealed when the stranger beside the stage spoke again, this time to the third man blocking the street: "Get around to the other side. We'll find out who's inside. And I just hope it's the son-of-a-bitch who pushed over the stove tonight." The gun was pointed now at the driver, but its holder glanced toward the men along the Buffalo Chip porch. "All right," he shouted, "are all of you going to stand there like stumps? Get out here and surround this outfit! Damn it all . . . get moving! Something is fishy when a stage takes off after midnight—just after my warehouse was burned down!"

The words brought a surly reply from a tall, stocking-capped man near the door of the saloon. "Why, Halligan? Why? I don't recall you ever sticking your neck out to help any of us."

"I pay wages, don't I?" Blain Halligan replied angrily.

"Damn poor wages," another voice sounded. "Besides, Halligan, after the blaze tonight, you're out of business."

More would have been said, but then the stage driver squinted carefully toward his foremost team and the arm of Lenny still dragging at the bridle. Very slowly he lifted the whip. Then his arm moved in a powerful sweep. The long lash executed a looping swing far toward the rear of the coach. Then with the accuracy of a bullet, the tip of the rawhide thong leaped forward. It caught Lenny's hand and ripped through the flesh. Lenny jumped back, and as he did so the horses and the stage began to move ahead. Blain Halligan, whose hand was about to open the stagecoach door, stumbled and almost went to his knees.

A shot sounded then, from a weapon Lenny had pulled from his belt. The bullet, meant for the irate driver, missed its mark. But it tore through the chest of Sam Douglas, who gave forth only a last gasp of breath and then slumped lifeless onto the coach's roof. Blain Halligan was striving to come to his feet as the stage team, which the driver had whipped into a run, tore down the darkened street. From his seat on the far side, Robert Lowell stared backward as he thrust a wind curtain aside. Then very methodically he fired the pistol he had grasped throughout the encounter. The bullet fell short of Lenny. And now the coach was beyond accurate pistol range.

Inside the coach, Lowell and Jim Plunkett stared at each other. Neither of them was yet aware that Sam Douglas lay dead upon the roof above them.

"They are bound to follow us," Lowell said at last.

"Maybe so." Plunkett's voice carried doubt. "But not many of them natives seemed anxious to join up with Halligan." He paused to assess the speed with which the stage was now departing Grangeville and plunging along the snow-patched road. Then he added, "Likely we will meet up with Henry and Jeff—if they got to the waiting place with whole hides. It's only a mile or a little more down the road. If we can—"

His words were cut short by a loud and urgent call from the driver: "Your partner was shot back there. I think he's dead . . . sprawled out back of me."

"Oh, Christ! No!" Jim Plunkett rasped aloud. "Sam couldn't be—"

"Stop the rig!" Lowell shouted. "I'll crawl up!"

"And let them fellows pick me off too!" the driver shouted back.

Jim Plunkett had stuck his head out the window as he yelled, "Any minute now you'll come to a crossroad where a couple of our friends are waiting! Stop right then!"

As they clattered on, both men in the coach were stunned and silent. How swiftly their escape had turned into tragedy. Presently Plunkett said softly, "If Sam has played his last hand, he did it damned well . . . getting that box out at Halligan's place."

"The box," Lowell repeated almost with fright. "I wonder where it is now?"

He did not have to wait long for an answer. Three minutes later the team slowed as the driver reluctantly tugged at the reins. Almost at the same moment Henry Carswell and Jeff Harding emerged from a shadowy patch of timber. Without a word, Robert jumped from the coach and swiftly climbed to the roof. There was a silence broken only by Plunkett's voice. "Climb aboard. Sam is on the roof. He's been shot. Dead likely." He peered about in the darkness. "Where's your team and sled?"

"In the grove, where we've been waiting for you," Carswell replied.

"Then you'd better pull off the harness and turn the team loose; they'll head back to the livery stable. Besides, on this contraption you'll be riding with the U.S. mail."

They turned to follow his suggestion. When they again neared the stage with its restless team and driver, Lowell was climbing silently down. After a moment of seeming hesitation, he held out an object toward Carswell. "Take this box and be careful of it. It may contain things to save all of our necks." He fell silent, and then moved to again climb to the roof. "Sam is dead, all right; probably he was gone within seconds of being hit."

The stage moved out. There had not yet been indication of pursuit. Around them was the night, the forest, and a vast silence in which the noises of the horses and the coach seemed loud and reassuring. Ahead stretched the curving and often treacherous stage road. To Boise.

Chapter 22

Deborah learned of the return of the committee from Mollie Plunkett just past dawn. Searching for words, she said, "Jim got home last night . . . after midnight. From Grangeville. Jim is all right. So are Mr. Carswell and Jeff Harding . . ." Her voice trailed into silence, and she sat squeezing Deborah's hand. She appeared about to say more, but the stress about her seemed not to permit it. Then she managed a smile and said, "And you know what, honey? That Lowell chap—your Robert Lowell came into town with them."

The words seemed to skip over Deborah, who was staring into her friend's face. "Don't try to hide it, Mollie. You didn't say anything about Mr. Douglas . . . Sam. What is it? I have to know."

"He was shot. Killed. They left his body upstate a way. It will be shipped into Boise in a day or so."

A frozen bleakness was upon Deborah; her fingers seemed cold and lifeless as she squeezed Mollie's arm. "Oh, God—no. Mollie," Deborah said, "am I a witch, someone possessed? All I have done is to meddle into other people's affairs and . . . and bring death and destruction." Her eyes were wide, stricken, haunted. "If only I had never snooped around, looked into that Nampuh thing."

Mollie Plunkett slid an arm about the girl. "Hush. Hush right now. You did what was the only decent thing . . . to try to protect the sheep-men and others you work for. You never asked any one of those men to go up there to Grange-ville. They did it because they admire you—and want to keep you out of harm's way."

Deborah strode to her bed, to throw herself face downward. The tears came then, racking sobs that Mollie was wise enough to realize marked the torture of realization. Tiredness would come now. And hopefully sleep.

Shortly after one o'clock that afternoon, they gathered in the sun parlor of the rooming house. Henry Carswell was the first to arrive. He was standing beside a corner table and toying with a fuchsia plant when Deborah came into the room. Without words, she moved toward him. He turned . . . and she saw the tiredness of his face and the marks of the ordeal through which he had come. Her arms went about him and for a while her head lay against his chest; then she looked into his face and murmured, "Thank God, you came back. Henry, why do you and others risk so much for me?" Before he could answer there was the sound of footfalls in the hall. She swung about, and de-spite being forewarned, a gasp escaped her. Rob-ert Lowell was standing in the doorway with both his stance and his gaze uneasy. "Hello, Deborah," he said. The words were just above a whisper. "I finally got here—didn't I?"

She walked with quick steps toward him. "Rob-ert, do come in."

He reached out his hand tentatively. "I have so much to tell you, Deborah."

Now there were more footfalls in the hallway.

Into the room came Mollie and Jim Plunkett—and directly behind them were two men, silver-haired Frank Wentworth and tall and dominant Jeff Harding. The roster of the meeting was complete.

One by one, they related what had happened in Grangeville.

A shadow of doubt came into Deborah's face after they finished, and she said, "Was it really worth it . . . all that each of you went through? True, Bearpaw is out of business. But both of the Halligans are still up there on the ranch. What is to keep them from creating another cheating concern?"

Carswell listened and shook his head. He rose, then moved to a chair where he had placed his folded topcoat. From beneath he pulled a gray and somewhat soiled paper filing box. He held it up. "Deborah, this is what may be your hole card . . . the last one ever to leave the hands of Sam Douglas. This morning I had a chance to skim through what is in this box. I've a gut feeling that its contents could destroy Blain Halligan. They could surely send that brother of his, Lacey, to jail—for keeps." He paused, and reached out as though to lay the box in Deborah's hands.

She drew back, pale and shaken, without touching it, and her gaze was imploring as it sought out Frank Wentworth. "I . . . I can't take it. I want no part of a means of destroying a man . . . even Blain Halligan. God help me to never again be part of causing any living soul's death."

As she spoke, a vivid picture was coming into Jeff Harding's mind—the utter abandon of her face as it had been that day high on Greys River

461

when an outlaw's bullet had torn through Bishop Joshua Stannard. Harding came to his feet, paced across the floor, and stopped in front of Frank Wentworth to say, "Frank, I think you should have this box of proof—of dynamite. Why don't you keep it for now?"

Wentworth stared thoughtfully at the box. "Thanks for the trust, Jeff, but I don't think I . . . Hold on! Don't we all know where this box belongs? In the hands of a man Deborah knows. A man just about everyone in Idaho respects and trusts—William E. Borah, the lawyer." They all agreed.

Moments later Deborah voiced concern about another facet of the committee's efforts. She turned to Carswell and asked bluntly, "Henry, are you willing to proceed with our plans to elect you Idaho's secretary of state? Time is running short for an announcement."

"Sure I will run for the secretary's office, if all of you think I should. We've started a cleanup. Now may be the time to get on with it—over at the Capitol. Do you think I should give it a try?"

Almost in one voice they chorused their "Yes" and smiled their approval.

As the meeting began to break up, it dawned on Deborah that for the first time two men—the two men who had been closest to her heart and to whom she had given herself—were in the same room with her. Almost furtively she glanced from one to the other. Jeff seemed to sense her scrutiny and smiled toward her. She lifted her head and studied his face with level and thoughtful eyes. Of those who went North, she thought, he seems the least tired or disturbed. Perhaps because the seeking out of crime and violence has become his way of life. How can he be so stern and unrelenting toward the men he hunts down and yet also be gentle and understanding? She was aware of the years between their ages; yet, since that night together in Wyoming, the span meant nothing to her. And now a thought came strangely to her. He is still almost a young man, despite that graying hair and the lines about his eyes. Young enough to enjoy life . . . to want the companionship I can offer. Yes, and to become the father of my child. The thought brought a blush of color to her cheeks, and she moved her gaze from Jeff.

Henry Carswell had moved across the room and now blocked her view of Jeff Harding's face. And at that same moment she felt a touch on her arm, turned, and looked into the eyes of Robert Lowell. Then she said with simple sincerity, "I am glad you could be here, Robert."

His gaze seemed to seek a clue as to what her reaction had been, over the months, to learning of the Nez Percé Indian girl pregnant with his child. His words came in a bantering way, but were fraught with uncertainty. "I was late getting into town, Deborah; that affair at Grangeville sort of slowed me."

She was holding his hand as she said, "I'm glad it happened that way. Now you know the truth about that wretched dismissal from the university in Seattle. You are a free man . . . you can go back there to finish—"

"It won't be that easy," Robert replied, and then hastened to add, "Don't think I am ungrateful. You brought about the solving of it.

Debbie . . . thank you. You are a very special person."

She felt the nearness of him as he leaned to touch her cheek with his lips. What words she would have spoken in reply would never be known. A movement among those within the room caused her to glance about—and to realize that now the scrutiny of Jeff Harding was silently and quietly upon her. Within moments he turned his gaze away, but instinctively she knew his mind had grasped the intensity of Robert Lowell's face and voice. He knows, her mind whispered. Knows perhaps as well as though I had told him.

And now there was a reserve and a stress about her that caused Lowell's next words to take on a matter-of-factness. "Deborah, as I said in my letter, I must talk over some business matters with you. It is urgent and we will have some decisions to make about our timberlands. When would it be convenient—?"

"Perhaps I should suggest dinner together this evening, Robert. But I'm too emotionally drained to enjoy going out. And I know you must be also. Why don't we just stay here and talk . . . after the others have left?"

His reaction was one of evident relief. "This would suit me . . . just great. I should be on my way back to the Clearwater day after tomorrow—with an answer. Yours and mine."

She rose, mingled with the others, and saw them out. When she went back to the sun parlor, she smiled. Robert Lowell was asleep, stretched on a sofa and with one arm thrown across his eyes. He seemed both disarmed of pretense—and pathetic. She noted more clearly the shabbiness of his clothing, his need of a haircut, his scuffed boots, and the etching of lines she had never before seen on his face. He seemed to have retained little in common with the lively-eyed prospector she had met that first day on Jordan Creek. She wondered if ever again the two of them would rekindle the urgency of intimacy . . . of love . . . of passion.

He stirred presently and his eyes opened. Then he sat up, brushing drowsiness from his eyes and letting scuffed boots drop to the parlor rug.

"Debbie . . . it's . . . it's you . . . ?"

"Who else would tolerate your snoring?" she teased. Then she added, "There is a bathroom at the end of the hall. Go down there and wash some of the sleep out of your eyes. And for Lord's sake, comb your hair. Then get back here so we can talk over the business you are so mysterious about."

He rose and moved to the door, then over his shoulder commented, "Still the same old Deborah . . . has to be sprucing up the whole world for that big pie-in-the-sky tomorrow." He ducked and disappeared as she tugged off a slipper and flung it at his head.

When he returned and dropped onto a chair facing her, there was an air of soberness and indecision about him. He leaned forward and spoke abruptly. "We have a big decision to make. It likely could involve more money than either of us ever dreamed of having. Listen, Debbie. Listen closely. Even then you may not believe me. One of the biggest lumbering outfits in America wants to get hold of the two hundred acres of timber we have up on the Clearwater River."

"For what?" she asked. "A sawmill site? A mine?"

"Neither. The Weyerhaeuser lumbering interests are after it for an ingress road. They sent fellows to look me up. Asked me to get in touch with my co-owner—you."

"The Weyerhaeuser Company," she repeated after catching her breath.

"That's right. They have made a deal with a railroad—I suspect it is the Northern Pacific—and together they have gotten hold of that God-awful big lot of timberland beyond our two hundred acres. It is the government . . . mostly . . . that is bringing it about. That and the fact that forests of the Midwest, in Michigan and Wisconsin and Minnesota, are beginning to play out. The government has its eye on northern Idaho for immense federal forest reserves. It is coming, Deborah. Before long all that beautiful timber country up North is going to belong to Uncle Sam, to the railroads, and to giant timber and logging interests."

She looked at him thoughtfully. "I have heard that already most of Idaho's timberland is in the hands of a dozen men."

"Part of the shame of our self-serving state officers. Present and past." Lowell had drawn a small pad of notebook paper from his shirt pocket and had a pencil poised. "What the Weyerhaeuser agents are offering is a timber swap."

Wariness sprang into Deborah's eyes. "You mean they want us to give them our two hundred

466

acres for land somewhere else . . . something we have never seen?"

"Not exactly. The first thing I did was to get legal descriptions and cruise the areas they mentioned. Mostly it is in the Pend Oreille area. Some magnificent stands of white pine and spruce. Some Douglas fir."

"Then why don't they log off what they already have?" Deborah asked doubtingly.

"They will a lot of it. But they really want a way into those thousands and thousands of acres beyond our little gateway on the Clearwater."

"We can keep them out, Robert, if we want to."

"Not forever and probably not for long. They can afford a battery of lawyers to outmaneuver us and bring pressure."

"Through that eminent domain thing, I suppose," she fretted.

"So . . . you have studied law?" he said, grinning.

"Not exactly. A lawyer I know, William E. Borah, explained it to me."

At sound of the name, he whistled softly. "Borah, eh? Just about the most noted lawyer in Idaho. Lady, you keep some illustrious company."

"What sort of acreage would they sign over to us in return?"

"I may have euchered them a bit on that. They began by talking of a one-for-one swap. Two hundred acres of theirs for what we have. I pointed out how much farther the Pend Oreille is from either my abode at Orofino or yours here in Boise. Also, I delicately mentioned how slowly seizure by eminent domain often works."

"Well?" Deborah asked impatiently.

"I ended up with two alternatives. We can get five acres of theirs for one of ours on a straight trade. And something else: I managed to get an option promised us for another two thousand acres of that Pend Oreille timber—there's no road into it—at one dollar and twenty-five cents an acre, provided we let them start an access road across our present holdings within six months."

Deborah straightened and looked at him in mingled admiration and anger. "And how," she demanded, "do you propose for us to come up with twenty-five hundred dollars to pick up such an option?"

Robert Lowell had slowly wormed his feet free of the scuffed boots and now his toe, showing through a hole in his sock, pushed them savagely about. "Damn it, Deborah, you're the schemer . . . the opportunist . . . the big-tomorrow promoter. You will come up with the money. I told the Weyerhaeuser land agents that you could."

She glared at him in utter amazement. "You did that? You . . . you . . . without even consulting me! Damn it, Lowell, I think you had better leave. Tomorrow I will make an appointment for us to talk this over with Mr. Borah." She waited, and her chin lifted before she faced him with unwavering eyes to say, "Bob, thank you for trying and for coming here. And one more thing: If we make a deal, somehow I will bail us out by exercising that option."

He heard her out and pulled on his boots. Then he rose and strode to the door. Before opening it, he said softly, "By the way, that option will be entirely in the name of one person—Deborah Dexter."

At late afternoon of the following day they entered the office of William E. Borah, attorney-at-law. Deborah introduced the two men and then said, "Mr. Borah, we appreciate your arranging to see us on such short notice. Robert has to catch a stage back to Orofino in the morning."

Borah watched Lowell draw a large and travel-worn envelope from his jacket. The scrutiny also encompassed the stranger's features, his wrinkled and worn clothing, and the nervousness with which Lowell was glancing about the book-lined office. "Take your time, Mr. Lowell," he said. "I understand that you have undergone quite an eventful—and traumatic—past few days."

Both Deborah and Lowell glanced at him in surprise.

"Frank Wentworth was here yesterday afternoon," Borah said. "To leave a file box. He gave me a summary of what took place in Grangeville."

"Have you examined the papers yet?" Deborah had come eagerly upright in her chair.

"Only cursorily. But I have them in a place of absolute safety."

Deborah's eyes raised to hold level with the kindly but unrevealing intentness of his face. "Mr. Borah," she said slowly, "those papers were stolen. I have not seen them, but I have been told they have the power to discredit and disgrace Blain Halligan."

"Wentworth has told me as much," Borah said.

469

"It is utter tragedy that lives were lost. If only there had been due course of law."

"What law?" Robert Lowell flared. "Halligan has flaunted every law and every principle of decency that he took an oath to uphold. And nobody did a damned thing . . . until Deborah had the guts to begin to smoke him out."

"He is right about Halligan, Mr. Borah," Deborah affirmed. "But it was my friends—Henry Carswell—Jim Plunkett—Jeff Harding—Sam Douglas—and Robert here who carried through to see that an . . . an end was put to Halligan's criminal swindle of the ranchers." She paused, caught her breath, and then went on. "Now likely there will be attempts at revenge. Even attempts on our lives, if I know Blain Halligan and his brother."

"Perhaps not. I would be careful but not overly concerned. Deborah, let me explain. That file . . . the canceled checks . . . the correspondence . . . Halligan's records. If they are as incriminating as I'm led to believe, they may be a deterrent. Safety insurance, as it were. Blain Halligan is obviously a crooked officeholder and promoter. But he is no fool. He isn't likely to attempt serious reprisal knowing that you may have documents that would discredit or even destroy him."

Lowell had listened carefully. Now he drew a relieved breath. "Deborah, I believe Mr. Borah is right. What I would like to hear now is how he sizes up this timber-swapping deal." He drew the papers from their crumpled envelope and laid them on the desk.

"You told me once, Mr. Borah, that it might be well for me to have you look over any legal papers pertaining to our two hundred acres of woodland up on the Clearwater. These papers were prepared by the Weyerhaeuser lumber mills people." She fell silent, noting that already Borah's gaze was rapidly scanning a letter, a trade proposal, and the option.

There was a long period of silence in the office. At no time did the unrevealing aspect of the attorney's face give hint of his thoughts or evaluation. Then at last he looked up, seeming to study Lowell's face. "I see nothing basically wrong with these documents. I think a change or two should be made to clarify and assure your rights, but the Weyerhaeuser Company is well funded and reliable. They do have some sharp people representing them. Knowledgeable. Shrewd. Ambitious."

"That is exactly why we came to you," Deborah answered.

"My thanks to both of you," Borah smiled proudly.

"Deborah will handle things for both of us," Lowell spoke up, "after my return to the Clearwater country tomorrow." He smiled wryly and added, "Besides, she has to figure out how to raise those twenty-five hundred dollars in option money. Thank God I don't. Not with my houseful of Nez Percé relatives."

Deborah could not suppress a gasp. It was the first time Lowell had spoken of his household . . . and possibly his marital status. By now the quiet-faced girl Deborah had seen at the cabin must surely have borne his child.

They walked from the law office and came onto a street drenched with warmth and evening sunshine. Robert stopped at the sidewalk's edge and peered about the town and the sweep of mountains beyond. "Deborah, would you walk with me for a while? Perhaps there is a park where we can talk." His face tightened as he went on. "I would like to rent a team of fast-stepping horses and take you for a ride so you could show me the town. Even better, I would like to ask you to have dinner with me in a swanky restaurant . . . and even buy you a whopping big bunch of roses. Well, damn it to perdition, I can't do any of those things. I have just money enough for my stage ticket home and a meal or so on the way. But will you go walking with me?"

"How about me renting that team and making the dinner reservation? I still haven't spent my last paycheck from the association. It'll be your turn next time."

Both pride and stubbornness surged across his face. "Thank you, Deborah—*but no, thank you.* I'll wait until a boat carrying my fortune sails up the Clearwater."

She caught his hand impulsively. "Why didn't you let me know how things are? We could have arranged to sell some timberland, or you could have borrowed against it." She was still holding his hand and they moved aimlessly toward the south. Finally they came onto the bank of the Boise River; there was a bench of stoutly woven wire, and they sat down. They spoke for a time of inconsequential things, each seeming to wait for the other to probe the chasm between them.

At last Deborah looked up and studied his face.

"Robert, now that you can be clear of the abortion affair, will you return to medical school?"

He rose to his feet and thrust his hands in his pockets. "Do you have any idea what that would cost?"

His tone caused her to flush and answer, "I got through college on precious little, except for what I could earn. There are bound to be jobs. Scholarships. Loans. Or we could sell the timber holdings—"

He turned, and although the setting sun was beating into his face, he eyed her in exasperation. "You never give up, do you, Deborah? And what the hell makes you think I want to go back to Seattle?"

"But you could be—" she floundered.

"I could be middle-aged and maybe potbellied by the time I finish an internship. Can't I make you understand? I don't give two whoops in hell now about being a doctor. I am over that stuff, Deborah. Maybe I just don't have the drive and the hopes and the trust in tomorrow that you have."

He had prodded deeply with both the words and the sting of his voice. And she replied in exasperation, "So . . . all you want is a few patched pants, a bellyful, a bottle—and a half-breed girl to carry off to bed."

She expected that he would lash out, either with furious words or his fist. Instead he seemed to have calmed. "Deborah, you have never forgotten that morning—when she came upon us in bed, have you?"

"Should I?" She realized that now tears were perilously close.

473

"Not really, I suppose. But there are things you should know. That Indian girl is not a half-breed. She is a daughter of one of the most respected leaders of the Nez Percé tribe. She has a son now, her son and mine. And another child is on the way. And Deborah, don't get so wrought up. She is my wife—and I am proud to have it so."

Chapter 23

SPRING came a little late to Boise that year, but Deborah Dexter seemed scarcely aware of the changing of the seasons. The shipments of wool to Ohio were now on a regular basis and required bookwork that seemed logically to be a part of her duties for the association. Also, Henry Carswell made it plain that he would be content only if she would take an active part in his campaign. Strangely, as the weeks wore on there was no repercussion from the havoc wrought by the committee at Grangeville. But Sam Douglas' name was now on a marble shaft in a quiet Boise cemetery. And a man had been left dead at the Halligan ranch house. Someday there would be a reckoning.

This spring morning Jeff Harding appeared shortly before noon, to stand in the hall doorway and look at her with an ironically puzzled smile. He had been at the association's office rarely since returning from Grangeville. Without greeting, he said, "How in thunder did a quiet, hardworking, and order-loving person like you get peeved enough to smash a boxed telephone into the face of a defenseless intruder?"

"Just the way I am going to throw this inkwell at you, Jeff Harding, if you don't come in here, sit down, and behave yourself."

"Lord, the misery of having two women ordering me about," he said, then walked in and sat down with easy grace on the corner of her desk.

"Don't you dare knock over my inkwell," she warned. "Now . . . what's this about two women?"

"You and Mama Echiverri. This morning she said, 'Harding, before you leave Boise again, you get yourself over to Deborah's office.' And you know what was on her mind? She thinks you are overworked. And you are, Deborah. Today or tomorrow you find a capable assistant. The association can afford it now—thanks to you and that mill in Ohio."

She leaned back—and realized that his searching eyes saw the tiredness and the despondency and the frustration on her face. His next words took her by surprise.

"Deborah, why don't you take a vacation? Go up North, maybe. It is darned pretty up on the Clearwater River this time of year."

"What would I possibly do on the Clearwater?" she asked, and she closed her eyes in weariness.

"Rest, for one thing—and maybe do something about the fellow you've been pining over."

Her eyes flew open and she stared at him. "Jeff, surely you can't—no, you wouldn't mean Robert Lowell."

He leaned forward, his eyes questioning. At the moment she was aware of his nearness, the clean correctness of his work clothes, and the manner in which the muscles of his supple form coordinated for quiet but alert movements.

"Yes, I mean Lowell. He proved right handy for

us to have with us up North. And, Debbie, be truthful with me and with yourself: You are in love with him."

She rose to her feet, grasped the edge of the desk, and stared at him. She said, almost in a whisper. "No, Jeff. I am *not* in love with Robert. Not anymore. There is an emptiness . . . a desolation. But whatever remains is not love." Her hands went out to grasp his shoulders. "You have to believe me, Jeff. There was a time when I thought Robert Lowell was my reason for living. A long time ago, over on the Yankee Fork. And . . . and later when I met him up in northern Idaho. Jeff, listen, please. Do you remember what I told you that night in the cabin in Wyoming when you said you wanted me? I told you I was no longer an innocent schoolgirl. I wanted you that night. Just as you and I were. Just as now I want you to know I cherished that night."

He pulled her to him and held his arms tightly about her. For a moment his cheek was pressed to hers. Then he rose to his feet and held her at arm's length. "Why in hell do there have to be these years between us?"

She would have answered, but suddenly Jeff Harding . . . the lawman . . . the enforcer . . . had fled into the hall.

The following day Deborah began searching for a person to take over some of the office duties. She also had a midday visitor; William Borah dropped unexpectedly into the office. After an exchange of pleasantries, Borah glanced about, assessing their privacy, then said, "Deborah, I think the time has come for you to accept the offer of the Weyerhaeuser Company for those two hundred acres you and Robert Lowell own. If you agree, I can send the necessary papers to Lowell later today. Also, I am convinced it would definitely be to your advantage to exercise your option on the 2000 acres at one twenty-five per acre. I just don't see how Lowell managed to wrangle such a concession from them."

She was about to nod her consent but stopped abruptly. To exercise the option would require an immediate twenty-five hundred dollars. Her face grew troubled. She looked at him ruefully. "Just where in creation can I come up with twenty-five hundred dollars? I think I have just over three hundred dollars in savings. Less than that in a checking account."

Borah ran a hand through the dark thickness of his hair. "I don't think you need to worry, Deborah; I know officials at the Boise City National Bank. Perhaps . . ."

"Wait a minute!" Deborah's voice was excited as she cut him off. "We may not have to do that."

"I'm listening," Borah said pleasantly.

"I just remembered something . . . about the house I am having built. The day before yesterday, I was down to the architects' office. I was told that a real-estate agent had been telephoning them. Someone already wants to buy my house and the lot I bought."

He peered at her in a sharply questioning way. "Would you want to do that? Sell your home before you have ever lived in it?"

"I can always build another house, Mr. Borah. Besides, nobody ever went broke making a profit." She did not reveal her inward reluctance; she would be parting with the home she had so carefully planned with the thought of the blind boy, Peter Moffitt within it.

"Would you look into the matter for me? Call the real-estate people. Drive a hard bargain, Mr. Borah. I want enough profit on that property for two things: I want to buy those two thousand acres of Pend Oreille timberland. And . . . and damn it, Mr. Borah, to have enough to pay for a surgical operation. A delicate one."

Borah came to his feet and approached her; his face showed concern. "Deborah, you mean you are—?"

She read his thoughts. "No . . . no, I am perfectly well." Then she was telling him of her stopover in Ogden, of the side trip to Salt Lake City, and of her meeting with an eight-year-old boy named Peter Moffitt, a boy for whom an operation might mean the wonders of eyesight.

"Is he related to you, Deborah?" There was deep interest in the lawyer's words.

"Not really, but we had the same stepfather—Bishop Joshua Stannard of the Mormon Church. But what matters is for Peter to have the chance to see. Mr. Borah, I have thought often of adopting Peter. But . . . but he is a Mormon. I am not."

He rose to leave, obviously moved by what she had revealed. "Deborah, I will get right on this matter of your house." He paused and grinned. "And I won't be offering it too cheaply. After all,

479

the services of eye specialists do not come for any paltry sum."

He had scarcely left when Deborah picked up a blank sheet of paper and began to write:

Dear Mother:

I should have answered your last letter sooner but circumstances seemed to delay me. I trust all goes well and that you are finding the satisfaction you looked forward to in serving those of your Church.

May I persuade you to do something for me? You know, of course, of the boy, Peter, whom Abrigal Stannard had and may still have in a Salt Lake City home for blind children. He is, I believe, nearing his ninth birthday. I want to send him a birthday present and need to know what he would really like. And beyond that I would like to have the names and addresses of the doctors who have examined him.

Mother, I want so much to adopt Peter; but because of my being single—and not of the Mormon faith—that is doubtless impossible.

But more important—I want, if it is humanly possible, to give him back his sight. I was told that an operation may help him to see again. Now, what I have in mind . . .

She continued writing, then paused to realize that this letter in a sense brought her closer to her mother than they had been since leaving Nebraska. When the letter was finished, she went directly to the post office to mail it. Then she realized it was long past noon and she was unusually hungry. She tossed her head as a decision was made—and then she was walking with long strides toward the home of Mama Echiverri.

An hour later, with her hunger satisfied and a glass of elderberry wine before her, Deborah sat across a red-and-white checked tablecloth from the Basque woman. They talked for a time of ranch conditions and the wool market.

"It is easier now for our people, Deborah," Mama Echiverri said. "The money from your friend at the big mill back in Ohio lets us have more things. Here in Boise. Out on the ranches. You helped bring about miracles."

"Deborah," she said presently, "listen to an old lady . . . to Mama. You need two things, my child. To not work so hard . . . maybe go on a vacation. Yes—and to get married."

Deborah answered, "Marry whom, Mama? There isn't anybody. Not one man anymore."

"Your common sense has deserted you." The tone of the older woman's voice had changed. Now it was higher pitched and almost derisive. "Nobody, eh? You are like a snow-blind sheep dog. Running and thinking in circles. *Don't you know he is in love with you?*"

"Who?"

"Who? Are you so stupid? Do I have to tell you? Or are you trying to keep the truth from yourself? Deborah, do you know why he stays away from Boise . . . and from your office?"

"You mean—"

"Of course that is what I mean. That Jeff Harding thinks the sun and moon and stars set or rise because of you. He loves you, child."

The wine was stealing away Deborah's inhibitions and her reluctance to reveal her thoughts. "I think you imagine a lot," she said and shook her head. "If not, Jeff has a way of keeping his feelings to himself."

"He may think he has good reasons," Mama Echiverri answered firmly. "He thinks there are too many years between you two. That he has no right—"

"But shouldn't I have something to say in deciding that?"

"Of course. But that lawman is uneasy, Deborah. Timid . . . afraid to let you read his inner thoughts . . . and hopes . . . and dreams."

"How could he ever—?" Deborah began. Then she fell silent. She remembered the meeting of the committee in the sun parlor of her rooming house—and the immobilized face of Jeff Harding as he had watched when she talked to Robert Lowell. She peered into Mama Echiverri's solid but kindly face. "Where is Jeff, Mama? I haven't seen him anywhere lately."

Mrs. Echiverri threw her hands aloft. "Who knows where that man is? Where there is a livestock man, or many men, needing help. But I know that he will be back for our Basque fete; it begins the second Friday from now."

Urgently Deborah wanted to think over her self-doubts. Why had it been so inevitable that she send Lemuel Froman away because of his beliefs? Why had Fate and time and loneliness driven Robert Lowell into the arms of an Indian woman? And now . . . why must Jeff Harding be torn with belief he must not again touch her? Is it because things just work out this way? she asked herself. Or is there something about me, something destined to destroy every chance I will ever have for a man's love . . . for marriage . . . for a child of my own? She stared unseeingly at the kitchen wall. Then she rose a bit uncertainly to her feet. "Mama, thank you," she murmured. "And Mama, when Jeff does come back to Boise, tell him not to be afraid . . . but to come see me."

The days that followed seemed to Deborah among the busiest she had ever known. She spent long hours at the office, glad that they caused time to rush by and eased the seeming futility of returning each evening to her suddenly lonely and somewhat unbearable room. The campaign of Henry Carswell for secretary of state had gained momentum across the state; the reaction to his candidacy was reassuring. It indicated the likelihood that Carswell would win by a large majority. Studying the reports and statistics, Deborah often pondered one aspect of such a victory. The present secretary was not campaigning actively; he was known to be searching for a position with the federal government. What would this change by Blain Halligan's superior and his confidant bring about? Surely Halligan would retaliate, venting his wrath and frustration. She surmised the moves would be against the committee. But who had organized the committee? There was no denying her role had been the major one—and Blain Halligan's vengeance must surely seek her out eventually.

Other matters were working out far more to her liking. William Borah's negotiations with the buyer for her lot and unfinished house brought an early closing. She no longer had an

483

obligation to the Boise City National Bank, and she had realized a profit of seventy-two hundred dollars.

As Deborah discussed these matters with him in his office, his eyes appraised her carefully. "Deborah, either you are working too hard or something is plaguing you. Why don't you take a real vacation—a trip? You have help in the office now, and there is no reason Henry Carswell shouldn't let others handle all that campaign correspondence. Fact is, it's a waste of time and postage. Carswell is going to win by a big majority."

She propped an elbow on his desk and let her chin sink into her palm. Then she said decisively, "You are right, Mr. Borah. And I know just what I would like to do. Before I pay out twenty-five hundred dollars for an option on that Pend Oreille timberland, I want to see it. Maybe dabble my feet in a creek. Try to climb right to the top of a big white pine tree. Look out over two thousand acres of trees and grass and meadow and let it sink in that it can be *mine*."

He looked concerned. "You'd have to go North, Deborah. Through Grangeville—all the stages stop there. It might be unwise . . . or dangerous."

"But I wouldn't be going that way," she answered with a reassuring smile. "I have always wanted to have a genuine boat trip. Why can't I take a train to someplace in Oregon? Then I'll catch a boat up the Snake River to Lewiston; I know a Colonel Sanderson in Lewiston who has a lot to do with boats on the Snake River and the Clearwater."

Borah nodded his head. "It is an excellent idea. But, young lady, are you acquainted with everyone in Idaho? It sometimes seems so."

"Friend of all but dearest of none," she answered, and her bitterness caused William Borah to sigh.

Then Deborah drew a letter from her purse. "About that other matter of mine you consented to look into—have you had time?"

"You're wondering what progress I have made about the little blind boy, Peter Moffitt. Deborah, adoption may be impossible. It is certainly going to be difficult because of his being a Mormon, presently in a Church facility in Salt Lake City." He spread his hands in a futile way, and added, "I understand your desire, Deborah, your concern—"

"No, you don't—that is, I have not explained yet." Her eyes were holding firm to the attorney's face, and an excited flush mounted her cheeks. "There is a possibility that Peter might be given his sight through the operation. A Salt Lake City doctor has urged that Peter be taken to a specialist in San Francisco. I want him to have that chance. So does my mother. She has even offered to go as an escort with Peter if the trip can be arranged."

"But the expense, Deborah. It would cost a lot."

"That is what I was coming to. Mr. Borah, you handed me a profit of seventy-two hundred dollars. Let's take out the twenty-five hundred dollars we will need for the timber option. Then—if necessary—use every remaining cent to get Peter to San Francisco and to pay for an opera-

485

tion. Do you think it is enough?" Her tone showed anxiety.

"It should be. Almost five thousand dollars. But Deborah, have you thought this over thoroughly? You would be sacrificing so much. And there is a chance Peter may not see."

"I will take that chance," she answered fiercely.

A little later he walked with her to the outer door of the office building as she was leaving. Then he asked, "Deborah, who is going on the trip with you—your good friends the Plunketts?"

"I hadn't thought about it," she replied. "Perhaps this time I will go by myself; I feel the need to be alone and free to do whatever I wish . . . even to do some soul-searching."

"Which may be just the thing, provided you temper it with a lot of rest and recreation and fun. And there is one more thing. Tomorrow I will drop by your office with the updated option papers on that timberland. That way you will have them whenever you wish to sign and deliver them to the Weyerhaeuser lumber people; I understand they have a regional office in Lewiston."

Deborah nodded. Then impulsively she asked, "Mr. Borah, have you seen or heard of Lemuel Froman lately?"

His eyes widened in surprise. "Haven't you heard? Froman is leaving Boise. He has closed his law office, and his house is up for sale."

"But why . . . where?" she stammered.

"All I know is what Lemuel told me when we lunched together a week ago. He decided a law practice wasn't for him. He applied to the Mormon officials in Salt Lake City for missionary duties; they offered him a responsible position in Sydney, Australia. He accepted it, but I don't know just when he is leaving."

"But his little girl?" Deborah asked. "Is he taking her?"

"He didn't mention the child to me. Surely either he or the Church has made arrangements for her care here in the United States . . . or possibly in Sydney."

The Basque festival was scheduled that year for the first week of August. Deborah wanted to attend it before beginning her trip northward. The festival would give her an opportunity to visit with Antonio Onederra and his wife, who would surely come in from their ranch. And there would be others of the Basque people whom she had grown to like and respect, especially Mama Echiverri. But her real reason for lingering in Boise was that Jeff Harding would surely be among those coming for the occasion.

Deborah was not destined to know the excitement of the Basque festival that year. Just three days before the start of the fete, her telephone rang. It was the Union Pacific ticket agent she had asked to book passage for her. The trip was scheduled to start August 2—at the beginning of the Basque festival.

Outside, the heat of Boise's first sultry day was beating at the window. Suddenly the office seemed small . . . restrictive . . . dull. She tossed her head, grasped the telephone more tightly, and said, "I will want the reservation for the second."

* * *

Just before sunrise on a morning ten days later, a Pullman porter awakened her. "Miss Dexter, we will be in The Dalles, Oregon, in forty minutes. Just leave your luggage when you're ready. You will have time for a bite of breakfast in the dining car."

She dressed quickly, choosing a white blouse and dark blue skirt. The shorter length of the skirt, and also the low-heeled shoes, would enable her to move more securely about a boat's deck. There were only half a dozen other people in the dining car at this early hour; she had her pick of white-linened tables and chose one on the right side of the car. She placed her breakfast order and then glanced out the window. The train was moving along a sizable curve between an immensity of brown and folded hills. She noted also a small stream fringed with willows; the train was moving next to this in a direction she judged to be northwestward. Later in the day this Union Pacific train would arrive in Portland, only a couple of hours from the Oregon coast. She pondered what it would be like to continue westward. She had never seen the Pacific Ocean. Would it be like the Great Salt Lake?

Soon she sensed that the train was slowing and coming onto a straight and level piece of track. She glanced again out the window—and gasped in amazement. Off to the north lay an expanse of river wider than she had ever thought could exist. "It's the Columbia," she murmured, and then watched the progress of a stump-nosed tug that lay down a streak of black smoke as it labored upstream. Far across the water she could see the buildings and trees and streets of a small settlement, and she sensed that it was in the state of Washington. Where must it come from, and how many lesser rivers must have fed into it? She thought of the Snake and Clearwater rivers as she and the Plunketts had seen them at Lewiston. She again studied the tug and its white-water wake. I wonder if it came from down by the ocean or from Portland. Why, it may even be going all the way to Lewiston . . . hundreds of miles from here. A thought thrilled her: *And so am I!*

Deborah would always remember the days of her launch trip up the great northwestern waterways. She could have made faster time continuing to Seattle by train and transferring to either the Northern Pacific or other rail lines that served Idaho's Northland. But the few days to be saved seemed of little consequence when weighed against the adventure and excitement of wending upstream on a steam-driven launch.

Six days later, at sundown, the panting launch reached the juncture of the Snake and Clearwater rivers. There were two towns now in view—Clarkston, Washington, on the western bank of the Snake River, and Lewiston, Idaho, sprawled along both the Snake and Clearwater on the eastern bank. The launch made a brief stop of Clarkston, then plied its leisurely way to the larger and busier docks of Lewiston.

Deborah walked ashore with a sense of well-being and enjoyment. The days of her river travel, with the continual possibility of new sights and sounds around each riverbend, had lessened her thoughts of Boise, of the association, and of every perplexity in her life. She had become tanned and lost weight. She had an eagerness and zest she had not felt since before her trek with Jeff Harding into Wyoming's Greys River country. She headed toward the hotel where she and the Plunketts had stayed on her first trip to this wooded and river-laced land. Tomorrow she would drop in on Colonel Sanderson. And tomorrow, she could either continue up the Clearwater for a closer look at the two hundred acres of timberland for which the Weyerhaueser Company was trying to deal —or she might continue by stage into the Pend Oreille country to determine whether to exercise her option. Tomorrow . . . tomorrow! Again its promise was a warming aura about her.

Deborah would have been far less entranced had she known what had happened this very afternoon in Boise. It began suddenly, when a man turned from the street and strode through the cases of ore specimens to approach the assay room and office of Frank Wentworth. The man rapped at the door, and when there was no immediate answer he pounded with loud insistence. Seconds later the door swung open and Wentworth stood peering at the man who had summoned him. The assayer's face took on a wary and noncommittal aspect. Then he asked, "Are you looking for me, Halligan?"

"If you could spare me a little time, Frank. I don't seem to see much of you anymore over at the statehouse." There was a taut uneasiness, and a masking of irritation in Blain Halligan's voice. Wentworth stepped aside and waved his visitor toward a chair. As they sat down, Wentworth scrutinized this man who had so unexpectedly appeared. He had always considered Blain Halligan to be a handsome and intelligent man. But now the well-chiseled features bore the marks of indecision, of sleeplessness, and possibly of fear. "Now, Blain," he asked in a not unfriendly way, "what is on your mind?"

Halligan forced a weak smile. "Frank, I just came from my boss's office."

"You mean our secretary of state?" Wentworth queried.

"Yes. And he gave me some damned disturbing news. His advisers tell him he can't be reelected. That Carswell, that fellow from down around Pocatello, will be a shoo-in at the fall election."

"Likely that is so," Wentworth agreed. "Carswell has come up with a lot of backing."

"But the man is a damned arsonist and a thief!" Halligan flared. "Did you know that he and some followers destroyed my business building up at Grangeville? They also prowled my home; one of my men was killed!"

Wentworth's expression took on simulated surprise. "I heard there was a sort of commotion up there—about the same time Sam Douglas was bushwhacked."

Halligan chose not to reply. A little time passed as the two men appraised each other. At last Halligan said tentatively, "Frank, I have been asked to persuade you to support the present secretary. He has been my friend for a long time, you know."

Wentworth's face was unrevealing as he poked tobacco into a pipe and touched a match to it.

Then he looked straight into Blain Halligan's face. His voice had sharpened as he said, "You are wasting your time, Blain. I have come to realize that your boss is both ineffective and given to lining his own pockets in devious ways."

"That is only hearsay," Halligan rasped. "Besides, hasn't that been a part of Idaho politics ever since territorial days?"

"Perhaps so. But it is time for a change. For some fiscal integrity. That is why I plan to support Henry Carswell. His business record is pretty damn clean."

Blain Halligan came angrily to his feet. "So you persist in supporting an arsonist. Well, Frank, it won't work. I intend to see that that stupid ass Carswell gets what he deserves—a few years behind bars."

The words failed to arouse Wentworth. "Sit down, Blain. Listen to me. You'd best think twice about going to the law against Carswell. Do you remember that when he first went to Grangeville he ordered a selection of the Bearpaw Enterprises veterinary medicines? I believe they were shipped to him at Pocatello about two days before your unfortunate fire. And Blain, he has had them analyzed by chemists. Need I say more?"

Again Halligan jumped up, his face livid and his fists clenched. "So that's the way it is, Wentworth. Well, by God, I know how to stop all of this . . . just as I know how it started . . . when a slut named Deborah Dexter started prying into things that were none of her business."

"Like the Nampuh Distributing Company?" Wentworth challenged.

"Yes! And like her coming so innocentlike to

my place up at Grangeville, claiming that a couple of doddering old fools named Plunkett were her parents." He paused and turned toward the door. "Frank, I see there is no use talking to you. But I am not the kind to tuck my tail and run like a whipped pup. Mark my words: I am going after Deborah Dexter, and when I am through, she will be whimpering to Jesus to let her get out of Idaho on the double."

Wentworth laid down his pipe and rose to his feet. Then he said in a voice practically void of emotion, "Halligan, before you do that . . . before you or any of your associates lay a hand on that young woman . . . you had best consider one thing: the records, the checks, and the correspondence that your brother, Lacey, let Sam Douglas and Robert Lowell remove from a desk in your home."

Halligan's face whitened. Then he said, "So you know about that, Wentworth. Likely they came running to you with what they stole from me." He looked searchingly about the room as though to see the filing box.

Wentworth answered slowly, choosing his words with infinite care. "Blain, you are wrong. I do not have those papers, although I admit that I have seen them. Do you suppose I would be fool enough to have them here, unprotected? All I have to say is this: Before you file any legal charges against Deborah Dexter, I suggest that you get the advice—and follow the suggestions—of the best and shrewdest attorney you can find. Then consider the consequences . . . for yourself and for your brother."

Halligan's eyes were both baffled and hate-filled as he jerked open the door. "It is all a damnable plot! A conspiracy against me! Hatched by a bitch who has mesmerized every last one of you!" Halligan's fingers, on the knob of the door, were white and trembling and his voice uncontrolled and shrill. "I'll remember this, Wentworth, if ever you want a favor! I'm not giving up! There are ways—" his voice trailed off as he stalked through the display room and onto the street.

Three hours later, a less urgent but firm rap sounded on Wentworth's workshop door. He grinned as he opened the door and Jeff Harding stepped in.

"Frank," Harding said, "has Blain Halligan been here today?"

Wentworth straightened in surprise. "Yes, he has. But why?"

"Because there may be hell to pay, Frank. I just came from the association office . . . where I went to see if any mail had been held for me. The girl there, Deborah's helper, was scared out of her wits. Crying. Just about ready to lock the place up and leave."

"Why? Get on with it, Jeff."

"Because Blain Halligan had been there. Mad and rampaging. Maybe out of his mind. He'd left ten minutes before I showed up." Harding looked searchingly at the assayer and then asked, "Was he like that here? Did you say something to set him off?"

"Maybe," Wentworth murmured. "We had some straight talk, and it got pretty hot. But he didn't abuse that office girl, did he?"

"He didn't lay a hand on her. He was looking for

Deborah. When he found she wasn't at the office, he got real nasty. Scared the new girl enough she told him of Deborah's being out of town—and that she had gone up North to look at some property she owned."

"Damn it . . . just what we wouldn't want him to know," Wentworth said uneasily. "Jeff, he may be off his rocker a bit. I told him there was no way I could support the present secretary of state against Henry Carswell. Halligan knows that means the end of his own political job and his opportunity to dip into the resources of the state and the ranchers."

Jeff Harding's face had taken on a harshness that the assayer had never before seen. "Frank, I don't care a tinker's damn about Blain Halligan or his future. It is Deborah I'm worried about. Before he tore out of her office he muttered something about seeing that she was put out of his way and his life once and for all."

"Now what are you going to do, Jeff?"

Harding glanced toward a wall clock. "In less than two hours I can catch a train to Seattle. With any luck, I can be up on the Clearwater River, around Orofino, day after tomorrow."

"But can you find Deborah?"

Harding's answer came in a strangely tense way. "Perhaps I can't. But I have an idea who can. You stay here and keep an eye on Halligan's office, Frank. If anything breaks, wire me at Orofino, through the sheriff's office."

Frank Wentworth nodded, then asked, "What if Halligan climbs on the same train you do?"

"That isn't likely." Harding laughed in a brittle way. "He will probably stop at Grangeville to reinforce himself with one or two of his thugs. He'll have to go by stage to do that. And besides, Frank, Halligan won't be climbing aboard the Union Pacific anytime tonight. I have friends in the Boise police who can detain him—just long enough—at the depot."

Chapter 24

EVEN BEFORE her arrival in Lewiston, Deborah had become aware of the drought that summer had brought to eastern Washington and the great forestlands of northern Idaho. As the launch forced its way up the Snake River, the seared hills lay in shimmering heat in every direction. For days a hot and dry wind had blown in from the vast Columbia Basin, bearing no rain clouds and causing the humidity to drop ever lower. At times it seemed that the air itself was laden with a static electricity that at any moment might burst into flames.

There had been talk of shriveled or dry creeks, of wheatlands lying in scorched desolation, and of grasslands and forests set ablaze by savage electric storms that carried only scattered drops of rain. The orchards and the fields lay piteously dry and devastated, even where streams or lakes were tantalizingly close. Even attempts at digging irrigation ditches seemed to no avail because of the dry and superheated air of each cloudless day.

These facts and their ominous portent were about her as, the day after her arrival in Lewiston, she boarded a stage that would take her northward to the university town of Moscow and onward to Coeur d'Alene. She hoped that from the latter town she could find some well-established and reliable means of getting into the Pend

Oreille area and to the timberlands for which the Weyerhaeuser Company had offered her an option. The trip was a sobering experience; with each passing mile there was new evidence of the lack of rain. Her memory went back to the green timber and lush meadows . . . and the refreshing rains . . . of the Yankee Fork valley. Things should be even greener and more lovely here in far northern Idaho, for wasn't this the area of rain and of mists and of fogs? But now the grass was brown and brittle, the flowers either dwarfed or lifeless, and the vistas of pine and spruce and fir somehow inert and despairing under a brassy sky and the occasional swirl of a heat devil.

The stage stopped for lunch and a change of horses and driver in Moscow. When it again got under way, she found a new passenger seated beside her. For the first hour he seemed to ignore her and quietly read a book. When she glanced at the title, she read: *Principles of Silviculture.* Moments later the stranger glanced up, saw that she was staring at the book, and smiled.

"Silviculture," she said aloud. "Isn't that something about forestry?" She was aware that the man was young, hardly out of his teens, with blond hair and intense blue eyes. At the moment he was obviously bashful.

"Yes, ma'am," he managed to reply, "it is the study of forests and their management."

"There is precious little management of our Idaho forests," she responded caustically.

"I know. But it will change when the federal forest reserves are established. And that is coming."

"So is the Second Coming of Christ," Deborah

498

said doubtfully, and then looked about to see if her utterance had offended others in the coach. Only the man beside her seemed awake, and now he was becoming wary and reopening the book. Deborah laughed a bit ruefully and said, "Excuse such plain talk. It is only because I get so wrought up as I see our heritage of timberlands being ravaged. Do you know that less than a dozen men control most of the timber resources of Idaho?"

"Yes," he answered, "and when I see the carelessness with which they log such magnificent areas as the Coeur d'Alene and the Pend Oreille—"

"The Pend Oreille," she broke in excitedly. "Are you familiar with that area . . . with its forest cover?"

"Not entirely; but I spent much of last summer there as a timber cruiser for a big lumbering concern."

Deborah was digging a folder of papers from her overnight case. "Then perhaps you can help me. And . . . by the way . . . my name is Deborah Dexter, from Boise."

The youth marked his place and laid his book aside to accept the hand she was holding out. "I am Erik Bertelsen. I study part of the year at the college back at Moscow. My father is a mine foreman up at Wallace."

Deborah had located a page of legal descriptions and now smoothed it on her knee. "I need to know something of the timber on these townships and sections. Do you think you—?"

He silently scanned the descriptions and then drew a topographical map from his pocket. "I have cruised some of these locations, ma'am. Here . . .

and here . . . and just a part of this." His finger was tracing across the map.

"What is it like? The timber? The land and the roads? You may save me having to inspect it myself." Deborah's voice was becoming excited.

"You would have an awful time cruising those areas, Miss Dexter. It wouldn't be easy . . . or perhaps safe."

"You mean that these areas aren't in good timberland?"

He shook his head. "I don't mean that. Not at all. On those sections you have listed are some of the finest stands of timber I have ever studied. White pine mostly, interspersed with larch up to two hundred feet tall. There is also Englemann spruce and a sprinkling of Douglas fir."

"Is it good, merchantable timber?" Deborah urged.

Erik Bertelsen hesitated. "I . . . I suppose it is. Yes, of course. But ma'am, it shouldn't be cut."

"Why?" she asked.

"Because some of those groves are spectacular and likely can never be replaced. To walk among those trees . . . those giants . . . is like treading the aisles of a vast cathedral. The rays and shafts of sunlight breaking through . . . the murmur of branches so high above as the wind searches through them. The green softness of the needle-carpeted floor. The chuckling streams. The animals that claim this as home."

"Forests mean a lot to you," Deborah murmured. Then she asked, "Why would anyone who owns such woodlands—especially a very practical and successful lumber company—offer to trade them?" Doubt as to the motives of the Weyerhaeuser Company was building within her.

"That is easy to answer," young Bertelsen said quickly. "The terrain of this area of the Pend Oreille is such that access to the groves would be prohibitive in cost. Even logging railroads and skidways would cost a fortune to build and maintain. There are narrow canyons. Cliffs. Precipitous slopes of granite and basalt stone. In other areas are bogs and swales that would become impassable after rains."

From the fierceness of his tone, she sensed that he was defending the sanctity of the virgin forest that seemed to mean so much to him. So she asked, "Do you think the area will always be like that—impractical or overly costly to lumber?"

"No. Not forever. Perhaps not many more years. But perhaps by then the government will have acquired the groves and included them in reserves. Besides, ma'am, before long there will be less expensive ways of getting into the remote and difficult areas. We'll see gasoline motor trucks able to travel trails where railroads can't possibly go. There are bound to be small sawmills too; from them lumber will be moved out. It will all come when lumber prices skyrocket."

Deborah quietly replaced the pages of legal description in her case. Then she turned to her companion. "When are we due to reach Coeur d'Alene?"

"After midnight. There is a lot of bumpy road ahead." He glanced at her with mingled bashfulness and curiosity and asked, "Will you be going on north . . . to the Pend Oreille?"

"No." She sighed in a relieved way. "Thanks to you, there will be no need."

Deborah remained in the town of Coeur d'Alene for three days. Despite the heat hanging over northern Idaho that August and the frequent scent of smoke from burning timberlands beyond the horizon, she found the community ideal for relaxation. From the edge of town stretched a lake with which she instantly fell in love. It stretched for miles between heavily timbered shores and reflected the sky with a blueness so vivid that she took every opportunity to gaze upon it. Each day she swam and lounged on a sandy beach. Twice she was invited aboard a sailboat to go racing around a cape and into the main length of Lake Coeur d'Alene. There were a few mining camps along the shores, as well as the cabins of those who claimed the lake as their recreation haven.

She took on added tan; her form became leaner, more erect, and more supple.

She tried her hand at tennis and ventured onto a lake steamboat that brought silver ore from a distant inlet of the lake.

She returned to Lewiston and to the hotel after being gone five days. With her mind now at ease, she took a bath, changed from her travel clothes, and put on a light green linen dress that she hoped was right for an active business person. Then, at a few minutes after ten o'clock in the morning, she made her way to the offices of the Weyerhaeuser Company to search out a legal representative whose name Robert Lowell had written down for her.

The transaction took little time. When she emerged from the office building half an hour later, she had spent twenty-five hundred dollars. In her purse were documents, attested by a notary public, transferring to her clear and valid title to two thousand acres of timber holdings on the Pend Oreille. She had never glimpsed a single acre of it and had only the word of Robert Lowell and of a young timber cruiser named Erik Bertelsen. And now, because of other documents that Lowell had already signed, neither of them had any claim whatsoever to the two hundred acres on the Clearwater river, that strategic wedge that guarded the entryway to timber stretching upward to blue infinity. But jointly they now held title to an additional one thousand acres near Pend Oreille as a result of their one acre for five trade. The canny agents of Weyerhaeuser had had their way.

She returned to the hotel and had a leisurely lunch. A hot and somewhat hazy afternoon caused her to sit for an hour on the hotel veranda gazing out over the wide joining of the Snake and Clearwater rivers and studying the movement of both pleasure and commercial boats. The glint of light on the water caused Deborah to become drowsy. Presently she shook the lethargy. Why not walk the three blocks to the office of the Columbia Navigation and Forwarding Company? She told herself that it would be interesting to again chat with Colonel Sanderson. But she was acutely aware of a deeper urge—again to board the work launch and let it carry her upstream through the beautiful valley of the Clearwater River, all the way to where its North Fork diverged to turn northward. There would be a settlement nearby called

Orofino. What harm could there be in going? A few days of her vacation still remained. Perhaps . . . just perhaps she would catch sight of the rivershore cabin of Robert Lowell and his family. She also wanted to see the two hundred acres of timberland that she had, until today, jointly owned with Lowell. She had glimpsed it only that once, when he had pointed it out from a distance.

At the office she was disappointed to learn that the kindly Colonel Sanderson had left for Portland the previous week. Nevertheless, she arranged for passage on the boat, to leave at eight o'clock the following morning.

Later that day, she was climbing the steps to the porch of her hotel when she sensed that she was being watched. Men were sitting on the porch, close to the hotel's entrance. She forced herself to keep her gaze seemingly unconcerned and straight ahead. Then a few steps later she swung her head quickly to gain full sight of the one man she knew was staring at her. For a second or two their eyes locked—and realization and recognition swept Deborah. The man seated within arm's reach of her was Blain Halligan.

She would have swept by him, without a sound or a hint of recognition, but was momentarily forestalled as she yielded progress to two lumberjacks who staggered from the doorway. Blain Halligan rose quickly to his feet, his face inscrutable as it came close to her own. He spoke then, low-toned words that came only to Deborah's ears: "I had an idea you'd be up here. Now it's your turn . . . understand?"

She pushed ahead as though not hearing or heeding him, but her pulse was beating rapidly, and anger was rising at the callousness of his words. Moments later, within the quiet of her room, she locked the door and dropped onto a chair. *He has somehow traced me up here, followed me.* She was unaware of what had taken place in Boise during her absence and of how the words of Frank Wentworth had forecast for Halligan the loss of his political protection. Yet, ever since the return to Boise of the committee from Grangeville, Deborah had known that someday a reckoning such as this would surely come. And tonight, alone and a stranger in this river city, she knew that only her own actions might bring her through to safety.

Later, when she surmised the hotel's dining room would be well filled, she left her room and descended to the lobby. She glanced about, but there was no sign of Blain Halligan as she walked into the dining room and was seated. Despite the stress within her, she ate hungrily and studied those about her. *Halligan is not stupid enough to try anything or make a scene in a busy place like this,* she reasoned. *But he is trailing me. Waiting for some sort of opportunity.*

Her thoughts were interrupted by the entrance of three men. She looked at them with instant interest. She had seen each of them before—as crewmen of the launch on which Colonel Sanderson had sent her up the Clearwater River. Although washed and tidied up, the three still wore work clothing and sat at a table somewhat removed from the other guests. They noticed her scrutiny of them but only grinned and went about ordering their meal.

They were well along with their meal when

Deborah rose and walked up to their table. "Excuse me," she said quickly. "You probably don't remember me, but I went up the river on your launch last year."

"That is where I've seen you," one of the men said while the others eyed her curiously.

"And I am going up to Orofino again tomorrow," she explained carefully. "Will all of you be making the trip?"

"Unless we get fired before then," one of them spoke up.

"Then would you mind very much if I walk down to the docks with you in the morning?"

They were all staring at her now, and the oldest one eyed her a bit doubtfully. "But why?" he demanded. "We have to get aboard and load cargo . . . an hour before it is time to shove off."

She leaned forward and dropped her tone to a confidential whisper. "Because of a man, that's why," she said urgently. "He is bothering me. If I get up early and go with you, maybe I can slip away from him."

"He won't try to come aboard, will he?" It was the most burly and silent of the group. "We can drop him in the river, sort of accidental-like, of course."

"No, I just want to get away from him . . . a long way from him," Deborah said, smiling.

She slept fitfully and with a chair propped against her door. Despite the warmth of the night, she kept her windows closed and locked tightly. When shortly after sunrise a solid rapping sounded at her door, she was already dressed and her suitcase and overnight case were packed and waiting. All three of the boatmen were in the hall.

As they picked up her luggage and made for the street, she sensed that they had already eaten. She peered about the lobby, but it was deserted save for a bleary-eyed night clerk. There was no sign of Blain Halligan; his absence caused her to heave a sigh of relief.

The journey of the launch up the Clearwater that day was somewhat faster than it had been on her previous trip. She was shocked by the change in appearance of the great river valley. There were still the great mountains and sweeping forests that had so intrigued her. But now they lay under a brassy sun and seared by a continuous southwest wind. The stream was much lower than she remembered it, with protruding sandbars and with low waterlines along the shores. Drought had dried much of the grass to a brittle brown and deadened the wildflowers. As they ascended within twenty miles of the junction at the North Fork, there was a constant haze of woodsmoke that lowered visibility and burned her nostrils.

She noted too the increase in small boats with engines that enabled them to speed easily by the launch. Had distance allowed her carefully to scan one such craft, carrying only three men as it went upstream, her perplexity and anxiety would have soared. One man was the operator of the boat. And behind him, with their eyes glued to the launch they were outdistancing, were two men she would surely have recognized: Blain Halligan—and a man called Lenny.

She thought of the reality and urgency of her position. Why had she, after hearing Halligan's threat, persisted in making such a wilderness side trip as this? Greater safety would no doubt have been hers in a fast trip by train back to Boise. She shrugged as though to rid herself of whatever might loom ahead. "I am going to see this vacation out without panic," she muttered half aloud. "I'll never be quite satisfied that I was wise in selling those two hundred acres until I see them for myself." Her inner thoughts might have silently added: And I have to see that cabin again. The Indian girl. Her child. Yes, and Robert too. Then I can feel free—and forget.

Now there was a familiar appearance about the shoreline and the wooded slopes beyond. Then she spotted the cabin. She caught her breath at sight of its log walls and roughly shingled roof; it seemed unchanged . . . unchangeable . . . and standing expectant of her coming. It is nonsense to feel this way, her mind cautioned. But to one of the boatmen she said, "Could you let me ashore there?" and pointed to the small, log-formed dock beside which an empty rowboat was moving restlessly about. The launch edged cautiously closer, and she could distinguish the path ascending a grassy crest to the cabin's front door. The boatman came to her side. "Are you sure you want to get off here, miss? It is a lonely spot . . . and if someone is following you—"

Deborah faced him, her eyes excited but level upon him. "Yes . . . put me ashore. There are people here I know, and I will be all right. And it may be several days before I'll be going down to Lewiston with you."

Moments later she was standing on the dock, her luggage about her, watching the distance widen between her and the launch. Seconds passed, and then a shadow on the planks of the dock, and a sense of someone near, caused her to wheel about. A gasp of unbelief broke from her. She was staring, wide-eyed and unbelieving, into the face of Jeff Harding.

"Jeff," she managed to ask, "how . . . why are you here?"

He looked at her with a somber and unrevealing gaze and made no move to touch her. "Deborah, I am here because I knew . . . realized for sure . . . that this is where you would come—and because you are in danger."

Deborah's face crumpled. "Oh, God, Jeff! I keep asking myself why I came. Perhaps to end a dream—or to rid myself of a nightmare." She glanced up the path toward the cabin. "Are they there? The girl . . . his wife? And the child? Is he . . . Robert?"

"No," Harding answered reluctantly. "They haven't been for at least two weeks."

"Then where—?"

"Deborah, I have talked to the girl's father. He is a Nez Percé leader and quite a decent sort. As soon as Robert got back from Boise, he rounded up his family and moved on . . . to some isolated spot in the back country." Jeff reached for her hand. "I'm sorry . . . about his leaving . . . and about my being here. But I had to come. Blain Halligan knows he is on the verge of disgrace and ruin. He ranted and raved to Frank Wentworth. Threatened to—"

"I know, Jeff. He was in Lewiston, at the hotel, but I managed to slip away. He said there that *it is my turn.* Jeff, is he dangerous . . . insane?"

"I don't know, Deborah, but I am sure of one thing: To get to you now . . . he must dispose of me." Jeff Harding fell silent, staring at the luggage at their feet. After a time he asked, "Shall I put these in the rowboat and take you into the settlement? Or is it best to wait until the launch returns . . . in a couple of hours?"

"Jeff, there are things I must do," she answered, "but neither of those. I want to go into that cabin. And . . . and I want you there with me. It will take only a few moments. But can't you understand? I want to put some ghosts to rest. Come." She grasped his hand and tugged him toward the path.

They pushed open the door of the cabin, and in its subdued light she looked about. Presently her face whitened into torment. Then her hands reached out to clasp Jeff Harding's shoulders. "Jeff, listen . . . please listen. You have to know." She pointed to the far end of the room and the bed from which all blankets were now removed. "I slept with Robert right there—gave myself to him. In love. In fulfillment of my longings."

"Deborah, don't. You don't have to—"

"Hear me out, Jeff. The next morning she came through that very door. The Indian girl. Wordless. Her face without emotion—and her belly large with his child." Deborah lifted anguished eyes. "Now, Jeff, you know and can despise me. But it is over. You know—and I am free."

"Deborah, I have much to tell you," Harding said at last. "But first let's get out of this place, into the sunlight. I'll get a bedroll I have up the slope under some pine trees. Then we can flag down the launch." He seemed to strive for more words, then his arms swept her to him. "Let me take you home to Boise, Debbie."

"I want that too, Jeff," she answered. "But later. There is something else. Can we get horses and ride up the mountain. I . . . I . . . and Robert owned some timberland there that I never saw save from a distance. We traded it off. But I want to ride through it once—the two hundred acres of it and perhaps a bit beyond, into the vast forest it sort of guards. Then I can feel free of it. Yes, free of it as I feel now about this cabin—and those who lived here."

It was well after noon when they rode onto the narrow saddle of woodland that both of them were satisfied comprised the two hundred acres. A hot wind had blown ever since midmorning, and now the forest gave off a deeply resonant sigh. They checked their horses at the top of a ridge where the timber was thinner and allowed sight of an immensity of pine and spruce and fir ahead. In the settlement, they had found a hotel, and while Jeff had secured their mounts, Deborah had changed into an outfit that would let her ride astride. Because of the wind, Jeff cautioned that they take jackets.

And now as they studied the forest floor and the trees bending before the wind, the dull dryness of the area brought worry to both of their faces.

"This whole part of Idaho is becoming a tinderbox," Jeff said and reached down to snap off the stem of a shriveled bit of mountain lupine. Then he added, "Debbie, it's pretty evident why the timber company felt they had to get hold of this saddle, the acreage you and Lowell held. You had them blocked from all of that"—and his hand swept the infinity of forest climbing to the northern horizon.

She did not answer, and Jeff glanced quickly toward her. He noticed too that the heads of the horses were lifted and their ears were toward the course over which they had climbed from Orofino.

"Jeff, there is someone back there. Just for a second or so I saw two riders; they've disappeared now."

He studied the ground and pointed to hoofmarks where their own horses had not trod. "Very likely there are others up here; I have an idea that the Weyerhaeuser people aren't losing time getting surveyors and cruisers into that wilderness ahead."

Deborah kept silent, knowing that he might only be trying to ease her mind. She was aware that he was still searching the timber behind them. "Perhaps we'd best make tracks back to town," he suggested.

"No, Jeff." She shook her head. "It is a couple of hours until sunset. And it is cooler up here, even in the wind. Let's ride ahead; perhaps there will be a meadow and a stream."

They rode on, and after a few backward glances Deborah's sense of uneasiness lessened. The thickness and size of the trees about them increased. This, they knew, was virgin forest where some of the giant trees were three hundred years or more old. They had ridden half a mile farther into the splendid isolation when voices sounded ahead of them. They came upon four men with surveying instruments. The men answered their greeting but proved to be tight-mouthed and obviously anxious to be rid of them. So they rode on.

As she hoped, their way led a little later into a meadowed opening. Across it ran a stream, now shrunken and listless but moving from one beaver pond to another. They gazed about, and abruptly Jeff was pointing to a ridge perhaps a hundred yards to the east. "Deborah, this area isn't as isolated or as deserted as we thought. See that black spot up there, just below those big white pine trees? It is a mine tunnel; and there is a waste-rock dump that has signs of mighty recent workings."

She studied where he pointed, then turned away with evident disinterest. "Mining doesn't excite me anymore, Jeff. Not since I worked like hell all summer over on the Yankee Fork and ended up with less than Mom would have paid me to wash dishes in her restaurant."

Harding eyed the lowering sun. "We had better be going back pretty soon."

"Pretty soon," she agreed. "But first let's peek into one of those beaver ponds. There may be some big trout . . . or we could be lucky and surprise a beaver at work."

"They work mostly at night," Jeff answered. "But we can have a look."

They rode close to a dam, tethered their horses to a willow sapling, and came noiselessly to the pond's edge. There were no beaver to be seen, but through the clear water they watched the movement of a dozen sizable and not too wary trout. Presently Jeff's arm went about her, and Deborah laid her head contentedly on his shoulder. His face softened, and he started to speak. What he might have said was lost in the sudden threshing of a whirlwind across the pond. It flung water in their faces and whipped at their clothing. When it quieted, Jeff's eyes followed the direction of the miniature waves. "The wind has changed," he said aloud. "Now it is from the southeast." As he spoke, he turned to face into the wind and back over the course that had brought them here. He remained momentarily with his gaze glued to what was visible of the saddle formation and the two hundred acres. Then aloud and harshly he said, "My God, Deborah, look back there—the whole damned world is afire!"

Within minutes there was proof of his words. A gale had followed the errant whirlwind, and now a haze of acrid and stifling smoke was about them. It deepened quickly to a twilight and then almost to the darkness of night. Far off there was light cast by fire racing through the crowns of lofty and closely spaced trees.

They would have remained a little longer, entranced and in mute horror, save for the frightened whinnying of their horses. As they turned to hasten to the animals, there was something akin to the patter of raindrops about them. This was not born of moisture, but a showering of pine needles before the wind. They were within a few steps of their horses when a flaming piece of bark came like a meteor above them. It was quickly followed by others, and with a scream of terror Deborah's horse tore free of its bridle and raced across the clearing. Jeff calmed the remaining horse by tying his jacket about its eyes.

The rain of windblown twigs and bark and needle clusters continued, but now most of them were passing overhead; spot fires sprang up across the dry meadow. Already smoke plumes were swirling in the wind far in advance of where they huddled near the pond. Deborah's eyes widened with concern and disbelief. "Jeff, what can we do? The entire ridge back of us is almost one solid fire. We can't—"

"No," he interrupted, "there is no chance of going back. Not for a while." Jeff's face was grave as he sensed that all too quickly every avenue of escape might be cut off by the inferno of fire, of choking smoke, and the menace of falling firebrands.

"There is water here, Jeff," Deborah spoke up. "If . . . if the meadow burns, we will have to get into the pond for a while."

"Deborah, there would probably be hell to pay even there." Jeff pointed toward the dry lengths of log above the waterline of the dam. "That dry wood is apt to catch fire and burn; if it does, the water could become hot. I've seen fish literally boiled in such situations."

"Then God Almighty, what can we do?" she cried out.

Instead of answering, Jeff was staring back over the course by which they had approached the stream. A man was moving toward them in a stumbling and half-blind way, his jacket wrapped about his face. As he neared, Deborah saw that his arms, now outthrust, were burned, with shirt sleeves torn and charred. His hat was missing, and his hair was filthy with the dirt he had pawed onto it to beat out fire. He came within a few yards, and she said aloud, "It's . . . it's one of the surveyors." Then she fell into sickened silence. Three more men, the remainder of the crew, had broken into view and were treading toward them.

All showed the ravages of smoke and scorching; two of the men had their arms around the third and were practically dragging him.

At first all four of the crew ignored both Deborah and Jeff; they dropped close to the water and scooped handfuls of it to wet their faces and to drink in quick gulps. Deborah watched them in a horrified and yet fascinated way. By the groping of the man who had been dragged in, she was certain that he was blinded . . . at least for a time.

She was walking the few steps to his side when the wind and the sound struck her. She had never felt a blast of hot wind such as this. It seemed for an instant to crush her on all sides, then threw her mercilessly into a clump of streamside brush. There was the roar then—of thousands of trees, of the forest giants, being mowed down by a vast hurricane the fires and the wind had created. When she dared look up, it seemed the end of the world. Southward was a vast wasteland of fallen timber, while overhead smoke billowed in great clouds. With fearful eyes she saw one such cloud explode into flames as its gases ignited.

Deborah rose to her elbows, to realize two things: Jeff Harding was moving toward her on his hands and knees. Just beyond him lay the jacket he had used to cover the eyes of their remaining horse—and the horse had vanished into the dark haze that defied the probing of her eyes. Jeff reached her side and peered into her face. "Debbie . . . Debbie . . . are you all right? Can you hear me?"

She nodded dazedly and would have spoken, but one of the survey crewmen had staggered to his feet and now was towering above them.

"Damn you," he said, "you've caused us to be in this mess . . . maybe burned alive!"

Jeff Harding clasped the surveyor's arms in a restraining way as he said calmly, "Ease down, fellow; all of you are still alive."

"You lit a fire back there, didn't you?" the other man accused.

Deborah had listened and now she flared, "You're crazy. We haven't lighted even a match, let alone a campfire." As she spoke, her mind was recalling the backward look she had taken from the ridge atop the two hundred acres. Now she turned to Jeff. "Those men I saw on horseback. Maybe following us—who disappeared?"

"You mean there were others back there?" the surveyor asked doubtingly.

"Likely there were. This fire started somewhere in that direction." Jeff was surveying their plight when he added, "It sure wasn't lightning started it. Not today." He was quiet a while and then spoke again. "We've got to get the hell out of here—all of us. The wind. It is sure to swing back to the southwest. When it does, this whole area is going to burn. This meadow. Even these beaver dams."

One of the crewmen was stumbling toward him. There was a torment of fear in his eyes, and he was sobbing wildly. "There is no other place! We're all going to burn to death! Oh, Christ!" He flung scorched hands up and buried his face in them. The others stared at him with somber uneasiness.

Into Deborah's thoughts had come an intolerable self-accusation. Have I, by coming here, marked these men for death? She thought dully of

Bishop Stannard and of Sam Douglas. Is it to go on as long as I live . . . a procession of death stemming from my actions? She too began crying, an abandoned and hopeless sound.

Jeff Harding had come to his feet; now he peered quickly at her. Moments later he motioned for the survey crewmen to listen. "Fellows, we can't stay here. Without something over us, protecting our heads above water so we can breathe, we'll be scorched or suffocated if the water gets too hot to endure."

"But what in Jesus' name can we do?" one of the surveyors asked. "Just run into a fire wall . . . or in circles?"

"Not by a damned sight," Jeff snapped. "Now, listen. Up on the slope, maybe eight hundred yards, there is a mine portal." He pointed, but the dark portal was obscured by thickening haze and windblown smoke. "I think we can still make it up there—if we hurry and stick together. Let's get going!" He turned to place a hand under the arm of the still sightless crewman. "Up with you . . . and hang on." His other hand went out in an effort to clasp that of Deborah, but she had moved from his side.

Jeff turned his head in alarm and called her name.

"I'm coming," she responded, and he saw that she had picked up his jacket, crumpled and dirty, where the horse had shaken free of it. For a moment Jeff Harding stiffened, and he eyed the jacket guiltily before saying, "Debbie, hang onto it. There is a letter in it. I plumb forgot to give it to you. A letter from Borah, that lawyer in Boise."

They spoke no more, saving their breath, their

518

strength, and their determination for the slow and steep and timber-impeded crawl up the mountainside. When it seemed that they had no strength to walk or crawl farther, the dark portal of the mine's tunnel broke into view. On its every side were tall conifers, mostly white pine, thrusting upward from the steep slope, their crowns now obscured in smoke. Jeff and the strongest of the crew lowered the sightless crewman just within the tunnel, and then Jeff shouted, "Anybody here?" There was only the sound of his own voice reverberating loudly against walls of solid rock. He turned to look about; a small stream of clear water trickled near the tunnel's edge.

Within moments the oldest of the surveyors glanced into the darkness of the tunnel. "We had better pray that this place has an air shaft. Over near Wallace last year a crew was killed by suffocation in a mine. Bad air and smoke and gases got them."

Deborah scarcely heard him, for now there was a resurgence of the wind. Nearby a giant pine crashed, partially blocking the entrance. Outside there was a blackness similar to night, broken by the eerie glow of endless acres of timberland aflame.

Now a member of the survey crew stared into the tunnel's depth and came to his feet. "Why the hell didn't you guys answer our call?" he asked angrily.

The words caused the others to turn and gaze into the yawning depths—and then to fall silent. Outlined before them were three men moving stealthily forward. In the hand of one was a leveled and menacing Colt revolver. "Raise your hands and get your backs against that wall. Damn it, I mean now!"

Deborah heard the words but scarcely comprehended them. Her eyes had steadied but in them was recognition as she looked beyond the gun's menace and squarely into the face of the second man . . . and said almost tonelessly to Jeff, "That second one—it is Blain Halligan!"

At mention of his name, Halligan thrust his way forward to stand beside the gunman. "Yes, Miss Plunkett—excuse me, I mean Miss Dexter—this time I can't offer dinner and a drink."

Before she could reply, she heard Jeff Harding catch his breath. His gaze was holding to the man with the pointing revolver. "And wouldn't you know it—Lenny is here."

"You're damn right I am. Now get against that wall."

Deborah moved closer to the rock. Now she was staring at the third man, who had fallen a couple of steps behind Halligan. That man is not one of them, she thought. His clothes. His bewilderment. His way of walking. He is a miner—and likely the one who somehow brought Halligan and Lenny here.

Lenny was drawing closer and waving the weapon. "You're getting out of here. Just as soon as you clear everything out of your pockets."

Jeff Harding at that moment felt a slight tugging at his trouser leg from the hand of the blinded surveyor. Very cautiously he began to bend over. He heard another voice asking of the gunman, "Why do you want to rout us out of here? Drive us into that hell of fire outside?"

"Because there is bad air here. Maybe two or

three of us can pull through. It's that simple."
Lenny's voice was becoming shrill. "Besides,
you're the sons-of-bitches who burned down
Bearpaw back in Grangeville. Well, we're about
even." He thrust his face, torn with wild fury, toward Deborah. "And you? Remember how you
heaved that box . . . damn near tore off my head?"

She kept silent, knowing that this man, in almost insane rage, was preparing to use the revolver.

"So you're not going to talk. Well, little good
it'll do you," Lenny stormed, and pointed his free
hand toward the red fury outside. "See that fire?
It's burning everything. And that means those
two hundred acres you thought would make you a
fortune. That's where the boss said to start—"

"Shut up, you damned mouthy idiot!" The command broke from Blain Halligan, and his arm
shot out as though to stifle further words. But
Lenny stepped free of him. "Get out of here—and
burn—or I'll shoot!"

In the tenseness of the moment, none of them
noticed that Jeff had leaned farther toward the
man sprawled at his feet. Jeff lowered his hand,
blessing the semidarkness, and felt the metal
shoved into it. It was his starting to come erect
that caught Lenny's attention. He swung about a
little for better aim. And the delay—only a frac-
tion of a second—cost him his life. The weapon
in Jeff Harding's grasp belched fire and lead.
The slug caught Lenny just below his lungs, tore
through him, and knocked him backward. For a
little time he lay silent and writhing; his fingers
twitched in vain for the revolver that slipped from
his grasp. Then he lay in the quiet of death.

521

Harding turned to Halligan, his eyes and voice cold. "Do you want to take up where he left off?"

There was a pastiness about Halligan's face as he said, "Why should I? None of us are going to come out of this alive." And then he smiled slackly at Deborah. "You and I could have gone a long way together. Well, by God, at least you're not going to be a timber baron. Just look outside."

They all stared into an outer world that had become an inferno. There was an eerie light reflected in crimson by low-hanging smoke clouds. Even as they watched, another forest giant crashed somewhere on the slope above them and shot root-end first down the flaming mountainside.

"There won't be anything but stumps on your timber patch, *Miss Plunkett*," Halligan said loudly.

She heard the words and moved closer. "You had him set a forest fire in this wind—just to get even with me?"

"I watched my warehouse burn. Remember?"

"But didn't you know? I haven't owned any timberland within a hundred miles of here since yesterday. I sold every inch of it to the Weyerhaeuser Company."

The man who had lurked behind Halligan came haltingly forward. Then he pointed at Lenny's body and at Halligan. "I didn't have anything to do with that burning. I was coming back to the mine—I work here—and I led these fellows here. Hell, maybe I shoulda let 'em burn up."

Jeff turned to him decisively. "If you work here, you know the layout. Are there air shafts?"

The miner nodded. "There's one back quite a piece, but it is in a drift. Not this main tunnel."

"Then we'd best get back there," one of the surveyors said, choking. "Half an hour from now . . . the way these gasses and the smoke are pouring in . . . we'll all be as dead as he is." He thrust an indifferent thumb toward Lenny's form.

They stumbled and groped their way deeper into the mountain, slowed by a rough floor of uneven rock and by the ties of a makeshift rail line. Although near exhaustion, they took turns guiding the man whose sight had not returned. When they came to the diverging drift, Deborah felt a slight movement of air—cooler and cleaner air. They had come to the air shaft.

As they used fingers against the damp rock of the wall for guidance, Jeff spoke up. "You—the mine employee—is there any chance of getting light in here?"

"Nothing but a carbide lamp like us miners wear. There's a couple we keep stashed. But mister, they help foul up the air."

"Get one," Deborah spoke up. "We'd have to use it but moments at a time." Then she added, "Is there anything here we can use to hang across this smaller tunnel? To block off smoke?"

The miner answered, "Maybe there is. Back a ways are a couple of old blankets and a sort of stretcher. We have them here just in case. I'll mosey back and take a look."

"I'll go with you," the chief surveyor said. "Maybe back there is a spot level enough so we can lie down; I'm about tuckered."

When their shuffling footsteps had faded, Jeff

523

said regretfully, "I wish we could pull off another miracle . . . find a handful of salt."

"Hell, what kind of a miracle would having salt mean?" a crewman said, irritated. "We don't have steak or potatoes to sift it onto. Not even a blaze to cook it over."

"Seems to me you're pretty helpless," Jeff Harding bantered back. "Just try running up to the portal and shoving it outside—that steak you don't have." He had sensed a lessening of the men's fear and tension and was striving to stir their hope. Presently he said to the sightless surveyor, "I've heard of an Indian cure for eyes in your condition. Pour a bit of salt into each of them."

"Jesus, no!" the blinded man groaned. "They burn like there's a red-hot poker in each of them right now." He quieted, then asked in a calmer way, "Do you suppose it just might work?"

The answer came when the miner and his companion returned from the rear of the drift. With the aid of a cap-mounted carbide lamp, they were carrying a battered stretcher, three blankets, and a small chest. "These are all I could find," the miner declared. "Some canned beans, beef jerky . . . and . . . yeah, and some sugar and the like." He did not add that there had also been a pint of whiskey, which he had pocketed.

In the uncertain light of the lamp, Deborah rummaged through the chest. "I thought so," she said aloud. "Here's a carton of salt."

Only one agonized groan broke from the smoke-blinded crewman as Jeff carefully applied the salt. "Steady, fellow," he encouraged. "The Indians say this works for snow blindness. And most anything else. Sort of makes tears flush out the corruption and swelling and the like." He finished the painful application and said, "Now . . . it will take some time."

Deborah had been watching in fascination, but suddenly she rose to her feet and stared about. "He is gone! Jeff, Halligan was standing over there a few minutes ago. Now he isn't here."

The light was swung about to send its feeble rays in one direction and then another. Nothing was revealed except the gloomy rock walls and the loneliness encroaching upon them.

"Maybe he just stumbled back where it is darker to relieve his bladder," the miner said at last.

But at the end of an hour Halligan had not reappeared. More time passed, and they watched for his return. They had darkened the carbide lamp, but at Harding's suggestion they relighted it. "We'd better get those blankets strung across this drift somehow," he said calmly. "The air is getting hot and heavy in here."

They managed to seal off all but a small portion of the drift. There was grim silence about them now and an unspoken thought: Only the thin shield of hanging blankets might protect their lives by holding back the suffocating smoke and the gases now filling the tunnel.

It was decided that for the hours to come two men must be close to the blanket barrier at all times, to rehang it if a blast of air caused it to fall, or if it caught fire.

Far back in the inky darkness of the drift, and just beyond the ventilating shaft, the others sought out places to lie and hopefully to get needed sleep on the rock floor, which seemed to offer the only coolness within the mine. Without obvious intent, Jeff positioned himself between the drift's approaches and the place where Deborah lay. Nearby, the smoke-blinded crewman said that his pain had lessened. He fell into a restless sleep.

For many minutes there was no word spoken. Then Deborah sat up, startled. "Jeff, are you there?" she whispered.

"Yes, Debbie, right here."

"Do you suppose he is somewhere about . . . Halligan? Maybe trying to sneak up on us with a club or something?"

His hand went out to seek and grasp hers. "Don't worry so, Debbie. I made sure he isn't this side of the blankets we hung up."

"And if he is in the tunnel . . . or . . . outside?"

"It may be what he chose," Jeff said thoughtfully. "Either to try to make a run for escape or—" His voice trailed off. The other possibility, that of Blain Halligan knowingly leaving the mine and plunging down the hellish, burning slope, he could not bring himself to mention.

She turned and moved closer to him. "Jeff, I am scared. Hold me."

Hours went by, and she slept with her head pillowed on his arm. When Deborah wakened it was to say, "That letter . . . the one in your jacket. Do you suppose I will ever get where there is light enough to read it?"

He would have spoken to reassure her, but now another voice cut the darkness, that of the crewman. "Say!" he shouted excitedly. "The pain . . . in my eyes . . . it's about gone. I think that if there

526

was one bit of light maybe I could see. I am going to light a match."

"Not yet. Not for a while," Jeff cautioned. "We can't burn up any good air. Besides, a little more darkness will likely help."

Time seemed endless then, time in which Deborah's mind searched the days and the years. She felt the nearness of Jeff Harding and the warmth of his body. She doubted that he had yet slept.

"Jeff, do you feel like talking?" she murmured.

"Of course . . . if you wish."

She let her fingers lace with his and asked, "Why is it you are always near when there is trouble—when I need you?"

"Because you were born to get into trouble, Debbie."

She moved as though to flounce from him and then lifted a hand to assure herself of his presence. "Jeff, do you remember that night up on Greys River . . . and the cabin?"

His breath quickened. "My God, Debbie, how could I ever forget?"

Her voice had tightened as she whispered, "Jeff, I love you. Just you. Only you." And then, gathering her courage, she added, "Jeff . . . ask me to marry you."

"Deborah . . . stop. If . . . if only I could."

She moved so that her lips were but inches from his ear. "You can, Jeff, you can. Unless there is one of two reasons. Because I have been with another man, or—"

"That means nothing. You were honest. You told me."

"Then," she answered, "it is because you've

527

convinced yourself you are so old . . . so ancient . . . so doddering . . ."

"Deborah, I am in my forties. Middle-aged."

Her arms were crushing him closer. "What is twenty or so years? Love is what counts. And trust. And a future together."

"Is it possible? Debbie . . . Debbie . . . is such as this possible? I love you." And his lips upon hers were an affirmation of his words.

They talked softly for a time. Then Deborah chuckled. "Why am I always selling something, Jeff? I was building a house in Boise. But I sold it to buy timberland. And now we'll need it, you and I."

"Likely we could have used it, Debbie. I am going to take a new job that was offered me. Foreman on a canal that is to be built to water more land down around Caldwell."

They fell silent as approaching footsteps sounded and the gleam of the carbide lamp fell upon them. It was the miner who spoke. "Just checking up on you folks; seems the air is a mite lighter and fresher up by the curtain we hung. If you—"

"Get that damned light out of my eyes. No, don't. I can see . . . honest-to-God see!" The grin that was breaking over the crewman's face seemed as broad as the drift into the mountainside.

The miner pulled the whiskey bottle from his ragged and singed pants. He eyed it ruefully and said, "I meant to keep this all to myself. Hell, drinking alone ain't that great. He peered at the crewman, then lifted the bottle. "Here's mud in your eye."

"Oh, Christ, no. First smoke . . . then salt . . .

and now mud." The crewman's words were plaintive, but he reached for the bottle. It went then to Deborah and then to Jeff—and circled until the last vestige of liquor had disappeared.

The rescue crew, a dozen dog-tired and blackened men, found them near midmorning of the second day. Only an occasional bit of smoke clung in the recesses of the mine as they made their way to the portal. Outside, the sun was shining with a brilliance that blinded them. As their eyes became accustomed to it, Deborah gazed in horrified silence across what had been a lush and green forest. Now it seemed to reach endlessly with tall, gaunt trees that were but burned-out sticks among smoking stumps.

Deborah sought out a weary-faced fire fighter. "It is ghastly. No life. No coolness. No birdsongs."

"We are lucky at that," he answered. "It burned about ten sections. Seven thousand acres, maybe. If the wind hadn't gone down it would have cleaned out maybe fifty–sixty sections." He pointed to the horizon, becoming visible through lessening haze. "See up there, miss. Green timber. Plenty of it left between here and the Canada line."

"At least we all came through alive," the miner commented.

"You think so?" the leader of the rescue squad spoke up. "Then how about that fellow lying down the slope fifty yards? Pinned down by a burning tree maybe thirty feet in girth."

Deborah threw her hands to her face. "You mean . . . there is—"

"Oh, he's dead, all right. Any of you want to

take a look at the remains? I warn you, it's not a pretty sight."

"I will go," Harding said firmly and followed the leader down the timber-strewn slope. He was back within five minutes to say tensely, "It was Blain Halligan. He has found his escape—of sorts."

In silence they began the descent of the slope, toward the water where there had been beaver dams but now was lifeless and brackish.

"Don't drink any of this stuff," the rescue chief ordered. "The ashes and the lye will make you goddamned sick."

Nearby a larger crew of fire fighters and rescue workers had gathered. One of them came forward. "If you can wait half an hour we can let the lady have a horse. The rest of you will have to hoof it out, but we can feed you first, and you will have an escort into Orofino."

Deborah had finished sandwiches and a cup of lukewarm tea when Jeff squatted beside her with a smeared and sooty envelope in his hand. "At last, Debbie, there's light enough so you can read this."

She unfolded the paper, recognizing the penmanship of William E. Borah on the first page: *Dear Deborah: This came yesterday from Lemuel Froman in Australia. Because of its urgency I am asking Mr. Harding to carry it North to you. We miss you. Come back safely and soon to Boise. Sincerely yours, William E. Borah.*

She lifted the enclosed letter.

Dear Deborah:

Does this surprise you, a letter from "Down Under"? I hope that you are your usual busy

530

and happy self . . . and that you have now moved into your new house. As for me, I am finding myself anew in the challenge of my work for the Church. Yes, Deborah, as you so clearly saw, my faith comes first and foremost in my mind, my soul, my life.

But yet, I am not so bound by Mormonism as to be blinded to the needs and the well being of my child—of Janice. She needs a woman's care and a home. At present she is living with a family in Pocatello, but they cannot take care of her permanently.

Deborah, how can I ask it? That you take Janice and give her all that you are capable of supplying? Love. Understanding. Motherhood. If you wish her with you as greatly as I do, my faith, my creed of the Latter-day Saints will not prove an insurmountable barrier. Take my child, raise her, watch over her. I only ask that someday, when you think the time is right, let Janice make her choice between my beliefs and yours—between Mormonism and what your own mother once termed "being a fighting Methodist."

There was more, but softly crying, Deborah handed the pages to Jeff. He read them slowly and smiled. "So, Debbie, we will have a family—one way or another. At least one child."

"You hush up, Jeff. We will have children, you and I—if we will it so."

"I am plumb willing to do my part," he said, grinning, and his manner of speaking caused a crimson flush to mount her smoke-streaked cheeks.

531

Epilogue

ON THE twentieth day of August in the year 1910, a forest fire swept northern Idaho that consumed three million acres of timberland in just two days. The mining town of Wallace had a third of its homes destroyed; smaller settlements, sawmills and homesteads, cabins and railroad structures were entirely destroyed. Seventy-two fire fighters lost their lives in the Coeur d'Alene forest; altogether, nearly one hundred people perished. It shocked America and brought about a new era in forest management and control. The already established U.S. Forest Service was strengthened and enlarged.

Later that year, Deborah Dexter Harding was asked to visit the offices of the regional forester at Missoula, Montana. To her surprise, she was greeted by Erik Bertelsen, now a regional assistant.

After they had talked a bit, he said, "Mrs. Harding, years ago when I told you of the timber on your Pend Oreille holdings, I hardly imagined that one day I would ask you to deed them to the United States government . . . to the Forest Service. But God knows that after this year's devastation we need your groves and meadows and streams." He looked at her and plunged on. "Nowadays your two thousand acres are pretty valuable, probably worth a lot more than I am authorized to offer." He became silent but watched her with eager eyes. Then hesitatingly he named a price per acre.

For a time she hesitated, but memory of a fire, a beaver pond, and a tunnel formed her words. "Have the papers prepared, Erik. I will deed them to the government to become part of the forest reserve."

The passing of title took place in Boise, with formal ceremonies marked by an address by Senator William E. Borah. They had scarcely ended when an elderly woman pushed through the crowd and neared Deborah. Beside her was a young man, wearing dark glasses and a somewhat stiffly formal brown suit. Deborah uttered a glad cry and said brokenly, "Mother, I didn't know you were here."

"Well, why shouldn't I be?" Rose Stannard answered with a bit of her old tartness. "We've seen precious little of each other. Besides, Debbie, nothing could keep him away," and she indicated the youth at her side.

Deborah stared at him in dawning excitement. "You . . . you? Oh, yes . . . you are Peter—Peter Moffitt."

He nodded. "I had to come, Mrs. Harding . . . to see you and to be here when you gave up a whole forest." His voice took on stress and he clung to her hand. "Just as you arranged an operation that let me see again."

He did not understand what she said in an awed tone. "Maybe, Tom Dexter . . . Father . . . you were right—and one can call up the morning."

THE CAVE DREAMERS

JEANNE WILLIAMS

THE CAVE DREAMERS is a vivid, passionate novel of the lives and loves of the women across centuries who share the secret of "The Cave of Always Summer." From the dawn of time to the present, the treasured mystery of the cave is passed and guarded, joining generation to generation through their dreams and desires.

83501-0/$7.95

An **AVON** Trade Paperback